Paradise Burning

by the same author

PLAYS
Away Games
Streetwise in Paradise
Treason's Peace
Double Tongue
Stand or Fall
A Terrible Madness
This Flesh is Mine
When Nobody Returns

NOVELS
Dead in the Water
The Invisible Exchange

EDUCATIONAL BOOKS
The Teaching of Drama in the Primary School
Pupils as Playwrights
Teaching Primary Drama

ACADEMIC BOOKS
Ben Jonson and Theatre (joint editor and contributor)
Jonsonians (editor and contributor)
Dark Attractions: The Theatre of Peter Barnes

http://www.brianwoolland.co.uk

Paradise Burning

a sequel to
The Invisible Exchange

Brian Woolland

PARADISE BURNING

Brian Woolland asserts the moral right to be identified as the author of this work.

This is a work of fiction. References to real people, events, establishments, organisations or local are intended only to provide a sense of authenticity and I used fictitiously. All other characters, and incidents and dialogue, are drawn from the author's imagination and are not to be construed as real.

Imprint: Independently published

Dedicated to the memories of John Airs, Peter Featherstone and Mario Reading, all of whom were inspirational and encouraging in ways they hardly knew.

And especially to the memory of my beloved son, Tom.

PARADISE BURNING

CONTENTS

PROLOGUE

On 15th September 1613, in the room where he was being held as a close prisoner in the Tower of London, Sir Thomas Overbury died in great pain. He had been coughing and vomiting for days. Such was his suffering that Overbury might well have prayed that his lungs would give out during one of his coughing fits. Many people thought that his death would be the end of his story.

Many people were wrong.

On 16th September 1613, in a room on the first floor of the stable block at Cope Castle near Kensington, Viscount Rochester (formerly plain Robert Carr) was attacked by one of his servants, a man known to the world as Matthew Edgworth. Fortunately for Rochester, his steward intervened to save his master's life, plunging a knife into the cutthroat's heart. As blood was pooling on the rough wood floor, Rochester instructed the steward to dispose of the body and make sure that the rogue's story was never heard.

Matthew Edgworth thought differently.

PART ONE

1
The day I died

A body. My body, lying face down in a pool of blood.

'Get rid of it, Colquhoun. And clean this floor.' Rochester's voice is trembling. If he had his wits about him he'd notice the blood's too dark and it's already thickening. But this is no time for inspecting the corpse of his would-be killer. He has to escape. If such a loyal and trusted servant as Edgworth can turn against him, where will the next attempt on his life come from?

Boots clumping on wood. Rochester leaving the room. I don't see him go.

'Is he coming back?' I say.

'He cannae bear the sight o' blood.'

'He should think himself lucky it's not his own.' If my dagger had reached his heart, the blood would have been his. That would have been the right colour. Nothing fake about the searing pain in my chest. I could have been kicked by a mule.

Colquhoun is standing by the window, looking out onto the yard below. Hooves clattering on cobbles, Rochester barking orders. He was down those stairs quicker than a scalded rat. Now he'll scurry off to his nest in Greenwich Palace, which is lined with royal favours, and the company of his beloved King James.

When the time comes for me to take my revenge, I will turn James against him. Royal grace and favour turns sour quicker than milk in midsummer.

2

'Rochester will nae be back today,' says Colquhoun. 'I'll get ye a mop and a pail o' water.'

'I'm not your servant. It was you he told to clean up.'

'This was your idea Edgworth. You clear up your own damned mess. I'll ha' nae more to do wi' it.' What does he have to be so angry about? He's just earnt himself a special place in his master's affections.

'I told you we should have rehearsed.'

'Ye think I ha' the time for your damned play acting.' He stares at me, glowering. 'Ye're nae better than him. Always complaining. I did as ye instructed. You're nae dead. And he thinks ye are. What more d'ye want?'

'I already paid you well for this, Colquhoun. But you'll not get the rest of your money til the job's done. So find a way to get me out of here.'

'You're a bloody mess, Edgworth. And you'll nay gang out o' here wi'out ma help. I'll get ye a pail o' water. And you scrub the damned floor.' With that he leaves, locking the door behind him.

My own dagger, a real dagger, lies where it fell. Reaching for it makes me gasp. I thought I was bruised, but it's worse than that. I undo the buttons of my doublet, remove the leathern bag which I'd filled with fresh pig's blood, and feel round the undershirt. It's bloody, but not torn. The stage knife hasn't penetrated. But Colquhoun lunged harder than he needed to. The bastard must have cracked my ribs.

I spit. No blood. So it could have been worse. The players' knife has a blade that's sprung and designed to retract, but for the illusion to work that blade has to be real. And palpably sharp. And the hilt and handle have to be as solid as any fighting knife. I'd spent hours oiling the mechanism, checking the blade would slide back, all but that small half inch needed to puncture the leathern bag of blood. But the players are wary of these knives, knowing that the mechanism sometimes seizes up. I should think myself lucky to be alive.

I wait for Colquhoun to return. He's been gone too long. Is there more to his anger than indignation about cleaning floors? Is he gathering the groom and stable boys to turn my feigned death into a real one?

A heavy wooden door banging shut somewhere in the stables below. Boots on wooden stairs. I'm breathing too fast. Even that's painful. So, I stay where I am, sitting on the floor, surrounded by drying pig's blood. In my present state, cold reasoning and warm persuasion will serve me better than a blade.

A key in the lock. The door flies open.

Colquhoun's alone. He has a pail of water and a scrubbing brush.

'Ye're still here,' he grumbles. Colquhoun was often dour and surly, wearing his Scottishness like a shield. But in the time that I'd been working for Rochester, he and I had struck up something akin to a friendship. I have no choice but to call on that and hope the angels of his better nature intervene on my behalf.

'You were right,' I say. 'I can't leave here without your help.'

He glares at me, saying nothing.

'And I will clean up,' I say. 'I owe it to you.' He looks suspicious. The Matthew Edgworth he knows isn't the kind of man to play the scullery maid.

'Here. Help me to my feet. Getting killed's more painful than I expected!'

4

He looks at me like this must be a trick.

'I'm grateful to you,' I say. 'You did well.'

'I was only doin' what ye' said. I did nae mean ye no harm.' Colquhoun's a man who needs to live by certainties. How can he live his life if he no longer knows who he really is?

He must have known I was right when I told him of the danger both of us were in. We both knew too much about what had taken place over the past two years. My escape was to stage my own death before Rochester ordered it. Colquhoun's was to retreat into an early dotage when it suited him. He'd once told me: 'I've nae mem'ry of all this you're talking about. Ma eyes are milked over and ma ears are blocked with wax.' As if that would serve as his protection.

In the end, Colquhoun will always do as bidden. Obedience will be his downfall.

I drop to my knees and, despite the pain in my chest, I start scrubbing the floor. He stands there watching for a while, his boot just inches from my face. One hard kick and those splintered ribs will puncture my lungs. But then, to my amazement, he kneels down and takes the scrubbing brush from me.

'Where will ye go?' he says, sounding almost rueful.

'I shall walk to Winchester,' I say. 'Money to be made in Winchester.'

I had no intention of going near Winchester. Colquhoun in his cups had been useful. But if I'd gained from his indiscretions, then so could others. And if in a careless moment he told the story of how Edgworth escaped from London to make his fortune in Winchester, that would suit me very well.

'I know. My first time too. When it comes to dying, I was a virgin.' He laughs at that. And offers me his hand. I grimace and hold back a cry as I struggle to my feet, but when I'm upright our eyes meet for a moment and he smiles. Then he looks away, as if embarrassed by the very notion of friendship. But there's something else that's troubling him too. He's said many things when drunk that betrayed his loathing of Rochester, but that doesn't count as disloyalty because he never remembers in the morning. Colquhoun's a man who needs to live by certainties. How can he live his life if he no longer knows who he really is?

He must have known I was right when I told him of the danger both of us were in. We both knew too much about what had taken place over the past two years. My escape was to stage my own death before Rochester ordered it. Colquhoun's was to retreat into an early dotage when it suited him. He'd once told me: 'I've nae mem'ry of all this you're talking about. Ma eyes are milked over and ma ears are blocked with wax.' As if that would serve as his protection.

In the end, Colquhoun will always do as bidden. Obedience will be his downfall.

I drop to my knees and, despite the pain in my chest, I start scrubbing the floor. He stands there watching for a while, his boot just inches from my face. One hard kick and those splintered ribs will puncture my lungs. But then, to my amazement, he kneels down and takes the scrubbing brush from me.

'Where will ye go?' he says, sounding almost rueful.

'I shall walk to Winchester,' I say. 'Money to be made in Winchester.'

Colquhoun in his cups had been useful. But if I'd gained from his indiscretions, then so could others. And if in a careless moment he told the story of how Edgworth escaped from London to make his fortune in Winchester, that would suit me very well.

2
The road to Oxford

I waited for the stables clock to strike midnight. Then the ghost of Matthew Edgworth walked out. There was a door in the north wall of the Cope Castle estate, with a gardeners' hut close by, where I found a spade which I took to a copse just outside the walls. I dug up a small knapsack I'd hidden there the day before, and changed into the clean clothes it contained, gentleman's clothes taken from the tiring house at Blackfriars Playhouse. I buried the bloody clothes in that copse, and with them all trace of Matthew Edgworth. After returning the spade to the gardener's hut, I headed for the road to Oxford where I had unfinished business.

I needed to be well away from Cope Castle by sunrise. But I was struggling for breath, and London was already tugging at my heart. The hubbub and the tumult, the chaos and confusion. I love it that it's so big and yet so small. Anything you want can be found in London. And there I was heading west, walking past endless fields and hedgerows with only a half a moon for company. Time would come when I might even miss the stench of the Whitechapel tanneries and the Fleet River in summer. I've got London in my veins. But I needed a new life, and London couldn't be part of it.

The sun was setting when I reached The George and Dragon in a village called Stokenchurch. I was exhausted and hungry, and the pain in my ribs so bad I could barely walk. The inn was welcoming, the food was good and the bed was comfortable. I was dog-tired but I still slept badly. Every time I breathed deep or turned, I was racked by pains in my chest and my back. But I wasn't coughing up blood. And that was a mercy. If I lay flat and breathed lightly, I fell into dreams, but instead of some lovely vision of Kate waiting for me in Canterbury and urging me on to meet her there, I see her head bobbing on the shit brown waters of the Thames. She's shouting to me. I call to her. No sound comes from my mouth. Then she sinks and it's my own damned fault. And Rochester is standing by the parapet of Fleet Bridge, laughing.

When I wake, the lantern in my room has long since died. A bottomless darkness, a darkness that engulfs and suffocates.

I struggle out of bed, shuffle across to the wall, edge along to the window. But when I open the shutters, the half-moon's concealed behind heavy clouds. Its ashen light gives no comfort. Is this the new Matthew? Afraid of the dark and my dreams?

I ease myself back to bed. When sleep finally comes, Kate's there again. With a man beside her, his hand on her arm. Have Rochester's thugs already tracked her down? Is she terrified? Or smiling? Has she given up waiting and found another lover?

I made my way slowly downstairs soon after daybreak. The new Matthew in an old man's body. I broke fast in the dining room. When I rose from my chair I was caught in a spasm of pain. Couldn't stand. Couldn't sit. The landlord came to my assistance. He was most concerned.

'A few days ago,' I told him, 'A dog ran out from a dark alley, barking at a passing horse, which threw its rider and kicked at the dog. Its hoof caught me in the chest. I was lucky it cracked ribs and not my head. But I have to get to Oxford.'

'There's a carter stops here every Tuesday morning on his way to Oxford. He'll be here before long. He owes me a favour. I shall ask him to let you sit with him, sir.'

So that was how I travelled on to Oxford. Not in Rochester's grand coach with Alice playing the 'fine lady' as she had when we travelled this road two years before, but beside a sullen carter on his creaky, overloaded cart. And although every bump and rut in the road made me wince, it was better than walking for six hours.

Despite my cracked ribs, I had reasons to be hopeful. I had money, good clothes, and in my knapsack the tools of my trade and those belongings I'd need in due course, including several little treasures from the Forman house. Two or three nights in Oxford, then quickly on my way. I could put my nightmares behind me. I'd be in Canterbury within three weeks, with enough money to see Kate and myself well set for years.

I took a room at The Crown, a well-appointed inn near the centre of the city. I was dressed as a gentleman and had enough in my purse to pay for a room with a comfortable bed, newly glazed windows and a simple tapestry on one of the walls. Luxury for a man whose master thought he was dead.

3
An Oxford education

I read Kate's letter – again. I'd read it so many times I knew it by heart. But I wanted to see those words written down.

I am safe. I am well.
We will be safe in Canterbury.
God bless you, Matthew.
Your loving,
Katherine.

Knowing that I'd want to read it again when I came to bed, I hid it under the pillow. Then I loosened one end of the mattress and pushed Doctor Forman's casebook and letters as far into the straw as I could reach.

I was tired, but not too tired to venture out and take a look round. The last time I'd been in the city there were more scholars than I could count, all dressed in long black gowns, a great flock of flightless crows, strutting and chattering. And all thinking their studies and their wealth made them wise. Who in the world is easier and more profitable to gull?

Had I come to the wrong city? Men and women going about their business. The clattering of horses and carts on cobbles. But not a scholar to be seen. Had they closed the university for the autumn, like they close the outdoor playhouses?

The Bear Inn was most welcoming. Half a dozen oil lamps, tables, chairs, warming fires in all three rooms. The smell of warm yeast and malt from the brewhouse out the back. And a promising hubbub. Wherever men gather after dark there are games of cards, and wherever there is gaming there are purses to be lightened.

'My young cousin's a scholar here.' I said. 'He recommended this inn, Master Goodstock, and said to meet him here.'

'You know my name?' I knew his name because a fellow had just called him, asking for his tankard to be refilled.

'*Master Goodstock's Bear Inn is the best in town*, so said my cousin. If you're not Master Goodstock, I've come to the wrong place.'

'This is indeed The Bear, but you won't find your young cousin here today because the scholars haven't yet returned for the Michaelmas Term.'

Those cracked ribs must have been dulling my wits. I should have taken a few days' rest. But I was impatient to get to Kate in Canterbury, and slavering at the sniff of easy money.

'My name's Matthew Lovall.' The name I'd given when I took the room at The Crown. I'd buried Edgworth in the copse by Cope Castle, but Matthew's common enough, so I thought to keep that.

'And who's your cousin?' said Master Goodstock. 'Many scholars drink here when the colleges are in session.'

'Nick Wellborn.'

'I'll let it be known you're looking for him.'

'Most kind of you, Master Goodstock.' I stayed by the buttery bar, talking with him, but all the while watching the games of dice and cards. No eager roaring boys, and not many greenhorns in The Bear that night. After a while I joined a table for a couple of rounds of cards and a quick game of dice. I lost at both. Not enough to trouble me, but enough to whet the players' appetites for when I came back the next day.

A porter greeted me when I walked into the Crown. He led me to my room and lit a lantern for me. I asked him how best to get to Warwick from Oxford – not that I planned going near Warwick. But porters tend to talk. So when the time came for me to move on, the hue and cry would chase a phantom to Warwick.

I returned to The Bear the following night. Master Goodstock was pleased to see me. He'd asked around, and reckoned my young cousin, Nick Wellborn, would be back in Oxford on Sunday.

'Excellent,' said I. And Prudence whispered, *Then, best get your business done before the weekend.*

A game of *Passe-dix* had started in the gaming corner. I don't normally bother with dice games. The only sure way to make a killing at dice is for two to work together. A mistake to work alone with loaded dice, for there's very little money to be made before someone gets wise to what you're doing. My interest was in the players. As Master Goodstock and I discussed the price of hops and barley, I kept an eye on the game. Who was winning? Who was losing? Who staked too high? Who stayed at the table too long? Faces and eyes. Who smiled and when? Like fishing. Watch the water carefully, you get an eye for the undercurrents. Most of the faces were familiar from the night before.

'You have house cards, Master Goodstock?'
'But of course. Why do you ask?'

'I am partial to a game of *Primero* from time to time. But, as you know, I'm a stranger in these parts.'

'There is no cheating in this establishment.' As if to prove it, he took a pack from the shelf behind him and handed it to me. I riffled through it. Good quality cards, and none of them marked. I gave them back. I'd have stayed talking a little longer, but a newcomer had arrived at the gaming table. Nobody seemed to know him, and that roused my suspicions. But if he was a cheater, who was his rook? I took my leave of Master Goodstock, walked over and asked if I could join the game.

'I thought we had a table,' says the wiry little fellow who's just joined, who I'm certain is a cheater.

'We do have a table,' says a burly fellow with a bushy red beard. 'More players, more at stake, more to win.' He gives me a wry smile, and pulls a stool over for me.

I thank him. They all move a little closer together, leaving a gap for me between Redbeard on my left and an old fellow with milky eyes and bald pate on my right. The cheater's directly opposite me. He scowls. With his pinched face, straggly beard and nose like a shoehorn, scowling suits him all too well.

Going round the table, we all say our names. Redbeard on my left is John. Next to him is Ben, a short fellow with a round face who has to reach over his belly to pick up the dice. The wiry little cheater calls himself Jack. Next to him's a young fellow, well fed and smooth hands. He's Michael. Not a working man, so perhaps a scholar, come back to Oxford early. Or abandoned his studies because he's fallen in with Pinchface Jack. And to my right is Amos, the old fellow. Six of us in all.

Every player takes a turn to be banker in *Passe-dix*. And the banker sits on the right of the dice thrower. For a cheat to work, banker and dice-thrower have to work together.

Redbeard starts as banker. The rest of us each put in our penny stakes. Small money, I know. But this isn't a game I plan to win.

Ben throws the dice. Two. Four. Three. Nine in total. Less than ten. So banker takes all. Big smile behind John's red beard.

Ben takes over as the banker. Pinchface Jack throws low. One and two threes. Seven. Ben takes all.

And so it moves on. When Jack's the banker, young Michael throws. High. A six and two fours. Banker loses. Young Michael looks worried. If they are cheaters, this is to set us at ease.

Next time I pick up the dice, I take my time. I look around. The door to the street swings open and bangs shut. The inn's filling up, but nobody takes much notice of a low-stakes dice-game. I wave to Master Goodstock that I'd like another jar of ale. Most of it will end on the floor. Pinchface Jack surely knows the trick. But this is for the benefit of the other players. And if things go as I plan, Jack and Michael won't be here tomorrow night. If the others think I'm fond of my drink I'll be more welcome at the table when I return on the morrow. I slow things down, weigh the dice in my hands, feel the corners. Honest dice – as far as I can tell.

'Your throw, Master Lovall,' says Jack. He and I speak the same language. It's a threat. He's feeling for his dagger, concealed beneath his doublet. There was a time I was more than a match for anyone in a knife fight. But Prudence reminds me, *You've cracked ribs, Matthew, and your left hand's useless.*

'Your throw,' says Jack again, like he's teaching his son to play.

I throw. I lose. The way it goes. I win the next round, then lose several more. The way it goes. And still the cheater keeps his loaded dice to himself – which is why I'm still in the game. He's watching me, wary. Saying nothing.

Several rounds later Ben suggests raising the stakes.

'Tuppence a throw?' says Amos.

'Straight to sixpence?' says Ben. 'I can't stay much longer. My wife'll have me darning socks if I'm late home.'

And so we go to sixpence. Amos doesn't like it. Two more rounds. The usual arguments. More tankards of ale. And still no cheating. Maybe I'm wrong. Maybe it's all honest after all, and I'm bringing my London ways to Oxford. Or is Pinchface Jack cannier than I thought?

Finally, he makes the switch. He puts a shilling on the table. Young Michael asks nervously if he means to put in that much. In the laughter that follows, Jack takes it back, puts in a sixpence. That's when he switches the dice. The shilling's the distraction. It's a trick I've pulled myself. Now Jack's the banker, with Michael throwing. And that's when Jack makes banker's call. 'Play your own stakes, gentlemen.' We can each put in whatever we like. If the banker loses, he pays each of us double whatever we put in. 'Your own stakes, gentlemen.'

That's when others start taking an interest. At first just a few men, who wander over to get a better view of the table. One of them's maybe a minder for Pinchface, though I can't tell who it is.

The thrower calls his stakes first. Michael puts in a shilling.

'Get on with you. Can do better than that young fellow,' says one of the onlookers. 'You've had lucky dice.' I mark that man, Is he part of the team? Michael looks up, grins sheepishly, takes his shilling back, puts in half a crown. The onlookers cheer. And what looks like Michael's heady recklessness brings others over, like crows around an ailing lamb.

Amos calls next. 'I'll put in a shilling.' Hands fidgety, top lip twitching.

Ben says he'll match Michael's half a crown. 'I've seen the way these dice are falling.'

'Me too,' says Redbeard.

Now me. The dice are on the table, waiting for Michael to pick them up. I could call them out now, show how they've been switched. But I'm biding my time.

'Your call, Master Lovall,' says Jack.

I venture a shilling and sixpence. I have to appear cautious. Best part of ten shillings on the table now. If Jack loses now, he pays out a pound. These are high stakes. By now a crowd's gathered. The other two rooms have emptied. The air is thick with smoke and sweat, slopped ale and the unheard farts of an evening's worth of strong ale and Goodstock's best mutton pie. We're all shouting to be heard.

I guess the dice are loaded low. So when Michael throws, banker takes all – and soon after that Jack and young Michael will quit the game.

Michael throws the dice one at a time. One. Low, just like I thought.

Then a four. The room falls silent. Michael has the last die in his cupped hands. He throws a five. Ten in total. The magic ten. *Passe-dix*. That means the stakes stay on the table. The crowd roars. Michael has to throw again, and we all have to double our stakes. I could almost admire them. Amos laughs nervously, a twittering, bird-like sound squeaking above the uproar all around. He fiddles in his purse, hands shaking, until he's finally got enough halfpennies and farthings on the table to make up his extra shilling.

'Your stakes gentlemen. Anyone for any more?' He's looking directly at me. I've already doubled to three shillings. I pull a face and shake my head. They've been playing a long game. I'm in for the longer one.

Every man in the crowd is roaring us on. The smell of stale sweat, spilled beer, tobacco smoke. I'm alive again.

'Pick up the dice, Michael,' says Jack.

Michael looks worried. The room quietens again.

The first die skittles and tumbles across the table. Four. Murmuring all around. The odds have just shifted against the banker.

One. Same dice as before, but in a different order.

This time the last die is a three. Eight in total. Banker takes all. Michael looks shocked. Groans and cheers filling the room. Any number of side bets out there.

Amos whimpers and slumps. Redbeard bangs his fist on the table in fury. But stops short of an accusation. He knows he's been set up, though he doesn't know how. Ben's grinding his teeth and clenching his fists. But it's me Jack's looking at. Quizzical but cold. Daring me to call him out.

'It's the way the dice tumble,' I say.

'And tonight,' says Jack, 'They tumbled low.' He shrugs and sweeps the shillings, half-crowns and sixpences into his purse, stuffs the small change into his pockets.

The crowd moves away. Amos gets to his feet and stumbles off without a word, leaving Ben, Redbeard, Michael, Pinchface Jack and me at the table.

'I've never had any luck with dice,' I say. 'You play *Primero?*'

Jack ignores this. He's getting up to go. But young Michael chirps up, 'I do. I want to win back some of what I just lost.' His first bad move.

Michael's up for it, and so are Redbeard and Ben. And Jack won't want to leave Michael alone with us. 'Three rounds. No more.'

We're all in. With Amos gone, we shift our stools a little. Redbeard's now sitting opposite Jack.

'Whose cards?' I say.

'House cards. Rules of the inn,' says Redbeard, getting to his feet.

'Glad to hear it,' I say.

Redbeard collects the pack from Goodstock. Then it goes the same as any game of *Primero*: bluffing and bluster, drinking and cursing, insults and laughter. I stay quiet, except when I make a bid. Then Michael makes his second mistake. Just before dealing he snatches a sideways glance to Pinchface Jack. When Jack picks up his cards, he hesitates and moves his hands a little to his right before holding the cards to his chest. It's a sign. I don't know their code, but Michael does. And, sure enough, Jack wins that hand. This should have been three rounds to show willing. If they were really good they'd lose a little now, then leave the table. But they've got greedy.

I don't say much. Just a little goading of Redbeard John. He doesn't know it, but he's going to play my foist. 'Fortune is a fickle whore,' I say, shaking my head in disbelief at John's poor run of luck as he passes over more coins to cheating Jack. The crowd's gathering again. I take a good look round, as if the presence of so many onlookers is making me nervous. But it's Jack's man in the crowd I'm looking for. If there is someone, I don't see him.

19

And on we go. No accusations of cheating yet, but Redbeard's been rumbling for a while. After two rounds the deal comes to me. I shuffle. Place the pack face down on the table, steeple my hands together, and shut my eyes.

'You praying?' says Redbeard.

'How else am I to win?' And I nod in the direction of cheater Jack, who fiddles with his beard. Everyone laughs. Even Michael and Jack, who slides his hand over that hidden dagger and gives me a warning look.

In goes the ante. Redbeard cuts the pack. I pick it up. First deal, two cards each. First bid. Redbeard's in. Everyone stays with him. Second deal. Second bid. Redbeard ups his stake. He's got a good hand, and don't I know it.

I lay the draw cards face down on the table. Ben and Michael change two cards each Jack and Redbeard both stick with the cards they've got. Jack raises his stake. Redbeard sticks with him. Ben and Michael fold.

'Show your hands,' I say.

Redbeard shows first. 'Primero,' he calls, triumphant. One card from each suit, and one of them a King. Cheers from the crowd. They don't often see a Royal Primero.

Now Jack chucks in, putting his cards face down on the table and shoving his stake across to Redbeard.

But Ben smells something's not right and turns Jack's cards over before the cheater can stop him.

Quartet. Four of a kind. The only hand to beat *Primero.* And all four of them Kings.

A hush of anticipation ripples out from the table; the ears of the crowd tuned to the unexpected silence.

'Only four Kings in any pack I've seen,' says Redbeard. 'And I had one of them. So where's your King of Hearts come from, you cheating bastard?'

And then, of a sudden, bursting up like a sprung trap, Redbeard rams the table forward, shoving cheating Jack from his chair, pinning him to the floor, then vaulting over, more agile than his bulk should have allowed. He grabs Jack by his beard and winds it tight, pulling him from out beneath the table.

'Cheat me, would you,' he shouts above the baying of the crowd. 'I been watching you. Four Kings? Where they come from?'

The game, the food and ale all gone: cards, tankards, trenchers of pickled herring and chunks of bread strewn all around; ale puddling on the flagstone floor.

'Four Kings!' shouts Redbeard. 'This for two of them.' With his right hand he lifts the flailing cheater to his full height, and with his left drives two straightened fingers up his filthy nostrils.

'This for the third.' A kick in the bollocks that leaves the cheater doubled up and gasping for breath.

'Four Kings!' roars Redbeard. 'And this for the fourth.' But what that might have been, nobody would ever know, for Jack has pulled his dagger.

The crowd falls silent.

What can I do? I can't let a little dispute about cards lead to murder. I'm on my feet. I squirm round. Get behind Jack. Michael's nowhere to be seen. Jack thrusts. Redbeard dodges, and tries to grasp the dagger by the handle. But Jack is slippery fast, even in his winded, nose-bloody, gasping state. So, I do what any good man would do. I wrap my arms round Jack to hold him back from striking again. Master Goodstock relieves him of the dagger.

Redbeard's about to kick him in the groin again when a couple of Goodstock's men grab Redbeard and bundle him out the door.

Pinchface Jack's a wiry little fellow, and my cracked ribs are stabbing from within. I can't hold him on my own. Goodstock's men are onto it.

It's over. Much blood. And maybe broken bones. But if they want to kill each other, they'll have to do it on the street outside.

Master Goodstock offers to buy me a drink on the house.

'I thank you, but may I take it up tomorrow? I should never have stayed this late.'

'There'll be a warm welcome for you, Master Lovall. I'll have no killings and no cheating in The Bear. I thank you for your help.'

It's good to be appreciated.

Back at The Crown, I sat on the bed, unbuttoned my doublet and emptied Jack's purse. As any common cutpurse will tell you, there's no easier way to relieve a fool of his money than restraining him from fighting. I counted the coins. Five pounds, seventeen shillings and fourpence. Not a fortune, and nothing like as much as I could have made if the scholars had been back, but more than most servants earn in year, and enough to get me to Canterbury and the bed of my beloved Kate.

I removed my boots, read Kate's letter yet again, and lay down on the bed.

I was woken by movement in the yard below. The ostler preparing a horse for a guest with an early morning start? I stilled my breathing and listened. Footsteps on cobbles. Prudence whispered *Time to go.*

I took my treasures from the mattress. Checked that those precious letters between Rochester and Forman were still there; letters that would be so valuable to Rochester's enemies when I returned to London because they implicated Rochester in Overbury's death. I rolled the letters tightly and slid them down behind the book's spine. I put Forman's casebook underneath my doublet then buttoned it tight. *A stranger on strange roads. You could lose your purse to highwaymen. Keep something back.* I found an angel in the cheater's purse and slipped that into my sock. Carrying my boots, and my knapsack, I tippy-toed along the corridor, down the stairs, and out into Cornmarket Street.

The sky was already lightening. Cocks had started crowing, setting off the dogs. I'd slept longer than I'd wanted to.

4
Madam Gossip's revenge

After half a mile or so, the cobbles of Saint Aldate's Street became a rutted track on a raised causeway across water meadows. Low lying mist hung softly in the still air, shrouding the river. I perched on the edge of a stone water trough, where I pulled on my boots, as stiff and as clumsy as an old man in his dotage.

I looked back. Not a soul walking down Saint Aldate's. Breathing was still painful. But I could walk without fear that Rochester's men or Oxford's cheaters might soon catch up with me. I didn't know where I was going. Certainly not Winchester after what I'd told Colquhoun. Perhaps Salisbury – wherever that might be? I knew it was south of Oxford, so I was heading in the right direction. There's money in cathedral cities, and church money always trickles down to nearby inns. Then from Salisbury to Canterbury with a full purse.

I hobbled over a wooden bridge which crossed the river. As I reached the far bank a pen of geese cackled furiously. That started the dogs. A red-faced girl looked up from milking a goat which was tied to a shack. She shouted at the dogs to hush, then turned to see what had set them off. I doffed my hat, bade her good day, and walked slowly on my way. I should have realised that when nothing much happens in your life, a well-dressed gentleman walking out of the city in the early hours of the morning is a tale to tell.

The track rose up a gentle hill. At the top of this I turned and looked back. Oxford was a dream of spires and towers and smoking chimneys thrusting out of low white autumn mist. I tapped my purse, the purse I'd filled last night. That was real enough.

I stood to one side as two carts came by, each laden with sacks of flour, followed by a boy leading a donkey laden with saddle packs.

'Good day to you,' I said. 'Have you come far?'

'Mill at Iffley. Saddle packs full of flour what they can't get on the carts. Go again tomorrow.'

'With the scholars returning, I suppose the colleges need to start baking bread.'

He shrugged. I guessed he was about ten years old. At his age I was working as the Boy of the House at The Cardinal's Hat, and I'd already learnt to cut purse strings.

'And how far is Iffley from here?' I said.

'Depends.'

'Depends on what?'

'How fast you's walking? When the old ass wants home and we're going back, it's near.'

'I have no time for riddling, boy.'

'You asks, I tells.'

He'd have got himself cuffed if he'd been talking to Matthew Edgworth. But Matthew Lovall smiled sweetly, amused by the boy's attempts at wit. And Iffley village wasn't far at all. A large water mill, a church, a few houses, another bridge over the river, and an inn. I was tempted to take a room and stay a few days, but I needed to get further from Oxford before resting.

The mist still hung over the river, but the sky above had cleared. As I followed the road out of Iffley a washerwoman who was going about her business in a narrow creek called out to wish me good day. Ever the gentleman, I wished her well.

I walked for several hours on paths close by the river – until I came to fields of wheat, where a dozen or so men and women were gathering the crop; the men scything, the women and a young boy tying it into sheaves and gathering those into stooks. They were singing as they worked. Ahead of me stood a large, stonewalled barn about thirty yards up a slight hill from the river. It had recently been rethatched – so there was money in these parts. The barn was raised on staddle stones, and no other buildings stood nearby. The doors were open. I climbed up and looked inside. I know little of the ways of country folk, but I do know that they don't bring in the corn until it's threshed and dried. That might take week or more. If I sat down to take my ease, I'd not be disturbed. I looked round carefully. The only doors were the ones I'd just come through. One side of the barn was full of hay, the other was empty, except for piles of hessian sacks. I sat down in the hay, opened my knapsack, broke bread and drank some ale from the leathern bottle I'd had filled at The Crown. I wanted to rest awhile, and then walk on for a couple more hours and find an inn where I could stay for a few days. My thoughts drifted to Canterbury, and the welcome I dared hope for. I shut my eyes, soothed by thoughts of Kate. As I reached for her letter I cursed my carelessness, for I realised that I'd left it beneath my pillow at The Crown. Far too late to go back for it now. I had it memorised word for word. But I felt foolish, and leaving it behind seemed like a betrayal.

I had no intention of sleeping, but that's what I must have done for I was woken by water thrown over my face and a pail clattering on the wooden floor. There standing before me was Pinchface Jack. And beside him, young Michael and a burly fellow I half recognised from the crowd watching on in The Bear. I jumped to my feet, and reached for my dagger. Pinchface Jack held it up to show me.

If I'd had the use of my left hand, if Colquhoun hadn't cracked my ribs, I could probably have been taken down Pinchface and Michael, and maybe even the other fellow as well, for I've always fought with my brain as well as my knives. But my wits had already failed me several times that day, for I'd left a clear trail out of Oxford: Kate's letter with its mention of Canterbury; the milkmaid, the donkey boy and then the washerwoman, all would have told of the well-dressed stranger heading south.

Never get into a fight you cannot win. I've said it more times than I can count. A wise old saw it may be, and it's served me well on many occasions. But it's not much use if you leave your wits behind, and the fight comes chasing after you.

5
The missing angel

The man with no name was shorter than me, shorter than young Michael, but heavily built and square faced, with one eye half closed by a thick scar that ran from his nose to his right ear. He carried a thick stave. He took a step closer, but kept his distance, holding himself just out of reach of a well-aimed kick, waiting for me to make my move.

'Not seen that trick before,' said Pinchface Jack. 'Four Kings. Where they come from?'

'You have my dagger,' I said. 'Three of you, just one of me. What are you waiting for?'

'And you have our money,' said Jack. 'Throw down the purse.'

I had to play this cautiously. Any more broken bones, I'd be as good as dead. Slowly, I removed the purse from my doublet, and held it out. 'Take it.'

'Throw it. At my feet.'

But they wanted something else as well. They could have stabbed me while I slept, and already taken the purse.

'Throw the purse.'

I held it out. 'Good money in there. Don't want it to spill.'

Jack gestured to Michael.

No-Name raised his stave. Michael inched forward, as if walking out onto a frozen pond. I dropped the purse into his sweating hand. He scurried back.

'Count it,' said Jack, not taking his eyes off me. Michael knelt on the barn floor, emptied the money and started counting.

'We could work together,' I said.

'We're not here to strike a bargain.'

'Maybe not. But I can offer one. You can't work The Bear again. They know you for cheaters now. Big Redbeard John. Not a happy man. He'll be looking for you. I'd guess word's already out. Oxford's not a big place. The scholars are back next week. We could work as a team. Those fresh young scholars. Wealthy parents. Full purses. Shame to let that go to waste. Rich pickings, easy pickings with the skills we have between us.'

He stared at me. Impassive. But the idea was there, floating in the air amidst the hay dust and the fetor of animal feed.

'Trouble is, Matthew Lovall, you ruined it for us.'

'Not if we work together.'

No-Name was breathing heavily. Grinding his teeth. Clenching and unclenching his knuckles. Jack had brought him here to do a job, not to listen to bargaining.

'You mock me,' said Jack.

'Not at all. We could do well for ourselves. All of us.'

'How?'

'Your faces are known in The Bear, so we don't go near The Bear. And the scholars won't know you. I scout for you. Lay the ground. Start the dice rolling. I lose enough to raise interest. You stay in hiding til I get word to you.'

'And how do we know you won't play another of your London tricks and cheat us again?'

'Your friend, whose name I don't know, can keep a watchful eye.'

Jack wasn't convinced, but he'd not yet dismissed the idea. I was sharper than any he'd worked with before. And I was still a fresh face in Oxford.

'And when we're done in Oxford, we go to Bristol, Exeter. Anywhere there's money.'

He nodded. The seed was taking root.

Michael looked up. 'I've counted it, master.'

'How much?'

'Five pounds, seven shillings and fourpence.'

'You sure?'

'I counted it twice,' said Michael. 'I reckon that's ten shillings short.'

'I reckon the same,' said Jack.

No-Name looked more interested.

'That's the purse from last night,' I said. 'I've not so much as loosened the drawstring.'

'Young Michael is good with money, aren't you lad?'

'Yes sir.'

'Throw the knapsack over.'

I did as he asked. Michael emptied it out. The only thing in it of interest to Jack was the tinderbox. He picked it up, ran his fingers over it appreciatively, slid the lid off and examined the phoenix rising from flames carved in dark oak.

'Well crafted, this. Where you get it?'

'I was given it,' I said. 'People I work for value my talents.'

He slid the lid back into place and tossed it to Michael. 'Give me my ten shillings, then maybe we can think about your idea.'

'I don't have it.' The angel was hidden in my sock. If I took off my boots, I'd lose the only weapon I had.

'Off with your doublet.'

No-Name lifted his stave. I undid the buttons on my doublet. I didn't want a fight, and so I had no choice. He searched the pockets, found Forman's casebook. He handed the book to Michael. 'What is it?'

Michael looked wary of the casebook. He ran his fingers slowly over the soft black leather, then opened it, fearful of what it might contain. He shook his head, baffled by the pages that Forman had illuminated with drawings of saints and angels. Others were filled with dense writings in Latin, Greek, and a script I didn't recognise. Whole pages were covered with interlocking squares and diamonds, all annotated with alchemical symbols. Michael seemed as enchanted as he was frightened. As if caught in the gaze of a deadly viper.

'The casebook was given to me by a cunning man to deliver to a great lord who lives near Salisbury. I've been trusted with delivering that book.'

'Salisbury? Eh?' He pulled out Kate's letter and brandished it. 'Not planning to join your lady friend in Canterbury?' So that was why they'd come south in pursuit.

Jack gestured to No-Name. I was expecting him to swing the stave. I was ready to grab it. But instead of swinging it like a club, No-Name used it as a pike, jabbing me hard in the stomach. I fell back, winded, gagging for breath. Then came the blow to my balls and the pain that tore at every nerve. I was doubled up in pain, couldn't get to my feet, couldn't crawl. I expected the kicking. But Pinchface was kneeling beside me, my own dagger at my throat.

'Michael. Leave the damned book. Take off his boots. I want our ten shillings.'

Clumsy, nervous hands unlacing my boots. Then pulling off my socks. How had I fallen so low? I could have kicked out and crippled young Michael, but Pinchface had the blade of my own dagger pressed to my windpipe. I keep that dagger well honed.

The clunk of a coin on the wooden floor.

'Ahh. What have we here? A pretty little angel. Ten shillings exactly. I thought I counted right last night. How did that get in your sock, I wonder?'

'What do we do? Finish him off?' The first time No-Name had spoken.

'Tie his hands and feet.'

I'd been so caught up in my dealings with the three cheaters from The Bear that I'd ignored the harvest songs wafting in from the fields. But if I could hear them, they might hear me. I managed one loud shout for help before Jack dropped the dagger and covered my mouth with grubby hands. I tried to bite, but he was pushing down with all his weight.

'Do it.'

Next I knew, No-Name grabbed both my hands, and Michael was sitting on my legs. I kicked as hard as I could. My bare foot made contact with something. That something gave a shout of pain. Jack took his hands away. I called out again. He rammed a handful of hay into my open mouth. I choked and coughed. He forced more hay in.

'His hands are tied.'

'Tie his damned feet, Michael.'

I kicked, I struggled, I did everything I could to break free. But my chest was in agony from the broken ribs, and I could hardly breathe.

'Now what?' said No-Name.

'Fill the doorway with hay. Matthew Lovall's about to learn what it means to steal from Jack Proudfoot.'

I watched them piling up hay in the doorway to the barn.

'The tinderbox,' said Jack. Young Michael threw it over. Jack gestured to the other two to get out. I cursed myself for keeping the box ready with highest quality charcloth, fire-steel and flints.

He set light to Kate's letter and used that as a taper. Flickers of flame soon became long tongues. He ran out. I squirmed and somehow wriggled to my feet. Flames, already taller than a man, filled the doorway. The barn was thick with smoke. The thatch would be ablaze in no time.

My legs were bound together, but I could jump. Instinct told me to hop like a frightened rabbit away from the flames. But that instinct was wrong.

The only way to safety was through the burning hay.

6

In the company of women

I cough. Then again. The smell of burnt hair, seared flesh.

The very act of breathing hurts.

I'm surrounded by darkness. A deep darkness that wraps me in emptiness.

I want to reach out. I can't lift my arms.

The sound of women's voices. Women talking quietly. Their words drift in and out. I call out – a weak groaning sound. My throat screams with pain.

I'm lying flat on something soft.

I try again. My voice so thin I can barely hear myself. My lips burnt raw.

'Hush you. Hush you. No need to talk.' A woman's voice. Soft and slow.

'Kate?' I say.

'Hush. Don't talk. Not yet. You're safe.'

'Can't see.'

'You have a bandage over your eyes. Your eyelids were burned.'

'Am I blind?'

'Agnes made a poultice. The bandage needs to stay awhile.'

'How long? I have to – '

'Hush you. No need to talk. Your throat and the inside of your mouth, that's burnt too. Just open your lips. Agnes made something to numb the pain, to soothe and help you sleep.'

'Alice?'

'Agnes.'

I whimper. A damp cloth between my lips. Cool liquid drips into my mouth. It soothes.

How long was I in that state? I remember it in glimpsed sensations – most of which were searing pains when they changed my dressings. I remember darkness, but not dreams; darkness and a numbness, where nothing touched my senses. Later, I discovered that I lay like that for more than a week. Hardly talking for the pain, drinking only when one of the women caring for me dripped spring water into my mouth, or the liquid that eased the pain. Eating only broth that's neither hot nor cold, fed to me in drips. Day, night, morning, evening, sunshine and rain, waking and dreaming – all merged into the same numbed fog of pain and sleep.

Until one day, though it could have been night, some thoughts become clear enough for me to whisper questions.

'My name is Constance. You've been drifting in and out of delirium. Agnes says it's best to keep you here.'

'Agnes?'

'Agnes saved your life. She makes the potions and the dressings.'

'Where are we?'

'Near Wittenham, a village not far from Abingdon.'

'I want to see where I am. Can you take the bandage off? I want to see you.'

'Agnes removed it yesterday to look at your eyes. Do you not remember?'

'No.'

'Your eyes need to stay bandaged for a few more days. Agnes knows. She is the wisest of women. 'Twas Agnes thought it best to bind your arms. You were scratching at your skin. Your arms are free now.'

'Constance?' I start coughing again. My throat still so sore. 'Constance? That your name?'

'Hush you, yes.'

She gives me a few more drips of the liquid.

I want to shout, to scream, to insist she take the bandage off. But I do what I've taught myself to do since I first learnt to pick locks. Breathe slow and calm. If I keep my mouth shut and breathe through my nose, it's less painful. At least the broken ribs are healing.

And so … time passes.

'Who are you, Constance? Tell me.'

'I will. In good time. But hush you now.' Calming, caring, soothing. Always talking quietly, gently, her voice as smooth as velvet, warm as new-baked bread. And well-spoken too, but not in the constricted Frenchified tones of court circles, nor the grating Scottish brogue that James and his sycophantic courtiers brought to Whitehall and Greenwich. I see a kindly, grey-haired woman, as old as my real mother would be if she'd not been taken by the plague; a woman who's been a nursemaid in some great house. I see parts of a story forming in my darkness. The Master has taken a liking to her, had her schooled to speak as he wants his children to speak.

'Adam heard your cries.' She interrupts my fancies. 'Adam was nearest to the barn. He shouted to us. Me and Sarah, Godwyn, Randall and Anselm. We'd been working the fields, cutting corn. We saw the smoke. We saw three men running from the barn. Anselm chased after them and caught the young one. It was the lad told us there was someone in the barn. We tried to beat the fire down, but it was too fierce. And the only pails to fetch water were in the barn. Then you leapt through the flames, your hair on fire. Randall pulled you away from the barn. Adam soaked his cape in the river, wrapped it round your head. Adam said to bring you here. He said Agnes would save you.'

'What is this place?'

'A room in the stables. Adam said to keep you here until your burns are healed and your sight restored.'

'And when the bandage is removed, what will I see from where I lie?'

She chuckles. I imagine a smile. A kind, good-hearted smile.

'We're on the ground floor of the stable block. The floor is bare earth, covered in rushes. One small window. The walls were limewashed, but they're greying now. There's green mould in the corner furthest from your bed, but the room's not damp. We have two lanterns. Both give good light. And a store of candles. There's a plain wooden chair, here at your bedside, which is where I'm sitting now. And outside, when you go to the window, look one way and you'll see a chase flanked by woodland that leads down to the river. Look the other way, and you'll see the rest of stable block, the coach house and a glimpse of the Hall. We give thanks that we can care for you.'

'I thank you for that.'

Constance spoke a lot about this Adam who wrapped me in his wet cape. Was he the Master of the Hall? Was she his wife? Or were they brother and sister? And Agnes? The wisest of women. A cunning woman, like Hannah? In one of my dreams, it was Hannah bathing my eyes, smearing ointment on the eyelids, although I'd not seen Cunning Hannah since leaving her to fend for herself in Epping Forest.

So many questions, but more pressing is my need to piss. How my life has changed, that I have to ask to take a piss.

Constance guides my feet to the floor. I'm sitting on the edge of the bed. I try to stand. My legs are weak. She gives me a pisspot. I ask her to leave the room. She laughs. Gentle, not mocking. I hear the door open and close. Muffled, distant sounds of dogs barking. But the room is silent. I'm alone. Then I realise that I'm wearing nothing but a long woollen smock. My clothes must have been so badly burned that these women have peeled them off me and dressed me as I am now. They had seen me naked, helped me piss and shit.

Despite the blisters on my fingers, I lift the smock and take a piss. The first time since being here I've done it for myself. I'm withered with shame, frustration, and a growing sense of rage. Rage against the women who are keeping me here coddled in infancy; against myself for being so damned foolish as to let myself get caught in that barn by Pinchface Jack. I should have known he'd come after me. I could so easily have ambushed them. I want to walk to the window Constance spoke of. But the bandage is so thick I can't even sense a source of light.

I hear the latch on the door. I panic. The pisspot drops, smashes on the hard earth floor. The door opens. The door shuts. Footsteps. Two women's voices. My hands reach for the bandage round my eyes.

'Best not touch that.' A different voice. Breathy. Not Constance. The sound of the forest, footsteps on leaves. 'You wish to see again, that bandage mun stay where he be.'

'Just a few days more.' That's Constance's voice.

I want to shout, to scream, to curse. But I can play meek when it's needed. I lift my hands to show it, and retreat into my sullen darkness. It's only the soreness of my throat – not wisdom or good judgement – that stops me from raging at my confinement.

Two women, one on each side of me. I can tell Constance by the softness of her touch. Agnes is harsher, her hands rougher. Outdoor hands. Together they lead me back to the bed and urge me to lie down.

'How much longer til I'm healed?'

'Mos' men burned as bad as you'd be dead by now.' Agnes talking. 'Healing takes its own time, but Adam says the Fullness dwells in thee, so who's am I to argue? We's waiting. We's all waiting. An' we mun be patient.'

'The Fullness?'

'Name he gives to God.'

'The Fullness dwells in me?'

'So say Adam.'

I've been cursed as a Godless bastard for as long as I can remember, and now this Adam thinks the Good Lord has made His house in me. Maybe Agnes thought I'd be pleased to hear such news, but God's never had much time for me. A cheater trying to burn me alive wasn't going to change that. Men go mad believing they're the chosen one. But if Adam believed it, and that was why these women were nursing me back to health, so be it. I'd soon be on my way to Kate and Canterbury. Then back to London to wreak my revenge on Rochester. For it was Rochester had brought me to this state, Rochester who'd driven me from London, Rochester who'd tried to have Kate drowned. And Rochester who would truly suffer for it.

But first to Canterbury to make sure that Kate is well and thriving. Then deal with Rochester in a way which causes him more pain and humiliation than anything I've had to suffer.

I said nothing of this to Constance.

7
There is danger in dust

Agnes didn't talk as much as Constance. And when she did, she used few words. She gave me potions which smelt foul and tasted bitter, but I did as I was told and swallowed. They eased my pain and made me drowsy. I looked forward to the relief, but resented the power it gave Agnes.

Constance at least had some grace about her, and she was kindly. She assured me that the burns were healing, and when she walked me round the room she told me that my legs were getting stronger. I struggled to believe it. I told her my name. Matthew. Not Edgworth nor Lovall. Plain Matthew. That was enough.

I wondered how I'd managed to shit and piss in the days before I emerged from my stupor. When Constance and I were alone in the room, I asked outright.

'We helped you, Matthew. Me and Agnes.' As they would have helped a sickly child. Constance made it sound so normal that it almost softened the shame.

The picture I had of Agnes in my head began to change. The rustling of leaves in her voice suggested a fairy-like wisp of a woman, slight and pale – until her hands touched my skin. She was firm and forceful when she and Constance helped me on and off the bed. Her hands were more like the rough bark of trees than the feathery touch that was Constance. In my head I saw a woman taking pigs to Cheapside market, so in my thoughts I called her the pig-woman, even though she smelt of herbs and garlic, trees and earth, not swill and dirt.

They worked together to change the dressing on my eyes, which they always did at night. They told me to keep my eyes shut all the while. But they needed a candle to see what they were doing, and I had to know whether I could see. And so I disobeyed – oh brave Matthew! But I saw only silhouettes, dark shapes in a dark room that looked full of mist. Both wore long brown skirts and plain woollen blouses, and both were recognisably female. One was short, the other as tall as I am. Neither of them was the pig woman of my imagination. Apart from that I was none the wiser. I had to accept that Agnes wasn't poisoning me, and that Constance was as caring as she seemed. Every evening Agnes helped to change my dressings, and every morning she brought the potions for my throat. She spent little time with me in between.

Time passed.

Then more time passed.

Constance told me when it was daylight outside, and when the sun set, but I lost track of days, of time itself.

'It's raining today.'

'I can hear it.'

'First frost of winter last night.'

'It does feel cold.'

I never thought I'd hear myself passing the time by talking of the weather.

'It's sunny today.'

'Will you take me outside?'

Agnes said I wasn't ready. So Constance walked me round the room and described what she could see when she went outside: deer on the chase, crows in trees, geese flying in formation. I was growing fond of Constance. Without Agnes's poultices, potions and remedies I'd not have survived. But it was Constance's care and kindness that saved me from the pits of despair.

'How long have I been here, Constance?' My throat was still sore, but I could talk in rasping whispers.

'You were barely conscious for the first week. Another week has passed since you first complained about the bandage.'

'I don't mean to complain.'

'I'm teasing. It's a good sign. It pleased us all.'

'Us? Who is us?'

'Adam, me and Agnes. And the others when we told them.'

'The others?'

'In good time you will meet us all.'

'And Adam? When will I meet him?'

'When the bandages are removed.'

'When will that be?'

'Agnes says soon. And Adam says to trust in Agnes.'

'Has Adam seen me?'

'He had them bring you here.'

'I would like to talk to him.'

'And he would like to talk to you. But when the time is right.'

'Tell me about him.'

'He is a good man, Matthew. We love him, and he loves us. Let him tell you about himself.'

The adulation worried me. I liked Constance. But the way she talked about Adam made me wonder whether she borrowed her thoughts from him.

'You said we're in a room in a stable block. Why do I never hear horses? Or grooms or stable boys or coachmen?'

'Best not talk so much. You'll hurt your throat.'

'When will I meet Adam?'

'Soon.'

'I know,' I snapped. 'Everything is 'soon.' But never soon enough.'

'Please, Matthew. Please be patient.'

I retreated into my thoughts, which grew darker. That notion of *before* was haunting me. There were two Matthews: Matthew Edgworth in London, with the use of both his hands, his sight and his wits. But he's an other man, for I am now this pathetic Matthew, cared for by two women I've never seen, doing exactly as I'm told. Helpless as a babe in arms.

'Adam says. Adam says. Everything is Adam says.'

'Hush you, Matthew. Let us walk.'

'Outside. I want to walk outside. I want to breathe the outside air.'

To my surprise, she agreed. It was the first time we'd been outside the room. Gently, but firmly, she took hold of my arm, and led me. Everything by sound and smell. She opened the latch on the door.

'A small passageway. Stay close.'

She drew me towards her. The warmth of her body next to mine, my upper arm against her breast. That shouldn't have aroused me as it did. So there was still something of that other Matthew.

Another latch. The creaking of rusting hinges. I followed her through. Breathing the chill morning air. The smell of woodsmoke. Chickens clucking. A dog barking in the distance. Rooks arguing.

'Careful. There was frost last night. The cobbles are slippy.'

We walked a few hesitant steps. My raw skin chafing sore against the woollen smock, my legs stiff and weak, my joints aching. I stumbled. If Constance hadn't had hold of me, I'd have fallen. Matthew, a doddering old man. In less than twenty yards, the dream I had of ripping off my bandage and escaping this darkness to Canterbury had become as fanciful as flying to the moon. We stopped for a while. I caught my breath. As if I'd just run five miles.

'Do you want to walk on? We must stay in the shade, but we can go a little further if you like.'

We walked to the end of the stables, then Constance suggested we go back inside and rest. Cobbles in the courtyard outside the stable block. But no horses. And yet the owners of the house were wealthy enough to have cobbles laid. I would have asked Constance why no horses, but I was sick of being told that Adam would explain it. So instead, I asked her, 'Talk to me. Tell me about yourself.'

She chuckled. I sensed the warmth of her smile. Her hand squeezed my arm. Gently. Like a breath of summer breeze.

'Adam doesn't like us talking about the past. Who we are now is what matters.'

'I'm not Adam. If I can't see you, Constance, at least let me hear you.'

'You don't need to feign an interest in me.'

'I ask because I want to hear.'

She was silent.

I tried again. 'I don't know where I am. You say Wittenham. I don't know where that is. Your name is

45

Constance. You've been as kind and as caring as anyone could ever be. But I can't see you. I want to know who you are.'

I stopped talking. For several minutes she was reluctant to fill the silence.

And then: 'My father was a cartwright. We lived in Abingdon, not far from here. I had two brothers and one sister. Is that what you mean?'

'Whatever you want to tell me.'

'My parents both lived long enough to see me married, when I was seventeen, to Richard Millward. His father worked the watermill in Nuneham Courtenay. You really want to hear this?'

The places meant nothing, but I liked hearing her voice. She was sitting close to me.

'Constance, I'm not Adam. I want to hear.'

'After Richard and I were married, I lived in the mill with him and his father. He'd lost his mother when he was just five years old. His brother, Ethan, worked at the Green Dragon Inn. His sisters had all married, and lived in Oxford. So, just the three of us at the mill, and the servants and labourers.' I heard distress in her voice, but urgency as well. She needed little more than gentle encouragement to continue.

'I know millers have a reputation for being bad-tempered and mean. But Richard was as kind a man as ever I've met. His father was too, though he died less than six months after Richard and I were married.' She fell silent, before adding, 'I am blessed, Matthew. I have been blessed with great happiness in my life. As well as suffering terrible sorrow.' It sounded like she was repeating someone else's sermon. Then she said in a whisper: 'We must treasure our fortunes. And ...'

'And what, Constance?'

46

Nothing. Silence. She sniffed. Were there tears in her eyes?

'We must treasure our good fortune, but not deny our sorrows, nor dwell in them.'

'I ask because I want to know you, Constance.'

Another long silence. And then: 'Richard became the miller. Despite losing his father, we lived happily together there for many years, and in due course we were blessed with three healthy children: William, Elizabeth and Thurstan. So, I have much to be thankful for.

'Then Richard took sick. He had such a fever that I took charge of the workings of the mill myself. It was autumn, almost exactly three years ago, and the corn kept coming in. Such a good harvest that year. The grain loft was full, and I didn't want to turn it away. So, I asked Richard's brother, Ethan, if he could stay with us and help. I thought it would only be for a few days. Looking back, I should have asked one of the mill hands to take charge. Richard never spoke ill of anyone, but I should have known that his silence about Ethan was in itself a warning. On the day of their father's funeral Ethan had drunk himself to a stupor. I'd thought it was because he was overwhelmed with grief. I should have listened to the gossip. The truth is he'd become a drunken sot. I'm sorry, Matthew.'

'I want to hear it, Constance. I like hearing you talk.' And even as I said those words, I felt a pang of betrayal, for I'd said the very same words to Kate. It was different, of course it was different, but I meant it when I said it to Kate, and I meant it to Constance. 'You asked Ethan to take charge of the mill.'

'He concealed his drinking. I never saw him take a drink. For a week all seemed well. He told me that the machinery was well-greased, the millrace was clear. And the mill was as

47

busy as it had ever been. I saw carters bringing grain, I saw bakers collecting sacks of flour. I saw everything was working well because that's what I wanted to believe. And it gave me time with Richard. There were times when we thought the fever had passed. He opened his eyes. He asked about the children. I never told him that I'd put Ethan in charge.

'Then came the day the fever broke. He was still weak, but the Richard I loved was back with us. He was so pleased to see the children when they sat with him. I thought the worst was over.

'Then all three children fell sick. I didn't want to leave them, but I needed help looking after them. I walked to my sister, Clare, in Nuneham Courtenay. Why not send a maid or a mill hand? Why? I don't know. I don't know. It's less than five miles. But in the time I was away …' She sniffed, and blew her nose.

'I'm sorry. I shouldn't have asked.' I wanted to put my arms around her, offer what comfort I could.

'I am glad to be telling you, Matthew. The others know I'm a widow. They know I used to be a mother. But I've not told my story to anyone except Adam. You've heard enough.'

'No. If you want to tell, I want to hear.'

She squeezed my hand. 'Clare agreed to come back with me and help nurse the children. But there were things she had to attend to. So, I waited. And that took maybe a couple of hours. By the time she was ready it was late afternoon. We didn't talk much as we walked. But Clare did her best to cheer me. She thought that all would be well now that Richard's fever had broken.

'The sky was darkening as we walked. We'd come a couple of miles when we saw the light in the sky over Abingdon.

You asked who I am, Matthew. For two and a half years I could only think of myself as a grieving widow. There was nothing else in my life. I was racked with guilt, and the conviction that if I'd stayed in the mill-house, I could have saved at least one of them. I blamed myself for leaving Ethan in charge, for in my heart I knew he was a drunk. One of the millhands thought the fire started in the grind floor, where Ethan was working. My beloved husband and my three wonderful children were all burnt alive. And a servant girl who was tending the children. The millhands did their best to save them, but fire spreads so fast in a mill. Always so much dust when corn's being ground. If that catches, it explodes as fierce as gunpowder. Richard explained that to me when he first took me to the mill and I asked him why he was sprinkling water on the grinding floor. There is danger in dust. That's what he said to me.'

Her voice had grown very quiet.

'So you see, Matthew, I know about burning. That's why I asked Adam if I could care for you.'

We were silent for a while. I reached out for her, to take her in my arms. But my hands met air.

'Constance?'

'I'm still here. I'm looking out of the window. Do you have children, Matthew?'

8
A fearful madness

'Do I have children? Not that I know of.'

'Might there be children you don't know about?' I heard a wry smile as she spoke.

'I'm not married. Never have been.'

'In your sleep you called out for Kate and Alice.'

Until then I'd told her nothing of my history. I'd grown fond of Constance. She'd cared for me very well. But my life was bound to Kate. I'd have no future without Kate. So I told Constance that Katherine was a fine lady's maid who I'd fallen in love with, and that when I was fully healed I planned to get to Canterbury, where Kate was now living.

But I said nothing about Rochester's attempt to involve me in the poisoning of Overbury, and nothing about the revenge I was determined to take against him when I returned to London. I didn't want her knowing that the man she was nursing back to health was capable of such dark thoughts.

'Are you and she betrothed?' I told her not. I don't know whether she was surprised, or perhaps relieved, because after that she asked nothing more about Kate, and I couldn't see her face to read her expression. But she did ask who Alice was.

'A close friend of Kate. She came to London with her family, fleeing persecution in Holland. But they weren't safe in London, and they knew others who'd settled in Canterbury.' I said nothing about finding Alice in a trugging house in Petticoat

Lane, nothing about the invisible exchange with Frances Howard.

'Should we be talking about the past?' I said. 'Will that not make Adam angry?'

If she heard cynicism in my voice, she ignored it. 'I have never been to London, Matthew. The farthest I've been is to Oxford. Richard sometimes took me there. When your throat is healed, perhaps you will tell me about London.'

What was to tell? That I learnt to cut purses before my tenth birthday? That my first employment was in a brothel in the stews of Southwark? That the Fleet River stank worse than an overflowing cesspit? Or perhaps tell her what she wanted to hear? That the streets were all cobbled, that Paul's was the finest church in Christendom and offered shelter to the sick and destitute, that the City Fathers used their wealth to welcome all within its walls, and London was a place where virtue was its own reward?

'I would be happy to talk about anything, Constance. But let me rest awhile for now.'

Time passed. For long periods we neither of us spoke, but I always knew when she was in the room, and was thankful for the sound of her breathing and the warmth of her body on the chair next to me.

More time passed.

Until eventually, I could bear it no longer. 'I have to know whether I can see. Call Agnes. If she'll not remove this bandage, I will tear it off.'

'Wait.' She took hold of my hand. 'I will find her. But I'll have to leave you here alone. I don't know where she is.'

I hear the door open, then shut. No key turning in the lock. I could remove the bandage and escape. Surely, I'm now strong enough to walk at least to the nearest inn. I reach for the bandage. My fingers grasp the cloth. But there they stay. I do nothing. I sit on the bed.

Is it because I have no money? Because I don't have good boots? Because, because, because. I could give a dozen reasons, but the truth is I'm frightened. I don't want to be alone when I rip off the bandage and find that I can't see. I've grown dependent on Constance. Agnes has healed my wounds, but it's Constance has been keeping me from the darkness of my fears: that I'll not have my sight, that my face will be so badly scarred that I'll be shunned wherever I go, and that Kate has given up on me. That's what truly terrifies me.

It's taking Constance an age to find Agnes. There's a voice in my head whispering that she'll never come back, that confessing my love for Kate has set Constance against me, and when the door opens again it'll be the steward of the grand house and his men come to throw me out. And I'll be forced to join some band of wandering beggars until I'm branded and whipped back to the parish where I was born.

I get to my feet. With one hand on the bed for balance I take a few shuffling steps. I feel for the pisspot near the foot of the bed. I lower myself and kneel. Piss in the pot. I can tell from the sound it's nearly full. Was Constance about to empty it when she went off to find Agnes?

Get back to my feet. Walk from bed to wall. I have my balance. I can walk without Constance's support. I shuffle round the edge of the room. I turn round, go back the other way, hands feeling my way over limewashed walls. I find the door. I lift the latch, move it backwards and forwards on squeaking hinges, as if it's some tuneless instrument. I can choose to stay in this room. I can choose to leave. I am master of my own fate.

I close the door. I can wait a little longer. I should go back to the bed, sit down, take stock. Maybe then I'll have the courage to take off the bandage. I will walk to the bed, then sit down and take stock. I will do it unaided.

Breathe in, breathe out. Hands away from the wall. Hold them out in front of me. A child's game of blindman's buff. I'm assaulted by a memory of Cousin Jacob, taunting me, prodding me, breaking a rotten egg over my pate as I career around to the mocking jeers of his fawning crew. That sets me going. I walk faster than I should. I take a step. I take two steps, then my bare foot hits the pisspot that Constance has left for me. The crock shatters as I trip and fall to the floor, into a pool of my own piss.

I cry out in frustration. Blaspheming, swearing. All those fucking Godless words that Constance has never heard me use.

I should pick myself up, get to my feet and wait until Constance returns. Explain quietly what's happened. But I scrabble around, trying to pick up the pieces of the broken crock, trying to clear up my own humiliation.

The latch clicks. The door squeaks open.

'Matthew.' It's Constance. I try to get to my feet. I slip on the wet floor, breaking my fall with raw hands in piss-wet rushes. It's a miracle I don't cut myself on pisspot shards.

'Wait. Let me help.'

Her hands on my right arm. Another pair of hands on my left. Hands I've not felt before. This isn't Agnes. The smell of a man. A man who spends time with dogs.

I'm back on my feet. They ease me onto the bed.

I want to ask the man if he's the one they call Adam, but I stink of piss and frailty, and I'm too ashamed to speak.

'We mun close the shutters.' That's Agnes.

Three of them. Constance, Agnes and the man who might be Adam.

Footsteps slop on the wet floor. Hinges squeal. Shutters being closed? Is it daylight outside? If the pisspot was full, is it early morning? I know about times of day in London, where there are chiming clocks and where the first cock crow sets off barking dogs, when the draymen and the carters, the barrow boys and hawkers are going about their business as soon as there's a hint of light. But here? This is the hell of nothing.

The three of them whispering. Even in whispers I can tell the man's voice. His grunts of agreement are deep and male.

'Stay still,' says Agnes.

Constance on the other side. The man breathing.

'I'll remove the bandage. Move your head forward.' Agnes speaking.

I do as she asks. Constance says nothing, though it's her hand on my arm. It does little to calm me. I have fought with men armed with knives in a Cheapside tavern, and suffered nothing of the fearfulness that grips me as Agnes slowly unwinds the bandage round my head. Once, twice, three times. Still another layer of bandage.

'Keep your eyes shut until we say,' says Constance. 'Your eyelids were burned.'

'They are shut.' In my darkness I remember Kate in the Wilderness at Audley End. You're not a man who does as he's told. But I do. I do exactly as Constance says.

The bandaging is fully unwound. I reach up.

'No,' says Agnes. 'Do not touch. Eyelids mun stay closed. Godwyn, light a candle.' Godwyn? Not Adam?

It's not obedience now. I'm terrified of what I'll not see when I do open them. The sound of clacking. Flint against fire-steel. I hear myself whimper. Will I ever be able to use a tinderbox again without feeling the terror, seeing the horror of Pinchface Jack striking sparks in the barn?

A hand close to my face, a fingertip touching an eyelid.

'Is that sore?'

I feel nothing on my skin. Pressure on the eye beneath, but the skin itself is numb.

'Godwyn. Bring light.'

Heavy footsteps. From behind closed eyelids I see the misted red of candlelight. Feel the warmth of flame near my cheek. I wince.

'You're safe. Be still, Matthew,' says Constance, who gently squeezes my arm.

I hear Godwyn's wheezy breathing. A large, heavy man by the sound of him. But it's Agnes who's close. I feel her every breath.

'Them be healing well,' says Agnes. 'Godwyn, stand back, and snuff the candle.'

Footsteps. Candle smoke. Beeswax candle smoke.

'Now, Matthew.' Still Agnes speaking. 'Open your eyes.'

A beeswax candle, not tallow? How can that be? In a room in a stable block?

'Matthew.' Constance speaking, like the mother of her sick child. 'Do as Agnes asks.'

9
Shadows in mist

'What you see?' says Agnes.

'Light through mist. Dark shapes.'

'The light's coming through gaps in the shutters,' says Constance.

I look towards her voice. All I can make out is shadow.

'You feel pain in your eyes?' says Agnes.

'They're sore. It feels they're full of grit.'

'Constance can bathe 'em. Then perhaps we mun open the shutters.'

Constance does bathe them with what she says is cool water from a nearby spring. Godwyn asks gruffly if he's needed. Agnes says he can go. Later, Constance told me that Godwyn was there to protect them in case I raged at discovering I'd been blinded. In the moment, however, I'm the frightened little boy still doing the women's bidding.

The latch clicks, the door opens. The room fills with hazy light. A shape goes out. It ducks its head as it walks through the doorway. Is Godwyn tall, or the doorway low? The door closes again. One of the women opens the shutters.

'Your eyes be foggy,' says Agnes. 'Healing be slow. Time be what he be. I leaves now. Back later.' The latch clicks. The door squeals open. Then closes. Am I alone in the room with Constance? I've spent long enough accepting the dark nothingness of my situation with the grace of the saint I'll never be, but my patience is running thin.

'How long do I have to wait? Midsummer day? Is that when Agnes works her miracles?'

'Agnes thinks your eyes will heal. She says if things look cloudy and it feels like there's grit in your eyes, it's because you have no tears.'

'I don't understand.'

'She says that every healthy person has tears in their eyes. Your eyes were damaged in the fire.'

'If I cry, then I see better?'

'Maybe.'

'Why can't Agnes tell me that herself?'

'Agnes doesn't like talking to men.'

She bathes my eyes again, and things are clearer. The cool spring water does my crying for me. I thank her, and ask her to sit beside the bed. I want to see this woman who's devoted so much time to me. I want to see how the woman I've pictured in my head compares with the woman who is Constance.

I see a round face. I think her cheeks are red. I think her hair is dark brown, almost black. I want to ask the colour of her eyes. I want her to come with me to the window where I can look at her properly. But outside, dogs are barking. Some way off, but approaching. Footsteps on cobbles. Striding, purposeful steps. Constance is distracted. She looks round. A man's voice outside. Not Godwyn's. 'Stay. Both of you. Stay.' I hear dogs being chained to a ring on the wall. Footsteps in the passageway outside.

Constance gets to her feet. A man comes in without ducking his head. Constance goes over and greets him. They kiss. Even through mist, I see that.

I will be on my feet when this man approaches. I will not be an invalid. My movements are clumsy, but I swing my legs off the bed, and I stand. He walks over to me. Constance hangs back. He's an inch or so shorter than me. He takes me by the hand. His face is in shadow, but he might be smiling.

'You are here with us, Matthew. You came from fire and through fire, and now you are healing. Godwyn and Randall thought you would die. I knew you would live. Welcome, Matthew. You are saved. You are born anew. As, in due time, we all shall be. My name is Adam Rowley. You have met Constance and Agnes and Godwyn. You may not remember Randall, but it was he who pulled you from the fire in the barn, Godwyn who carried you here. Soon you will meet us all. Praise God in The Fullness.'

I've not been a churchgoer since my mother, my father, my brothers and sisters, all of them were taken from me. I prayed for each and every one of them. I prayed in church. I prayed at home. I knelt beside my mother and I prayed for little Beth when she was taken by scarlet fever. Six weeks later, I prayed for little Edward, when he was taken by smallpox. And then for the twin babes as they sickened and died. When my mother sent me away to the care of Aunt Grace because father had taken sick, I was still the boy who prayed and implored Himself that He would save my parents, and that I could go back home. I even prayed when Cousin Jacob mocked me for it, though only after he'd fallen asleep. But if there is a God, he's long since given up on me.

'Thanks be to God,' I say. It trips off the tongue so easily. I said it often enough when I was a child. If there's truth in what I'm being told, I owe my life to these people: Randall for pulling me from the flames, Godwyn for carrying me here, Agnes for her deep and ancient wisdom, her potions and poultices. Constance for her loving tenderness.

'The miracle of your rebirth and recovery has given us all strength,' says Adam.

How can my recovery give others strength? What can I say? That I'm glad? The patter, the banter that used to come so easily in London has all dried up.

'Agnes says you must stay in dark places until your sight is fully returned. She tells me that your throat was burned. So it would not be right for us to feast while you can only sip at your broth. But we shall most surely give you the welcome you deserve when you are ready, Matthew.'

'I thank you, sir.'

'My name is Adam. Please don't treat me as your lord and master. We are equals, Matthew. The poorest beggars, the rogues and thieves, the whores and cutpurses, all are every whit as good as the great ones of the earth.'

A rogue and a thief! Does he know me by repute? He bows his head, picks up my right hand and kisses it. Rochester surely does the same when he takes his leave of King James.

'I will leave you to rest now, Matthew. But may we eat with you this evening? It will not be the feast that you deserve, but it will be our way of welcoming you, marking the beginning of our journey together.'

There's something unsettling about his presence, but he has the unwavering respect of Agnes and Constance, so he has me wholly in his power. I lie shamefacedly, and I tell him I look forward to that.

Constance follows him out. The dogs greet him with barking. I'm alone. Has Constance's duty of care ended?

Matthew, the child on his sick bed, abandoned and close to panic.

I can see. Everything is clouded, unsteady, as if through thick glass. But I can see. I get to my feet. I may be weak, but I can walk. And maybe my wits are returning after learning the lessons so generously doled out by Pinchface Jack. An idea is forming. I hadn't understood why Constance has been so attentive, but now I do. She belongs to Adam Rowley and is following instructions. For years I lived by the maxim to trust no-one. I've said it more times than I can count. And yet I've abandoned myself to this invisible woman. And now she's abandoned me. I can walk slowly round the room without using my hands for balance or support. Without help from Constance. I can get out of this prison. Without help from Constance. Just find the road, follow the sun, walk south. Keep walking. From the bed to the wall. From the wall to the bed to the wall to the bed. Along the wall and back. Until then I'd not noticed the pile of straw in the corner. Was that where she'd been sleeping?

Keep walking. I want to look out of the window. Get a better sense of where I am before I venture out. The light is dazzling. My eyes feel are still so full of grit. If there's a bowl of spring water somewhere in the room, I can't find it. Where is she? Damn her?

'Constance?'

I curse myself for calling out. I don't need her. I can walk. I can see. I can walk out and find the spring myself. My eyes will heal. It's only a matter of time. I don't need these people. I can be Matthew Edgworth again as sure as the sun comes up each morning. And Matthew Edgworth can surely find his way to Canterbury.

But for now ... I close the shutters. The light's too bright. I need to rest awhile.

A hand on my forehead. I've been asleep. I recognise the touch before she speaks. 'Matthew. I'm sorry. I didn't want to leave you.'

'You didn't leave me. You had business to attend to. I was here on my own for a few minutes. That's no hardship. But I couldn't find the bowl of spring water. Where did you leave it?'

'Agnes says it has to be freshly drawn.'

'Then show me the spring.'

'I've already drawn some myself and filled the bowl. It's by the door.'

'I don't need you fussing over me, Constance. I can do things for myself. Just show me the spring.'

'Are you angry with me?'

'Why would I be angry with you?'

'When things start to improve, that's often the most difficult time. Richard was bad-tempered when he started to recover.' She puts her hand on my arm.

'I am not Richard. Don't pretend that I am.'

I can't see Constance's expression, but her silence seems pained. Let her stew awhile.

'And nor am I the man your beloved Adam Rowley thinks I am.'

She takes her hand away. Is she so easily offended? I can see enough to watch her walking to the door.

'Go on. Leave me. I don't need you now.'

I'm like a dog that's been chained too long. Snapping at whoever comes near. Even Constance. Especially Constance.

She opens the door. She bends down to pick up something. Shadows in mist. She comes back into the room. Puts the bowl on the chair by the bed. Sits on the bed.

'Do you want me to bathe your eyes?'

Does she really need to ask? But I don't stop her, and her touch is as soothing as ever. When she's finished, she asks, 'Would you really like me to leave?'

'Your choice. I'm not your keeper. And you're not mine.'

'I can leave you alone for a while if that's what you want. But be careful. The bowl of water's on the chair. There's lint cloth beside it if you want to bathe your eyes.'

'Did Adam instruct you to come back? Did Agnes tell you to bathe my eyes? Are you always so obedient?'

I want to see her expression, but I can't read her face. A long silence. Outside, the dogs are barking – but some way off. I hear a wind blowing, and a flurry of leaves whirlpooling into a corner nearby.

'Constance?'

She waits before answering. 'Yes.' She's close by the door. I feel a sudden flurry of nerves in my stomach, and I silently curse myself for needing her so much.

I do my best to sound conciliatory. 'You told me there were rushes on the bare earth floor. You said nothing of the straw in the corner. Have you been sleeping on that?'

'Someone had to stay with you. Your life was in danger.' There's a chill in her voice.

'Why is my wretched life so damned important?'

She doesn't answer. Despite the bathing of my eyes, they still feel sore and prickly. It's easier to shut them, to choose darkness.

'Are you still a widow, Constance?'

'Of course I'm a widow.'

'Are you and Adam not man and wife?'

'Adam has been good to me. There are things we share. But he and I are not man and wife.'

'What time of day is it?'

'Afternoon.'

'I want to go outside again. I want to see where we are.'

She nods and murmurs agreement, but she's distracted. 'Shall I take your arm?'

'Let me try on my own.'

She stands nearby as I get to my feet, then leads me to the door. She holds it open. I follow her down the passageway. There's a lingering dank smell of horses that had once been here, but no sound now. No neighing, no whinnying, no chomping on hay, no clattering of hooves.

'There's another door,' says Constance. 'That takes us outside.' I can see her well enough to watch as she lifts the latch, and see the door swing open. She takes hold of my arm to guide me through. I'm glad to feel the warmth of her touch.

'How far do you want to walk?' Her hand still on my arm.

'Hold still.' It's not walking that interests me. It's being outside. Trying to see for myself where I am. And having Constance near. I'm angry with myself for having been so short-tempered with her.

My sight is still as if through thick, cloudy glass. But I can see that we're standing on cobbles. The sky is grey. There are buildings behind us and to either side. Fallen leaves have been blown into the corner. I hear a parliament of crows bickering as they return to nearby trees. What I can't see or hear are people.

My irritation with Constance is forgotten. And she chooses not to remind me of it.

'Help me, Constance. Tell me what I'm looking at. We're standing on cobbles. I know that. The stable block is behind us. We've come through a door and we're standing in what seems to be a courtyard.'

'The stables and coach house surround the courtyard on three sides. But from where we're standing, we can look down the chase and across to the other side of the valley. Can you see the large oak tree?'

'I see the shape of a tree.'

'That's good.'

'And I see that this is grand for a stable block. It has a cobbled yard. It must be part of a fine estate. But no horses? No grooms? No stable boys?'

'Not now.'

'Why? Where are they? Has half the world died?'

10
A child's face

I ate with Adam and Constance that evening. Good claret wine, warm bread, fresh from the oven, and a rich broth.

'Breaking bread together,' said Adam. 'Bread and wine in your honour, Matthew.'

Bread and wine in my honour. No mention of God. What I'd learnt from the actors has stood me in good stead over the years. With the help of costumes and face paints from the Blackfriars tiring house, I'd played Sir Haughty Disdaine, the strutting courtier who could charm and smarm through the grandest of houses, Martin Farnworth, the rank beginner who would fumble his cards but walk away with a full purse. But who was I now? They honoured me, when I was nothing but a half-blind weakling, dependent on the kindness of women? More to the point, who did Adam think I was?

When Constance told me that Adam believed God was in me, an image came to mind of those stone-faced puritans who plagued the courtyards outside Saint Paul's ranting their hypocrisies to all who'd listen: Humble yourselves in spirit that ye may walk the true path – while all the time parading in their capotain hats and clothes so very plain that nobody could pass without noticing them. Blessèd are the meek for we shall inherit the earth. Even I knew the Good Book well enough to hear that we slip in for they.

But Adam Rowley was no puritan. He wore his fair hair curling in long ringlets, his beard neatly trimmed in the fashionable style, and a leather doublet with polished brass buttons; the attire of wealthy gentleman squire. After breaking bread, his talk was not of the Great Tribulation that would soon come amongst us, but of the unexpected bounty of this year's harvest, the clemency of the weather and the pleasure he took in his beloved dogs.

He could not have been more welcoming, yet the longer he talked, the more uneasy I became. I'd learnt early in life to avoid debts, but with the passing of each day, I owed Adam and his crew ever more. I've eaten with scoundrels in the kitchens of Petticoat Lane trugging houses. I've suffered the rankest of pies that the Mermaid in Paternoster Row has to offer. I have dined with nobility in the person of Lady Frances, the Countess of Essex herself. But I have never been so uncomfortable at dinner as I was that evening in the abandoned stables of Adam Rowley's grand house.

Eventually, he fell silent. I took it as my invitation to speak.

'Constance has been very kind to me.'

'Thank you,' said Constance. The first words she had spoken.

'She is a good woman, Matthew.' Was there a warning in that?

'I know,' I said, and looked over to Constance. I hoped she'd join the conversation, but she took it as her cue to leave.

I knew nothing of Rowley, except that Constance and Agnes were in awe of him. I had a sackful of questions, but in the dim light and with my clouded sight, I couldn't read his face, so I held back those that mattered most, and started with a simple, 'Beeswax candles?'

'You sound surprised,' said Rowley.

'Such luxury in stables!'

'Where tallow splutters and stinks, beeswax brings light to the darkness, perfume to the air and sweetness to the soul. We must take pleasure in what's given to us. I was born into a wealthy family. Some say that was good fortune. But for some it's a burden.'

'I'd say good fortune.'

'True wealth is only found in humanity and fellowship. The wealth I have now is with those who surround me, who give themselves to others, whose love is enriching.'

'Are these stables part of your family estate?'

He laughed. 'My family! My estate! Oh, Matthew. You and I could talk for hours about family – mothers and fathers, brothers and sisters, life and loss. In the fullness of time there will be no estates, no ownership. There will be love that's freely given and received with good grace.' He took my hand in his. 'I will keep no secrets from you, Matthew. But some things need time for the telling.'

'How long have I been here?'

'Just over three weeks. The speed of your recovery gives strength to us all.'

'Three weeks? It feels longer.'

'Randall and Godwyn feared you'd not survive. They saw a man with his hair ablaze in a burning barn, where I saw a sign of new life, the most precious of gifts.'

'You didn't know me then,' I said. 'You don't know me now.'

'I saw a man reborn from flames.'

'I had a life before that fire, and I will not let go of it.'

'It is not good to dwell in memories, not good to let them weigh you down. We have all done things we regret, deeds of darkness. But we can be so much more than the creatures of our deeds.'

'Creatures of our deeds?'

'Most men and women are trapped by their actions and mistakes. We do not have to be.'

'Are you seeking my confession?'

'I am not a priest.'

'What then? What do you want from me?'

'I seek nothing from you.'

Did he expect me to believe that? 'What do you know of me?'

He chuckled, amused by the question. 'We were working in the fields when we heard your cries and saw the barn on fire. Three men running away. Randall pulled you from the fire. Godwyn carried you here like a babe in arms

. Anselm caught the young one. We kept him with us until he told us what happened.'

'What did he tell?'

'His name was Michael. He said you stole money from him and men in Oxford. That your name is Matthew Lovall. That he had no part in the burning.'

'You believed him?'

He was silent for a while. I didn't think the question was that difficult. I noticed a strange buzzing somewhere in the room.

'Is that?'

'What?'

'It's nothing. I thought …' It had stopped. Had the noise been in my head?

'Young Michael said he tried to stop them. He was terrified we'd hand him over to the magistrates.'

'Did you?'

'I asked him if he wanted to join us. He said no.'

'You let him go?'

'He thinks you died in the fire.'

'You told him he could join you?'

'He chose not to.'

'He had my tinderbox – which they used to light the fire. He could have thrown it away.'

'He was a frightened child. Fear makes people do many things.'

'The boy told you I stole money. That makes me a thief. Does that not matter to you?'

'What matters is who you are, not the story told by some frightened boy child. How could you have stolen what they never owned? Can anything be truly owned when all is part of the Great Fullness?'

His evasions dressed as mystical wisdom were irritating me. 'Who do you think I am?'

'I think you are Matthew,' he said with the broadest of smiles. 'And I think you will tell me who you are when you know it yourself.' His gentle, warm-hearted laugh wrong-footed me again. I was annoyed that I couldn't read the expression on his face. 'I think you have a ready wit, and the men who tried to kill you are themselves cheaters. You may have a dark past. That may trouble you. But it's of no matter to me.'

'And you? Who are you, Adam Rowley? A preacher?'

'I mistrust the clergy, and have no time for the church – not for the papist Romans, nor for our English Protesters. The only robbers I cannot forgive are churchmen and their collectors of tithes.'

'But you are a man of God?'

'I am a man, and God, if you choose to use that word, is in me. But the Fullness that some call God is also in you, Matthew. And you are in him. He sees us more clearly than we see ourselves. And when He grants us His revelations, He shows us what we and the world might be.' He leant forward and said quietly: 'He shows us possibilities. He shows us what we might become in those days before the end of days.'

You see a possibility. You make it happen. I'd been saying as much for years. Wise Hannah knew it. Forman knew it. Was this Adam Rowley wise in the same way they were wise? Or was he something very much darker? I'd heard The End of Days so many times before, roared out by the blistering hellfire preachers outside Paul's. But Rowley spoke the words so softly he could have been hushing a child to sleep.

The buzzing had started again.

'Do you hear that,' I said. 'Are there flies trapped behind the shutters?' As I spoke, I heard another voice in my head. Jacob. Say the Lord's Prayer backwards. Conjure the Lord of the Flies. My loathèd cousin Jacob, conjuring the great darkness.

In my London lodgings I'd learnt to shut out all those noises I didn't want to hear: the yowling cats, the barking dogs, the bawling drunkards, the screeching gulls – I was deaf to all of them when I chose to be. But now, in this empty stable block, I found myself distracted by the buzzing of flies.

'Earlier today we harvested honey from our skeps. Some of the bees must have followed me. I can let them out if they concern you.'

I watched Rowley's shadow slip over to the window, open the shutters and fuss until he announced they'd flown. My sight was poor, the light was low, but I was convinced I saw a face outside. A child's face. I'm sure I saw Rowley wave his hand in a gesture of Begone before he closed the shutters, and sat back down beside me. My dreams had been haunted with nightmares of Jacob's death, and my sight was so poor that I assumed the face must have come from my own fevered imagination.

From outside, the sound of a dog barking.

'We learn much from the bees. The bee is the wisest of all animals. Each bee works tirelessly for the benefit of all. It is not jealous nor envious.'

'I know nothing of bees,' I said. 'What do you want from me?'

'Whatever you bring, whatever you choose to share with us.'

'Suppose I have nothing to give?'

'You have already given us more than you can imagine. Your presence is itself a gift.'

'I've done nothing.'

The dog still barking. Another had joined the chorus.

'Do you mind if I bring them in?'

'Why should I mind?'

They brought with them wet fur and the familiar dog-breath stench of rotting fish. I saw the shapes of two large dogs. They sniffed my legs, then padded off and lay down near the pile of straw that had been Constance's bed.

'Mother and pup,' said Adam. 'Martha and Toby. Devoted to each other. Very loyal.' And noisy too, as they slavered and licked themselves clean. I'm not used to sharing a room with dogs. Frances had her lap spaniel with her on the occasions she summoned me to Salisbury House. Kate once told me that Lord Essex used to bring his favoured dogs into Chartley House to eat with him, but I have never lived with dogs.

Rowley used beeswax candles, he was dressed in expensive clothes, he brought his dogs indoors. He had the manners of a gentleman and some of the trappings of nobility, and yet he treated me as the one to be honoured.

'Is God, or whatever you call him, is He in the dogs too?'

'God.' He said the word slowly and quietly, weighing the sound of it, in soft velvet tones, as if confiding a close personal secret to a lover. 'God, as some people call Him, is a Fullness, a completion. His essence is in dogs as it is in all creatures. They do not know it. But most men do not know it either.'

I'd have asked him to explain, but I knew I wouldn't understand, and in truth I didn't want to.

'You say, dear Matthew, that you have nothing to give. Before you came to us, Constance was sunk into a state of abject melancholy. Since you have been with us, her darkness has lightened. She has found herself again. Before you came to us she was weighed down with guilt. She blamed herself for the death of her husband and her children.'

'I've done nothing for Constance.'

'You accepted her love. Her love for you has been a healing – for you and for her. You come amongst us, and we are nearer completion. It was meant that you came to us. Your presence is a reminder that each of us has the Fullness in us.'

He could have been describing a New Messiah, but those weren't the words he used. 'Constance has been very kind to me.'

'She has indeed,' said Rowley, and then got to his feet. 'And now I must take my leave.' He clasped my head firmly in his hands, leant forward and planted a kiss on my forehead.

Then he called his dogs, and they were gone.

I was left alone with nothing but Rowley's beeswax candle, the strangeness of the encounter and the lingering feeling of his wet lips on my skin.

I wanted to plan ahead, not mull over the teachings and preachings of a man who despised the church. But I couldn't help myself. Maybe Rowley was wise in ways the churchmen weren't. But I had a nagging feeling that hidden beneath his gentle manner, strange words and seeming kindness, there lurked something much darker. And I couldn't put from my mind that clouded image of the child's face that appeared at the window when Rowley went to banish the bees.

11
All shall be shared

I don't know how long I was alone before Constance came back, but time enough for Rowley's candle to splutter and die, leaving me in the darkness of my own confusion.

When she eventually returned, Constance carried a lantern. She placed it on the chair, and sat beside me on the bed.

'Thank you for looking after me, Constance.'

'It was Agnes cared for you.'

'Agnes's potions healed my burns, but it was you nursed me back to health.'

'And soon you'll be leaving us for Canterbury.'

'How can I leave for Canterbury? I can barely walk to the end of the stable block. And all I can see are shapes in the mist.' But I knew that her shoulders were slumped and her head hung down. I took her hand in mine. She flinched. But didn't pull away. The softness of her hair nestled against my cheek. There was a raw vulnerability about her I'd not noticed before. I'll not pretend I wasn't aroused. Constance would have seen that for herself if she'd been more alert. But I held myself in check.

'We cannot stay forever in this place,' she said. 'Not you. Nor any of us. The Fullness means movement. It is what we are. Like rivers. Always flowing. There will be a new age, Matthew. We shall be the heralds.' She spoke quietly, as much to herself as to me, as if by parroting Rowley's words she could persuade herself of the truth in them.

'That doesn't seem to bring you much hope, Constance. You sound downcast.' I guessed it wasn't me she wanted, nor the salvation of Rowley's new age, but to stay close to the mill where she'd lost her husband and children.

'We have no choice,' she said. 'We cannot stay. We must all move on. The scavengers are circling.'

'You've been very good to me, Constance. I thank you for it. I will never forget you.'

She lifted her head. 'Nor I you.' Then she got to her feet and walked away.

'Are you angry with me Constance?'

'Not you, Matthew. I'm angry with myself.'

'Why?'

No answer. Her silhouette was close to the window.

'Is there moonlight?' I said.

'Nearly full. And cloudless. And little wind. It will be cold tonight. Perhaps the first frost of autumn.'

From outside, the call back and forth of owls. Then nothing. No howling dogs, no wailing cats, not even the skittering of rats in the roof. Silence swelling and filling the room – until Constance whispered something so quietly that I could only hear shushing sounds, not words.

'I can't hear you. Come closer. Say that again.'

She walked slowly back, sat down beside me again. The light of the lantern fell soft and warm on her face.

'All shall share.' She said. 'All shall be shared.'

'Is that what Adam says?'

'He said I am to tell you.'

'Tell me what, Constance?'

'In the Fullness, all shall be shared.'

So close. The movement of her lips. Her tongue. All shall be shared. So simple. So perplexing.

'I'm to stay with you, Matthew.'

'I know. You made me a promise some weeks ago.'

'It will be cold tonight. Too cold to sleep alone.' Her hands on my cheeks. Her eyes unwavering. Her lips just inches from mine.

'As brother and sister? To keep us warm?'

'As Constance and Matthew.'

There had been times while I was regaining my senses, and my eyes were still bound with bandages, when I'd wondered whether the Constance who aroused me was a dream of my fancies, and that when I could finally see properly, I'd find her to be an ageing, pock-marked greasy hag. But the Constance who sat beside me on my pallet bed had clean skin, long fair hair and clear eyes.

'Together? In the same bed?'

She didn't reply.

'Is that what you want? Or was that what Rowley says you should do?'

'All shall be shared. It is a truth he shares with us.'

I was minded to ask her where Adam found his great truths, but it was him I wanted to argue with, not Constance. She'd seemed so disturbed when she came back into the room. I wondered what happened outside. Had Rowley instructed her to share my bed? Was that what so disturbed her? Share and be shared. It might be what Jesus Christ taught, but no sermoniser I'd heard in church pulpits ever spoke of beds and bodies, except in the same breath as Hell and damnation.

All shall be shared. Was that his way of preventing me leaving for Canterbury? A devious way to possess me, the opposite of his claim that nothing should be owned.

'Matthew. Come back to me.'

'I'm here, Constance.'

And for all my qualms and hesitations, she was a woman in her prime and our lips were just inches apart.

We did share a bed that night. My hands, my face, my eyes, my lungs had all been burned, but I was still a man – although there'd been times in the weeks after the fire when I'd had my doubts. And I was glad for the darkness. My face has long been scarred, but that seems to have been an attraction for women. But no amount of poultices and potions could hide the ravages of the barn fire. I daren't ask her what I looked like in daylight.

The bed was as narrow as any pallet bed. There was less room for the two of us than when I lived at home with my own mother and father, and I'd shared a bed with my brothers and sister. But the thought of Kate in Canterbury, and my worries about what might happen in the days to come between me, Constance and Rowley meant that when we climbed into bed I was determined to stay chaste. It might be several weeks before I'd be fit enough to make my way to Canterbury. Leaving would be even more complicated if Constance and I did the jiggy business.

At first we lay together, nestled like spoons, with me turned away from her. But her breasts were pressing against my back.

I tried to think of things that might distract me from the warmth and softness of her body. I pictured learning to cut purses from the groundlings in The Globe, scrumping apples with Jacob over the walls of Tottenham Court. All to no avail. So I tried to fill my head with images of men and women who'd been destroyed by French pox, their bodies decayed from inside out. Even that didn't dampen my arousal. I asked Constance to turn away, so we'd be lying back to back.

'Do you not want me, Matthew? What am I to you? Am I only the nurse who cared for you in your blistered, burning darkness? Am I not also a woman, Matthew?'

'Of course. Yes. Of course, you are Constance.'

'Then hush you, and hold me.'

I was surprised by how much I wanted her, by the intimacy of our union. Constance gave herself to me, pulled me into her, with an urgency that none of the whores I've been with could ever have feigned.

And did I think of Kate? Was I racked with guilt? Not then. Not that night. Guilt had never been something that much troubled me. And that night I wasn't thinking ahead. As moonlight streamed through half-closed shutters, Constance and I talked, and we laughed together. Time slipped by. I thought I heard something outside. Constance covered herself in her cape and tiptoed barefoot to the window.

'A fox.'

'We should lock the door,' I said.

'There's no lock, no bolt.'

So, I tied the latch down with the lace from Constance's boot. And she laughed at our small conspiracy to stop Agnes and Rowley from disturbing us in the morning.

When we were back in bed, I asked, 'Why were you so angry earlier, Constance?'

She was silent for a while.

'Hold me, Matthew. Make this real.'

We wrapped ourselves round each other.

'I was angry because I couldn't put from my head the voices of Hell and Damnation that always so filled me with fear when I used to go to church. I was angry because I didn't trust myself. Because I was frightened of what my own body was saying to me.'

We slept very little that night. Indeed, I wasn't aware that we'd slept at all – until we were both woken by a knocking at the door.

12
Blood and splinters

Constance sits up, startled, breathing fast, warm light flickering across her bare breasts. There are lanterns or torches outside.

'Matthew Lovall? You in there?'

Neither Constance nor I say a word.

More knocking. Fists on wood. Then iron on wood. The pommel of a dagger?

No time to dress. But we grab what we can to cover our nakedness.

In the madness of the moment, I'm thrown back to the Matthew Edgworth of old. I search for my dagger. But there is no dagger. All we have is guile and surprise.

I take the pillow, stuff it under the blanket to make it look like there's a body in the bed.

'Constance,' I whisper. 'Look after the man in the bed. Here.' She understands immediately.

Silence outside. Flickering torchlight still visible through the half-shuttered window. They're not going away. I remove the other lace from Constance's boot.

A sudden banging and crashing. They're using a heavy stone or thick stave to break the door. The latch gives way. The door flies open. Splinters of wood, large and small, strewn across the floor. The first man through carries a dagger. He's not seen me. I'm behind the swinging door. But he's into the room too fast for me to catch him with Constance's bootlace and garrotte him. Behind him there's a man with a flaming torch.

'Where's Matthew Lovall?' says dagger man. I recognise the voice. It's Pinchface Jack.

Constance is kneeling beside the bed. If she so much as glances in my direction we're both lost. 'You're too late,' she howls, as if in pain herself. 'He's dying of his burns.'

'And where's the witch who's healing him?'

'There is no witch.'

'You lie. You're hiding her. Where is she?'

He walks over, dagger in hand. The second man strides in with flaming torch in in one hand, dagger in the other. No Name, his henchman from the barn. No other lights outside.

Constance draws them to my sham sickbed like wolves to an ailing lamb. If she wants me to sneak out for help, she's forgetting that I can barely hobble and have no idea where I might find Rowley and his men. But I can see a foot long splinter of oak from the smashed door lying on the floor.

My broken left hand, the hand I've always used for dagger work, is useless. And my right arm's weak. I have just one chance to make the blow count.

Holding his torch in front of him, No-Name steps further into the room.

'No,' screams Constance. 'Stay away. Leave us be. He's dying.'

I drop to my haunches. Reach forward, pick up the splinter. The tip's as sharp as any honed blade. But it's wood, not steel. The wood could snap. He's wearing a leather doublet, but woollen britches. I take a breath, then lunge. Hard and straight. Up, into the inside of his thigh, inches from his crotch. He screams. And falls. He drops the torch. My wooden dagger snaps. But at least three inches of it are buried in his flesh. I've severed an artery. Blood spurting, pumping onto the floor.

Jack has pulled back the blanket. The lump he thought was me is a pillow. His mate's lying on the floor, screaming, thrashing around, trying to kick me with the leg that still works. Jack turns, sees I've no weapon. I'm running out of lives.

Then Constance takes the blanket, flings it over him and pulls him back. He's flailing, his dagger caught up in the heavy cloth. I rush to help, but slip on pooling blood.

Constance is strong. She used to be a miller's wife. She can hold him wrapped like that, but not for long. He slashes. The blade appears, and then the hand that's holding it. I'm back on my feet, and onto the bed. I grab him by the wrist and bite. My legs and arms are weak, but there's nothing wrong with my jaw.

More howls of rage, and spurting blood. I yank the dagger from him. Pick up the flaming torch, thankful that it didn't fall and set light to Constance's straw bed. The fellow on the floor is squealing like a stuck pig as he tries to get to his feet. I cut his throat. Squealing turns to gurgling.

'Let go the blanket, Constance.'

As Jack throws it off, I thrust the flaming torch towards him. He backs away until he's up against the wall. I taunt him with the torch, waving it in his face. As he raises his hands to fend it off, I step forward and thrust the dagger up from below, so it slides behind his ribcage up into his heart. He sinks to the floor. It's the death I'd choose for myself. Quick and clean.

It's getting light outside. The sun is rising. I pick up the torch and wedge it in a crack in the splintered door.

'You've killed them,' says Constance. 'You killed both of them.'

'They came with daggers drawn.'

I put my arms around her. My sight's still misty, but I can see the woman I spent the night with. She's trembling. Her mouth's half open and she's staring straight ahead. She's locked inside the shock of what just happened. She grips my arm as if that will stop her falling.

'They were here to kill me,' I say. 'And they'd not have hesitated to kill you too.'

Constance sits on the bed. She says nothing. I wonder if she's going to throw up. I want to put my arm around her, hold her to me. But my hands are bloody, and I don't want to distress her further. So I sit close, hoping my presence will be a comfort.

And then, to my astonishment, she turns and says quietly: 'Thank you, Matthew.'

Now it's me who's struck dumb.

'You're right,' she says. 'Agnes warned us. She saw this. *There will be blood.* Those were her words.'

'Agnes said that?'

'She can see in ways that we cannot.' Like Cunning Hannah, I thought. Hannah, too, could heal. And Hannah, too, saw blood. As prophecies go, *There will be blood* doesn't count for much. There is always blood. But these Oxford cheaters knew about Agnes. *Where's the witch who's healing him?* She has a reputation. And these two aren't the only ones who know it.

'We cannot stay in this place,' says Constance. 'We must get word to the others. Tell them what's happened. But first I'll get water. You need to wash your hands.' She sounds unnaturally calm. But I'm not arguing. Let her be busy. I've never known how to manage wailing women.

She returns with a pail, puts it on the floor, kneels beside me, and washes my hands. I could be her small child who's been playing in the mud. But the washing of my hands, the squeezing, the gentle rubbing makes me feel like a man, not a child. There are two dead bodies lying in pools of blood just feet away, and I'm aroused again.

I turn to her. 'Constance.'

She's looking down, steadfastly focused on our hands. She doesn't respond. Doesn't speak. Doesn't look up. She's fighting something in herself. Anger? Rage against this man who's forced her into a world of violence when she thought he was the placid, patient man who made her feel better about herself?

Her hands are still kneading mine. She's no longer washing. She's squeezing my finger, rubbing her thumb in my palm, her breaths are coming faster. I hold her to me. We kiss. Then she pulls back. She's on the edge of tears.

'What did we do?'

'The killings? Or our night together?'

She looks at me, wide-eyed, her mouth half open. She murmurs, 'Yes.'

Gently I remove her hand from my arm. 'We're safe now,' I say.

She shuts her eyes and gives a quiet moan. And her whole body seems to sink.

There are footsteps in the passage outside.

'Constance?' Rowley's voice. He's standing in the doorway, the splintered remains of the door beside him.

Constance sits up and pulls away from me. 'We're unharmed,' she says.

Rowley's in the room. He steps round the bodies. He goes to Constance. Takes her by the hand.

'Are you hurt?'

'Not a graze. Matthew saved us, Adam. He saved me. He saved Agnes. He saved us all.'

'I knew it,' he says, holding Constance's hand to his chest. 'Give thanks.'

He can surely smell our mingled sweat. He must know we've taken him at his word and shared each other's bodies. And yet he turns to me and gives thanks. I've fucked his mistress all night til dawn, and would have done again if he hadn't interrupted us. He surely knows it, yet it's me he thanks. Is the world turned upside down?

He leaves go of Constance's hand, takes hold of mine, and solemnly asks, 'What should we do?'

No time to ask how the cheaters knew where I was, or how they knew that Agnes had healed me. So many questions, which would have to wait. The matter in hand was the corpses and what to do with them.

'The bodies have to disappear,' I say. 'We have a choice. Fire or water.'

And now the horror of what's happened catches up with Constance. She starts to shake and moan. Her hands go to her mouth, she drops to the floor and retches.

'Get her water from the well,' I say. Adam does as instructed, without question. He gives her water to drink, then washes her face. When she's breathing easier, he asks her to get help. 'Randall, Godwyn and Anselm.'

She still seems dazed, but she does as bidden, leaving me with Rowley and the two corpses in the bloody stables.

'I did the killing,' I say. 'But without Constance's help it would have been me lying there in my own blood, and those two would be coming after you for giving me sanctuary. She's as strong as any woman I've ever known. She has a ready wit and fierce intelligence.'

'I know.' He sounds almost rueful. Is that a hint of jealousy?

'Fire or water?' I say.

He looks puzzled.

'You asked what we should do. We burn the stable block. Cremate the bodies, destroy the evidence. Or create another story.'

'What do you mean?'

'There's always a story, Adam. They came looking for me. Nobody here. So they rest for a while, get drunk. A flaming torch falls onto straw. The stables burn down.'

He gave this more thought than it deserved. Then slowly shook his head.

'Then water. We wrap the bodies, stuff them in sacks. Weight them. Dump them in the river. But this floor must be spotless. No sign of blood. The door replaced. Can that be done?'

13
Truly one of us

There was a bend in the river where a dark pool had formed and the waters lay flat and calm. Rowley agreed that the bodies should be hidden until nightfall, then taken to the river, weighted and dumped silently in the dark of night.

The men Constance brought to help worked quickly and efficiently. Randall was at least six inches shorter than me, but thick with brawn and taut with gristle. He wrapped the first corpse in hessian sacks, picked it up and flung it over his shoulder as a kitten to be drowned. Not the kind of man you'd want as an enemy. Anselm and Godwyn carried the other corpse between them. Anselm was a big man, no taller than me, but strong and heavy set. Later, I discovered he'd been a ploughman; and Godwyn, the tallest of them all, a groom in the very stables where I'd been nursed back to life.

When they returned from hiding the corpses, they brought another with them to replace the smashed door. Gabriel. They said he'd been a carpenter before joining Rowley's crew. His eyes were blue, he had curly fair hair. As a boy, he must have looked quite the pretty cherub. Perhaps he would have done so still if the skin of his face hadn't been so heavily pock-marked. He didn't speak to me, and hardly said a word to the others, but he smiled as a man who feels blessed. If he survived smallpox, then I suppose he was indeed.

Constance had found boots for me, an old leather jerkin, and a long cape. She took my arm, and led me away from the stables. I hobbled slowly, unsteady on my feet. I still couldn't see as well as I did before the fire, but the sky was blue, and I was pleased to feel the warmth of the sun on my face, although that was a mixed blessing because my eyes still felt gritty and that was worse in bright light. I could, nevertheless, see better than before. The stable block surrounded a cobbled yard on three sides, with a covered well in the middle. The house which the stables once served enjoyed a fine view over the river valley. In the darkness of my temporary blindness I'd pictured something as large as Cope Castle or Salisbury House. Those had at least a hundred rooms. This house was timber framed with a stone-tiled roof, two gables and high, brick-built chimneys. Hardly a palace, but even with my cloudy sight, I could tell it was as grand a house as I'd seen since leaving London, and with a view that looked over a long chase that stretched down almost to the river.

'Is that Rowley's house?' I asked.

'It used to be known as Rowley Hall, but in the true Commonwealth we seek, there will be no such thing as ownership.' I held my tongue. The time to question Rowley's madcap nonsense would surely come, but Constance was keen to walk on. She led me across the chase and along an ancient track, up a hill and away from the river. I asked to stop and rest on the bough of a fallen tree. I was out of breath, my body ached and I struggled to keep my eyes open in the bright light. I was angry with myself for feeling so weak. Constance gazed into the far distance. What did she see? Burned-in memories, secret yearnings? Or had the shock of the killings caught up with her?

She turned and offered me her hand. 'Come. We must be on our way. Agnes says the weather will turn. We don't want to be caught in the rain.'

The track led into thick woodland between high ditches, with gnarled ancient trees curving over, a long tunnel into darkness. Constance called it a holloway.

'We go through here?'

She took me by the hand. I said nothing, not wanting her to hear my unease, though she sensed it, I'm sure. Even if I'd wanted to tell her, I could never have put words to the strange, unexpected fearfulness I experienced in that world of knotted trees and ancient banks. It was the kind of darkness that pulls you in and suffocates. I understand the dangers that lurk round the corners of buildings, the menace that takes cover in London's dingy alleyways. This was a world I didn't know, a world I'd never known, and didn't want to.

'It's an old road, Matthew. Over hundreds of years thousands of folk have walked this way.' That didn't make it easier, but I allowed her to lead on. We emerged from woods into an open meadow with a view of two nearby hills, one of them topped with a copse of old trees, the other ringed with banks and ditches.

'The Clumps,' she said. 'A place of ancient magic.' She said it with awe in her voice, not fear, although for me those words, 'ancient magic', confirmed a place of dread.

We crossed the meadow, and then the track led back into more woodland. The first drops of rain were falling on the canopy above. After a few hundred yards we came to a clearing, where a large circular wooden shelter had been constructed. Tree branches had been cut to make low walls and the frame for a turf-covered roof. I was reminded of the abandoned charcoal burner's hut in the woods near Hamsted where I first found Cunning Hannah, except that this was much bigger than Hannah's hovel, and far more substantial.

In the middle, a large black cooking pot was hanging from a metal tripod over a firepit enclosed with stones. Smoke rose slowly, disappearing through a hole in the roof. Two women were sitting nearby on joint stools with their backs to us.

'Agnes,' said Constance. She stood up and turned to face us. The other woman turned, but stayed seated. I was taken aback by how small Agnes was – not much taller than a ten year old child – with long dark curly hair which hung down her back to her waist.

'You bring him here.'

'He saved my life,' said Constance.

The other woman said nothing, but gave me an embarrassed smile.

Constance introduced me to Agnes's companion, 'Marian.'

'Good day to you, Marian,' I said.

'And to you, Master Matthew.' She knew who I was.

Agnes, however, had no time for pleasantries. 'Our men saved him from the burning barn. Me what give him healing.'

'And I thank you for it, Agnes,' I said.

She glared at me. My eyes were not yet strong enough to see the colour of hers. But I knew that look. I'd seen it before. It was the way Simon Forman used to stare at me, unblinking, reading my deepest fears, sucking my thoughts from me.

'Saved your life, did he? Did he?' She was talking to Constance, but still staring at me.

'They'd have killed me, Agnes, if Matthew hadn't – '

'So now his debts is paid. And he's up an' walking. So surely that's an end to it.'

'May be he saved your life too, Agnes. They were looking for you.'

She glowered.

'Matthew is a good man, Agnes.'

'So he stay with us? That it? That what Adam say? Eat with us? Sleep with us?'

'Adam has offered me shelter and sanctuary,' I said. 'You and Constance, Adam and Randall. I owe my life to you. You have all been very generous.'

'Constance gives too much.' Was that to inform me or to chastise Constance?

Agnes sat down. Marian leaned across to her. They whispered to each other. Then Agnes went back to stirring whatever was bubbling in the pot.

I became aware of another kind of gurgling. Constance led me across to a wooden bench on the far side of the shelter, where a woman was sitting with a babe at her breast. Constance introduced Felicity, then lent over and kissed her forehead.

'I have heard much told about you, Matthew.' There was a warmth in her voice.

My eyes were growing accustomed to the dim light, and I could see more of the building – if that's what it could be called. Wooden benches had been arranged in a rough circle around the fire. Piles of straw lay further away, by the walls of the shelter.

The women all wore thick skirts over pale cream smocks. And the men I'd briefly met, Randall, Godwyn and Anselm, wore simple leather jerkins and tunics, yet Rowley dressed as a gentleman in a doublet with gilt buttons. All shall be shared. Yet Rowley set himself apart by what he wore. Still playing the master with his servants.

Constance led me to a pile of straw. We'd surely only walked a few miles, but my legs ached, and I was weak with exhaustion. 'No shame in feeling tired, Matthew. You will recover your strength soon enough. Lay yourself down. You are safe here. You are with people who will welcome you and care for you.'

Agnes cast a look in our direction that suggested otherwise.

I lay down and fell into a deep sleep almost immediately.

The next thing I knew there was singing and laughter and the smell of roasting meat. The place had filled – with people and smoke from a fire and flaming torches. I stayed where I lay in darkness, the outsider watching on from the edge of the shelter.

I am used to the raucous hubbub of London taverns. And although there were far fewer people in this creaking wooden shelter than in the crowded smoky rooms of Cheapside or Thames Street, I felt overwhelmed at first. In London, I know what I'm looking for. I can scan a room and smell trouble, sense the cheater and his rook, sniff out where violence might start. In deepest Rusticshire, I could only glean impressions. The cooking pot that Agnes and Marian had been tending had been set beside the fire, which now blazed where before there'd been embers. A man with his back to me, silhouetted against the fire, was sitting on the joint stool where Agnes had been earlier, turning a skewered animal carcase on a spit over the flames. I looked for those I knew. Gabriel – I think it was Gabriel – was playing a fiddle. I saw Randall emptying a sack of wood and stacking it near the fire. I thought I recognised Anselm and Godwyn in a group of maybe half a dozen men and women, and a small boy in the middle of them. Felicity's babe was strapped to her chest, and she was shuffling in time to Gabriel's fiddle. I didn't recognise the other women, but one was older than everyone else. The boy was standing between Godwyn and the younger of the women I'd not seen before. They were all holding hands and dancing, singing a chorus whose words I couldn't make out. It wasn't what I'd call carousing.

Rowley's dogs lay on the floor, near the man who was turning the spit. He let go the handle and got to his feet. I recognised him as Rowley himself. He called out, 'John.' The boy broke from the dancers and walked over. Judging by his height, I reckoned he was about seven years old.

Rowley raised his hand. Gabriel stopped his fiddling and lowered his bow. 'We shall feast soon,' Rowley announced. 'But first I must speak. There is purpose in our gathering. Sit here, sweet boy. Take my place. Turn slow and steady. All of you, find somewhere to sit. He is come among us and must be welcomed. I shall wake him now.' I shut my eyes and made the gentlest of snoring noises. How could he wake me if I wasn't asleep? I like to please.

A hush fell.

Rowley's footsteps approaching. A hand on my shoulder.

'Stir yourself, Matthew.'

I grunt in surprise, sit up, look around in amazement.

'We are all here, gathered to welcome you.'

Crackling from the fire. Fat spurting from the carcase that young John is struggling to turn. Slow he can manage, but not steady. I can see it now, a small deer on the spit, heavy for a boy. Rain loud and heavy on the roof. The weather has indeed turned. Canterbury seems further from here than the Fortunate Isles.

'Come forward, Matthew. Come out of the shadows.'

I stand up. Rowley takes me by the hand and leads me towards the fire. Everyone approaches, like they're all moving in to get a better view. I catch sight of Constance, who's with Agnes on the opposite side of the shelter. I smile at her. They both take a step forward, but Constance doesn't smile back. Has she been crying? Or is it smoke in her eyes?

Rowley's grip on my arm is firm. The rain on the roof is steady, the spit squeaks in its cradle as John labours to keep it turning. But the hush is oppressive. All gawping at me as if I'm the Bearded Mermaid in a stall at Bartholomew Fair.

Rowley urges me closer to the fire. What was it he said before? You came through fire. I look across to Constance for assurance. Her face looks blank. I stop where I am, maybe a yard or so from the flames.

Rowley looks at me. Is that the ritual? The man who came from fire sacrificed to it?

'We wish to welcome you, Matthew.' He pulls at my arm. I hold still.

'My face. The skin's still sore.'

'I understand,' says Rowley. But he doesn't let go. And Randall now approaches and takes my other hand. He's a deal shorter than me, but so very strong. I'm no match for him without a weapon of some kind. All are still, except for the boy John who's toiling away with the squeaking spit. Rowley nods towards Constance. She walks over, takes my head in both her hands and looks me in the eye. She speaks slowly: 'I, Constance, welcome you, Matthew.' Simple words, but such weight in them they might be marriage vows, sealed with a kiss on my forehead. I have never heard Welcome sound so like Farewell.

Felicity steps forward. She passes the babe to Constance.

'I, Felicity, welcome you, Matthew.' Followed by the kiss on the forehead.

And on it goes. After Felicity, then Marian and the two women I'd not yet met: Joan and Sarah. There's a pause. Rowley looks around. With the firelight behind him I can't read his expression. But something's wrong. He beckons Marian to come forward, whispers something in her ear. She whispers her reply. He shrugs. Then beckons to Godwyn. Who comes forward and takes his turn.

'I, Godwyn, welcome you, Matthew.' It's the first time I can see his face properly. He has a scar on his right cheek. Healed long ago, but visible even in that half-light. I wonder what happened to the man who gave him that.

After Godwyn, comes Anselm. Then Gabriel, the angelic, pock-marked fiddler, and Randall, who has to reach up on tippytoes to kiss my forehead. Rowley gestures to Gabriel to take his turn at the spit and for the boy to greet me. He stares at me like he knows me. After a prompt from Rowley, he goes through the strange ritual, though he has to stand on a stool to reach me, and his kiss is so wet that it dribbles onto my nose. Then he jumps off the stool and runs back to stand between Sarah and Godwyn. His mother and father?

And finally, Rowley himself. 'I, Adam Rowley, welcome you, Matthew.' He kisses my forehead, then takes a step back. 'You have come amongst us, and now you are truly one of us. The Fullness is in you. He has brought you to us. The same which is in me is in thee. The same which dwells in one dwells in each and all of us.'

The Great Fullness inspires him to a Great Sermon. His less than merry band of followers seem impressed by the Great Wisdom of his words, though it all makes less sense to me than a Game of Vapours in Bedlam. What comes next is easier: 'Now let the Feast begin.'

The venison is served on wooden trenchers. Leathern bottles of wine and a barrel of ale appear, though I've no idea where they come from – nor the tankards and goblets. The drink begins to flow. And yet again Prudence abandons me.

It had been years since I drank as much as I did that night. I've played the drunkard often enough – people drop their guard (and as often as not their wits too) when they think you're in your cups. Maybe I was relieved that Rowley's welcoming ritual didn't have me roasted on the flames. And I was indeed grateful to them all for welcoming me and caring for me, so I wanted to show willing. I accepted the first tankard of ale and drank a health to all. It was refilled without my knowing, and one cup became two, and three became too many to count. So my memories of that evening are few and hazy. But I know that there was a heated conversation between Constance and Marian, who was worried about Agnes. Neither of them knew where she was. At the time I didn't understand why it mattered so much.

After much talk and more drink, and Gabriel's fiddle growing ever louder and faster, I retreated to the edge of the shelter to sit for a while and rest on a bale of straw to put a stop to the slow somersaults that the world was turning.

I drifted between watching the merrymaking and something like sleep.

I open my eyes and look around. Gabriel has given up trying to scratch a tune from his fiddle. The fire has died down. Constance and Felicity are sitting together, the babe fast asleep held to his mother's breast. I try to name all those whose faces I can make out in the gloom. Anselm, Randall, Godwyn and Sarah with John now curled up asleep next to them. Joan is the oldest of us. She's talking to Marian.

I look for Agnes. She must have slipped out of the shelter into the night. And that's when it dawns on me that she alone of all Rowley's jovial crew hasn't kissed my forehead.

I shut my eyes. I'm cold. I stand up, unsteady on my feet. I want to be with Constance. I want to be wrapped in her warmth.

A hand on my shoulder.

'Matthew.' It's Adam Rowley. 'You bring joy to us all.'

I thank him, and grunt something incoherent about the welcome I've received.

'Agnes will find her own way to welcome you.' I think he's trying to reassure me, but he can't disguise the anger in his voice.

14
The Clumps

I woke before dawn – my head pounding from all the cider and ale I'd poured down my throat the night before. Constance didn't stir when I staggered to my feet, put on boots and donned a cape. I just made it out of the shelter before throwing up. The rain had passed through in the night, but my belly was still in turmoil. The ground was sodden, but the clouds had passed and the sky was lightening. I found a grassy clearing and was sitting on a fallen tree trunk, arms wrapped round my stomach, when Agnes appeared, silent as a ghost in the early morning half-light. She startled me. I retched again. It wasn't the way I'd have wanted to greet her.

She held out a leathern bottle. 'Spring water. Clean your mouth.'

I grunted my thanks, took the bottle, and was about to drink when I stopped myself.

'You think I'd give you poison after all those weeks I been healing you?'

'I'm not used to trusting people.'

'You mistrust the wrong people.'

'What do you mean by that?'

'What I mean, Master Matthew, if that be your real name, is drink this to clean your mouth of vomit, ease your aching head.'

I took a drink. The water was cold. But my mouth still tasted sour and full of grit. Had she been expecting me? Watching and waiting for the intruder she wanted rid of?

'I healed you 'cos that's what Adam Rowley wanted. But you's not what you seem. I known that from the first.'

'I've not lied to you, Agnes. Nor to Constance, nor Adam, nor any of you.'

'But you's hiding things. I do know that.'

'What's past is past. Adam Rowley says we shouldn't dwell there.'

'Adam Rowley ent always right. An' besides, there are things you ent tol' him. Things he's not tol' you.'

'I thank you, Agnes, for everything you've done for me. Without your healing I would surely still be blind, and more than likely dead.'

She gave that strange half grunt, half growl that I'd heard in the stables when my eyes were still bandaged, before I knew who she was. I was still sitting on the fallen tree. She was standing in front of me, but she was so short that I hardly had to look up to meet her gaze.

'What you want from us?'

'You've already given me more than I could ever have expected. You, Constance, Adam, all of you. I didn't seek you out. And I'll be on my way again as soon as I have the strength. I swear to you, I mean you no harm.'

She stared at me. Looking into me. Then she did the strangest thing. She knelt down and took hold of my hand. When she spoke again it was in a soft, almost singsong voice that belied the harshness of her words: 'Yous may not mean to bring harm. But you brings it just the same. I sees it. And I knows it. I's always known it.'

'I am not what Rowley thinks I am, whatever that might be. But I've done nothing to deceive him. Nor you, nor Constance.'

She shut her eyes, conjuring a picture of something in her mind.

'The boy Michael carry summat with him that made him sore afeared. You know what that was?'

'I have a raging headache, Agnes. I can hardly think straight.'

'More fool you for drinking so much.'

'I don't expect sympathy. But I beg you let me go back to the shelter and sleep this off. I will happily talk later.'

'It were a book, Matthew. Michael said you had it concealed about you when they found you in the barn.'

Agnes could argue with me all she liked, but she was far too small and frail to keep me there against my will. I stood up. She stared, unblinking, daring me to push her aside.

'Why?'

'Why what, Agnes?'

'Why was you carrying that book? You wrote it, did you?'

'No. I didn't write it. It belonged to a doctor, Simon Forman.'

'Not you what wrote it then?'

'No.'

'Rowley thinks you wrote it.'

'No. It was Doctor Forman's book. His casebook he called it. Do you have it?'

No answer. From the opposite side of the valley came the faint sound of a cock crowing, muffled by the mist.

'I thought it was lost,' I said. 'Burnt to ashes in the barn fire. Do you have it?'

'I knows where it is. Who's this Doctor Forman then?'

'You've not heard of him?'

'No.'

'He had a reputation. He was well known in London.'

'What do I want with London?'

'Can you give me something to cure my raging head?'

'Maybe.'

'Please. I beseech you.'

'Who's this Doctor Forman.'

'He was a fine physician. He died a year or so ago.'

'What's it he wrote in that book?'

'Some people said he was a sorcerer, a necromancer. I knew him for a physician and an astrologer. His widow, Anne, gave me the book for safekeeping. She said it contained great wisdom, and she wanted me to take it to his brother who lives in Salisbury. I was heading there when I lay down to rest in that barn.'

'You wants to see it?'

She knew. She knew how much I wanted it. How much I needed it if ever I was going to return to London, and do what I planned. 'You have it?' I said.

'Poppy juice will ease your aching head. But 'twill make you sleepy.'

If Agnes hadn't healed my wounds, I'd have dismissed her, mocked her as a common simpleton. But she had the power of knowledge. When my eyes were still bandaged and I only knew her by her voice and her touch, I'd heard her breathy, half-whispered words like leaves on the forest floor. She'd brought poultices and potions, ointments and salves. Her hands were rough, but there was a soothing tenderness about her. In my imaginings I'd seen an elderly woman, steeped in ancient wisdom. Maybe that's what she was. But she inhabited the body of a child. And her voice, too, shifted: strange low growling sounds one moment, soft whisperings the next. A she bear in its dark cave.

'Do you have the book, Agnes?'

'I take you,' she said, getting to her feet and offering me her hand.

Of course I wanted Forman's casebook – if she actually had it. But I went with her because I was so desperate for a draft of poppy juice. And because I'd be better off with Agnes as an ally than an enemy.

She led me across the wet grass of the clearing to a narrow track that led through the woods and away from the shelter where the rest of Rowley's crew were still sleeping off the feast. We emerged from the wood onto a field, where barley had been recently scythed. I followed her until she stopped and waved an arm in the direction of the valley, where a long, wide ribbon of white mist lay like a pristine shroud over the Thames, splitting the landscape in two. The tops of willows that grew along the banks sprouted from the mist, as if growing out of some great white lake; and behind them the spire of a church floating on clouds.

She turned to me and gave a twisted smile – as if she herself had conjured the picture, and the mist had settled over the river to her bidding.

'It is beautiful,' I said, hoping that was the response she wanted from me. But she'd already walked on. We crossed several more fields, where mown corn had been gathered into rows of stooks. Agnes strode on ahead, knowing I'd be hobbling along after her.

She squeezed through a gap in a hedgerow. I duly followed, although the pounding in my head was worse with every step. She was leaning against a large hayrick at the far side of the field, waiting for me. No sooner had I arrived than she was back on her feet. She took me by the hand again. 'Come.' As we rounded the hayrick, I realised that the hill before us led up to those strange ancient earthworks I'd seen the day before. I stopped.

'You wants to see your Doctor Forman's casebook.' A reminder, not a question. Her grip on my hand tightens. We arrive at the first deep ditch that stretches round the hill. We cross it on a causeway, then up and over the first high circular bank. Not a breath of wind. A raven croaks, lifts into the sky from the woods beyond the earthworks. It glides slowly down, a bird-shaped darkness against white mist in the valley below. A bird-shaped glimpse of that dread dark world beyond.

Walk on, Matthew,' she says, as if I'm a broken nag that's just seen a snake.

Why has she brought me here? When did I first catch sight of this place? Yesterday? The day before? Time itself is cast adrift and floating loose. Yesterday, today, tomorrow. It all means nothing. How long since I was trapped in the barn fire? Ten days? Ten months? My childhood terrors at the Spital Fields seem closer in time than the feast last night. Is that why Agnes has brought me here? To force me back to my own wordless terrors? To the memories of the Spital Fields and what I saw there?

She grips my hand tighter. We walk side by side until we reach the middle of that huge ring of earth. She stops. 'Shut your eyes.'

'Why?'

'You feel it. I knows you feel it, Matthew.' I'm breathing too fast. 'Tell me what it is. Tell me.'

'I'm sick, and my head aches like I've been kicked by a mule.'

'Do not deny me. Do not deny yourself. You feel it. What happened here?'

'Just take me to Forman's damn book. And give me something for my head.'

'Tell me what you knows about this place.' She's growling again.

'I've never been here before.'

'But you know. You's shivering, Matthew. But it's not freezing.'

It's the same unnamed terror I sensed when I first caught sight of Forman's scrying mirror, that depthless darkness I glimpsed on the walls of the ruined Priory close by Spital Fields, something worse than death itself. A band of iron crushing my skull and a dark void beneath.

'There is death in this place, Agnes. Many deaths. And something worse than death itself.'

'You do know then,' she says, and sets off again before I can ask what it is I'm supposed to know. She leads me across another causeway. It's not until we're in the copse that Agnes stops, lets go my hand.

'My head is raging, my bones ache. Just tell me what you want with me?'

'Whatever truth you care to tell.'

'Is this where you've hidden Forman's book?'

'Tell me who you are, Master Matthew, and the truth of why you had the book. Then maybe I answers your questions.'

We're in a circle of trees, standing at the edge of a glade with cropped grass. In the centre there's a great slab of a boulder lying flat.

'I have enemies in London who want me dead. I worked for a man who considers himself a great lord. He hired me to make things possible between him and a lady who was married. Things that others weren't to know about. But they did know. His closest friend knew, so he had him imprisoned in the Tower and poisoned. And the lady's maid knew. So he arranged for her to be drowned in the Thames. His coachman knew. He fell down stairs and broke his head. And I knew too. I'd have been next. That's why I left London. And that's why I don't want people to find me.'

'Come closer. Sit you down.'

I'll do whatever's needed to set Agnes at her ease. I lay down my cape and sit on it. She places her hands either side of my head, draws me towards her. She insists I shut my eyes, as if she can read my thoughts better like that.

'You killed two men in the stables.'

'They were the same men tried to burn me alive in the barn. They were looking for you as well Agnes.'

'You killed them.'

'Yes. I did.'

'And before. When you was in London? Who you kill there?'

'I swear to you I am not a murderer, Agnes. And I'm a man of my word.' Nausea is welling in my stomach.

'Is that what you are? A man of your word? Now there's a thing. And have you killed before?'

'Rowley says to leave the past behind.'

'Me who asks. Not Adam Rowley. Me who asks who you are. And what you are.'

'Yes, Agnes, I have killed before. I take no pleasure in it. Never been something I do lightly. But I am not a killer. That is not who I am. Kill or be killed, Agnes. That's the world I come from. Sometimes there is no choice.'

'You talk in riddles, Matthew. I heal people, I'm a healer. Constance married a miller. She was a millwife. Anselm be a ploughman 'cos that's what he do. Gabriel a carpenter. How so you're not a killer?'

'If I tried my hand at ploughing, that wouldn't make me a ploughman. Same with killing. I do what I have to.'

'You kill, you're a killer.'

When I choose not to answer, she falls silent, but places a hand over my eyes. I don't resist. Neither of us moves. Time passes. She takes her hand away. 'What you see now?'

The only thing to have changed is the rising of the sun.

'What you see?'

'Trees losing their leaves. Shadows. Grass. Sunlight on that slab of stone.' A shaft of light has penetrated the circle of trees and fallen on the boulder in the centre of the glade. 'That what you want me to say?'

'You see what you see. See it, Matthew.'

'See what?'

'Open your eyes to what be here. Or close them and feel it.'

'You mean the light on the stone?'

106

'The sun moves. Moon waxes and wanes. Shadows move round. All things change. Turning and changing. They grows and they dies. But this place is different. I's known it since I were a child. And you, too, Matthew. You knows it too, even though you never seen it before. You pretend that you don't. But you do. You know death when you feel it. You sensed it in the earthworks. And you shivered. But here it's different. You sense that too. Say what you know. Say what is here.'

'Why do you so dislike me, Agnes?'

'I don't like or dislike. I only asks you this – tell whatever truth you knows.'

'Is this where you've hidden Forman's book?'

'You want to see it?'

'Of course I want to see it. I want to know whether you really have it. How do I know this isn't where you plan to poison me?'

Silence. The air so still.

'I show you the book if you tells truth about it.'

She tugs at my hand. And I'm back on my feet.

'Can you read?' she says.

'I can read English. And a little Latin.'

'This book you call Forman's book. Can you read that?'

'There's names in it. They're in English. I can read them. But not the other stuff, the Greek and Hebrew, if that's what it is. Not the signs and symbols.'

'You understand it though?'

'No.'

'Then why's you got it?'

'I told you – '

'What you said before worn't true.'

How does she know? And why in Hell's name does it matter?

'Prove to me you have it,' I say. 'Let me see it.'

She leads me to the boulder at the centre of the copse. 'First rays of sun have passed. We can sit here now. Shut your eyes. Cover them with yer hands.' As if this is some children's parlour game. But I do as she asks. I hear her walk quietly away. Footsteps kissing grass. When she returns, she puts a hand on my shoulder. Forman's book lies beside me.

'You says you don't understand what's in it. So, Master Matthew, tell me why you have it.'

I pick the book up. Run my fingers over the soft calfskin black cover, now hard and brittle from the heat of the fire. The edges of the pages are singed, and some are stuck together and the ink has run from being dowsed in water. But it's survived the fire. And the letters between Rochester and Forman, Forman and Frances, they are all still where I slid them – in that gap between the pages and the spine which only appears when the book is opened.

'Are those rooks or crows nesting in the trees?' I ask.

She looks up. I poke the letters out and slip them up my sleeve. Agnes might know all there is to know about herbs, potions and mystical stones, but she's childlike when it comes to the simplest cheater's sleight.

'Ravens,' she says. 'If the book ent yourn, Matthew, why you have it? I won't tell no-one else. Some things Rowley don't never need to know.' In that moment of confidence she's given away how wary she is of Rowley, how much she resents his power. And I'm guessing that her mistrust of me is at least partly because Rowley treats me like I'm special.

'The truth then, Agnes. I knew Forman. He did indeed have dark powers – far beyond my understanding. I didn't like the man. He didn't much like me. But I never wished him harm. He had many enemies, but I wasn't one of them. My master had dark dealings with Forman that he didn't want anyone to know about. After Forman died, I took the book from his workshop. I'm convinced my master had him poisoned. Forman was another who knew too much. I kept the book for myself. It's a weapon I might yet have to use in my own defence.'

It might have sounded like a confession to Agnes. It wasn't the whole truth, but it was a good deal more than half. Agnes looks puzzled and disappointed. I think she expected occult powers and deeds of darkness. But who am I to tell such tales?

'What else be in the book?'

'I know not, Agnes. Horoscopes? Astrological calculations? Recipes for remedies and ointments? Ancient wisdom – beyond the grasp of a mere rogue such as I.'

'But you feels it, don't you. You feels its power.'

I hold the book to my chest and shut my eyes. 'Oh I do indeed. Of course I do. I know how powerful it is, and how dangerous. I used to think that by carrying it I would keep myself from harm.' Now at last I'm on safer ground. Tell her what she wants to hear. And not so far from the truth.

'Same with this place,' she says. 'Feel the spirit. Don't understand it though. What I knows for sure is this. In ancient times this was a place of power. I saw your book, your Doctor Forman's book. I thought 'twas you what wrote it. Thought you'd be the one to understand The Clumps.'

'I wish I were that man, Agnes. But I hold Forman's book as a soldier might hold a shield. I know there's wisdom within. Just as I know the spirit of this place is good. But the book is my protection.'

That pleases her. Her mistrust seems to have faded, as the rising sun has burnt off the autumn mist in the valley below.

She led me slowly back to the shelter, avoiding walking through the earthworks. Thinking that perhaps I now had an ally in Agnes, I asked what Rowley thought Forman's book contained.

'He thinks you wrote it, your own true Testament, that Special Book you bring for us.'

'He can think what he likes, Agnes. It's Forman's book. I've told you the truth.'

She nodded slowly. 'I knows when a man speaks truth. It be such a rare thing. Rowley's a fool.'

'If he's such a fool, then why do you stay?'

'Safest place for me. An' besides, he speaks truths. Sometimes. Talks babble-brook nonsense too. Trouble of it is, he don't know the difference. But mos' men's much worse than Adam Rowley.'

That gave me pause. But my head was still pounding, and I was in no state to ask Agnes which of Rowley's babblings she thought were truths. 'You said you'd give me some poppy juice.'

'I will. And 'twill ease your aching head. But here's a warning for you, Master Matthew – '

'Just give me poppy juice, Agnes, I can't think straight to heed your warnings. Not now. I'll talk with you later, I promise.'

'Don't cross Adam Rowley. He don't take kindly to it. And don't think I'm simple jus' 'cos I'm small.'

'I don't think you're simple, Agnes. Far from it. But let me have Doctor Forman's book.'

'Rowley wants to see it. I'll give it him.'

'I beg you tell him nothing of what I've told you. Not a word about Simon Forman.'

'All safe wi' me,' she said with the faintest twitch of a smile. 'And I won't be telling nothing 'bout those letters either, those letters you tucked up yer sleeve.'

15
A beauteous commonwealth

The shelter was quiet when I woke. I reached out for Constance, but I was alone on the bed of straw. I was unsteady on my feet and my head was woozy, but no longer ached. The embers in the firepit were warm, but no flames, nor any smoke.

How long had I slept? I remembered Agnes, our walk to the earthworks, what happened at The Clumps and the draft of poppy juice. I'd not dreamed it because I still had Forman's letters. But Agnes wasn't in the shelter. The whole crew had slipped out without waking me. But someone had placed men's clothes beside our makeshift bed. Britches and a doublet, socks and boots. Assuming they were for me, I dressed, slipping the letters into an inside pocket.

I'd woken with a yearning for Constance and my prick standing proud, but I was hungrier in my belly than I was in my groin. I'd eaten more than my fill the previous night, but I'd thrown up most of it. I found a bowl with a ladle, and dipped my finger in what looked and smelt like frumenty porridge. It had long gone cold, but it was sweet with honey, and it eased my hunger.

I sat for while thinking about Agnes and Rowley. If he was mad enough to see me as his New Messiah, bringing with me Matthew's Book of Mystical Wisdom, maybe I shouldn't disappoint. There'd be no need for trickery. I could teach some of his crew to do my work for me, bring me all I'd need to set up home in Canterbury.

*   *   *

'We cut wood for burning, we fish, we forage for fruit, hunt deer, trap rabbits and hare. And sometimes we labour in the fields.'

'Hunting and trapping?' I said. 'Is poaching not dangerous?'

Rowley had been the first to return with his dogs padding after him.

'Poaching is not a word I like,' said Rowley. 'We take what is rightfully ours. In good time, all land and its fruits shall be shared equally again. Before good English men were trapped by the Norman yoke, this land belonged to all. We cannot own land any more than we can own water or air. They call it enclosure. I call it theft. We show the way, Matthew. In the Fullness, there will be no poaching or stealing because none will take more than they need and all will share in true common wealth. Until that time we have to tread carefully. Soon we will move on. We will find us a place.'

'A promised land,' I suggested.

'A place of safety, where others trust us and we trust them.'

'Where all shall be shared?' I asked.

'Yes.'

I was happy, for the moment, to play by his rules, even if his earthly paradise wasn't the place where I'd choose to live. But Rowley had a quiet, calm dignity about him, and the way he spoke made what he said sound almost reasonable, although the

113

courtyards of Bedlam echoed with similar rantings. All shall be shared? It was the All that grated with me. If it's stashed away in Greenwich Palace or one of those grand mansions on The Strand, I'm all for sharing. If it's mine, I'll be the one to choose who I share it with.

Felicity returned to the shelter, holding her babe in her arms. She smiled and bade us both good day, sat down on a joint stool by the firepit, lifted her smock and put the babe to her breast. Could the child be Rowley's?

He seemed to read my thought, for he said, without lowering his voice, 'In her previous life, Felicity was a maid to Lady Roche. The Lord grew bored of his wife, and he raped Felicity. When her belly grew swollen, she was accused of shameless depravity and dismissed.'

I'd heard many such stories before, but was struck that he spoke so openly of Felicity's previous life, as if anyone joining this strangest bunch of vagabonds was being offered a kind of resurrection.

Felicity's babe fell asleep at the breast. She laid the little fellow down, and asked Adam, 'Will you rock his cradle?'

He stood up, kissed her on the forehead, and took her place by the cradle. I followed him over. And Felicity left us to go about whatever her business was outside.

The cradle squeaked as Rowley rocked it slowly back and forth, regular as the pendulum on a long-case clock. A while passed before he spoke again. 'All amongst us here have suffered great adversity. Felicity was fleeing from the Lord and Master who raped her. Constance from the tyranny of widowhood and a brother-in-law who thought she was his by right. Agnes we saved from accusations of witchcraft. And you we rescued from the murderous gang who would have burned you alive.'

'Did they escape with the money?' I asked.

He laughed.

'I had a purse with me when I arrived in the barn. Did they escape with it?'

He knitted his hands together as if about to give a sermon. 'There was a feast last night. Or is your head still too sore to recall? We don't yet have our own brewery or cider presses. The coins were scattered in amongst the ashes. What use is money if you don't spend it?'

'And so that money became part of ...' I checked myself. 'Our common wealth.'

'You make our future possible.'

'That pleases me greatly.' As big a lie as any told to the King by his parasitic courtiers.

'I brought with me a book as well as money,' I said.

His lips lifted into half a smile. Had he been wondering when I would speak of it?

'Was it burnt in the barn fire?'

'The boy John saw it. One of the men dropped it as they fled.'

'So the book survived?'

'I showed it to Agnes when none of us knew whether you would live. I hoped she might understand what it contains. She disappointed us last night. I apologise for her absence from your welcoming feast.'

'She found me this morning and gave me poppy juice to ease my aching head. It's why I slept so late.'

'She returned the book to me after leading you back to the shelter. She is foraging for mushrooms. She says they are most plentiful on a warm autumn day after a night of rain.' Then he looked me directly eye to eye. 'She sometimes says she would rather live alone. But she knows she would not survive if ever she were to leave us.' Was the threat in that directed at me as well as Agnes?

He unbuttoned his doublet, reached into an inside pocket. He'd had the book on him all this time we were talking.

'Do you know what it contains?' I asked.

He smiled knowingly, but said nothing. Was he playing me?

Felicity's babe whimpered in his sleep. I guessed he was no more than three months old. Rowley looked worried, almost fearful. Most men do their best to stay away from crying infants, but Rowley's reaction seemed excessive. The child was only whimpering.

I bent over and hummed some wordless lullaby that came unbidden from the depths of my memory. Adam's dogs pricked up their ears. The babe calmed.

Each of us waiting for the other.

'Will you allow me to show you something?' I said. I held out a hand. He passed the book to me.

I held the brittle leather cover between my fingers, sniffed at the singed pages, feigned astonishment that it had survived the fire. I leafed slowly through, until I found a page covered in Forman's strange signs and symbols that I knew weren't Latin or Greek. I ran my fingers slowly over the page.

He looked at me quizzically. 'What? What are you? Are looking for something?'

I might not yet have him hooked, but he was nibbling at the bait. 'Hearing you talk, Adam, listening to all you say, I have begun to wonder ...' Slowly, slowly, reel him in gently.

'Yes?'

'To wonder ... whether there was something in me that was drawn to you and to this place, even though I didn't know it. Something I wrote more than a year ago.' I showed him the page. 'Something that might interest you.' Something I hoped nobody but Forman would ever understand.

He scrutinised it. Was I taking too big a risk? He was well spoken, had all the signs of a good education. Surely he couldn't read Hebrew – or whatever these occult signs might be?

'Did you write this?' he asked.

Oh Agnes, are you true to your word? If she had spoken of Doctor Forman, Adam would know what I was doing.

'Shall I read what's here?' I said.

'Please you.'

I intoned with the utmost gravity: 'The poorest beggars, the roaming vagabonds, even rogues, thieves, whores and cutpurses are every whit as good as the great ones of this earth.' I'd heard enough of the tinpot preachers in the courtyards of Paul's to know the form.

Rowley watched wide-eyed as my fingers traced the shapes on the page. 'Can anyone say that God is in one, and not in another? He is in all. When we know that, then The Fullness will be IN us, and OF us.'

Rowley shut his eyes and breathed deeply, inhaling the miracle of Matthew's wondrous words.

At that moment, the dogs started barking. Rowley and I both looked over to the door. The boy John was standing there, staring at us. I expected Rowley to shoo him off, for he was clearly troubled by the boy's presence. But he simply quietened the dogs, and then: 'Go on, Matthew. Say more.'

'You want John to hear this?' I whispered.

'We have no secrets. He is the future, Matthew.'

But the future chose not to come in. The future stood in the doorway, looking in on the present, where Matthew the Mystic wove his twisted tale.

'When each he and she hears The Fullness within, we shall truly find us.' I edged the book closer to the light, and took a pause. I have learnt much from the playhouses. 'We shall find us in His most beauteous Commonwealth.'

'His most beauteous Commonwealth?' Rowley chorused. 'You wrote that?'

'It's there. In the book.' I showed him Forman's mysterious scribblings.

And it no longer mattered what Agnes had told him. He wanted to believe his New Messiah's Great Wisdom, for it chimed with his own.

John stood where he was, not moving, his mouth half open. Was the boy a fool or a simpleton? What terrible adversity had he suffered to end up with Rowley's crew?

The babe whimpered again. In his wonderment, Rowley had forgotten to rock the cradle. Whimpers turned to cries, then cries turned to howls. The dogs sloped off outside the shelter with their tails between their legs. Rowley reached into the cradle, picked up the child and held him aloft. 'Praise be to thee, for thy cries are a sign that thou shalt grow to manhood in the most beauteous true Commonwealth.'

I think in truth the little fellow needed his mother's tit.

16
Mothers and sons

'I shall find Felicity,' announced Rowley. He handed the babe to me, and was gone before I could protest.

When my mother was still alive she used to say that I was the only one could calm my little sister Beth. But that was more than twenty years ago. I walked around with Felicity's mewling, stinking infant in my arms, wet shit leaking through its swaddling clothes. So easy to put it back in its cradle and walk away. And yet I held him to my chest, rocking him gently back and forth, humming a lullaby my mother sang to me, whose words I'd long since forgotten. He grew calmer. Maybe he even smiled, although more likely he'd let rip some wind. Nothing like a good fart to bring a smile to the face.

When Felicity returned, her face was like warm sunshine in a rainy April. 'Do you have children of your own?'

'No.'

Felicity took the babe from me. His name was Samuel. Mother and child were easy with me.

'Would you like to be a father?'

I laughed. 'I'd like this afternoon to be warm and sunny. Doesn't mean it will be.'

Felicity was young and healthy, and her skin was unblemished. Did Rowley want me to bed her too? Share and share alike. But fathering a child with her…. Whatever the benefits of Rowley's Commonwealth, I wouldn't want any child of mine to grow up in it.

I spent the afternoon with them, and the time passed very pleasantly. We took the child to a stretch of the river with a shingle beach on our side.

'You asked for a warm and sunny day. And now it is,' said Felicity. 'As warm as it was in August.' She gave me a look of admiration, as if it were my doing.

She removed Samuel's soiled swaddling clothes, lifted her skirts, waded in to the river and washed them. I watched little Sam crawling around on the grassy bank, and tried to stop him from stuffing his mouth with every twig and acorn he could find.

When the swaddling clothes were clean, it was Sam's turn in the water. He screeched so fiercely that every nearby woodland bird took flight. She passed him back for me to dry him.

'He's comforted by your presence.'

We sat for a while on the riverbank. She put Sam to her breast. We sat back in the unseasonably warm sunshine, as small birds skimmed the surface of the river, all so easy in each other's company.

'Why do they do that?' I said.

'What?'

'The birds, flying like that so close to the water.'

She laughed at my ignorance, but with no hint of mockery. 'Swallows, catching flies.'

'The only river birds you see in London are gulls screeching and squabbling as the fisherboats unload at Thameside wharfs.'

She had never even been to Oxford. Sitting there, watching swallows darting back and forth, thinking about nothing much at all. Maybe that's what people mean when they talk about being at peace with the world. I knew it wouldn't last. It never does. But in that moment, I didn't care.

Until ...

I heard something in the trees behind us. I looked around. Saw nothing. But the feeling of being watched didn't go away. I know so little of life outside London, but even I know that foxes and wolves hunt by night.

Someone had crept up on us. I'd dropped my guard in the barn and was almost burned alive. And so nearly been murdered in the stables with Constance. My father died when I was seven years old. Ever since then I've carried a perfectly balanced razor-sharp dagger. But here, in the depths of Rusticshire, all I had was the clumsy knife I'd taken from Pinchface Jack in the stables. I'd been softened by the company of women, lulled by the slow flowing river. I didn't look round, gave no indication that I'd heard the movement. Instead, I slipped down the gently sloping bank, nearer to Felicity and started throwing pebbles into the water.

One stone. Two. Three. And again. One, two, three. Set up a rhythm. One, two. And then I leapt to my feet pulled out the knife, and turned ready to do what I could.

A child's face was peering out from behind a tree. He tried to hide, but didn't flee. It was the boy, John.

'What are you doing? Are you alone?'

He looked at me, wide-eyed, blank faced.

'What are you doing here?'

'Adam said to watch and learn.'

'Did he send you?'

'No.'

Felicity was watching warily, clutching baby Sam to her. I crouched down to talk to John. 'I can teach you things,' I said quietly. 'Tomorrow. But leave us be for now.'

'What things?'

'Be patient.'

'What things?'

'Tomorrow. Would you like that?'

'Yes.'

'But for now, just leave us be.'

And he did.

The sun was warm, the slow-moving river rippling on the shingle bank was soothing, and I loved the sound of little Sam's gurgling as I played peekaboo with him. But I couldn't relax. The business with John had unsettled me more than it should have. Had Rowley sent the boy to spy on me? Or perhaps to take back Forman's book. I resolved to hide it in a safe place as soon as I could.

By the time we got back to the shelter, the sun was low in a clear sky, and the air was cooling fast, perhaps heralding the first frost of autumn. Most of Rowley's crew had returned. The fire had been lit, Joan was sitting beside it, occasionally stirring a stew in a large cooking pot. Agnes was sitting on her own, surrounded by piles of mushrooms, berries, nuts and crab apples, putting some into cooking pots, some into storage jars.

Candles had been lit. Adam Rowley raised his hand to acknowledge me, but he and Gabriel and Randall were talking earnestly. The boy John was sitting on the ground near Godwyn and Sarah, playing with sticks. What a sad life for a boy, without others to play with.

Constance lay asleep on the pile of straw which had become our bed. I watched her breathing, her lips making gentle purring sounds every time she breathed out. I kissed her on her cheek. She opened her eyes.

'Matthew.' She put her arms around me. 'I was worried about you. Agnes said you were sick.'

'I drank too much last night.'

'I see you found the clothes.'

'Thank you.'

'Thank Adam. They were his brother's.'

'I'll thank him when I talk to him.' I asked what she'd been doing all day.

'Working with Agnes mostly. Foraging and harvesting. Collecting herbs and mushrooms, pears and berries.' Her hands were stained red with the juice.

'What happens now?'

'We all eat together whenever we can. It'll not be a feast tonight, and there won't be much meat, but it is good to be together.'

'Were they all living here in the woods while I was in the stables?'

'For some of that time.'

'Did it not matter that you were separate from everyone else?'

'Agnes and I had work to do. We do not always do everything together.'

'But they all slept here while you had a roof over your head? Did that not make others resentful?'

'Their work was to start preparations for our journey. Mine was nursing you back to health.'

'And where did Adam Rowley sleep?'

'Sometimes here. Sometimes in the house.'

I looked over to see him still deep in conversation with Gabriel and Randall. Maybe Constance caught something in my expression. 'Is something wrong?'

'No. Nothing. But I'm puzzled.' I needed to choose my words carefully. 'There is much I don't understand. All's to be shared, but Adam stands apart.'

'He has given everything. We trust him.'

'Who is he, Constance?'

'Ask him. Let him tell you himself.'

'Yes. I will.'

'You seem troubled, Matthew.'

'Puzzled and confused. That's all. I've never lived like this.'

'None of us has. It wasn't easy for any of us at first. But Adam has given us all strength and purpose.'

They were all so devoted to him. Even Agnes, who was more suspicious than any of the others, had clearly tied herself to this strange way of life.

'Where did you spend today?' said Constance.

'Agnes insisted on showing me The Clumps before she gave me poppy juice to ease my aching head. I talked to Adam, and I helped Felicity with baby Samuel.'

'She likes you.'

'She likes it that I was happy to play the nursemaid for a while and comfort little Sam.'

'That's as may be. But she does like you, Matthew.'

'Tell me about the boy.'

'Baby Sam?'

'No. The one they call John.'

'Nothing much to tell. He rarely speaks. He was living with Sarah and Godwyn at the Hall when Adam offered me shelter. They say the boy has no memory of his own true parents. Godwyn and Sarah took him in when he was not yet weaned. Sarah had recently lost a child of her own. Adam asked her to act as John's wet nurse.'

'What's he to do with Adam?'

'Only that he cares for others. John was the bastard child of a maid on a nearby estate. The maid died of childbirth fever. Sarah had recently lost her own son, and a babe had lost his mother. Adam simply sought a safe upbringing for him. He is a good man, Matthew. Adam's parents were happy with the arrangement. Sarah and Godwyn have raised John well. More than that, I know not. Adam teaches us not to chase down people's pasts. Why do you ask?'

'Something about him. I don't know. He follows me. Just stands, watching me.'

'He has no brothers and sisters. He means no harm. He's not used to strangers.'

Felicity looked over at us. She smiled.

'You can go to her if you like,' said Constance.

'What do you mean?'

'Go to her. She likes you.'

I looked at Constance, trying to detect in her face some trace of bitterness that was absent from her tone. What I saw was weary resignation. Perhaps it was what she expected of men in Rowley's madcap world of sharing.

'I don't want to go to Felicity. I like her. I like her child. I like it that they both like me. But I don't want to go to her.'

I wanted to assure Constance that all would be well, that I was there for her, that I would stay with her. Wasn't that what any woman wanted if she'd given herself to a man? But the truth is, I no longer knew what I wanted. Constance or Kate? Stay with Rowley? Or get out with Constance's help as soon as possible? But, until I had clearer plans, I couldn't talk to her about that. And so I took her in my arms and told her in whispers that I wanted her more than words could say. And there was truth in that, for I did want her. And I had no words for my confusion. But something was changing in me for I was also beginning to yearn for certainty – whether it was Constance or Kate – when all my life before the barn fire I had thrived on chaos. And in my uncertainty, I could also see why Rowley's magical promises of salvation were so appealing.

I said nothing of this to Constance. We held each other close. And the warmth of her body, our bodies together, was more of a comfort than I could ever have imagined.

17
Old money, new truths

Rowley was bringing wood in from outside and stacking it near the edge of the shelter. The younger of the dogs followed his every footstep, out and back. The boy was there again. He said he wanted to help. Rowley told him to sort the driest wood and take that to a pile beside the firepit. He did as he was told, but all the time he kept his eyes on me, as watchful as the old bitch Martha, who lay nearby.

Rowley sat down. I joined him. Both of us on sturdy oak chairs with fine barley twist legs and carved backs, which I'd not noticed before. They would have graced the grand entrance hall at Audley End. But here, beside the firepit, beneath a roof of turf-covered rough-hewn timbers, they could not have been more out of place.

'No more dry wood,' said John, his eyes still fixed on me.

'Then gather up some kindling.'

The boy didn't move, still staring.

Rowley put an arm on his shoulder. 'We need kindling, John.'

'Now?'

'You'll find sacks by the entrance.'

At last he did as bidden, leaving just Rowley and myself in the shelter. I thanked him for the clothes he'd found for me, then came straight to the point.

'If I'm to come with you, Adam, there are things I need to understand.'

'Of course.'

'A few days ago you said you'd keep no secrets from me. I understand that. But you, and now I, wear different clothes from all the others.'

He smiled. The question seemed to please him. 'Many in the world out there are easily impressed by a man's apparel. I still have dealings with those people. I dress as I do in the interests of us all. And as for you, clothes should be worn, not moulder in a drawer.'

'The clothes you wear are yours though?'

'They are no more truly mine than the water in the river, the sunshine that brings us warmth, or the land beneath our feet.'

I cocked my head to one side, hoping to disguise my irritation as curiosity.

'My family was wealthy, Matthew. It is not in itself something I'm proud of. But we must treasure whatever gifts we receive. We had a fine estate. As a child I attended Vespers in our own chapel every evening. On Sundays we went to the nearby parish church. It wasn't til much later that I saw it all as the rankest hypocrisy.'

Both dogs lay still, snouts between paws, eyes shut, but alert to their master's every change of mood.

'I was the eldest of six children. James and Abigail both died in infancy. But Peter, Judith and I were healthy. Franklin was born five years later. He was frail. Mama read every sneeze and whimper as the first sign of the sickness that would take him to an early grave. He grew used to getting whatever he wanted. My father was maybe too soft-hearted, but he was a good man,

Matthew. A profoundly good man.' He gave me his carefully studied look of sincerity.

'Sometimes he allowed tenants to forgo their rent if they were in trouble. But Franklin took delight in being cruel to the servants. I saw him take a riding crop to Godwyn because he'd tried to stop him riding a horse that was lame.'

'Godwyn who carried me from the barn?'

'He worked in our stables, and his father before him. Godwyn and Sarah, Randall, Anselm and Joan, they all worked on our estate. I have always been especially fond of Godwyn. I've no doubt that's why Franklin set upon him. I pulled the crop from Franklin. But Godwyn nearly lost an eye. He still bears the scar to his face.

'Later that day I heard Franklin telling father that it was me who'd lost my temper with Godwyn. And Franklin was believed. Franklin could do no wrong. Franklin would never lie.' His voice trembled. Martha looked up, her ears fell back.

Rowley looked me closely eye to eye. 'I don't talk about this to others.' Of course he didn't. I was the special one, the only one he could really trust. He was so earnest I thought it had to be a cheat. But why so elaborate? And what was it leading to? What could he possibly want from me?

'Not long after that I left home to become a scholar at Morton College in Oxford. I missed home. But I was glad to be away from Franklin, and fortunate to have an inspirational tutor, the Reverend Sedgwick. He taught me to seek truth in unexpected places. In the Fullness of Time, he used to say, Men will come to understand. He was a small, quiet man. He rarely spoke louder than a whisper, but his words had more impact upon me than any ranting preacher. When revelation comes, do not hesitate to act on it. His Word is more mysterious than the church allows.'

Rowley got to his feet, put wood onto the fire. The dogs looked up. He prodded the fire until flames took hold and lifted the smoke through the hole in the roof above. He sat down. Martha moved over and rested her muzzle on his boot.

'You want to hear more?'

'I'm honoured that you confide in me.'

'Reverend Sedgwick often spoke about learning from adversity, but nothing prepared me for what happened in that winter vacation. I had steeled myself for spending time with Franklin again, but not for what happened on Christmas Eve. My brother Peter fell from his horse while out riding with father. With Peter on the ground, father's horse shied and he was thrown. He cracked his head on a rock and died where he fell.'

'Oh Adam.' But he stopped me before I could offer any commiseration.

'I don't seek your sympathy. I tell you because this is something I want you to hear.' But he took a pause before continuing. 'Peter was paralysed by his own fall.'

Rowley was about to continue when there was a noise behind us. The boy John was standing silhouetted in the doorway. He put down the sack of kindling. And stood there, motionless.

'Bring it here.'

He brought the sack over, laid it down, then stood looking at me, his strange expressionless stare more unsettling than Rowley's tale of woe.

'John. Leave us,' said Rowley.

'Should I get more kindling?'

'Fill as many sacks as you can. But leave them outside.'

'I want to stay. Matthew said he'd teach me things.'

'Then I'm sure he will. But for now, he and I are talking.'

'I want to stay.'

'I said no.' Rowley clenched his fists, and almost immediately opened them, stretching out his fingers in the hope I hadn't noticed. But I'd caught a glimpse of a man who had to fight his own quick rage.

I walked over to the doorway and crouched down to talk to the boy. 'I will teach you things, young fellow. I will teach you things that will bring you great fortune. Would you like that?'

He nodded.

'Then you must be patient.'

He nodded again.

'Good. So now you must do as Master Rowley asked, and gather more kindling. When we've finished talking, I will seek you out.'

The dogs watched as I returned to sit beside Rowley. His hands were knitted together, and he was rocking gently back and forth. He looked calm, but the movement troubled me. It reminded me of madmen in the cells of Bedlam.

'Peter shouldn't have even been out riding that day. Father had asked Franklin to go out with him, but Franklin had drunk himself into a stupor the evening before, and refused to rise from his bed. Peter only went because father was so disappointed.' He stopped. Shut his eyes. The calm in his voice belied turmoil within. When he leaned down to stroke Martha, his hand was shaking.

'Peter couldn't speak. The doctors could do nothing. I prayed. All the household prayed. Mother was distraught, seeing Peter lying in bed, barely able to eat and drink, moving his mouth but not speaking.'

I tried again to offer my commiserations to Rowley, but he was determined I should hear him out.

'Mama was more distressed by Peter's paralysis then she was by father's death. She was by his bed all day. I was with her when the parson, Geoffrey Benson, came to visit. He asked us to kneel with him at Peter's bedside. He prayed for father's departed soul and for Peter's recovery. Then the sermonising started. God sees your tears, he hears your weeping. God's purposes may be an ineffable mystery, but we must yield to them. Mother sank ever deeper into the pit of melancholy. And that was itself a revelation. Benson's preaching was bile. If we are to learn from suffering it is not by dwelling in the pain of it. We must rejoice in this life while we still have it. The preaching brought no consolation, only a flood of sorrow for my mother, a flood which soon drowned her.'

Rowley stopped. Looked at me, then closed his eyes. He wanted me to see that. Wanted me to witness him trying to shut out the memory. I don't think he was feigning his distress. But there was something about the story which came too pat. And we didn't have to wait long before he started again: 'Benson came every day. He preached and he prayed. And he brought infection with him into the house. Peter caught a cold which quickly turned to fever. Mama caught it too. In less than two days the fever took Peter from us. First father, then Peter, then mother two days after that. A year's grief in less than a month.'

He fell silent. Eyes shut, head bowed.

I waited awhile before asking, 'These clothes, the clothes I'm wearing, were they Peter's?'

'They were clothes he sometimes wore.'

I thanked him for letting me wear them, and was glad to be out of the long woollen smock, but to be filling a dead man's britches and boots and wearing his doublet was unnerving.

Rowley continued as if it were quite normal for a stranger to be dressed in his dead brother's clothes: 'My mother and father were dead. Peter was dead. So I became master of the estate. Franklin cried and he cried, but what I saw were tears of anger, not sorrow. And the true cause of his fury was that I steadfastly refused to give him money to pay his mounting debts.

'After the funerals, Franklin left us to go scrounging from a cousin in Warwickshire. As soon as he was gone, I sold the horses. I have never enjoyed hunting, and they were a constant living reminder of the riding accidents. I sold all except two carthorses and a donkey, all now kept at Manor Farm.'

'I'd wondered why the stables were so quiet when I was being nursed back to health.'

'I can hardly imagine how distressing it must have been for you, Matthew, to wake and find yourself unable to see.'

I thanked him for his concern, but I was bemused. Being without a horse in rural England is no less foolish than braving the Cheapside taverns without a dagger. Selling his horses because he didn't like hunting – even in the depths of such grief – that was surely the action of a simpleton or madman. And Rowley was no simpleton.

'And Judith? Your sister?' I said.

'She married. William Harpole. A lawyer from Oxford. Ten years older than Judith. There'd been a grand wedding in August the previous year. After the riding accidents she came back, had her old room. Did her best to support mother. The husband stayed in Oxford pleading his cases, reaping his fees. He didn't appear until the funerals.'

'Do you not like him?'

'Not my business to like or dislike. It was Judith agreed to the marriage. And father to the dowry that Harpole insisted on, which meant that the estate was becoming depleted. After the funerals Judith returned to Oxford with Harpole. And soon after that Franklin slunk back to the Hall. He wanted me to evict those servants and labourers who were sick or unable to work for any reason. I refused. They'd been born on the estate. How could I evict them for the sin of falling sick? You are soft in the head, Adam, said Franklin. There are thousands roaming the roads of England who'd be willing and able to work these fields and pay rent. Franklin could scoff all he liked, but I was the eldest son, and I was now the master of a great estate, if not of my own feelings. I'd lost everything that was dearest to me. My parents both dead. My younger brother dead. My sister lost to a lawyer who was already betrothed to the law and his fees. My youngest brother lost to vulgar appetites and gross debts. What was I to do? I had nothing save my beloved dogs and servants. Old Joan brought me food, but for a week I couldn't eat.

'And then, while I was still in that place of darkest despair, I woke one night. There was no blinding light, no shimmering vision, no angels manifesting themselves beside my bed. But I did hear a voice, an ethereal voice. I'd heard the words before, I'd read them many times without ever truly understanding, words from the Gospel of Saint Matthew: Blessèd are the meek.' He paused, looking at me again with that intense stare, as if I were that Matthew.

I gave my own dutiful response: 'For they will inherit the earth.' I remembered it from my own childhood, for I, too, had suffered droning sermons.

'Indeed, Matthew,' he whispered. 'In my grief and desolation, I heard the truth. And with that understanding came a glorious lightening of my spirits. I would open my doors to those in need. And they would inherit the bounties of this earth. Through great pain came understanding, and from that understanding came great joy.' He spoke with rapturous pride in this great revelation. There wasn't much meekness about it.

His story wasn't that different from mine. I lost my mother and father and all my brothers and sisters. But that taught me to make my way in the world, not to conjure up some fine vision of a Great Commonwealth, and gather a ragged crew about me and lead them on a trek to my very own promised land. He remained as opaque to me as smoked glass. Maybe the real difference between us was that he knew nothing of poverty.

'If your servants have become the inheritors, why choose this rough shelter when all could live in Rowley Hall?'

'For a while that is where we lived. Some who'd been servants and labourers at Rowley Hall accepted my offer. Old Joan already had a bed in the servants' quarters. Godwyn and Sarah lived in a room above the stables; Gabriel and Randall in cottages nearby. They joined us in the Hall itself. Other servants were suspicious. I let them leave. Perhaps they thought I was trying to trick them. I think it more likely that the parson warned them that my actions were the work of the devil.

'In the beginning, I hoped word would spread, and many would want to join us in Rowley Hall. I thought the estate itself would become an earthly paradise. I even dared to hope that other landowners would follow my example.'

What chance of that? I thought. The more men have, the more they want is my experience. He'd have a better chance of reaching paradise by paying sixpence to a London wherryman and asking to be taken to The Fortunate Isles. But I cocked my head to the side and made a show of listening.

'Word did spread quickly, but not as I'd hoped. My sister Judith tried to persuade me that my actions were the folly of grief. Sweet Judith, I told her, you too will see the truth. You would be welcome to join us. She said she'd think about it.

'When Harpole, the lawyer, visited, he said that if Franklin went to the law, a court would deem my actions proof that I was not of sound mind, and the estate would pass to him. We had dinner together, we discussed the matter. We drank wine. In the eyes of the law he was right. And he knew I would do anything to prevent Franklin holding the deeds. So we came to an agreement. That was in May of this year. I agreed to transfer title to the estate from myself to William and Judith. The deed of Indenture is already drawn up. I promised I would sign on the first day of November on the condition that they left us alone until then. They agreed. What else could they do? As a gesture of goodwill, I agreed to oversee the bringing in of harvest.'

'Which you were doing when I sat down to rest in the barn?'

'Yes, indeed.'

He continued to confound me. I thought he was a madman. But I had never seen him shirking any labouring tasks. His hands were scratched by thorns and brambles like everyone else's. He often worked alongside his ragged crew, even though the others were outdoor men and women, and Rowley was an indoors man, a soft-skinned landowner who'd enjoyed being a scholar.

'A transfer of title?' I said. 'Are you selling to them?'

'Any monies will become part of our common wealth. While the rest of the world still has need of money, we must put it to good use, Matthew.'

'From the beginning of next month Judith and her husband will own the estate?'

'They will have legal title. Judith rides over to speak to me, to make arrangements, and when I speak with her, I dress to reassure her that I am still her loving brother, and that I'm not mad, even if the law thinks I am. I have no desire to distress her.'

'And Franklin?'

'The agreement I struck with William excludes Franklin. But once the transfer is made, it's her business what she does.' He stood up. The dogs stirred. 'We lived in Rowley Hall for much of the time you were recovering in the stables. We built our shelter on land that is part of the Rowley estate. We built it to prove that we can live like this when we need to. And now we need to move on, Matthew. We need to find a place where we can settle in peace. There is nothing noble about living in the woods.'

'Amen to that. Where will you go?' Even as I said it, I knew that you should have been a we.

'We will know the place is right when we find it.'

'And will we live like this until we do? In woods and forests? Living the life of a jovial crew of beggars?'

'We are not beggars, Matthew.'

'I know that. But there will be many who think of us that way. England is full of beggars and vagrants. Many bear scars from being soundly whipped. There are no delights in beggary.'

'We are not beggars,' he insisted. 'And we never will be.' His lip twitching as he spoke.

I hesitated before responding. I'd seen how quickly he could fall to rage. But I owed it to those who had cared for me to save them from the brutish cruelty of English law.

'You've signed nothing yet?'

'I am resolute.'

'I do not wish to dissuade you, Adam. But if you were to delay signing over your estate, we could set out in spring, when it will be easier to recognise land of real promise, land that will be right for us to settle, land where the true Commonwealth can set down roots and grow.' I hoped he heard that we and us.

He nodded and pursed his lips as if giving the matter some thought, although I wondered whether he ever heard anything or anyone except his own inner voices.

18
Keys and locks

I'd heard the story he wanted me to hear. He'd suffered great loss. He was a loyal son. He loved his family – except for Franklin, who'd betrayed them all. He'd learnt from the pain of his grief. He had enemies who didn't understand his noble ideals. For much of the time he spoke quietly, and although his obsession with the Great Fullness made the Puritans who rant outside Paul's seem mild-mannered and sane, the promises he made to his devoted followers sounded almost plausible.

For my part, I hope I convinced him that his story touched me. But I have learnt to seek out those stories that people want to keep hidden. The story Rowley didn't realise he was telling was that he would still be rich, even after transferring the title of his estate. And the story I didn't tell him was that his New Messiah would happily relieve him of the burden of that worldly wealth.

I sought out John. It wasn't difficult. He was lurking nearby.

'Would you like me to teach you to read?'

'Can't read,' he mumbled. But he looked interested.

'Can Anselm read?'

He shook his head.

'Or Godwyn?'

'No.'

139

'Gabriel?'

'Don't know.'

'You ever seen Gabriel reading?'

He shook his head again.

'But you, Master John, you have the wit and spirit to learn quickly. You learn to read, and your skills will be greatly prized. How does that sound?'

His expression didn't change – it rarely did – but he nodded, which I took to mean it sounded good.

'It will be easier for me to teach and for you to learn in Rowley Hall.'

His mouth was hanging slightly open.

'Can you take me there now? I don't know the way. So I need you to guide me. Can you do that?'

He looked as if no-one had ever before asked for his help.

'Master Rowley says it was you rescued my book from the fire in the barn. That was very brave. If I teach you to read, that could be my way of thanking you.'

He almost smiled. Taking that for agreement, I put on the cape and boots that Constance had found for me, and we set off.

'Did you live at the Hall?' I asked.

'Yes.'

'How long for?'

'Don't know.'

'Did you know Master Rowley's mother and father? And his brothers and sister?'

'They lived in the big house. We lived in the stables.'

'With Godwyn and Sarah?'

'Yes.' He didn't say much, but seemed to warm to the task of playing guide.

The sunken path between the ancient trees was the one that Constance called the holloway. My sight was much improved, and I saw it more clearly this time. Perhaps that's why it no longer held such terrors for me.

The trees were soft with moss, and long strands of lichen dangled like pennants. We walked on, and out onto a path in a riverside meadow. I noticed the church whose spire I'd seen emerging from the mist when I was on The Clumps with Agnes. It was a couple of miles away on the far side of the river, and surrounded by houses. A small town.

'What's that place?'

'Dorchester, I think.'

'Have you ever been there?'

'No.'

We walked on.

'Did you know I come from London?'

'Yes.'

He'd heard of London, but never even been as far as Oxford.

'Some day, young John, I'll show you London, and you will see such sights as you could never dream of. Bigger than Oxford. Much bigger than Dorchester. A river runs through it, a river so wide there's not a man alive that's strong enough to throw a stick from one side to the other. And a great stone bridge crosses this river, a bridge so big that houses five storeys high have been built along each side of it. There are many grand houses in London, banqueting halls and a palace called Whitehall so big it has two thousand rooms. I'll take you to a hill at night where we'll look down and see the city spread before us.

Look up and see the stars in the heavens. Look down and see a hundred thousand candles and lanterns still burning bright.'

I was tempted to tell of mermaids and unicorns, carriages that move without horses to pull them and shimmering towers reaching high up into the clouds, but there was no need, for he was enchanted by the reality – though I was careful not to mention anything that might frighten him. So I said nothing of the gangs of roaring boys, nothing of the taverns where blood was spilled as often as beer, nothing of the horrors of Newgate or Bedlam. But I did tell him of the wonders of the playhouses.

'You will never see such finery as you can find in the theatres.' I sat down on the bough of a fallen tree and John sat with me. 'When you come with me to London, I will take you to the tiring house of the Blackfriars Playhouse. And there you will see skirts and cloaks made from the finest silks and velvets; and more crowns and sceptres than in the Court of King James.'

'Can I be a player when we go to London?'

'First, you'll have to learn to read, for the players have to say the words the poets write for them. And for that – to learn to read – we have to be in Rowley Hall.'

The house stood on the brow of a low hill, about half a mile up from the river. He took me to a porch at the front of the house. The floor of this porch was tiled, there were wooden benches built into the walls, as you often find in churches.

'Shall we open the door? Will you show me inside?'

'Are we allowed?'

'Of course we're allowed. All shall be shared. Isn't that what Master Rowley says?' I turned the large iron ring attached to the latch. But the door was locked.

'When you used to go in the house with Sarah, which door did you use?'

He took me round to the kitchens. That door, too, was locked. And John didn't know any other way in. So I showed him how to prise a window without breaking glass. I lifted John up and he scrambled through. It brought back memories of my first time into a locked up house – that delicious combination of fear and excitement. Once inside, he found a larger window and opened that for me to climb through.

'You've done well, young man. I'm proud of you. Master Rowley will be too.' It tripped off my tongue all too easily. John nodded, and his mouth twitched in the beginnings of a smile.

We stood together in the entrance hall. A wooden staircase led upstairs. The walls were panelled in dark oak. Nails in the wood suggested that pictures had once hung beside the stairs. But the walls were now bare, except for two wall lanterns and a silent lantern-clock. I wondered when it had last been wound, and whether Rowley had sold the paintings, or his sister had removed them?

There was no other furniture in the entrance hall. In a house of this size I'd have expected a chest and at least a pair of chairs. But nothing.

'Do you know the house well?'

'Mum brought me with her sometimes.'

'You mean Sarah?'

'She says to call her Mum.'

Unsurprisingly, the kitchens were at the back of the house. A long table stood in the centre. The andirons were still in place by the fireplace, there were hooks on the beams, shelves on the walls, and a single corn dolly hung from the ceiling beam nearest the fireplace.

I often used to find my way into London houses that had been abandoned in haste – for the threat of plague is never far away – with the furniture and kitchen goods left behind. I always find an empty kitchen unsettling, for the kitchen is the beating heart of any house. Having John with me made this one less so, but it was strange in other ways. Although some of the paraphernalia you find in kitchens was still there – pots and pans, jugs and bowls, ladles and other ironware, and there were still trenchers, tankards, cups and glasses on the shelves – there was less than I'd have expected for a house of that size. So the kitchen felt at once abandoned, yet still in use. Rowley must have had his crew remove those things they might need on their great journey to nowhere. But there'd surely still be some keys. And that's what I wanted. Maybe one in the backdoor lock? Or perhaps a set of keys hanging somewhere? But no. There was a cubby hole labelled 'keys' in the wall beside the door, but words alone don't open locks.

In the dairy – a large room off the kitchen – most of the wooden pails had been removed, but the cheese press, the wooden paddles and a butter churn had been left behind. Much more useful to me and young John, was a coil of cheese-wire sitting on a shelf, and in the corner a box of meat skewers in a variety of sizes. The skewers might be too wide and the wire not stiff enough for a small lock, but for a big old lock like the one on the back door, a couple of those skewers would probably do the trick.

John was looking puzzled.

'If I'm going to teach you to read, young man, we need to unlock some doors, then find some books. Where should we start?'

'Don't know.'

'Your first word's in here. Look by the back door. What do they usually keep in that cubby hole?'

'Keys.'

'So, what do you think that word says?'

'Keys?'

'See. You can read already.'

It was the way my father had taught me. I was intrigued by the books and pamphlets that he brought home. He never forced me. But I'd always liked the game of chasing words.

'There are usually books in a study,' I said. 'Do you know where that is?'

He shook his head and shrugged.

'Then we must explore the house together.'

The withdrawing room seemed much as it must have been when Rowley's parents were still alive and the Hall was thriving. Long damask curtains were still hanging by the windows, and three long couches were arranged in front of the large fireplace. The floor was covered with fine Turkey carpets, and a fire had been laid, ready to light – and beside it a basket of dried logs.

In the dining room we were greeted by a strong smell of beeswax. When my parents were alive, we had tallow candles every night of the year, except for Twelfth Night. Then, the house was filled with the smell of honeyed beeswax. And despite Rowley Hall feeling abandoned, that's what it brought to mind – the festivities and laughter of Twelfth Night.

There were two large cupboards and a wall lantern on each side of the large fireplace. The windows were framed with heavy curtains, but the tapestries, wall hangings, rugs and carpets had all been removed, leaving the wooden floor covered with rushes – as if this dining room with its finely crafted wood-panelled walls was a low tavern. In the middle of the room was a long table with place settings for thirteen diners: each with knife and spoon, wooden trencher, drinking glass and linen napkin.

Thirteen place settings, but only twelve chairs.

Thirteen place settings. And twelve of us in Rowley's crew, including me and John. Thirteen with Rowley. The strangeness of that table laid for a banquet – with everything ready, except for the food and drink – was such that I didn't give much thought to the missing chair. Maybe Rowley planned not to sit, but to kneel in a performance of great humility.

The study lay behind a door concealed in the wood panelling in the dining room. It was about four yards wide by three yards deep, not quite as large as the room in the stables where I'd been nursed back to health. Every wall was filled with shelves of books. A finely crafted desk stood before a shuttered window. On it, an oil lantern, two pewter candlesticks, each with a new candle prepared and ready for lighting, a goose quill, inkwell, and a tinderbox. The room had been in use in the past day or so. Was Rowley still managing the estate? So many maybes, so many riddles.

'Can you teach me now?' said John.

'You've already started. You read the word KEYS in the kitchen. So let us look for a book that has the word key in there somewhere. Chase the word, John. Key. At the beginning is a letter that looks up, at the end a letter that looks down. Or if it's keys, it has a big squiggle at the end. I found some paper in a drawer, dipped the quill in ink and slowly wrote the letters as large as would fit on the paper.

k e y s
'There. That's what we're looking for.'

We took it in turns to get a book. He chose one. I chose one. His first was *Good Councell Against the Plague*. It might have held good advice, but neither of us could find a key in it. My turn next. I was pleased and surprised to find copies of several plays. *A Wittie and Pleasant Comedie called The Taming of the Shrew*. No keys in that either. But I was most impressed that John recognised the key in lackey and Turkey.

'The extra letters turn key into a different word,' I explained.

'What's a tur key?'

'A faraway place where carpets come from.'

'The words look different in the book you chose, Matthew?'

'The words are the words that actors say in plays.'

'They say all those words?'

'They read them and then they learn them. So when they speak you wouldn't know they'd ever been written down.'

The next book he chose was also a play.

'What's this one called?'

'*An EXCELLENT conceited Tragedie of Romeo and Juliet*.'

We leafed slowly through. And there it was: keys. He found it for himself.

'What do these other words say?'

'Hold, take these keys, and fetch more spices, nurse.'

He looked puzzled.

'Lady Capulet says that. She's one of the people in the play.'

'Why?'

It was the first time he'd used that word why. Every child of his age that I've ever known asked WHY all the time. He was a bright boy with a sharp mind, but fear had been holding him back. He wasn't an easy child, but I was beginning to warm to him.

'Why does the Lady ask the nurse to fetch more spices?' I said. 'I'll tell you as we're walking back to the shelter. But for now, let's do a little more reading.'

He learnt to write the k, the e and the y. We found other words with the letter k in them. I taught him the sounds of other letters.

'Are all those books different?'

'Most probably,' I said.

'So many words.'

'So many words. So many stories.'

While he was looking at the books in Rowley's library, I slipped the tinderbox in my pocket. It was a good one. Almost as good as my own, the one used against me in the barn. When next you come to light a candle, Adam Rowley, remember what you told me. In your brave new world there shall be no such thing as stealing.

I think John would have happily stayed in the study for the rest of the day. But I thought it best to stop while he was still full of enthusiasm. And besides, I had other things to teach him.

'Did you used to sleep in the house?'

He was more forthcoming than he had been earlier. He showed me the bedchambers. Four of them had a view down to the river. There were two at each side of the house, and three in the servants' quarters at the back. John used to sleep with Sarah and Godwyn in a room above the stables.

The bedchambers looked much as they must have done when the house was full of life. Curtains hung by the windows, each of the six main rooms had its own wash-stand and basin.

And on the floor: 'Look John. A Turkey carpet.' He knelt down and ran his hands over the fine weave. In the finest of the rooms, where I guessed Rowley's mother had died, a door led to a small parlour with a tall wardrobe and dressing table. Laid out neatly on the dressing table were a hairbrush, comb, scissors and a looking glass. And in the drawer beneath, a collection of hatpins which I slipped into my pocket. John didn't even notice me open the drawer, for he was intrigued by the looking glass. While he was admiring his own reflection, I pocketed the scissors and a silver bracelet. I'd have taken more, but John turned the glass to show me my face. It was a sight I would rather not have seen. I knew I must be scarred, but until then I'd not realised just how badly burned I must have been. My face was no face, a featureless blotchy pink. My eyebrows hadn't regrown. My hair had all gone, and was regrowing in tufts. Little wonder John had stared at me. I tried to smile at him, though after what I'd just seen in that glass, I wondered what he saw.

We returned to the kitchen, where the table was big enough for us to work on. I lit several candles and a lantern. And there, as John watched wide-eyed, I turned hatpins, meat skewers and cheese-wire into a set of picklock wires.

I'd enjoyed teaching John the beginnings of reading, though in truth I did little more than whet his appetite for words. But this, the business of making picklock wires, was really why I'd wanted to bring him here. I needed an apprentice – for my left hand was still of little use, and it was taking longer than I'd hoped to develop fine control of my right.

The outside kitchen door had an old-fashioned one-lever lock. London locksmiths stopped making these when Good Queen Bess was still on the throne and my parents were still alive.

'Take the first wire, John. Push it gently into the lock, through the keyhole. Stop when you feel it touch the lever of the lock. Now take this stiffer wire and gently, gently, gently push it in so it sits underneath that lever. Now twist and lift.'

We heard a heavy click as the lock slid back. I opened the door for him to walk through. For the first time his whole face smiled.

'I'm proud of you John. Are you now my prentice boy?'

He grinned and nodded. We went back inside and tried the front door. The lock on that was more modern, and required a bit of patience, but he did that too. Young John was a quick learner. I could see us becoming a good team over the next few weeks.

19
Why do brothers fight?

I wanted John to practice his new skills with different locks, so we made our way to the stables. The door to the room where I'd been nursed back to health had been replaced. If this was Gabriel's work, he was a fine carpenter. John led me upstairs to the room above, where he'd spent much of his young life with Godwyn and Sarah. I suggested he go back down on his own and try a couple of locks without me watching him. I promised to help if he called out, but he was excited to be allowed to do something for himself, and that gave me time to hide Forman's casebook and letters. I'd noticed there was a loose floorboard by his bed. As soon as John was downstairs, I lifted the board, slid Forman's book and the letters as far I could reach, replaced the board, threw straw over it and moved the bed a few inches to make the loose board less obvious.

As John became more confident with the picklock wires, he grew more talkative. I told him about London and the places I'd show him. I encouraged him to talk about himself, and how things used to be. Slowly, slowly, little by little, I got a sense of how his life had been at Rowley Hall.

Godwyn had been head groom. He and Sarah were married, and had a room on the first floor of the stable block, which was where John slept too. Some days he helped his mother in the house, some days he worked with Godwyn and the horses.

'You like horses?'

He nodded and smiled.

'You have a favourite?'

'Athena.' He said quietly.

'Athena? A mare?'

He nodded.

'You ever ride her?'

He looked nervous.

'Did you?'

He grinned.

'Did you sneak into the stables and ride her bareback when everyone was busy?'

'No.'

'I'd wager you did! Brave boy. I can just see you riding out. A fine mare would love being ridden by a boy like you. Light on her back. Such delicate hands.'

He stifled a laugh.

Keep tickling, Matthew. Find the right lever. Slow and gentle. When the lock clicks, the door will open and young John's story will see daylight.

'Athena was Master Franklin's horse. He used to lift me up and let me sit with him.'

'And you rode out with Master Franklin?'

He nodded, but looked down. The memory was troubling. I told him how I learnt to ride horses at a livery yard on the edge of Lincolns Inn Fields.

'When Master Franklin took you out on Athena, did he sometimes let you take the reins?'

He nodded.

'Did you like Master Franklin?'

'Yes,' he whispered, as if ashamed of it.

'The first time I took the reins,' I said. 'I loved that. I remember it so well.'

Another smile breaking through.

'Did Godwyn mind you riding out with Master Franklin?'

'No.'

'What about Master Rowley?

He shrugged.

'Did Adam not like it when Franklin took you riding?'

He closed his eyes. He was shutting something out – or keeping it in. He told his story as much in silences as in words. I could well imagine Rowley's fury if the child and Franklin got on well – if only because it was something Rowley couldn't control.

'I've never had a horse of my own,' I said. 'But I do love riding. And I think you do too.'

More nodding.

'So when you and I go to London, Master John, I will teach you to ride myself.'

The biggest of grins.

'Has anyone ever started teaching you to read before?'

'Master Franklin showed me writing on the horse saddles.'

'Where the maker's name is written?'

He looked away.

'So Franklin started teaching you to read?'

'He said he would. Uncle Adam didn't like it.'

'Was Franklin kind to you?'

He nodded. But there was nervousness behind his eyes. I wondered if Franklin's attempt to cultivate the boy had been a way of getting at Rowley. My thoughts started racing. Could it be that John was Franklin's bastard son? That Franklin had got a maid with child, but taken no responsibility? Then Rowley paid Godwyn and Sarah to bring up the child? Perhaps he really was the good man that Constance said he was. And if Franklin was as dissolute as Rowley painted him, he'd want to prevent him having any influence on the boy. It was possible. But the boy was clearly frightened of Rowley, not Franklin.

John interrupted my thoughts.

'Are you my father?'

I laughed. 'I like you, John. And you are a very fine prentice boy. But no, I fear I'm not your father.'

As we walked back to the shelter John wanted me to tell him the story of *Romeo and Juliet*. I couldn't remember it all, but I got the heart of it.

'There are two families in a faraway place.'

'Turkey?'

'Near Turkey.'

'And these families are at war.'

'Why?'

And so it went. He interrupted again and again, asking all the *whys* he'd kept in hiding for years.

'We should call you John Robins.'

'Why?'

'Because robins are the chirpiest of birds. And you are the chirpiest John I've ever met. And John Robins sounds better than plain John Robin.'

'John Robins?' he said proudly.

'Why not?'

He liked that. He was more interested in the family feud and the fighting than he was in the two lovers. He kept coming back to wanting to know why the Montagues and the Capulets were at war. I had to fob him off with, 'I think they always had been. That's all they knew.'

He was silent for a while. And then he said. 'Sometimes brothers in the same family fight. Don't they?'

'Sometimes.'

'Why?'

'Lots of reasons.'

'Did you fight with your brother?'

'My brothers and sisters all died before we were old enough to fight. But I fought with my cousin, Jacob.'

'Why?'

'Because he was mean, because he mocked me in front of his friends, because he made me do things I didn't want to do.' Because, and because, and because. But Jacob's death still brings me out in chills. And even though he terrorised me, he taught me things that stood me in good stead for years. If I'd not forgotten them in Oxford, I would never have been trapped in the barn fire. But that wasn't what was obsessing young John.

'Is that why Uncle Adam fought with Uncle Franklin?

'Did you see them fighting?'

'Don't remember.' That came too quick. Then a whispered, 'I saw lots of blood.'

'Whose blood?'

'He didn't mean to hurt Godwyn.'

'Who didn't, John? Who didn't mean to hurt him? What do you remember?'

I thought I'd stepped too far, for he slunk back into silence for several minutes. We'd reached the path by the river bank, and I was about to change the subject, lighten the load for the little fellow, talk about the church a mile or so away on the other side of the river, and how small it was compared to Paul's, when the story came bursting forth: 'Master Franklin took me out for a ride, and I was sitting in front, riding on the saddle with the name on it. And I was holding the reins. And when we came back to the stables....'

'Yes, John. Go on.'

'When we came back to the stables, Uncle Adam was there, and he was angry. He pulled me off the horse. He shouted at me. He told me to go away. And I did go away. But I ran and hid and I watched and Uncle Adam was shouting at Uncle Franklin. They were both shouting. I didn't understand the words. Uncle Franklin had a riding crop. He lifted it up, and Uncle Adam said *How dare you*. And I was hiding 'cos I didn't want Uncle Adam to see me. And then Godwyn came in because Athena was rearing up and Uncle Franklin fell off and dropped the crop and Uncle Adam picked it up and said *How dare you threaten me?* And Godwyn tried to catch the reins and stop him hitting Franklin. And that's when Uncle Adam hit him with the crop.'

'Adam hit Godwyn with the crop?'

'There was lots of blood. But he didn't mean to hurt him. I know he didn't mean to.'

20
Sweet kisses, dark whispers

The rains came again that night. Pounding on the roof of the shelter. Nobody ventured out. The fire was built up and we all ate together. A meaty venison stew. Knowing what I now did about the size of Rowley's estate, and that the ownership hadn't yet transferred to his sister, I guessed the deer in the pot had been hunted and killed on Rowley's own land. How much easier to live like a beggar when you have a thousand acres to call your own.

I wanted to hear from Godwyn and Sarah what Rowley had told them when he asked them to bring up John; and from Godwyn himself about how he got his scar. Who was he defending? Franklin, or the boy? And what else was Adam lying about? Those weren't conversations to be had when anyone else was in earshot.

Talking wasn't the only reason I needed time alone with Constance. Had it not been raining so heavily, I'd have suggested we walk up to the Hall and spend the night in one of those grand four-poster beds. It was ever more frustrating to be lying with her on our bed of straw with the others all nearby. I wanted her. And having seen the remains of my face in the glass earlier that day, I was desperate for her to want me. I whispered in her ear that if we covered ourselves with a blanket and were very quiet, nobody would know.

'I would know, Matthew. And I don't want to be quiet about it.'

'We can kiss, and we can touch.'

And so our touching was soft as whispers, and our whispering light as feathers. But there was only so long I could resist. My hand slid over her stomach, down to her thigh. She took hold firmly.

'No, Matthew. I'm sorry. Don't. Please, don't. Not here. Not now.'

In amongst the snoring, the coughing, the grunts of slumbers, came regular drips of water hissing in the embers of the fire. But there was no longer that pounding, thrumming on the roof. The rain had eased.

'We could go outside.'

'Matthew.' Her face just inches from mine. 'Don't try to force me. After Richard died I never expected to love any man again. He was the first man I ever kissed. And until you, the only one. I gave myself to you because I thought you understood me. Don't destroy my faith in you. I cannot give myself to you with the others so close.' She kissed me chastely on the forehead. I held her to me and returned her chaste kiss.

'Tomorrow, Matthew. There's a room above the stables, where Godwyn and Sarah used to sleep. We won't be disturbed and we'll have all morning.'

'We could go to the Hall. There are soft beds there.'

'Have you been to the Hall?' she whispered. I couldn't see her face, but the stiffness in her body spoke of disbelief – and fear.

'Today. I went with the boy, John. He wanted to learn to read.'

'John hardly ever speaks.'

158

'John's anxious. But he's no fool. He carries a heavy burden that he doesn't understand. He chose to bury himself in silence. But there's a bright flame of intelligence burns inside him.'

'You went inside the Hall? Was Adam with you?'

'I couldn't find him to ask. John led me to the Hall. We found a way in.'

'Oh, Matthew.' That shiver of fear again.

'What?'

'It's not wise to upset him.'

'Why would he be upset? He wants us to share everything.'

'You don't understand. Adam has been so good to us.'

I could feel her breath on my skin, but could see nothing of her face. There was no light in the shelter – no moonlight from outside, and nothing within. The embers of the fire had faded.

'Adam and I talked this morning. He told me his story. He told me of the deaths of his mother and father, and his brother, Peter. He told me about Franklin. And how he plans to transfer the estate to his sister. He's generous, I know. And he's been good to you and the others. But he's troubled, Constance. Very troubled.'

'He won't like it, you going inside the Hall without him there.'

'John wanted to learn to read. I wanted to show him some books. The boy said nothing against Rowley. But some of the things he told me…. Either Rowley or the boy is lying. And the boy has no reason to.'

'Adam has no reason to.'

'Then why is he so insistent that people's pasts aren't important?'

'We have to escape the traps we make for ourselves. Adam saved me from myself. And if he hadn't freed me, I would never have been able to love you, Matthew.'

I still didn't know what it was I feared about Rowley. I'd seen no obvious sign that he was a danger to others – except for that scar on Godwyn's face, and that may have been a story that the boy made up. Indeed, Godwyn was as devoted to Rowley as every other member of the crew. Rowley's Great Fullness was a strange god, but not so strange as the God of Hellfire and Damnation I'd been threatened with as a child. I could even see the sense in *All shall be shared*, although I'd never want to live my life that way. I thought Rowley a hypocrite. But aren't we all in some way? It wasn't that. From the moment when Constance first talked about him, I was troubled by the way she held him in such devotion – and indeed all of them did, even Agnes. But the other side of devotion was that shiver of fear. He terrified her – not for what he had done, but what he might do. And that convinced me that we had to leave as soon as possible. I yearned to be lying with her naked, to feel her skin against mine, to be inside her, and to experience again that special closeness we'd known in the stables. But even more than that I wanted to extricate her from Rowley's madness and get us both out while we still could.

I'm convinced that she sensed the darkness in Rowley even as she needed to believe that he was her saviour. But I knew not to persuade her with argument. Better to be a listener. Let her be her own persuader.

'What drew you to him, Constance?'

'I will not speak ill of him. Nor should you.'

'I don't want you to speak ill. I want to hear the good. I understand why Godwyn, Sarah, Felicity and many of those who worked on the Rowley estate might choose to throw their lot in with him. But what persuaded you, sweet Constance? What drew you to him?'

One of Rowley's dogs yelped in its sleep. Outside, the rain grew heavier again.

'We ground corn at the mill for the Rowley Estate. On Twelfth Night each year, Adam's father invited us to the Hall for a feast – Richard, me, the children, a few families from Abingdon. Adam, Peter and Judith were there; and even Franklin when he was younger.

'When Adam heard about the fire at the mill, he rode over to offer his condolences. He said there was a room at Rowley Hall where I could stay until the mill was rebuilt and working again. At first I declined. I wanted to be with Clare, my sister, in Nuneham Courtenay. But she has children of her own. And being with children all day was too painful a reminder of the loss of my own. So I accepted Adam's offer. He gave me a room of my own in Rowley Hall. I was treated as a member of the family. Adam was kind, and asked nothing of me. I feared he might try to kiss me, but he never did. At the time I was too caught up in my own grief to think about it, but I look back now and see that he was struggling.'

'With what?'

'With himself. I don't know. Something he wanted to tell me. But whatever it was, he kept it to himself. He made no demands. He never even kissed my hand. I was relieved. But I confess I thought it strange.'

I, too, thought it strange, for Constance was a woman in her prime.

'I had no interest in men. But he was kind to me. The family were kind. The world is a harsh place for widows. Adam and his family made it safe for me. He's made the world safer and fairer for all of us. I wasn't drawn to him. I learnt to trust him. I know there are times when he sinks into melancholy. And that can sometimes seem like rage. But it's rage against himself.'

The most dangerous kind, I wanted to say. But I didn't. Instead, I asked her, 'Were you in the Hall on the day of the riding accident?'

'I went into Abingdon for the morning. I got back early afternoon. I knew even before I went in the door that something terrible had happened.'

'Was Franklin at home?'

'He'd come back to stay for a few days. I knew he sometimes drank too much. I knew that he and Adam sometimes fought. He usually smiled when he saw me. But that morning, he was very distressed. He kept saying, *It should have been me*.'

'What do you think he meant by that?'

'He said he should have been the one who was riding, not Peter.'

'Franklin should have gone riding with his father?'

'He wanted to be reconciled with the family. He knew how much his father loved those early morning rides while there was mist on the chase. But he'd stayed up late with Adam. Had too much to drink, and in the morning – '

'He was too hungover, so Peter took his place. Yes?'

Had anyone been near enough to hear our whispers and not make out the words, they might have presumed we were lovers arranging a secret tryst. But Desire had limped off. My head was far too full of Adam's feud with Franklin.

162

'Athena and Peppercorn had already been saddled up when Old Master Rowley and Peter got to the stables. Franklin was sobbing when he told me this. I had never seen him so distressed.'

'Who saddled them?'

'Well, Godwyn of course. Who else?'

'I don't know. That's why I ask. Was Peter a good rider?'

'They all were. They'd all been riding since they were very young. But Peter was the best of them.'

I thanked Constance and kissed her on the cheek. We held each other. There were so many more questions I still wanted to ask. But they could wait til morning.

'I do understand why you might be wary of Adam,' she said.

I was more than wary. But dripping poison into her ear about Rowley would turn her against me and not him.

'Good night, sweet Constance.'

'Tomorrow, Matthew.' She kissed me. Such sweet promise.

21
Witch water

We'd planned to be up early, but we'd had little sleep, and neither of us stirred until we were woken by the morning hubbub. The fire had been rekindled. Joan was stirring frumenty porridge in the cauldron that hung over it. The rain had stopped at last, and through the entrance I saw a shaft of sunlight piercing the canopy of leaves.

Constance whispered in my ear: 'Do you still want to go to the stables?'

'A bowl of porridge first?' If we didn't eat when food was prepared, we'd go hungry.

So it began as the most ordinary of mornings. Joan and Marian stirring the pot, ladling out into bowls. Felicity bouncing the babe on her knee. Agnes sitting with Marian, young John with Sarah, but his eyes still fixed on me. Was he obsessed by the charred remains of my face? Or did he still imagine I might be his father? Rowley's dogs scrounging for scraps. And Rowley himself holding court. Gabriel, Randall and Anselm in close attendance, all leaning forward attentively. I should have marked that as different, for at this time of day it was usually only Gabriel he talked to so earnestly. Had I been more alert I might also have noticed that Godwyn was missing.

We finished our bowls of porridge. I looked at Constance. She looked at me. We got to our feet. No harm in going together. I was the New Messiah, I could make my own choices. We were about to leave when Adam Rowley stood up. 'Today, friends, is a day like no other. After today we enter the new age, and shall be released from old bondage. Today we throw off our chains.' His eyes were shut as he was talking, and he was rocking slowly back and forth in time with his own breathing.

Now that he had our full attention, he lowered his voice. 'When we still lived in bondage we often heard the bible words: *The Lord saith I am Alpha and I am Omega, I am the beginning and the ending, I am the first and last.* Soon, there shall only be WE, not I. For WE shall see the last and will become the first. All things hidden shall be known, all things secret shall be revealed. We shall move from ignorance to understanding. Do not be afraid. Just as rivers flow to the oceans and there is nothing men can do to stop them, so WE shall flow into the Great Fullness. We shall be born anew.'

The crew all gazed at Rowley with rapt attention. All except Sam, who had a great fullness in his mouth and was sucking on it.

'But first, before we celebrate, there must be a cleansing.'

He waited. Nobody spoke. Was I to be his Matthew the Baptist?

'Agnes, step forward.'

She walked slowly over to him. Had she been preparing some strange concoction for us all to give our bodies a little evacuation? Was that his idea of a cleansing? Standing before him, Agnes's head reached to his chest.

'Agnes, we love you. And we treasure the wisdom you bring.'

Martha, the bitch, got to her feet and slipped away to lie by the entrance to the shelter. Then Rowley put his hands on

Agnes's shoulders and turned her round to face us. He repeated the words, more slowly this time. 'We treasure the wisdom you bring.' And then to us: 'Say it.'

All repeated: 'We treasure the wisdom you bring.' It was a wholehearted chorus – not the kind of mumbled response I'd heard so often in church in my childhood. Constance took my hand and squeezed it, urging me to join in.

'Agnes?' said Rowley.

Agnes said nothing.

'Say it Agnes – I am treasured.'

'I am treasured.' She said the words in that strange, growled whisper of hers.

'Say it again.'

Agnes glanced at me. Did she expect me to rescue her? I acknowledged her, but until I knew what Rowley intended, I thought it best to go along with his flummery.

'I am treasured,' she said, louder this time.

'Each one of us is precious. And we hold you to us.' That was the cue for Anselm and Randall to step forward, stand either side and take hold of her arms. She didn't resist.

'Before we make our great journey, there must be a cleansing.'

'There must be a cleansing,' all echoed back – including me this time, to my shame.

'We love you, Agnes. And we treasure you. But there have been times you have chosen to separate yourself. When we gathered together to welcome Matthew, you chose to absent yourself.'

Silence.

'Your wisdom is a threat to others, which is why they call you a witch. But we have given you protection and saved you from your persecutors. You must therefore be reminded of what awaits you if you walk away, if you deny us.'

My gaze flicked between Rowley and Agnes. There seemed no animosity between them.

'Let us walk.'

Anselm and Randall led the way, with Agnes held between them. Rowley and Gabriel next, the dogs padding obediently behind. Then Marian, whose face was ashen, more distressed than Agnes herself. Sarah followed, holding young John by the hand. I glanced a querying look at Constance. She would have gone next in the procession, but I held her back.

'Did you know about this? Has Rowley been planning it.'

'Hush, Matthew. Not now.'

'What in Hell's name does he mean by a cleansing?'

'Adam knows what is best for us all. Agnes is walking freely. She understands.'

Anselm and Randall still had hold of her arms. Not what I'd call walking freely. But she was making no attempt to break free.

'Constance.'

'Hush.' She squeezed my arm.

The sun shone brightly on the strange procession. I thought we were heading up to Rowley Hall. But instead we emerged into a grassy clearing, which sloped gently down onto a shingle beach.

On the grass before us stood a large wooden engine mounted on the back of a four-wheeled flat cart. Godwyn was holding the reins of a heavy horse, harnessed between the shafts of the cart, which he backed down to within a few yards of the shingle, so that the rear of it faced the river. This strange engine – a small scaffolding tower about four feet high and wide and firmly fixed to the cart – must have been what had kept Gabriel so busy for the past few days, for it was solidly constructed and clearly the work of a skilled carpenter. I had no idea what it was, nor what its purpose might be – until Rowley gave the order: 'Attach the plank.'

Rowley held Agnes by the arm while Randall went round to the other side and lifted a long plank, balancing it on the cross beam of Gabriel's wooden engine, where he secured it with leather straps, so that the plank could now pivot like a child's see-saw. A chair with arms and high upright back had been fixed to the end nearest the river. The missing chair from the dining room at Rowley Hall? Gabriel had spent the past week making a portable ducking stool.

With the plank strapped firmly in place, and the end with the chair on it resting on the shingle beach, Rowley took Agnes to the chair. She stared at him, wide-eyed, unblinking, but still she made no attempt to break free. He sat her in the chair, tied her wrists to its arms, and her ankles to the chair legs.

She looked so small in the chair. I tried to chase away the thought that if she'd been at table in Rowley Hall they'd have given her cushions.

She turned to us, looking into the eyes of those who claimed to be her fellows, still not crying out for help. Staring at us, looking into us. She was met by blind obedience to Rowley, the leader who claimed not to be our master. I think Marian and I were the only ones to meet her gaze. The others all looked down. Even Constance. The grass beneath their feet more interesting than Agnes's plight.

With Agnes firmly strapped in, Anselm and Randall climbed up onto the cart. They pushed down on the plank until it lay horizontal, with Agnes in the chair at the other end – now

168

six feet up in the air. Still she said nothing. But she did shut her eyes, and it seemed to me that it was Agnes who conjured the wind, for until then the air had been calm, and yet a breeze blew up. And in that moment all I saw was Agnes in space, her long dark hair streaming out behind her. The chair, the long plank, Gabriel's wooden engine, the cart, the horse, Rowley and his crew all seemed to disappear.

Then Marian ran to Rowley. 'Let her down, Adam,' she wailed. 'Agnes meant no harm. She will not leave us.'

'We all love her, Marian. Which is why she must be cleansed.'

'No. No. No.' Marian beating both hands on Rowley's chest. 'She will drown.'

Gabriel restrained her, holding her arms to her side.

'Your concern touches my heart, dear sweet Marian. But Agnes is safe. She will come to no harm.'

When nobody came to support her pleading, Marian allowed Sarah to lead her away. Rowley climbed up onto the cart. Toby, the younger of his dogs, tried to jump up with him. Rowley shouted at it to lie down, then addressed us from his new pulpit: 'Agnes, we love you and we need you.' He opened his hands, and lifted his palms, exhorting us all to join with him again.

'We love you and we need you,' chimed the response.

'We treasure your presence. And the wisdom you bring us.'

'And the wisdom you bring us.'

'That is why there must be a cleansing. To protect you from yourself. From this you will learn not to fight against the communion of souls. The water may feel cold to the skin, but it will nurture your soul, for water is the giver of life. And we,

Agnes, do what must be done to protect you from those who wish you harm. The Fullness is in all of us, and will surely keep you safe.'

Agnes opened her eyes and gave him a strange beatific smile. But she remained silent. I could only think that she had somehow disconnected herself from Rowley's madness, that she had slipped into a trance. Perhaps that was her way of protecting herself. But her self-assurance was almost as unsettling as Rowley's insane brutality. And there was some small part of me that half expected Agnes to perform some kind of miraculous escape.

My fanciful thoughts were interrupted by Rowley leaning over the side of the cart and saying to Godwyn, 'Move the cart down to the river.' He spoke softly. No trace of anger in his voice.

Godwyn whispered to the horse in the way that horse people do, and put a hand on its chest. The horse took a step back. The cart moved down towards the river. Agnes, the tiny child-like figure with long dark hair, now sitting six feet above the fast-flowing river on a fine dining chair from Rowley Hall. The river swollen from all the recent rain flowing fast beneath her.

The cart wheels squealed, the wooden joints creaked, as it moved ever closer to the shingle strand. Agnes still silent as she and the chair moved out over the water.

Then suddenly the right hand wheel nearest the river sank a foot or so deep into a bog concealed beneath the grass. The cart lurched wildly to the right. The opposite front wheel lifted into the air. Agnes broke her silence with a piercing scream. Rowley was knocked off his feet, and lay winded, clinging to the scaffold of Gabriel's engine. Godwyn urged the horse to push harder. But even the strongest horses have no power when walking backwards. The cart was stuck. If Anselm and Randall let go the see-saw plank, Agnes would drop into no more than three feet of water. It was not the dunking Rowley had in mind.

'It is a sign,' I said, as much for the assembled crew as for Rowley.

Rowley said nothing.

So I took my chance. 'Godwyn,' I called. 'Lead the horse forward. Pull the cart out of the mud.'

'Adam,' said Godwyn. 'What should we do?'

Rowley was staring into space. I walked round to him.

'Have the horse pull the cart back up onto solid ground,' I said. 'Then we can fill the rut with stones.'

Rowley hesitated before agreeing. Then signalled to Godwyn to do as I suggested. Godwyn pulled on the leading rein. The horse took up the strain, the wheel rose a little, but no more than an inch or two. Then the horse slipped, and the cart jolted back. Agnes was shaking. Her head, her hair, her whole body. The chair was shuddering, the long plank exaggerating every juddering movement of the cart as Godwyn's horse tried again to pull it from the mud. But every movement of the cart took the wheel deeper into the bog. Despite the shuddering and shaking, Agnes was staring at Rowley. I marvelled that she wasn't releasing a torrent of curses. But there was no hatred on her face. She looked uncannily calm.

I have never set much store by talk of witches. The only acts of witchcraft I've ever seen are theatre tricks and the cheats of mountebanks. Doctor Simon Forman and Cunning Hannah both had powers and knowledge I could never understand. But Hannah was no witch, and Forman was no sorcerer, no matter what some have said about them. I do confess, however, that when Agnes smiled at Rowley then shut her eyes, I would not have been surprised to see her tormentor struck down by a bolt of lightning. In truth, I'd have been relieved to see the end of Rowley. Even if his intention was really just the warning that he claimed, the river was so high, the current so fast flowing, that even the shallowest dunking would surely drown her.

Why was I so concerned about Agnes, given that she was so bad-tempered and disliked men so much? Why should I care what happened to her? She had none of the grace about her that Cunning Hannah did. But she'd saved my sight and healed my wounds. I owed my life to her. That was reason enough to save her. But I had also grown very fond of Agnes.

The cart was now listing so far one side that she'd have tipped into the river had she not been strapped to the chair. But she was now just a foot or so above the water, as Anselm and Randall struggled keep their end of the plank weighed down.

Until then, Rowley's dogs had been obediently lying down. Then the cart lurched again, Marian shouted out to Agnes and ran towards her. Chaos and confusion erupted. Marian calling to Agnes. Joan and Felicity calling to Marian to stay back. The horse whinnying, struggling to stay standing as its hooves slipped in the mud. It was too much for the dogs. They ran to the water's edge, barking furiously at Agnes.

'It is a sign, Adam Rowley,' I yelled. But the mayhem was now so great and Rowley had fallen so deep into his private madness that he didn't hear me. But I was shouting for all to hear, and not just Rowley. 'Agnes has already understood her warning.' I grabbed him by the shoulders. Forced him to look at me. He was wild-eyed. 'She knows what will happen if ever again she resists the power of our Commonwealth.'

At last my words broke through. He nodded, as if remembering that I was his anointed Messiah.

'Godwyn' he called. 'Take the cart forward.' Had he not seen what was happening?

'The cart is stuck,' said Godwyn.

'Do as I say,' shouted Rowley.

The wheel lifted a few inches, but then the horse slipped and stumbled on the mud. It whinnied, close to panic. Godwyn tried to calm the beast. The wheel had sunk down to the axle.

Anselm and Randall did their best to tie the plank down. But the cart was so unsteady they could no longer hold it. The chair splashed down. Agnes now in the river to her neck. Still strapped to the chair. Screaming for help.

Marian shrieked and waded out. Only a yard or so from the shore, but already waist deep in churning, muddy water. Agnes's head just above water. The chair and the plank were buoyant. But her clothes were heavy. And every time she screamed, she gulped in a mouthful of surging river.

'Anselm,' I shouted above the pandemonium of cries and shouts and barking dogs. Unfasten the plank from Gabriel's engine.'

The flat bed of the cart looked like the deck of a ship in a storm.

Rowley standing, watching. Eyes wide. Mouth half open. He made no attempt to stop me taking charge. 'Grab hold of the plank,' I shouted. 'All of you. Pull it back on land.'

Anselm and Randall understood immediately. They knelt beside Gabriel's engine. Struggling to keep their balance and untie the lashings. Then the plank was free. Anselm still had firm hold of it, but with the current dragging Agnes and the chair downstream, it pulled him off the cart and crashed down, swinging round with the current, knocking Sarah on the head and off her feet. As she fell, she took the boy John down with her.

And in that moment, I see disaster. I see Agnes, the chair and the plank all now caught in the current. I wrap my arms around the plank to hold it. Shout to others to do the same. A wild tug of war against the river itself. Boots slipping in mud. Bodies falling. Struggling back up. Agnes sinking as her clothes grow heavier. Dogs barking. Agnes screaming.

And then, just as it seems we're edging the chair towards the bank, I see Constance let go the plank. She runs into the water, Rowley's dogs snapping at her heels. She's shouting out to Marian. But Marian's already fallen. Her head is bobbing downstream.

I'm confident now that they can pull the plank to the bank, and Agnes with it. But if Constance falls, there'll be no way of saving her.

'Constance,' I scream. My boots have already filled with water and are heavy as granite.

'Constance.' Can she even hear me above the chaos of roaring water and barking dogs? 'Agnes is safe.'

I edge forward. If I go much further out we'll both be swept away. 'Constance.'

At last, she turns. A look of terror on her face. She seems paralysed, unable to move forward or backwards for fear of losing her footing and drowning.

I edge forward. My foot hits a rock. I stumble. I could so easily have gone down. And Constance knows this better than me, for she's a yard further out. I take off my cloak. Bracing myself against the current, I throw it towards her. It falls in front of her.

'Grab it, Constance. If you fall I'll pull you back to land.'

I throw again. Still she doesn't move. I daren't go any closer. If I fall we'll both be lost. I throw again. This time she catches it.

'Hold with both hands, Constance. Hold tight.'

We stay like that too long. Constance staring at me. But I can't move until she's ready. And the water is so damned cold. My hands are numb.

'Hold tight to the cloak, and move to me.'

She's terrified, but moves slowly forward. Six inches, a foot, leaning against the surging waters. I haul in the cloak, as if it's a rope and I'm pulling a sinking boat to shore.

I stumble again and ...

... then we're on the shingle beach. Somebody – I don't know who, don't even know if man or woman – somebody has an arm round me and is helping me walk. Somebody else wraps a cape round Constance. We collapse on the sodden grass. I'm shivering. Shaking. Felicity is holding a bloody kerchief to Sarah's forehead. Is that the chair lying on its side on the shingle beach? Is that Rowley kneeling beside me?

I'm struggling to keep my eyes open, and can't feel my hands and feet. Constance is beside me. Her eyes are shut. Is she breathing? Her chest is moving. She must be alive. And I'm aware of it, so I must be too.

Or maybe not. Because I've stopped shivering and I no longer have the energy to keep my eyes open. Sleep – or whatever – is such a blessèd relief from Rowley's madness.

22
Not what I expected in Hell

There's a strong smell of wood smoke.

Wood smoke and onions.

Wood smoke, onions, beeswax and meat broth. Not what I expected in Hell. And I've surely not wheedled my way into that other place.

I dream sounds as well as pictures, sometimes I even dream words. But I don't dream smells. And the air is warm, not Hellfire roasting. I open my eyes. There are flames before me. In a hearth, not some raging inferno.

I'm lying on a couch, wrapped in blankets, dressed in one of those undyed woollen smocks they put me in when I was recovering from my burns. Agnes is here too. I think it's her. Lying on the floor, in front of the hearth, wrapped in blankets.

Constance is sitting on the other couch. Old Joan has a bowl of broth and is spooning it into her mouth. Constance looks at me. I think she smiles.

Time passes. I drift in and out of something like sleep.

Somebody comes and makes up the fire. But still I feel cold. Somebody male? Godwyn? Gabriel?

I think I recognise the withdrawing room in Rowley Hall. But Rowley's not here. Was he the one who drowned?

Joan feeds me some broth. Constance still wrapped in a blanket on the couch. Near the fire, a wooden rack with clothes draped over it, some of them the clothes I was wearing when I waded into the river, the clothes that had once been worn by Rowley's brother. Steam rising from the britches and doublet.

Time moving in strange ways. In and out of not quite sleep. I open my eyes again. 'Thank you,' says Constance. 'You saved my life.'

'And you saved mine.'

'I was merely your nurse.'

'Did I dream it? Or did I see Agnes there, in front of the fire?'

'That was Agnes. Wrapped up warm.'

'She didn't drown?

'Joan said she got wet and cold. But they got her out before you and me.'

'Where is she?'

'In the kitchen, I think. Adam wanted us all to spend the night here, to feast together and sleep in comfort in the Hall before we set off tomorrow.'

'Agnes in the kitchen with Rowley? After what he did to her?'

'She wants to help.'

And I want to get away, far from Rowley. I want Constance with me. And I feel a strong urge to protect Agnes – and young John too.

'Agnes wants to be part of us,' says Constance.

'Rowley could have drowned her. And she wants to help him?'

Constance cradles my hands in hers and leans forwards. Her face just inches from mine.

'He meant no harm to her.' She's speaking quietly, softly. 'We need Agnes. We want her safe. Sometimes she wanders off like a child. She needed to understand that actions always have consequences. She knows that now. She can see how we all love her.'

I pull back and look around, half expecting Rowley to be sitting behind us. I assume Constance is talking for an audience, but there's nobody. She gets up, puts a couple of logs on the fire. Turns the rack round, moves the clothes about. 'Nearly dry,' she says. The curtains have all been drawn, the wall lanterns are lit, a dozen or more candles as well. And, of course, in Rowley Hall they're beeswax candles.

I'll not change Constance's mind about Rowley while we're still in Rowley Hall. But I can't stop myself. 'You went in the river to save Agnes. You thought she would drown. Do you not remember that?'

'Yes, I do remember. And you threw the cloak for me. You saved me from drowning. Of course I remember.'

I get to my feet. 'I need to walk outside. Come with me.'

'Not yet. Maybe later. You need to warm through properly.'

'I'd like to talk, Constance. And not in here.'

'Do *you* remember what happened?'

'I threw my cloak for you. We struggled back against the current to the shingle beach.'

'You fell, Matthew. You not remember that?'

'I nearly fell.'

'We took a few steps together, then you fell. I tried to hold you, but the current was too strong. It was Adam ran into the river. Adam who grabbed hold of you. Adam who pulled you out.'

I have no memory of that.

Time passed. I maybe slept a little. Sarah came in with John, who looked at me with almost a smile.

'You're alive, Master Matthew,' he says.

'I hope so.'

'And I shall bring you some more broth,' says Sarah. Her forehead's bandaged.

I call out as she turns to go, 'Is it night?'

'Mid-afternoon. We drew the curtains to keep in the warmth.'

Sarah wants John to go back with her to the kitchens. He pleads with her to stay. She insists he, 'Leave Master Matthew be.'

He follows her out.

'Where is Adam now?' I say to Constance.

'I don't know. With the men, I think. Getting things ready for tomorrow.'

'I want to thank him.'

'Stay in the warm. Thank him later. At the feast.'

'Where's Marian?'

Constance looks away.

'Constance? Where's Marian?'

She shakes her head and whispers.

'I can't hear you.'

'The river's in flood. They said she was swept off her feet and washed downstream. She'll find her way back. I know she will.'

Later Sarah told me that Randall and Godwyn ran down the path beside the river until they found her drowned body about a mile downstream, her clothes tangled in the branches of a fallen willow tree.

Time passed.

Constance told me my clothes were dry and said she had to go and help prepare the feast. She promised we'd talk later.

'Where nobody can overhear us,' I said.

'Yes. If you like.'

She left me alone in the room. The clothes were dry. I couldn't rid myself of the thought that they were Rowley's brother's clothes. But I'd rather wear them than the grey woollen smock.

Agnes came in with a cup of some potion she'd concocted, shutting the door behind her. She said it would help me get my strength back. I thanked her, then lowered my voice: 'Why are you still here, Agnes? I'm glad you are. But why – ?'

'I do as I'm tol'. I needs to be safe. I thanks you for what you done at the river. I'll not forget. Now drink your potion. Get you back your strength.'

'What's in it?'

She shrugged.

'Not poppy juice?'

'You in pain?'

'No.'

'You want to sleep some more?'

'No.'

'Then you don't be wanting poppy juice.'

'More riddles, Agnes. What's in it?'

'An' besides. I don't have none. All my poppy juice is packed away. Not my choice, Matthew. 'Twas Adam Rowley said she has to go in a safe place. So that's where she be.'

'Agnes, what's in this potion?'

"erbs. Leaves. Seeds. Crushed bark. Me to know what goes into my potions. You to drink it.'

I lifted the cup to my lips and pretended to drink. It smelt sour and bitter. I pulled a face and coughed. 'Leave it with me. I'll drink the rest soon.'

I hoped she'd be satisfied with that and leave me to stay warming myself by the fire. But she sat down next to me on the couch.

'You not trust me, Matthew? You thinks I wants to poison you?'

I shook my head. 'I don't understand you, Agnes. But I do trust you.' And I did, at least I did at that moment – as much as I ever trust anyone. A strange and unexpected bond had grown between us. Sitting beside me on the couch, she was smaller than young John. Close to, I could see she was older than I'd thought she was. Lines and wrinkles. Old scars and pock marks. All the marks of age on a small child's body.

'Don't ask you to understand me,' she said. 'I healed you. An' you helped save me from the waters. You has a plan, Matthew. I knows it, sure as I's always known you'd bring trouble. You didn't mean to bring it, I knows that now. But it come with you just the same. I seen it from the first. I's always known it.'

'I don't understand why you want to stay with Rowley.'

'Who says I do?'

'Then why? Why do you stay?'

'What he say. Safest place for me.'

'Your friend Marian is drowned, Agnes. Drowned because of Rowley's madness.'

'Safest place for me is what I said. 'Twas never safe for Marian.'

'You talk in riddles, Agnes.'

'No riddling in your plan, though, Matthew. I knows what you want. I seen it clear. Wait til after the feast, then off you goes with Constance.'

We were the only ones in the room, and the door was shut. 'Constance hasn't agreed to it, Agnes. But if she does agree, then you can come with us. We'll look after you. And we won't be dunking you in any rivers.'

''E won't allow it, Matthew. Won't let any of us leave. You seen what happen when I stay away from your welcome feast.'

'How can he stop us?'

She shrugged. 'More o' them than there is of us.' She looked at the cup I was nursing in my lap. 'Give you strength, Matthew. You might need it.'

I drank the potion as she bade me. It tasted less foul than it smelt. She took the cup and went back to the kitchen, leaving me with my thoughts all mingle-mangled.

Agnes's potion did indeed make me feel awake. Maybe the time to go would be early the next morning. Rowley seemed happy for me and Constance to share a bed. We could talk later. I didn't want to rouse suspicions, for the business by the river had shown me that Rowley's crew were loyal to him to the point of blindness, so I stayed where I was, warming myself by the fire.

The door opened slowly. John looked in. Furtive. Scanning the room. When he was certain that I was alone, he tippy-toed over.

'Can we go to the study again? Do some more reading?'

Why not, I thought. The worst that could happen was that Rowley could find us there, and scold us.

23
The end of days

Nobody saw us leave the withdrawing room, cross the hall into the dining room and walk through the panelled door into the study.

'Shall I find another key?' said John.

'In the books?'

He nodded eagerly.

'Let's start with *key*, then see what else we can find.'

While John was leafing through pages, I pulled back the curtains. The shutters had been closed and barred from the outside, so it wasn't possible to open a window. I thought it strange, but nothing more than that. Constance had talked about going into Abingdon when she was living in the Hall, and Wittenham wasn't far away. So I assumed Rowley didn't want anyone seeing lights in the house that evening. I lit a lantern and a couple of candles.

John found some more *keys* in another play, *The Tragedie of Macbeth*. But he wanted more of *Romeo and Juliet*. He was obsessed with family feuds.

I showed him the word Capulet, and asked him to look through the play and find all the times the word was written. While he was doing that I did my own search. In a drawer in the desk was a large parchment document, folded, but not yet sealed.

This Indenture it began in large letters. After that, the lettering was small until the words *Transfer of Legal Title*. Soon after that came *Adam Rowley*. And on the next line: *Judith Harpole*.

'How many you found?' I asked.

'No more keys. But here's Capulets.' He'd found old Capulet calling for his sword. 'Did you have a sword when you lived in London?'

'No, John. Real swords are heavy and burdensome. When I'm fit and healthy, I like to be fleet of foot and quick in my wits.'

'That's what I want to be,' he said, looking at me with such simple admiration that I experienced strange pangs of regret about leaving in the morning, and that I'd have to stop playing the father that he so wanted me to be. And that set me thinking. If Constance and I were leaving, we'd need money. But the picklock wires that we'd crafted so carefully the day before had been lost in the river – along with the dagger I'd taken from Pinchface Jack in the stables. I struck a bargain with John. I'd teach him more words, and read some of the play with him if he could bring me half a dozen more hatpins.

He scurried on his way. And I returned to the indenture. The writing was small and hard to read – until I came to the words *John Brown*. With Rowley I'd come to expect things to be not quite what they seemed, but what followed astonished me, not because it was unlikely but because it had been staring me in the face from the moment my sight was good enough to notice John watching me.

> *… the boy known as John Brown, whom I hereby declare to be my true and only son … Although he*

was born out of wedlock, it is agreed between the parties to this indenture that when he doth come of age he shall inherit ...

John was Adam's son, not Franklin's. No mention of the mother. He wanted John looked after. But the boy's mere presence touched raw nerves in Adam. When he'd seethed about the wickedness of Lord Roche raping Felicity, he was raging against himself. Had he taken her and baby Sam into the fold of his magical commonwealth to appease his own guilt?

I folded the indenture and slipped it into an inside pocket. In the morning I'd show it to Constance, and maybe then she'd believe me that Adam wasn't what he seemed.

The door squeaked open. John appeared, clutching a fistful of hatpins. 'I got them, Matthew.' So proud of himself. It would be a wrench to leave him with Sarah and Godwyn, but the skills I'd already taught him would stand him in good stead.

'Watch me, John.' I bent the tip of one of the hatpins. 'Now you.' And he did the next. Until we had a set. 'I keep three. You keep three.' He grinned.

I'd have gone straight upstairs and emptied the drawers in the bedchambers, but John wanted me to keep my side of the bargain. Knowing that he found the family feud more fascinating than anything the star-crossed lovers might get up to, I leafed through, until – 'Here. I have it. You can be Tybalt.'

'Is he a Capulet?'

'He is indeed.'

'Does he have a sword?'

'In this scene he does. And I shall be Benvolio.'

'That's a funny name.'

'The poets often give the people in their plays the strangest of names.'

At that moment, the door opened. Adam Rowley stood there, shocked and surprised to find us. For a moment, however, he seemed transfixed by the clothes I was wearing. Did he see the ghost of his dead brother? John pricked the haunting with a jaunty, 'Matthew's teaching me to read.'

Rowley forced a smile, a half-hearted attempt to hide a scowl. 'How pleasing,' he said, though he clearly felt usurped.

'Young John is a quick learner,' I said.

John beamed, but the mask of Rowley's smile slipped. 'I came for more candles. We are about to sit down to eat. It will be a celebration.' But the tone of his voice implied a funeral.

He picked up the two candlesticks, then ushered us out of the study.

In the dining room some of the crew were already seated at table. A high stool had been brought for Agnes, replacing the chair that had been used for the dunking. She was sitting near the door to the hallway. Rowley asked me to sit between her and Constance. He had John sit near him at the opposite end of the table, close to his study door. Sarah and Joan, Godwyn and Anselm brought the food in, then took their places at table, although there was to be no eating until Rowley had given another sermon. This was mercifully short – not much longer than the Grace my father used to say at home. He stood beside John and announced: 'Tonight we celebrate our wondrous coming together. After this feast we leave our old lives behind and we set forth together on our journey. All things are now possible because the Fullness is in us.' He raised his glass. 'Let us drink and be jovial. Enjoy the food before us, and fill our souls with rapture.'

I don't know whether rapture filled our souls, because I don't understand souls and I suspect what I mean by rapture wasn't what Rowley had in mind. But we certainly all intended to fill our bellies. And now that the food was on the table, Rowley insisted that he, and he alone, would serve our drinks. He asked whether we wanted ale, mead or claret wine, and ensured that our tankards and glasses were all filled.

He made no mention of Marian. And there was no place for her at table. Nor any talk of Agnes's punishment. Life was to go on as normal – if such a fine feast is normal. Joan and her helpers had been busy in the kitchen. In the centre of the table was a roast suckling pig and two hare pies. At each end of the table a roast hen stuffed with onions. And after that came pippin tarts, gingerbread and marchpane. Gabriel's fiddle lay on the floor beneath his chair. The merriment came from food and drink and so much talk and laughter that we were soon all shouting to be heard. They all knew that it might be days or weeks or even months before their bellies would be full again.

And as for me? I ate my share of food, but I'd learnt my lesson from the feast in the shelter when I was welcomed and Agnes stayed away. I did what I've been doing for years when people around me are getting drunk. I pretended to drink and I played the drunkard. Anselm was sitting on my left. He chose ale when Rowley first offered. I chose the same. And every time that Rowley filled my tankard, I waited awhile then poured mine into Anselm's. So nobody thought it strange that in due course I had to visit the privy.

That's when I found the front door locked.

No surprise in that, for if the curtains were drawn and the shutters were closed to stop neighbours seeing what was going on inside, it would make sense to lock the doors against intruders. Perhaps that was why the kitchen door was also locked.

I had my own picklock wires, but I wasn't confident I could pick a lock in low light. I grew up left-handed. Picking a lock with my right is like wearing thick gloves and trying to thread a needle. If Constance and I were to escape, we'd need John's help.

I returned to the dining room. Gabriel had his fiddle under his chin, and was playing a merry tune. Joan, Sarah and Felicity were singing the verses, the men the chorus.

Constance had fallen asleep. And Rowley's dogs weren't with him, which was unusual, for they followed him everywhere. I thought Constance was asleep because she and I had hardly slept the night before. But Agnes knew something wasn't right. She was nudging Constance, trying to wake her. That was the point when I should have seen it, when I could have stopped it. But I was too busy making plans for our escape.

'Play us a jig,' I shouted to Gabriel. That was greeted with a cheer. Gabriel got to his feet, and most of the others too, though Joan had also fallen asleep. Rowley had left the room, so the raucous merriment seemed an ideal opportunity to get John out. In the hallway I asked if he'd had anything to drink.

'A sip of mead. Uncle Adam thought I'd like it because it was sweet.'

'One sip?'

'I didn't like the taste. It made me feel sick.'

'Are you going to be sick now?'

'I poured it away.'

'Very wise.'

We were still standing in the hallway. The kitchen door was open. The sound of Rowley pouring ale into a jug. While he was busy in the kitchen, John and I could go upstairs. I removed my boots, and told John to take off his shoes.

The locks on the drawers in the bedchamber were too small and finicky for me to pick, and even the few sips of mead that John had drunk made him unsteady. But he managed to open one. In amongst some trifling trinkets sat a silver bracelet, a pair of ear-rings, and a brooch that took the form of a butterfly with filigree wings and tiny blue jewels for eyes. There were also two velvet-lined boxes. One contained a pearl, the other a gold ring, which I slipped onto the fourth finger of my left hand. It fitted perfectly. I guessed it had been Rowley's father's.

'What are we doing?'

'Taking them for safekeeping.'

That seemed to satisfy him. We tiptoed silently back down the stairs. Rowley must have returned to the dining room because there was nobody in the kitchen.

'What are we doing now?'

'Shh. We have to whisper. What we're doing is secret. Come with me.' I led him to the back door. 'This was where you learnt to pick locks. Show me you're still as good as you were.'

Hatpins weren't strong enough to shift the lever. We needed a meat skewer. I found one in the pantry. I was about to go back into the kitchen when I heard Rowley's voice.

'I've been looking for you, John.'

'I wanted some more gingerbread.'

'Then you must have some. There is plenty. Did you drink the mead I gave you?'

'I didn't like the taste.'

'I am sorry to hear that John. Mead in moderation is a fine drink that will fill you with goodness. You must try some ale.'

'Don't like it.'

'Then small beer. Or maybe watered claret wine? You may be young, but it's not right for you to be the only one of us who doesn't take a little drink.'

The sound of liquid poured into a cup.

'There.'

'Don't like it.'

'Drink it, John.'

The boy choked.

'Now take the cup, and drink a little more.'

Silence.

'Have you seen Matthew?' asked Rowley.

A moment's hesitation, and then: 'He went to the privy.' In that moment I felt so proud of him. But now I curse myself for not having the wit to put an end to Rowley's madness there and then. He wouldn't have been ready for me, and even without the use of my left hand it would have been easy to skewer him.

'Come with me young John,' said Rowley. 'We must return to the feast. We must all be together when the feast comes to an end.'

Footsteps as he and the boy walked out. The door to the hall banged shut. One greasy meat skewer was enough to shift the lever of the old lock on the outside door. I had no idea what Rowley was planning, but I wanted to be sure we could escape through it. I didn't want him locking it again, so I found a wooden spoon, whittled the handle to a point and forced it into the keyhole, hammered it in with a cast iron skillet, then snapped it off. In my trade, we call that spiking a lock. Then I found a carving knife, and hid it up my sleeve. Not my weapon of choice, but needs must.

Even as I left the kitchen and walked down the corridor to the hall, I felt the strange silence which had fallen over the whole house. The dining room door was open. No caterwauling fiddle, no stomping feet. Rowley was waiting for me, standing at the far end of the table, candlestick in one hand, bottle in the other. John was sitting in the chair beside him, his head slumped to one side, mouth hanging open, the cup of small beer fallen from his hand to the floor, where it had smashed into pieces. Even Felicity's babe was asleep. Rowley must have poured mead down its throat. He and I the only ones in the room still conscious.

He held out his arms. 'Welcome, Matthew. We are now complete.' He put the bottle down. Picked up another candlestick. 'We have light,' he said, holding both candles in front of him as if in some grand ceremony. 'You are the light, Matthew. You showed us the way.' His smile as fixed as a vanity portrait.

Anselm, sprawled across the table, groaned in his stupor. I put my hand to Constance's brow. She was warm, and she was breathing. It could have been worse. My first thought on hearing the silence was that he'd poisoned everyone. So foolish of me. Why had I not seen it before? Agnes's poppy juice hadn't been stowed away. Rowley had used it to spike the drinks.

I put my hand on Constance's shoulder. 'Constance.' She moaned and stirred, but didn't wake.

'Leave her. She's at peace. She's ready.'

'Ready for what?'

'Our great journey.'

I look back and think how many things I could have done differently. Could have, but didn't. In my miserable defence, I had never before encountered anyone who saw the world as Rowley did, and even the few sips of ale I'd taken must have slowed my wits. I could have slipped the knife down my sleeve and thrown it. But a carving knife, however sharp, isn't weighted like a dagger. Even if my aim had been true, there was every chance the handle would hit first, and the knife would fall harmlessly to the floor.

My best weapon was what little wit I had left. I walked slowly towards him, picking my way between broken tankards, smashed cups and broken glass.

'Sit you down, Matthew.'

I chose to stay standing.

He shrugged.

'Tell me what I need to do,' I said. 'I want to be sure I understand.'

He had that look of wide-eyed rapture about him again. 'You do understand, Matthew, for it was you who taught us what we must do.'

I edged closer, sliding my feet on the wooden floor awash with spilt drink.

'You came through fire, and you were reborn. You, better than anyone, must know that when you pass through fire you emerge into the light, into a new world. I know the rebirth will be painful, but we are all now ready to make that journey. Drink with me, Matthew. It will make the journey easier.'

'Thank you, Adam. You are right. Yes, I do understand.' I did indeed. I understood why the doors were locked and why the shutters were barred shut. And I understood that Marian in her watery grave, and John, Constance, Agnes, and all we chosen ones were prisoners to his blazing madness.

I could have simply turned and walked away. But that would have meant leaving John and Constance, Agnes and

Felicity, all of them. I had to stay and play his game. I found an unbroken tankard, reached for the jug of ale to fill it, and edged closer to Rowley.

I lifted the tankard. 'Will you drink with me, Adam?'

'Finish your ale,' he said. 'Then let us drink brandywine together.' He glanced at the bottle he'd put on the table.

I put the tankard to my lips. The trick of it when you can't pour the stuff away is to toss your head back, hold the drink in your mouth and feign gulping it down while not letting anything pass your gullet. It takes practice, but it's a skill well worth acquiring.

'I owe you so much, Matthew. Before you came to us, I thought we would have to live like beggars and vagabonds until we found a haven of safety. I always knew we would succeed, but I thought it might take several years. You showed me another way, the true path to rebirth that takes us through fire.'

I thanked him and smiled. With one hand clutching the tankard to my chest, I reached for the jug with the other. A man needs to top up his drink.

'These are simple gentlefolk, Matthew. They fear change. My love for them is stronger, more enduring than any carnal love. So they sleep to make the journey quick and easy. Soon they will know true ecstasy.'

'I would dearly like to make that Great Journey with you, Adam, but I fear I will not be welcomed into the Fullness, for I am a great sinner.'

'No, Peter. You must not blame yourself.' Did Adam just call me Peter? No matter to me. I could play Peter if that gave me more time.

'I fear the afterlife, Adam, because I have killed.' I feigned drinking some more, hoping he'd do the same.

He put the candlesticks down on the table, and clasped his hands together. 'Not the *after*-life, Peter. We journey to a new life.'

'I am not worthy.'

'There are some truths in the Bible, Peter. Truths that have become entangled in the webs of deception woven by the church and the priests. Jesus died to save us from our sins. His death absolves us of our sins. He will journey with us.'

'I am too fearful. I have killed more than once.'

'I, too, have killed a man,' said Rowley. 'And yet the journey holds no fears for me.' He shut his eyes. That slow rocking motion. 'We will travel together.'

Perhaps now would be the time. I reached for the jug of ale. But he opened his eyes.

'Matthew?'

'Yes.' I could be Matthew again if that's what he wanted.

'My brother Peter has gone before us.'

'You killed Peter?'

'It was never my intention. I love Peter as I have never loved any other. Man or woman.'

'I though Peter fell from his horse.'

'He fell from Franklin's horse. I loosened the girth of the saddle. If I'd known Peter would ride instead of Franklin, I would never have done it. I killed you, Peter. And then you showed me the true way. You have already made the Great Journey once. And now we shall do it together.'

'Then pour the glasses of brandywine,' I said. 'And let us drink to the ecstasy that will soon be ours. To the Great Journey that we shall make together as true brothers.'

He reached for the bottle.

I said a silent prayer. Not something I've done in many years, not since my mother fell sick. I prayed that my aim was as true as it used to be. Then I threw what was left in the jug of ale at the candles. One was doused. The other spluttered, then flickered back to life.

I hurled the jug into Rowley's face, and sent him reeling. I slid the knife down my sleeve, pulled John's chair out of my way, grabbed Rowley by his hair and held the knife to his throat.

Blood was pouring from a cut on his forehead, but he looked at me with no more fear in his eyes than if he'd allowed a favoured child to beat him at arm wrestling, as if he had always wanted me to fight him.

'You cannot stop it,' he said. 'The Fullness is ready to welcome us.'

'Then drink mead,' I said.

'I *want* the pain of burning. I need my flesh to feel the pain you felt. I seek its purification. I have no desire to sleep through the journey.'

'Drink the mead, Adam, or I'll cut your throat and you'll bleed to death before the fire takes hold.'

And then. At last. That sickening smile fell from his face.

'Drink, Adam. You shall not be lord and master making choices for us. All shall be shared. Remember. Now drink.'

With the knife still firmly on his throat, I seized a handful of hair in my other hand and forced him back to the table. He put the cup to his lips. And took a tiny sip.

'Fill the cup, Adam. Drink it.'

He filled, and drank.

'Again.'

He gave me a look of glowering rage. And then, of a sudden, reached for the burning candle. I let go his hair, grabbed the bottle of brandywine and smashed it over his head. He was soaked with the spirit and blinded by blood pouring from his head wounds. Despite this, he still flailed around knocking over the candle. Tongues of blue flame slithered across the table, dripping onto the floor and up his brandy soaked arm.

His clothes soon caught light. As flames reached his face he howled with pain and stumbled across to the windows, where he tried to wrap himself in the curtains to smother the flames. I had no choice but to cut his throat. He was a human torch setting light to anything he touched. His blood spurted across the detritus of the feast. He fell to the floor, gargled on his own blood which was frothing from his severed windpipe. And there, on the floor, his blood mixed with spilled ale, splinters of glass and the blue flames of burning brandywine.

Rowley had been thorough in his preparations. The layer of rushes between the table and the curtains was thicker than anywhere else in the room. The flaming brandywine had set the rushes alight. He must have soaked them in candlewax. When I first came here with John, the smell had prompted fond memories of that last Twelfth Night I spent with my own family. I threw whatever ale I could find on the floor to douse the burning rushes. But the curtains were already burning. I ripped off my doublet, Peter Rowley's doublet, and used that to beat out the flames.

Convinced that I'd killed the fire, even though the room was filling with smoke, I gathered John in my arms and carried him out to the kitchen. I sat him on a chair. Laid his head on the table. He didn't stir.

I went back in. The smoke was thicker, darker, foul smelling, acrid. Choking. But I could see no flames.

I don't know exactly what happened and when. But I do remember standing in that doorway, unable to move. Knowing I had to get people out. Holding my breath. Struggling to keep my eyes open.

Can't move forward. Can't run away. I'm back in the barn with the wall of flame in front of me. I can't jump through it this time.

Constance coughing pierces the dark trance of my terror. 'Get out,' I shout to her. Then choke as I take in a lungful of smoke.

She's moving. Constance is moving. She gets to her feet.

'Go,' I shout through my coughing fit. 'Go.'

She will never forgive me if I don't rescue Agnes. I force myself into the room. Hands on Agnes's shoulders. I shake her. She doesn't stir. I lift her from the stool, sling her over my shoulder like a sack of grain.

As I turn to leave there are flames racing up the curtains. A fierce gust of heat. I catch a glimpse of movement behind me. Constance stumbling out into the hall.

Agnes no heavier than John. I carry her out to the kitchen, sit her in a chair, lie her head on the table.

No Constance in the kitchen. No Constance in the hallway.

I shout for her. She must have run out into the night. I open the back door. Bellow her name into the darkness. No response. She must have taken refuge in the stables. After losing her husband and her children she has good reason to be terrified of fire. Smoke's already in the kitchen. But I have to go back.

I get as far as the dining room doorway, where I'm met by smoke so thick I can't see. And a fearsome wall of heat. Curtains aflame, greedy for the wooden ceiling. Above the roaring of the fire comes the sound of window glass shattering. Rowley's feasting room is a furnace.

I hate myself for abandoning the rest of Rowley's crew. Hated myself then. Hate myself now for what I didn't do. No matter that there is no-one alive could possibly have withstood that heat. Randall pulled me from the burning barn, braving fire himself. Sarah and Godwyn did their damnedest to bring up young John. Old Joan was a good, honest woman. Felicity a loving mother, Sam an innocent babe. None of them deserved to die. Not even Gabriel, who'd built the ducking engine. He'd only been doing what Rowley told him was necessary. It's scant consolation that at least John and Agnes, Constance and I have escaped.

I retreat to the kitchen, coughing, choking, eyes red raw and streaming. John and Agnes are still not moving. I take John first. Over the cobbled courtyard to the stables. And there I lay him on that bed, where Constance and Agnes nursed me back to health.

I go back for Agnes. The kitchen's filling with smoke. Just half a minute later and I couldn't have got her out. I glance back as I carry her to the stables. Flames have burnt through the shutters and are reaching up into the night sky.

I lay Agnes down beside John. They're both breathing heavily. Both still deep in the grip of the poppy juice.

I'm back outside. In the courtyard between the house and the stable block. My stomach churning with dread as I shout Constance's name.

I stand, watching. Not knowing what I'm doing, not knowing what I'm thinking. It's a clear night. The fire's lit up the sky. It must be visible for miles.

I can shut my eyes, but I can't shut out the roaring, the crackling, the smashing of glass, the crash of falling beams. And then another sound. Galloping, approaching horses.

PART TWO

24
Embers

Not a day goes by in London without fires breaking out. Runaway pig knocks over the chestnut man's brazier. Hot coals go flying. Half a dozen market stalls are up in flames. Every winter's night there are chimney fires somewhere in the city. Those pretty little sparks that take flight when a maid prods smouldering logs. They nestle on the soot, glowing in the darkness, waiting for a draft to blow them into life.

What a spectacle for gawping crowds! What a hubbub of noise and confusion! And what fine opportunities for the gossips and cutpurses to ply their trade. But I'm not cutting purse strings in London. I'm watching flames from Rowley Hall reaching up into the sky. Lead is dripping, stone tiles sliding from the roof, great wooden beams falling, sparks chasing ever higher into the night sky. I watch and I listen, transfixed. If it weren't for the sickening smell of burning flesh I could be marvelling at the fireworks for a royal wedding.

Then I saw the horsemen silhouetted against the blaze. I turned and walked away. I think back now, and wonder that I still had any wits about me. And yet I went back into the stable block and after checking on Agnes and John, I climbed the stairs to that first floor room, where John used to sleep when Sarah and Godwyn cared for him as their own. I moved the bed, kicked away the straw, lifted the loose floorboard, and retrieved

Forman's book. After making sure the letters were still inside, I tucked it into an inside pocket of my doublet, Peter's doublet, Rowley's brother's doublet. Then I went back downstairs.

I sat down on the bed where I'd been nursed back to health. Agnes and John both lying curled up together, safe in the comforting oblivion of Agnes's poppy juice. The only light cast on their nestled bodies was the warm glow from the distant flames, the peace of sleep dissolving the difference in age between them.

'You said you'd take me with you.' A woman's voice. Constance's voice. From outside a thunderous crash. A wall collapsing. Horses whinnying. Men shouting. Constance must be hiding somewhere in the stable block.

'Adam Rowley confessed to me,' I was whispering, not wanting to wake John or Agnes. 'He caused Peter's death, his brother's death. That's what drove him mad.'

'Adam wasn't mad.'

'He loosened the girth of Franklin's horse. He wanted Franklin to fall. But Peter took the horse instead. Peter died. Their father died. It's not what Adam intended. But it was his doing.'

'Adam gave us sanctuary. He welcomed us where nobody else would. He understands better than anyone how best to live our lives.'

'He was John's father, Constance. He kept it hidden. From John, from Godwyn, from Sarah. Was that a good way to live his life? Denying John knowledge of his true father? It's no wonder he taught you all to deny the past.'

'Who are we to stand in judgement over others? We are so much more than the worst of our deeds. That's what he teaches us.'

'Adam Rowley is dead. And Joan and Sarah. Felicity and baby Sam. It was Rowley set the fire. And the fire took them all. All except you and me and Agnes and young John. You escaped. I rescued Agnes and John.'

I wanted to hold her close. I wanted her to hold me. But she stayed in the shadows. Keeping her distance as if my telling her what Rowley had done made me the fire-setter.

'He dosed you all with Agnes's poppy juice.'

'He loved us. Even you, Matthew. Especially you.'

'When the embers have cooled and they search through the rubble, they'll find charred bodies. People will want to know how the fire started, and why so few people escaped. Ignorant people make ignorant connections. It's not safe for you here. Not safe for Agnes. They'll call it the vengeance of a witch, or a woman driven mad by her own grief. None of us is safe here. Half of Abingdon and all of Wittenham will be here tomorrow morning. Gossip, rumour and malice thrive on misfortune.'

'You want to go to Canterbury, Matthew. I understand. Take Agnes and John if that's what they want. But leave me here. I can fend for myself.'

'You'll not be safe here. Come with me. To Canterbury.'

There. I'd said it. For better or for worse, I'd said it. But still she didn't show herself.

John stirred first, making small whimpering noises. He'd drunk less than anyone else. I sat beside him. Took hold of his hand. He sat up with a start, groaned, clutched his head and vomited. I tried to reassure him that we were safe, but he was confused and frightened.

When Agnes came round and I told her what had happened, she understood immediately. She, better than any of us, knew what Rowley was capable of. She agreed that we had to use the cover of night to get as far away as possible from the ruins of the Hall.

She knew a way through the woods. We took a couple of leathern bottles and filled them with water from a nearby spring. Agnes knew the hidden tracks and byways better than anyone, and the moon was nearly full. I took John by the hand and followed.

'Is Uncle Adam coming?'

'No.'

'Godwyn and Sarah?'

'Just us.'

I don't know how many miles we walked, although mostly it was through woodland for that was where Agnes felt safest, and it seemed wise not to risk walking on open highways. I put my trust in Agnes, which was well because she had stores of nuts and fruit hidden in the woodland. If Constance was following, she was very quiet.

As dawn broke we found ourselves on the edge of a heath. The only shelter was a small shepherd's hut with stone walls, a turf roof and a low wattle fence in place of a door. Inside, it was empty except for a pile of straw. Barely enough room for the four of us. Sheep used it as often as their shepherd, for the fence had tufts of manky wool caught on it, the floor was covered in droppings, and the place stank of stale piss. We used handfuls of straw to sweep out the droppings, then spread what was left over the bare earth floor. It wasn't luxury, but it was shelter, and we needed rest before going any further.

I kept watch first while Agnes and John huddled together on the straw, keeping each other warm. They were asleep as soon as they lay down, looking like the sole survivors from a litter of puppies. I felt my own eyelids getting heavy.

'Why don't you rest too?'

'I've not forgotten what happened when I lay down to rest in the barn near Wittenham. You go in, Constance. There's room inside.'

'I'll stay here with you. Do you have a plan?'

'Our water won't last much longer. And those nuts and berries that Agnes squirrelled away in the woods won't sustain us for long. We need food and drink.'

'What will you do?'

'I'll walk on. Do what I have to.'

'And what of Agnes? Will she come with us?'

'She can make her own mind up.

'And John?'

'He'll be useful.'

'Useful? Is that why you've brought him? So you can teach him to pick pockets and locks? Cheat at cards and dice?'

'He needs a father.'

'Or is it you who needs a son?'

'We can care for him, Constance.'

'But you don't want to care for him. You plan to use him.'

I moved away from the hut.

'You don't want John to hear me, do you.'

'I'm not walking away from you, Constance. I don't want to wake John and Agnes.'

'Have you changed your mind about me coming to Canterbury?'

'I want you with me. How many times do I have to say it?' It was all I could do to stop myself from shouting at her. And

204

I was glad when she sank back into silence. I needed time to think, although it was a marvel I could think at all. My memories of the fire, the sounds and smells, the choking smoke, lay deep inside – smothered, but smouldering. Just waiting for the embers to be fanned back into flame.

The heat. The flying sparks. The falling stones and timbers. The smell of burning flesh. I still dread what should be the release of sleep, where my dreams are so often haunted by the burning dining room at Rowley Hall. Whenever I see velvet curtains or smell the honeyed glow of beeswax candles, I feel something close to panic. But there, on that heathland somewhere south of Oxford, I fondly imagined I could put those terrors behind me, and plan the way ahead. I conjured explanations in my head about why the four of us might be travelling together.

'Why do you want me to come with you, Matthew? To warm your bed and bring you comfort on the journey? Or do you worry that Kate has given up on you and married another man? What then, Matthew? Turn to Constance? I'd rather you abandoned me now than in some strange place where I know no-one.'

'You need to rest. We'll talk more after I've brought back food and a change of clothes. You'll not starve. And you won't go cold.'

She went quiet again. The only sounds were buzzards keening. Such quietness could drive a man mad. But I had enough of my wits about me to know that the sun rises in the east whether you're stumbling out of a trugging house on Petticoat Lane in the early hours or standing by a shepherd's hut in Oxfordshire. And by that compass of the rising sun I reckoned that the thin plumes of smoke I'd seen rising into the morning sky came from buildings a few miles to the south.

I roused John and Agnes and explained where I was going. Assured them I'd not be long. John looked downcast.

'I'm hungry,' he said.

'I'm hungry too. That's why I'm going to get food.'

'Can I come with you?'

'Not this time. I won't be long.'

'Why can't I come? You said I was your prentice boy.'

'I will get us food and drink and clean clothes. Constance will stay here with you.'

Agnes was staring at me.

'I'll come back for you, Agnes. For all of you. I'm not abandoning you.'

'Tell him, Matthew,' said Constance. 'Tell him about his inheritance.'

'It can wait.'

'What can wait?' said Agnes.

'I need to talk to John.'

'You said it can wait. What can wait?'

'I'm tired, Agnes. We all are. I need to talk to John. Something I wanted to tell him.'

'Secrets, is it? Secrets twixt you and the boy? I brought yous both here. I found us food. And nows you wants to talk wiz 'im alone. I grown to like you, Matthew. Don't throw that away by cloakin' yourself in secrets.. What you says to 'im you says to me.'

'There's a village or a town not far away. I'll bring back food and drink and clean clothes.'

'That's not what yous was going to say to the boy. If it needed saying a minute ago, it needs saying now.'

'It's up to John,' I said. 'This is something he might want to keep secret.'

'Go on. Tell me,' said John. 'I don't mind Agnes hearing.'

So I sat down and asked him to sit beside me. And then, as simply and as gently as I knew how, I told him what I knew of his early life. Told him that his real father was Adam Rowley. Told him that Rowley asked Sarah and Godwyn to take him in, and make sure they cared for him.

John looked at me wide-eyed. But he remained mute.

Agnes stood by the doorway to the hut. She didn't speak, she didn't smile, but every so often she looked at me and nodded. Maybe I was confirming what she'd already divined, or whatever Agnes did to understand the world.

'Are you not my father?' said John.

'I cannot be your father. But if ever I do have a son, I hope he's as strong-minded and as quick-witted as you are. Adam Rowley was your father.'

'Can I see him?'

How do you tell a seven year old child that his father set a fire which burnt alive the adults who'd looked after him for most of his life? I softened it as best I could. Then I reached into my doublet, Peter Rowley's doublet, and drew out the indenture.

'This is yours, John.'

His expression didn't change. But Agnes looked curious. I found the place in the document where John's name was mentioned. 'Your name is on this. Do you recognise it?'

The writing was so small and the script so convoluted that he couldn't read anything. I traced my finger over the words as I read them aloud: '... *the boy known as John Brown, whom I declare to be my true and only son ... It is hereby agreed between the parties to this indenture that when he doth come of age he shall inherit one fifth of the Rowley Hall Estate.'*

I'd hoped that would bring a smile to his face, but he remained as steadfastly inscrutable as I would be if ever I picked up four aces in an honest deal at primero.

'What do you think of that, Master John?'

'Don't know.'

He didn't ask what it might mean to inherit one fifth of the estate. He asked nothing more about the fire. No questions about Sarah or Godwyn. And he didn't ask about Adam Rowley. He said only this: 'Is it my job to be my father now that he is dead?' And then, before I could respond, 'I'm tired. I want to go to sleep.' He stood up and went back into the shepherd's hut.

It was Agnes who asked what it meant.

'The indenture? It means he'll have land of his own. Maybe a small farm on the estate.'

'No, Matthew. Not what I wor askin'. My job to be my father now that he is dead. What you reckons he mean by that?'

'I don't know, Agnes. You heard what I told him. He was Rowley's bastard child. Rowley wanted him to have a fifth of the estate. Maybe John's thinking he needs to start preparing to be a landowner?'

'That be not the way John thinks. Not what he wor' saying. He seen Adam the man who understand things mos' people don't.'

'I thought you didn't like Rowley.'

'Didn't have to like him to see he knew stuff. He saw things others don't. There was times Adam Rowley got things all tumbled downside up. But there was times he spoke truths, times he saw things clear. Childers see things too, Master Matthew. That's what the boy saw in Adam Rowley.'

From somewhere nearby came the sound of keening. I looked up. Two buzzards circling. Scavengers. Was there a dead sheep nearby? Agnes saw me look up.

'They knows, Master Matthew.'

'What?'

'When a beast is ailing.'

'You mean one of us?'

'Who knows? But all's not right, is it?'

'You talk in riddles, Agnes.'

'Who you talkin' to jus' now?'

'John.'

'Before that.'

I shrugged.

'*It can wait* was what you said.'

'I don't remember.'

'I do, Master Matthew. You was talking to someone. Not to me. Not to young Master John. I heard you.'

'I'm tired, Agnes. I need to rest. You take your turn as lookout.' I turned to go inside the hut with John. She took hold of my arm.

'Answer me. Who was you talking to?'

'I'm asleep on my feet. I have to lie down.'

'Tell me, Matthew. Where be Constance?'

'I don't know.'

I allowed her to lead me away from the hut because I didn't want John to overhear us.

'You have Constance with you?'

'I am not her keeper. Nor are you. Not in my power to make Constance do anything.'

'I gave you poppy juice, Matthew, to ease your aching head. Ointments to save your eyes. Poultices to keep your burns from festering.'

'You saved my life, I know. And I thank you for it. And I stopped Rowley from dunking you. And then I carried you from his hellfire. So now you and me are quits, Agnes. And Constance will do as she pleases.'

She drew me further down the gentle hill. We took a grassy path through the trees until we reached a clearing. Maybe she felt safer under the cover of trees. She sat down on a moss covered boulder and bade me sit with her. She took my hands in hers.

'Look at me, Matthew.' Sitting beside her there was little difference in height between us. She looked into my eyes. I looked into hers. Green eyes. The colour of elm leaves in early summer. For October, the sun was surprisingly warm. A last breath of mellow autumn before the rains and the chills of November set in.

'It were Constance you was talking to.' It wasn't a question. She knew. 'Do you see her, Matthew?'

I don't remember whether I replied.

'Do you see her when she talks to you?'

A light breath of wind. Leaves fluttered down. Damp moss, leaf litter. The smell of mushrooms in dank darkness.

'Do you see her?' whispered Agnes, her face so close to mine we could have been lovers. 'When she speaks with you, do you see her?'

'She keeps herself to herself. Stays in the shadows. Maybe her face was burnt, or she lost her hair. Maybe she's not ready to let me see her.'

'Tell truth, Matthew. I knows truth. You tell it, I can help.'

'I don't need your help.'

'Never needed no-one's help. Until you was in that burning barn. Needed help then didn't you.'

'You healed my burns, gave me back my sight. I thank you.'

'Your sight's your own. Not mine to give nor take away.'

'I've said it before and I'll say it again. I will never forget what you did for me, Agnes. But I'm going to walk to the next village, get us food and drink and clothes and – '

'Hush you. Listen to the forest. Listen. Then speak truth, or not at all.'

Her hands over my eyes. I didn't move. I look back and wonder what power she had over me – beyond my owing her the debt for my recovery. But on that mossy boulder in the woods, I wasn't thinking about deals and debts. I was only conscious of her hands over my eyes, her fingertips warm on my forehead, her palms soft on my cheeks.

'What do you see when you talk with Constance?' Her voice like the scurry of autumn leaves whirling in a courtyard.

'I don't know.'

'Is she here now?'

'I don't know. I don't think so.'

'Will she come back?'

'Yes. Yes, she will. I asked her to come with me to Canterbury.'

'Is she here now?'

Something rustling in the undergrowth. Maybe a weasel. Maybe a snake. Something shuffling or slithering in the darkness. Not Constance.

'I don't know where she is. She lost her husband and her children when the mill burnt down. She needs time. Surely you know that. You better than anyone.'

She removed her hands from my eyes. 'Tell me what happened.'

'I already told you.'

'You tol' me 'bout Rowley feeding us all poppy juice in our drinks. How he wanted us all to pass through fire to his promised land. 'Bout the curtains soaked in candle wax. How you carried me and John from the flames. You said nowt about Constance. You carry her too?'

'She was stirring when I went back in for her. She must have drunk less than everyone else. I shook her. Shouted at her. I saw her wake up. She didn't need my help. I could hardly see for smoke. She ran out as I was picking you up. She wanted me to rescue you, Agnes. She loves you.'

'You not rescue her?'

'She saved herself.'

'Know that do you?'

On the other side of the clearing a shaft of morning sunlight fell on the bark of a fallen tree.

'What you see?'

'I see steam rising from the moss on that fallen tree.'

'Has Constance shown herself when she talks to you?'

'Maybe she wants to keep herself hidden.'

Agnes gave a low hum every time she breathed out. Long, slow intakes of breath followed by this strange humming sound.

'Agnes?'

'Join with me, Matthew.'

I had no idea what she was doing, but I allowed myself to match her breathing.

'Rest your head against mine.' I sensed the vibration of her regular humming. I don't know how long this continued. Until … 'Is Constance with us?'

I opened my eyes, hoping to see her. I looked around like an expectant child. I felt a breeze on my face, and a chill in the air. The weather was turning. I got to my feet and called out for her.

'Be not a game of hide and seek.'

'Where is she?'

Agnes stayed on the mossy boulder, her eyes still shut.

'Where is she?'

'Sit you down, Matthew.'

'You're playing games with me. The two of you.'

'No games. No fooling. If you be ready to hear truth I's'll speak truth.'

'Where is she, Agnes?'

'Sit you down and hear me.'

'Constance.' I shouted her name so loud they'd have heard it in Abingdon. 'Constance.' I shouted again and again. 'Constance.' The thwacking of wings and screeching as a clamour of crows took flight. 'Constance.'

Agnes sat still and calm. Waiting for my frenzy to drain away.

Exhaustion got the better of me. She gestured for me to sit back down beside her.

'Constance's spirit is here. She is here with us if you quieten and listen.'

'Her spirit? No. If she's here, she's here. She is not dead.'

Agnes looked at me with a calm and generous kindness.

213

'Where is she?'

'Sit with me. What you saw running through smoke wasn't Constance making her escape. Her flesh was consumed in fire. Her charred bones are there in the embers of the Hall.'

'No, Agnes. No. She ran from the room. I've spoken to her.'

Agnes was again holding my hands. To my surprise there was some comfort, almost reassurance, in that. I didn't pull away.

'She be with us still. In spirit. Not in flesh.'

'I heard her. We talked. It was her voice.'

She took my face in her hands, looked into my eyes. 'You spoke with Constance. What did you say?'

'I asked her to travel with me to Canterbury. She wants to come with me.'

'Or was you talking to yourself?'

'She argued with me, Agnes. I know it was Constance. I know her voice. How could I not know it? I was so long blind, and in that time her voice was all of her I knew.'

'Her voice and her touch. But she be no longer with us in the world of flesh.'

'She wants to come with me.'

'Does she? That what she said? Be better for you an' I come wi' you on your Canting Berry travels. I'd be more use to you. 'Cept I don't want to.'

'You! You come with me! To Canterbury?!'

How could I take her with me? How could I walk into an inn with an old woman in the body of a child? This woman who hated men. Who sought out Rowley to escape those who thought her a witch. 'I cannot look after you.'

'No man's ever looked after me.'

'And when we reach a town and we want rooms at an inn? What then, Agnes?'

'You ent listening, Matthew. Hear me. I don't wants to come.'

'If ... Constance ... is really dead ...' I could hardly bring myself to say the words. 'Then maybe it's best her spirit stays with you, Agnes.'

'You made her a promise to take her with you. That's what you tol' me. And you tol' me you's a man o' yer word.'

I looked down. My hands were shaking. Overhead, the crows were screeching as they returned to their rookery high in the trees above.

'One moment you say that talking to Constance was talking to myself, the next you say I must be held to a promise made to a woman who doesn't exist. This is madness, Agnes. Madness. And I'm done with it.' I got to my feet.

I was just a few yards up the grassy path when I felt Agnes's hand on my arm.

'Where you going?'

'You know where I'm going. Canterbury. Alone. I would have taken Constance if she'd escaped the fire. But you tell me she's dead, and you want to stay here, so I go alone.'

'Do you indeed? And the boy? What of him?'

25
The Gift of Silence

I woke John. 'You and I are going to go foraging for food.'

I told Agnes she should wait in the shepherd's hut. 'I am indeed a man of my word, Agnes. Wait for us here, and we'll bring you food.'

She stared at me. I'd made a life by reading people and playing their hopes and doubts, their fears and dreams. But Agnes remained a mystery. I assumed she was suspicious, because I would have been, but she might equally have trusted me and been glad of the opportunity to rest.

John and I made our way across the wild heath, in the direction of the columns of smoke I'd seen earlier.

'Would you still like to learn to be a player, John?'

'Was my father a player?'

'Of a kind, yes.'

'Do I have words to say?'

'The first thing that good players learn is the power of staying silent. When they can do that, then they learn their words and their lines.'

John pursed his lips tightly together.

'Very good. You can smile if you like, but say nothing until I tell you.'

'Can I nod or shake my head if somebody asks me a question?'

'Is that talking?'

'Sort of.'

'Then what do you think?'

'I think I have to be a silent player.'

'Can you do that?'

He looked at me blankly, saying nothing, without the slightest twitch of a nod or a nay.

'Excellent, John. I think your silence will talk us into a fine feast.'

This time he did smile.

At first light I'd thought the smoke was coming from the chimneys of a town. We found it was a village, but well-kept and well-moneyed by the look of it. No cobbles on the streets, but no ruts in the roads either. A good honest village with no place for rogues or vagabonds, vagrants or beggars. It was as well I was dressed in Peter Rowley's clothes.

We walked past a manor house, a large church, and several fine houses. We stopped at an inn beneath the sign of The Bear.

'Are you ready?'

He put his finger to his lips.

I opened the door and went through. John followed. It was early and the place was empty. I called out for the innkeeper. The sound of a door opening somewhere upstairs. Footsteps on wooden stairs.

'He will probably talk to you, John. Don't answer. Say nothing. Just stare at him.'

Another door opening. He was a round-faced she, a woman who wore her hair tied up beneath a cap, revealing a rosy-cheeked and kindly looking face. Her smile drained away as she grew closer and could see how I looked. I was dressed like a gentleman, but smelled like a tinker. My clothes were filthy, and I knew from that brief glance in the looking glass in Rowley Hall how alarming it must be to see my scarred face so early in the morning.

She looked down at John, who stared at her wide-eyed.

'My son and I would like to break fast,' I said.

She shook her head. But seemed reluctant to turn us away.

Rowley's crew had grown used to the way I looked, and accepted me for who I'd become. They had only ever known me with my disfigured face. I could see how shocked this woman was, but I ignored her disdain – or was it her fear – and continued: 'My son and I have come from Banbury. We're heading for Salisbury. Prithee, forgive us our appearance. We stayed a night at in Woodstock. There was a fire. You can probably smell it on our clothes. We escaped, but the stables burnt down and we lost our horse and most of our possessions. We have walked here from Woodstock.'

She crouched down and spoke to John: 'You walked all the way here from Woodstock?'

His mouth didn't move.

'You must be hungry.'

The edge of his mouth twitched in the beginning of a smile, but then he stopped himself, as if smiling might count as breaking his silence.

'Shall we find you some food?'

For a moment I thought his stomach would get the better of him. But he simply looked at her wide-eyed.

'He is very hungry,' I said.

'Don't be shy, boy. I'm sure we can find you some food.'

'He's not shy, Mistress. He's deaf and he's mute. And he's very hungry. We both are. Neither of us has eaten since the day before yesterday.'

I thought she might pick John up and hold him in her arms, as Lady Frances used to hold her lapdog. It was well that she didn't, for that might have put his silence to the test.

There was indeed a White Hart in Woodstock, for I'd ridden through the town when taking Alice to Chartley. I hoped Woodstock was far enough away that news of an inn burning down there wouldn't yet have reached this village.

'Are you the innkeeper, Mistress?'

'My name is Jane Atkins. Yes, I am the innkeeper – ever since my dear husband, William, passed away.' The memory seemed to bring some warmth to her voice.

'We walked to Oxford, but the scholars are in session, and there was no room in the inns we tried. At least that's what they told us. But I suspect they took one look at us and took me for a vagabond and my dear son, John, for my knave.'

'Oh, my dear. You poor dear boy.'

John stared at her, soaking up her pity, playing his silence to perfection.

She took him by the hand. 'Come with me young fellow.' John held his ground and looked up at me.

I nodded to John, and he allowed himself to be led through to the kitchen. Although she couldn't bring herself to look at my face, she was curious about our story. She placed large bowls before us and ladled mutton stew into them, then cut several slices of bread and gave us each a tankard of small ale.

'Goodness me, you are hungry,' she said to John.

'My heartfelt thanks, good lady,' I said.

'Poor boy,' she said.

The poor boy shovelled another spoonful of stew into his mouth.

'You are most generous,' I said. 'But I fear I cannot pay you now, for I lost all my money in the fire in Woodstock.'

'Plenty of stew in the pot,' she said, still looking at John. He didn't look up.

I told her that for safekeeping I always kept my purse under a pillow when sleeping away from home, and that when the alarm was raised I needed to get the boy to safety and by the time I went back into the inn, the fire had taken hold. 'So you see, we have nothing except these ragged clothes. And I cannot pay you for your hospitality.'

'You're heading for Salisbury?'

'That was our plan. But we are both so tired that I'm not even sure where we are.'

'You're in Moreton. And you're very welcome. Will you be returning this way?'

She'd drawn up a stool and was sitting beside John, watching him eating his stew, still addressing herself to him as if he was voicing the puppet sitting next to him.

'I shall, yes. I am a widower, good lady. And John's mother's family came from Salisbury. John has an aunt there who has offered to look after him for a few months. After taking John to Salisbury, I shall return to Banbury, and from there to London, where I have business to attend.'

She turned to 'Poor, poor John. How long ago did you lose your mother, you poor, poor boy?'

He stopped spooning stew into his mouth. I was willing him not to answer.

'John was barely old enough to know his mother, my beloved wife Caroline.' I touched the ring that I'd placed on my ring finger, the ring I had taken from the bedroom at Rowley Hall. 'She died a few hours after giving birth to John's sister, Jessica.'

John turned to me, a quizzical look on his face. I could read the unspoken question. Is that what happened to my real mother? I put my hand to my mouth as if to contain my own grief and hoped he could read the gesture, and with it my thoughts: *Say nothing, I beg you. Don't ruin all. You're doing so well.*

'The babe lived for barely a week. So my dear son, John, is an only child.'

She seemed moved by the story, and thought about it for a while, before offering us a room for the night.

'I have no money to pay you, Mistress.'

'You're coming back this way. You can pay me then.'

'Then take my wedding ring,' I said. 'As surety.'

I thought for a horrible moment she would accept. But she waved the idea away. The offer alone was enough to convince her we'd be coming back. She opened a door onto a wooden stairway, and led us upstairs, along a passageway with bare white walls to a well-furnished room at the back of the inn. The four-poster bedstead was curtained, the wood-panelled walls boasted hangings, two chairs with cushions stood beside a table in the corner furthest from the door, a washbowl sat on a tripod stand. The window, which looked out over the yard at the back of the inn, was glazed and curtained. This was surely The Bear's finest room.

'I thank you Mistress Atkins. You've been more than kind.'

'I run an inn. We are here to offer good food and drink and shelter. My husband always said we should never turn away those in greatest need. I merely do as he would have done. If we'd had children, and one of ours had ever found himself in poor John's situation, I would like to think that others would have done as I do.'

And thereby hung a tale, I suspected. We owed our good fortune to finding a widow who wanted children of her own, and to the enigma of John's silence, for that allowed her to write any tale she chose onto the poor boy's blank face. And, despite my frightening appearance, I suspect that Peter Rowley's clothes also helped our cause.

'Do you need to rest?' she said.

'We could probably sleep all day.'

She called for a chambermaid and instructed her to bring us each a nightshirt.

'You can sleep all day if you so choose. I will arrange to have your clothes cleaned and dried while you rest.'

There was a time when I trusted no-one, but I accepted the offer. And was glad that the bed was wide enough for a family of four, for I'm unused to sharing a bed for sleep. Once we were in the room with the door firmly shut I took the rest of the Rowley jewellery from my pockets and hid it beneath my pillow – and with it Forman's casebook and the letters folded inside.

'Give me the picklock wires, John,' I whispered. 'The ones we fashioned from the skewers and hatpins at Rowley Hall.'

He looked at me wide-eyed.

'The picklock wires.'

He shrugged. Had he lost them?

'You can speak again now. You can speak quietly while we're here alone. This is not your stage.'

'Have I passed the test? Am I going to be a good player?' He spoke so quietly I could barely hear him.

'Yes indeed. You're very good. See what you've done. It was your silence got our bellies filled, your silence got us this room, and your silence that's going to get us clean clothes.'

We changed into our nightshirts, put our filthy clothes in a wash-basket outside the door, and went to bed.

I'd already slipped into the land of sleep when John rolled over to my side of the bed and nudged me. 'Matthew. Was Adam Rowley really my father?'

'That's what he told me.'

I glanced over at him. He was lying on his back gazing at the ceiling. After a few minutes' silence I'd dropped off again when he whispered, 'I want to be a player.'

'And you shall be, John,' I mumbled. 'An excellent player.'

'Adam told me he didn't like play acting. He said theatres are bad places.'

'Do you think they're bad places?'

'Don't know.'

Another long silence. I tried to keep my eyes open. 'But … but … but …' His whispered buts repeating like hiccups.

'But what, John?'

'I have to be my father. I am … I am his son. He …'

But he didn't have the words to speak his thoughts aloud, and I didn't have the energy to tease them out of him.

'John,' I murmured, 'You learn very quickly. And you have the gift of silence. Players who have that gift are rare indeed.'

He glanced at me. The beginnings of a smile twitched at the edges of his mouth, but his eyes were wet, and he quickly looked away, retreating back into a different kind of silence.

What damned right had Rowley to any place in the boy's thoughts? The child he'd always denied in life and only acknowledged in a scrap of legal parchment that would have been burnt had I not found it. How dare he, of all men, damn the theatres because they seethed with pretence?

I turned my head again to look at John. His eyes were closed. He was breathing heavily. And instead of cursing the man who would have killed us all, I lay still, hoping that John would sleep peacefully, and not be prey to the onslaught of nightmares that would surely soon be coming his way.

Knocking. I open my eyes. Darkness. Agnes gave me sight again. Now she's snatched it back. Cursed me for making false promises to Constance.

John calls my name. His hand shaking my shoulder. I sit up. See a narrow slit of flickering light. Remember where we are. An inn.

More knocking, louder. Is the place on fire?

'Matthew.' John shakes me again.

There was a window. I'm sure of it. We can escape through that.

'Somebody at the door,' he whispers.

'Don't. Don't open it. Keep the fire out.'

'What fire?'

And then from outside. 'I have your clothes, Master Matthew. And the boy's. Washed and dried. Can I come in?'

'Wait,' I shout. And I'm back. Back in our world. We must have slept all day.

'I'll go,' I whisper to John. 'And remember. Don't speak.'

I open the door. The maid enters the room, places a flickering lantern on the table. Looks across at John, smiles at him.

'You sleep alright, young fellow?'

John's sitting on the edge of the bed. *Don't speak, John. Don't even nod your head.*

'Nice bed,' says the maid. 'Best we have. Mistress Atkins took you to her heart.' Is this a test? Had she heard the boy's voice?

She goes back out. My finger to my lips. She returns with a wicker basket. Lays the clothes on the bed.

'Turned dreadful cold,' she says. 'I'm to lay the fire for you. I be back soon.'

'Don't trouble yourself.'

'No trouble. I got kindling downstairs.'

'We don't want a fire. We're used to cold weather.'

John looks at me. I'm willing him not to speak.

'The Mistress told me I should lay it and light it.'

'And I say we don't want it.' Doing my best to stay polite.

'Just lay it then, shall I? Light it later.'

'We do not want a fire.'

She looks hurt.

'You be staying tonight, though? Mistress thought you would be.'

'Maybe. I don't know. I need to talk to her myself. We need to dress. I prithee leave us.'

She shuts the door behind her. I wait awhile, then peer out to see she's not still in the corridor, for I know that John will want to talk to me.

'I'm cold, Matthew.'

'Then dress yourself.'

He removes the nightshirt and starts to dress.

'Why can't we have a fire, Matthew?'

'I have fucking told you, John. No.' I take hold of both his arms and hold him close. It's as much to stop myself from raging as it is to reassure him. 'Don't cross me,' I whisper. 'There will be no fires in this room.'

He shivers. I've seen children beaten for such insolence. But I let go his arms. Why doesn't he understand? Is he truly his father's son?

He sniffs, and looks away. Finishes dressing himself.

I'm minded to have him stay in the room while I talk to Mistress Atkins. But I want more from her than shelter and meals. And John's silence is more persuasive than any words of mine.

At the bottom of the stairs a wooden door opened onto a small room where a dozen or so men sat drinking and playing cards. A fire had been lit. I stayed at the edge of the room, but could feel the warmth from there. John was drawn to it like a butcher's dog to a bitch on heat. He stood in front of it, shielding it from me and from all in the room. It gave me the chance to slip across to the buttery bar. A couple of men shouted at John to move away. He took no notice; as good at playing deaf as he was at playing silent. I had to steel myself to go back in, take him by the arm and lead him away. I apologised and explained that he couldn't hear them. Murmurs of sympathy, but I was in no mood to stay and talk.

We found Mistress Atkins. I asked to speak with her alone. She called for a servant to take over from her. While we waited, she tried again with John.

'Did you sleep well, young man?'

He looked at me.

'He did. We both slept well. You've been very generous, Mistress Atkins.'

'Eleanor says the boy looked cold. Do you plan to stay tonight? She can light the fire in your room for you.'

John smiled. And I thought for a moment he was about to speak, and our story would come tumbling down around us. I squeezed his arm to remind him of the part he had to play.

'It's cold and already dark,' she said. 'You surely don't plan to walk on tonight?'

'Mistress Atkins, you've been most kind. But you know I cannot pay you for your hospitality, and I hate to carry debts.'

'Not a debt. A gift. The room would be empty if you weren't here.'

'Very well. I thank you.'

'Then let Eleanor light a fire for you. It's set to be a cold night.'

'Thank you, but no. After the fire in Woodstock ...' For a moment I forgot the name of the inn where I'd said we were staying when the stables caught light. She stepped in and rescued me.

'Of course. I understand.'

227

And so we stayed another night. She fed us well – in a snug without a fire, to John's dismay. Despite everything he'd witnessed, he still had a hearty appetite. Mistress Atkins found a woollen blanket to wrap around him until we took to our bed.

I had thought to use the picklock wires we'd fashioned from skewers and hatpins, and to go through the inn when everyone was asleep and fill my pockets with whatever might be useful on the journey ahead. But I was so shaken by Mistress Atkins's trust and generosity that I was stricken by what some might call a conscience. It was the strangest of feelings.

In the morning, I said we'd be on our way. She said a carter from the village could take us to Newbury later that same morning.

I would have readily accepted the offer if I'd not felt compelled to go back for Agnes. I said we'd rather get on our way as soon as possible. If the carter came by us on the road, he could maybe pick us up and take us the rest of the way. She said she'd ask him to keep an eye out for us. She gave us directions, and a knapsack for some bread and cheese and apples. And then, to my astonishment, she pressed a purse into my hand. 'You'll need a little money on your journey.'

'I will repay you three times over, Mistress Atkins, although I fear I cannot say when that will be.'

In response, she simply smiled. I felt quite weak. I have cheated at cards and dice, I learnt to cut purses when I was barely eight years old, I've stolen silver and gold from many of London's fine houses. I am well used to having money. But not for a simple drawstring purse to be filled with such straightforward kindness.

I pantomimed a goodbye wave for John to follow my example, and we set off walking south. There'd been a heavy frost overnight. The sky was clear, but there was little warmth in the sun and no sign that the ice on frozen puddles was melting.

'Whatever you want to say, John, don't say it. Not yet. Not til we're well away from the village.'

We crunched our way for a mile, maybe two, before he asked where we were going.

'You see that hill?' I gestured to our right. 'When we find a path, we'll head for that, then circle round, go back and find Agnes.'

'Why?'

'Because I promised Agnes I'd go back for her.'

'Why?'

'We have some food and she has none. We share it with her.'

'Why?'

'Because I made a promise, and that's an end to it.' And to think it was only a week before that I'd been delighted to hear John Robins chirruping his first whys!

I found an old path between hedgerows in the direction of the hill. We turned up it, John's steps slowed.

'Keep up, John.'

He trudged beside me as we climbed. 'I thought you said we were going to Salisbury.'

'I did. But first we have to go to Agnes.'

'Then do we go to Salisbury?'

'Maybe.'

'You told her my mother's family came from Salisbury. Do they?'

'I was telling a story. To get us a bed and food. I was play acting, John. Same as you were play acting the deaf mute. It's what we needed to do.'

'But you said – '

'I know what I said.'

'You said you never lied.'

'That's not what I said. I said I'm a man of my word, and that's different. It also means I don't make idle threats.'

We walked on. Or, rather, I walked. He trudged. After a few hundred yards of this, I came close to losing my temper. 'Walk with me John, or find your own way.'

After that he stayed close – and sullen.

'And don't sulk.'

'I'm not sulking. I'm being silent. You said I was good at being silent.' I didn't let him see my half a smile. I couldn't help myself from liking the boy, even when he was irritating.

With the sky so clear and the sun so bright, it was easy to find our way back to the shepherd's hut. There were half a dozen sheep inside and a dozen or so nearby. But no sign of Agnes.

I led John down through the woodland to the clearing where I'd talked with her about Constance. I didn't expect her to be sitting on the fallen tree awaiting our return, but I'd hoped she might have left some sign of where we could find her. I understood why she wasn't there – if there were sheep around the hut, it was more than likely that the shepherd wasn't far away – but I was disappointed by her absence.

'What are we doing?' asked John.

'We're waiting for Agnes.'

'She's not here.'

'And that's why we'll wait awhile for her.'

'Where is she?'

'If I knew that, I'd go and find her. I want to give her the food we have for her.'

'I'm hungry.'

'So am I. But we've been well fed the past two days. Agnes has had nothing.'

'Agnes finds her own food.'

'We said we'd bring it for her, and we are men of our words.'

'Are we?'

I sat down on the fallen tree where I'd sat with Agnes. Twigs and grasses were still glistening with hoar frost. Every shiver of a breeze brought leaves down around us.

John wandered around, scuffing at the leaves, impatient. A boy can only hold his tongue for so long. 'What are we going to do?'

'We're going to wait. I've told you.'

'How long?'

'Long enough.'

'Long enough for what?'

'Don't try me, John.'

He pulled a face.

'I've told you.'

'I'm not sulking.' But he was pouting. And although I didn't want him to see it, I was as impatient as he was. I was thinking the same. What do we do?

We waited.

But I have never been good at waiting, and the cold of the fallen tree was seeping through my britches.

'Shall I go and look for her?'

I shook my head. 'She's like a wild creature. She knows the forest. Knows the sounds. If she's anywhere near, she'll know we're here. She'll show herself is she wants to.' That's what I wanted to believe. That Agnes was safe and biding her time, that she had some den or cave where she could keep herself out of harm's way. But a fear was nagging at me that the shepherd had returned to find her in his hut. Word about the fire at Rowley Hall would have spread by now. But there was nothing I could do for her if she didn't show. And I still had John in my care. I made a decision. I got to my feet.

'Where are we going?'

'Abingdon.'

'Why?'

'Because you want to be your father's son. We'll find someone in Abingdon who can make that happen.'

26
Monstrous, truly monstrous

I knew from talking to Constance and Rowley that Abingdon lay north of Wittenham and Rowley Hall. The boy and I walked across heathland until we came to a road which ran from south to north. Before long we heard the heavy plodding of a carthorse pulling a rumbling two-wheeled cart.

'Should I stay silent?' said John.

'Your silence has served us well. You've turned it into a fine art.'

It was good to see him grin again.

The carter stopped, looked down at us. I smiled and bade him good day. He mumbled something in return, but was staring at my face. Being an object of fascination – and often revulsion – was something I'd have to get used to. He asked John where we were going. John said nothing. I told him Abingdon. He offered me a seat beside him on the driver's bench. The boy could sit behind us on a bale of straw.

'Have you come far, Master Carter?

'Today, from East Hagbourne. But I live in Oxford. Going back there now.'

He seemed a genial fellow, but thankfully not curious enough to ask why my face looked as it did. He wondered why we were walking. I told him that my horse was lame, and I needed a farrier to come out for it. After that, he asked no more questions, for he had stories of his own he wanted to tell. He regaled us with what he'd heard about the 'Terrible doings at Rowley Hall. Monstrous, it was.' His upper lip twitched with the horror of it as he spoke. 'Monstrous, truly monstrous.'

'Rowley Hall?' I said. And where is that?

'Not far from here as we drive. Not far enough, say I. Down a track over there. Not far from Wittenham. See the Clumps?' He lifted his right arm and gestured to show me. Two fingers missing on his right hand. 'Other side of them low hills.'

I didn't ask him how he's lost his fingers. He was, after all, a carter. A life spent lifting and loading.

'I been there, for my sins,' he said. 'To the Hall. Used to go quite reg'lar, when old Rowley was alive. Even then I could sense things not right. Monstrous, what happened. Truly monstrous.'

'What was it?'

'Whole place burnt down. Terrible fire. But that baint be the half of it.'

I encouraged him to talk, but was glad that young John was in the back, where the rumbling of the cart would drown out anything we said.

'Not the half of it, I tell you. Monstrous evil. I used to go to the Hall every six weeks or so. Old Master Rowley was a good man. As good as they come. Talked to me himself, he did sometimes. Never heard a bad word spoke against him. And us carters, we hear if things ain't right. Good man he were. Kind man.'

It seemed that carters in Oxfordshire carried gossip as the wherrymen do in London.

'What happened?'

'A curse laid on the place was what happened.'

'A curse?'

'Bewitching.'

'You believe in such things?'

'Not a matter of believing. It's fact is this. Old Master Rowley died. Fell from his horse. And the eldest son too. Both fell the same time. And both of them was fine horsemen. That don't happen for no reason. Bewitched they was. Cursed and bewitched. And things just got worse from there.'

'Bewitched? Who did the bewitching?'

He glanced across at me. 'I don't know they names. They change their names. But I tell you this. The mill at Wittenham burned down not long before. The miller and his three sons died. But not the millwife. There was evil lurking even before old Master Rowley was thrown from his horse. Monstrous evil. Then young Master Rowley inherited, and his mind was poisoned. He'd lost his father and his brother and then his mother too. So what's he do? Takes in all manner of rogues and vagabonds. Rowley Hall becomes a whorehouse. A seething den of enormities. And all around there's stillborn calves, cream going sour, butter turning rancid. Come as no surprise to me the Hall burnt down. Hellfire itself come to Oxfordshire.'

'Rowley Hall?'

'That's right.'

'Did anybody die?'

'All o' them is what I heard. Young Master Rowley, and all his gang of beggars and whores, thieves and vagabonds. All except the witch. 'Twas her set the fire. 'Twas her called up the gale that fanned the flames.'

'A witch?'

'A coven, I reckon. A ghastly coven.'

It was well that our clothes were clean, and that we didn't smell of smoke. If we hadn't come so close to being burned alive ourselves I might have asked more questions, dug a little deeper, tried to find out what he really knew. As it was, I played aghast, and turned round to check that John was safe. He was sitting with his back to us, bouncing up and down on the straw bale, as the cartwheels squealed and we lurched along the rutted, pot-holed road.

Abingdon came into view. As Master Carter fell briefly silent, I ventured, 'I've also heard rumours. I thought they were idle gossip, and couldn't possibly be true.'

'What? What d'you hear?'

'About a fire that killed a score of people, and dogs and horses too. They said it was up this way. I didn't know it was Rowley Hall.'

'Oh, that's where it was alright. I could take you to the ruins, 'cept I has to get to Oxford while it's still light.'

I shuddered at the thought of going back to the ruins. 'I heard about the witch too,' I said. 'Thought it was idle chit chat. Gossip and malice.'

'What you hear?'

'I didn't believe it.'

'What? Tell me.'

'More than one witch I heard. But I didn't believe it. I heard they were testing themselves for something much bigger.'

'Witches? More than one?'

'Poisoning water and casting curses. It was witches made the master set the fire himself.'

'Where d'you hear that?'

'I didn't believe it. Not til you told me about the fire at Rowley Hall. Now it all makes sense. But if that's all true about the Hall, then ...' I took a pause. He'd taken the bait. Now wait awhile before drawing him in.

'Then what?'

'I hardly dare think about it.'

'What?'

'When did the Hall burn down?'

'Two nights ago.'

'So even now, the ashes are barely cold.'

'Monstrous.'

'Then maybe there is truth in it after all. For that was the night when I saw something in the night sky. Three shadows passing in front of the moon. Made me shiver and feel sick to my core. I passed it off as ale-sickness, though I'd drunk no more than a couple of tankards. What I heard, Master Carter, was that there's a coven of three. An unholy trinity. And now that they've wrought their monstrous enormities here, they are planning something even more wicked. I thought it was tavern talk. Now I know it for the truth it was. Even as the fire took hold all three witches took flight. And that's what I saw. Darkness sucking light from the moon. The coven taking flight and setting off for London.'

'London?'

'What happened at Rowley Hall is just the beginning. They plan their revenge against King James for his tract against witches. *Daemonologie*. You know of that?'

'Of course.'

Highly unlikely, I thought. But who was I to challenge him?

'I fear that what happened at Rowley Hall is just the beginning, a way of putting themselves to the test. The King himself will be next. How long before we hear of a Great Fire of London? All the fine palaces burning.'

'You think they're in London already?'

'If they could poison the mind of good Master Rowley and lay their curses to such monstrous effect, they will most certainly be long gone from here.'

27
The business of law

That silenced him. But not the cart – which screeched and squealed til we came to a halt outside an inn by a stone bridge over the river. The painted sign, a golden crown set beside a dark blue thistle, squeaked to and fro as it swung in the wind. So the burghers of Abingdon had heard of King James and knew that he was Scottish.

Most carters I've known have bad backs. This poor fellow grimaced as he climbed down from the cart and limped slowly to the door of the inn. He'd injured a leg as well as losing fingers. Every trade carries its risks.

I lifted John down and whispered to him that while we were in The Crown and Thistle he should play deaf and mute again.

It was about midday. The place was busy and warm, the throng of bodies protecting me from sight of the fire. I bought Master Carter a drink, and drank a toast to his generosity. He soon turned to men he knew. The talk was all of the fire at Rowley Hall and the madness of Adam Rowley for playing host to a witch. I added nothing to the growing noise of gossip and rumour. Master Carter was doing my job for me. If he spread the story I'd told him with as much enthusiasm as he'd listened to it, Agnes might be allowed to live in peace a little longer.

Holding John by the hand, I eased my way back to the bar and asked the landlord if he could recommend a good lawyer. He gave me a name and directions to find him. We slipped out without saying our goodbyes. Let Master Carter tell the story in his own way. He'd enjoy being the carrier of big news.

The lawyer's house was on the other side of the river. We walked over the stone bridge. John stopped in the middle. I thought to look at the swans. But he wanted to talk.

'Matthew? What's a lawyer?'

'A man who sees to it that things are done properly.' Not the answer I'd have given in London.

'Do I have to stay with him?'

'If you want to be your father's son, then you'll have to live here or nearby until you come of age.'

'Can you stay with me?'

'I have to move on. To somewhere a long way away from here.'

'London?'

'Not yet. When you're older, you shall come to London. And there I will show you the theatres. And take you to all the places I told you about.'

He looked at the river. I suspect he was gazing at his own future. Then he turned back, looked up at me and solemnly announced, 'I want to come with you. I'm good at playing silent.'

'You're learn quickly. You'll soon be reading books on your own.'

'But who will teach me?'

'We'll find someone, John.' He sniffed. And retreated into himself. I took his hand. We walked on. I tried to stay calm, to keep a smile on my face. I didn't want him to pick up on my own concerns.

The lawyer's house was three storeys high with a stone tiled roof, and a wooden sign swinging from overhanging eaves. On it had been painted a partially unwound scroll with elaborate seal and beside it a lawyer's cap and gown, and beneath it the words.

Masters Benson & Powell
Civil Lawyers

We stopped outside.

'Did you ever meet Adam's sister?'

'Don't know,' said John.

'Her name was Judith.'

'I think so.'

'She married a man called William Harpole. So her name's now Judith Harpole.'

'People didn't tell me names.'

'Did she like you, John?'

'Don't know.'

'Did you like her?'

He shook his head and shrugged. As I went to open the door, he pulled me back.

'Do I stay silent?'

'I think so. Yes.'

'Am I deaf?'

I thought about this for a while. 'Maybe it's best you take a speaking part this time. Are you ready for that?'

The door opened before he could answer. 'We are not locked behind closed doors,' said the young clerk in a black gown. He gaped at my face before asking, 'Is it Master Benson or Master Powell you wish to see?'

We weren't ready.

'Please come in. Master Benson or Master Powell?'

'Master Benson,' I said. But only because his name came first.

He ushered us into a small hallway, with wood-panelled walls and tiled floor, and a couple of chairs on each side. He bade us sit down. 'I will ask,' he said, then left us on our own.

'No need to play deaf this time,' I whispered to John. 'But say nothing til I bid you to. If the lawyer asks you a question watch my left hand. If I put it on my chin, say Yes. If I scratch my head say No.' I was putting a lot of faith in the boy, expecting him to play his part extempore.

As my eyes grew accustomed to the dim light, I noticed the framed parchment document hanging on the wall opposite us. I knew enough Latin to recognise *Universitas Oxoniensis*, the University at Oxford; but the light was too dim to read any more.

The clerk returned. He asked us to follow him through a narrow corridor to a room at the back of the house. Benson stood up as we went in. He was short, with a long grey beard, and wore a lawyer's cap and gown. I couldn't see his eyes, for he was silhouetted in front of a long low window, and the light outside was bright. He sat down, and stared at my face before placing his hands flat on the desk before him and leaning forward.

'Forgive my appearance,' I said. 'I was born with my face, so I'm used to it. But it's troubling, I know.'

'Not at all. Not at all.'

But he was unsettled, and looked at John rather than me when he greeted us: 'Good day to you sir, and to you, young man.'

John smiled.

'Good day to you, Master Benson. My name is Matthew Lovall.'

'And this is young Master Lovall?'

'No. John is not my son. But for the moment I am acting as his guardian. I was a close friend of Adam Rowley.'

'The Rowleys of Rowley Hall?' He pulled back a fraction. He was a lawyer, and it was his profession not to be shocked or disturbed by anything his clients told him, but had the light in the room been better, I'm sure we'd have seen his face cloud over.

'Master Rowley and I were scholars at Oxford together.'

He pulled back a tiny bit further. It was almost imperceptible, but if you can read that hint of a twitch that gives a tell at primero, you can read behind a lawyer's good manners.

'Just over a fortnight ago, I received a strange letter from my dear friend Adam. He said he needed to see me urgently, and could I possibly visit him at the Hall. As you will probably gather from my accent, I've lived in London ever since I graduated from the University. But I did as Adam asked, Master Benson. Of course I did, for he had been a good friend to me at Oxford and had helped me out on many occasions. When I received his letter I'd heard none of the dreadful rumours about the goings on at the Hall which assailed me when I stopped at an inn in Iffley.'

'You visited the Hall?'

'I did indeed. Which is why I'm here now. I'd been to the Hall during vacations when Adam and I were scholars together. Adam's mother and father could not have made me more welcome. I never met his brothers, Franklin and Peter, nor his sister Judith.' If Master Benson had ever had dealings with the Rowleys, the names might lend credibility to my story.

'I am a lawyer, Master Lovall. I assume you wish to make use of my services.'

'I want to lodge an indenture with you. It concerns the boy.' I looked at John. 'I thought you would want to know how it came into my hands.'

'An indenture?' said Benson.

I removed it from my inside pocket, unfolded it and laid it on the table. I pointed to the seal and Rowley's signature. And beside it the signature of a witness.

'Adam Rowley,' read Benson. 'The indenture witnessed by Edward Strickland. A colleague of William Harpole.'

'Adam's brother-in-law,' I said, reminding Benson how well I knew the Rowley family.

'Harpole and Strickland have their offices in Oxford. This document is a transfer of title, Master Lovall. What does that have to do with the boy?'

'May I?' I took back the document and found the paragraph that had so surprised me just a few days before. I read aloud:

'... the boy known as John Brown, whom I hereby declare to be my true and only son. Although he was born out of wedlock, it is agreed between the parties to this indenture that when he doth come of age he shall inherit one fifth part of the estate, to include Manor Farm House and the field adjacent to that house known as Lowe Meadow.'

'Is the boy your ward, Master Lovall?'

'Not in law, though I have been caring for him since the terrible events at Rowley Hall. I didn't even know that Adam had a son until I arrived at the house some four weeks ago. That is when he told me about the boy and his inheritance. I was curious as to why he wanted me to know. And why at that particular time? He seemed in good health. Adam's letter told of the terrible accident that befell his father and his brother, Peter; and of the death of his mother. I thought perhaps he had intimations of his own mortality, and wanted to be sure the boy's legacy was secure. But.' I sniffed.

'But what, Master Lovall?'

'It is hard. It is hard to find the words.'

John was looking at me closely, watching my hand for his cue.

'I sensed something was wrong from the moment I arrived. Adam made every effort to appear delighted to see me, but the house was full of strangers. Servants spoke to him as friends. He seemed to glory in their company.'

Benson nodded. I guessed he'd heard similar stories.

'And Adam himself …' I paused again. Benson leant forward. Just a little. But enough. For a man of the law, he was surprisingly easy to reel in. 'Adam spoke to me as if enchanted, or enraptured. "In the depths of my grief I heard a profound truth," he said to me. "I had to open my doors to those in need. In the Fullness of Time these people will inherit true Common Wealth." His words, Master Benson, although I'm still not sure that I understood him. He often spoke of "The True Common Wealth." That troubled me greatly, Master Benson, and I feared that whatever great truth had been revealed him, I was losing a dear friend.'

Benson nodded and tutted.

'He showed me the indenture,' I said. 'And he explained that one copy had been lodged with Strickland, the witness we spoke of earlier. He wanted me to ensure that this copy was lodged with you, Master Benson.'

'Very well.'

'I don't think he entirely trusted William Harpole.'

'I cannot comment.'

'Of course not. Then he introduced me to young John.' I put my hand to my chin in thought, then turned to John. 'You remember that?'

'Yes, sir. I do.'

John was, of course, a minor and had no voice in law. But Benson seemed impressed by that.

'When Adam and I were alone again, he asked me to take John away from the Hall.'

'Did he say why?'

'I asked him. But he would only say that the boy was in danger. I asked him what kind of danger. He said he didn't know. But he was adamant. And he didn't tell you either, did he John.' I put my hand to my forehead and scratched my hair as if the very act of retelling the story was distressing.

'No sir. He didn't tell me nothing. He just said to go with you. And I liked you and you was kind to me.' Oh, John, I thought. The King's Men players at The Globe will be ready to welcome you to their company with open arms.

'Over the years Adam had been generous to me, and so I agreed. I liked the boy, and he seemed to like me. I had business to attend to in Newbury, and so John came with me. It wasn't until we were on our way back to the Hall that I heard the terrible news.'

Benson shook his head. Then seemed to stir himself. 'You can lodge the indenture with me, Master Lovall. It will be safe and secure. There is nothing more we can do in law until the boy comes of age.'

'I understand.'

He stood up and offered me his hand, which I shook. But he must have caught the expression on my face, for he answered the question I was reluctant to ask. 'I am a lawyer, Master Lovall. I give my services for a fee. I accept the indenture. My clerk will give you a receipt. The fees will become due when the boy, John Brown, comes of age and claims his inheritance.'

Lawyers usually cling to their clients like ivy to oak – but only when there's the prospect of money coming in to fill their coffers. There'd be money to be made from John when he was grown to a man. Until then, it seemed, Master Benson had no interest in him.

Or so I thought. We stood up to go. Benson walked over to the door and called for his clerk to escort us out. As we were waiting for the clerk, he took hold of my arm and said, 'The indenture will be lodged here. It is a properly constituted legal document and will have the full force of law, but I should warn you that William Harpole may well contest it. And that could be costly.'

'Contest it? On what grounds?'

'He may claim that Adam Rowley was not of sound mind when this was drawn up.'

'It is witnessed by Harpole's own legal partner.'

'He would be foolish to contest it. I merely warn you that he might.'

Was he playing lawyer's games with me?

'And … it is possible. I'm not saying it is likely …'

To the point man, to the point.

'Harpole might choose to sell Manor Farm House before John Brown comes of age.'

'And that would be legal?'

'Yes, it would.'

'So, what do you suggest?' And there, he had me, or so he thought. I was seeking his legal advice. So much law, so little justice.

'I can give notice that we hold a copy of the indenture here, and that its contents have been noted. That will register a charge against the legal title of Manor Farm House.'

He edged closer. Closer to the gull he thought would soon become his client. Ivy seeking oak.

'I would, of course, have to act on behalf of a client.'

'Of course,' I said. 'And will there be a fee for giving notice and registering the charge?'

'A small fee.'

'And when does that fee become payable?'

'Once the charge is registered.'

'And I will be more than happy to pay it if it means young John inherits what is rightly his.'

I was minded to give his clerk a made-up address in London where he could send his bill, then shake his hand and walk away. I could have played him at his own games, but that wouldn't get the bill paid, and without Benson's goodwill no amount of legal niceties would ensure John's inheritance. And, besides, I wanted to get away from Abingdon and Wittenham as quickly as possible. So I did what I have never done before. I asked to pay the lawyer his fee before it became due. It was indeed a small fee. Ten shillings and sixpence. But it didn't leave much in the purse that Mistress Atkins so generously gave me.

I took my leave of him and prompted John to do the same.

'I thank you, sir,' said John. He grinned, and gave a little bow – the player on the stage at the end of his performance.

28
Changes of heart

'You must remember this place,' I said as we walked out onto the street. 'You'll need to come back here when you're of an age to claim your inheritance.'

He grunted, and looked down at the cobbles. I took him by the hand and led him back to the bridge, where we stood together looking over the low parapet.

'Where are we going to go now?'

I knew where I was going. Back to try to find Agnes and warn her of what I'd heard from the carter, and then south to Newbury and on to Canterbury.

'I don't know. I need time to think.'

In a nearby street, opposite the Crown and Thistle, two women were standing, arms folded beneath their bosoms, talking energetically. Half a dozen children were playing nearby. Still holding John firmly by the hand, I approached and bade them good day and asked if they could look after 'my boy John' for an hour or so. They looked suspicious until I produced a penny for each of them, and the promise of another when I collected John in an hour or so.

The shorter of the two women called the eldest of the children over and told her to let John join their games.

John tried to follow me. I got down on my haunches.

'Stay here with these people. It won't be for long.

'Don't want to play,' he whispered.

'Don't then. No matter to me. I have business to attend to. Do as I say. I will be back for you.'

He turned away, and went to sit against the wall. He might have been crying.

I hurried up to the market place, seeking out a better class of inn than The Crown and Thistle. The Red Lion was welcoming, but most inns are if they think you're going to spend money.

It was time I wanted. Time to sit alone and think. I'd have sought out Judith, and persuaded her to take John in, except that I couldn't go back to Oxford.

I bought a tankard of ale and a trencher of bread and cheese. I told the tapster I was from London, and had recently journeyed to Oxford, and was now on my way to Newbury and then Salisbury. He was looking askance, trying not to meet my gaze. I thought for a moment that I'd said something foolish, until I remembered that it was my face that worried people. 'I know what it looks like, Master Tapster. But I was born like this. I have to be thankful I wasn't born a woman, for I would never be married off.'

That amused him – though not so much as to stir a laugh.

'So, I'm sure you'll understand, Master Tapster, if I ask to eat and drink alone, where I can sit with my thoughts uninterrupted. He led me through to a snug at the back of the inn; a room with one small window, a rush-covered dry earth floor, limewashed walls and no fireplace. Two tables, benches round the walls, and no-one to disturb me. I thanked him. He said he'd ask a maid to bring me bread and cheese – which she duly did; and a couple of apples too.

How things had changed for me. The surname was the least of it. I would never have chosen to sit alone at a drinking house. There's always money to be made when drinks are flowing, even in the middle of the day – especially in the middle of the day for that's when most tricksters are sleeping off the night before. Yet now all I wanted was to be alone with my thoughts.

I needed to find someone to take John in, a mother to treat him as one of her own. One of those women standing gossiping with the urchins playing on the dirt road? They knew about bringing up children. They'd give him a home. A roof over his head every night. There. The decision had been made. Now I could rest awhile, then find a carter heading for Newbury.

Why wait? If you've already made up your mind, why call in here?

It was her. I knew it without looking.

I asked to be left alone.

You are alone. I'm the only one talking to you.

I didn't want to look at her.

He wants to stay here, Constance. He needs to stay here. This is where he grew up.

He's a child, Matthew. How can he know what is best for him?

He told me what he wants. *My job to be my father now that he is dead.* He wants to grow up here.

He wants you to be his father. He told you so.

I am not his father.

You taught him to read.

I taught him to recognise a few words.

You took an interest in him. Why teach him if you care so little for him?

252

I needed his help. I taught him to pick locks. And if I hadn't, I wouldn't have got out of Rowley Hall alive, nor would Agnes, nor would he. I taught him to play silent when it suited me.

He liked that.

It was a game, Constance. A game to get a gullible old maid to take pity on us.

She didn't answer that. But I could hear her breathing. I shut my eyes. Sounds from the street outside. The rattling and squeaking of carts, clip-clop of horses' hooves, cries of a costermonger selling fruit from a barrow. Loud enough to hear through the thick glass of the one small window. But I could still hear Constance. Slow, regular, deep breathing. In through her nose, out through her lips. Almost purring. Just as she did when we lay together in the wooden shelter with the rest of Rowley's crew. Slow. Peaceful. Calming. If I reached out, I could touch her. What was it Agnes said? She is with us. In spirit. Not in flesh. Agnes has her ways. Her way of gentling it to me. Constance was dead. Burned alive in the fire. But she was close. I know nothing of the spirit world, save for the strange prophecies of Cunning Hannah and the curses that Forman left as traps in his workshop. I didn't understand what Agnes told me. But I knew that Constance was with me. I could smell the sweetness of her breath. And if I shut my eyes, she was indeed beside me. Turning to look or reaching out would drive her away. But her presence was enough.

Matthew. Why pretend you're so cruel? That is not who you are.

I am who I am, Constance. You only know the poor wretch you nursed back to health. I cannot be the boy's father just because he'd like me to be.

You've already given him more than his own father ever did.

Enough's enough. I've saved his life. I've risked coming to Abingdon to lodge his inheritance with a lawyer. I can't take him on the journey I have to make.

That quietened her for a while. I should perhaps have left then. But I had a fearful thirst on me, and there was a long journey ahead. I went back to the buttery bar to get my tankard refilled. I shut the door behind me when I returned to the snug. I sat back down. Took a drink.

You treat him like your son. Then you abandon him.

He'll be safer here than on the road with me. And he needs to be with other children.

He's not used to children. They'll bully him.

Did you not see where I left him? They were younger than him. All of them.

Him being older? You think that will protect him?

I think he has to live his own life, Constance. I can't live it for him.

Time to go. But I didn't. I sat for a while, not moving. My head full of maybes and what-ifs. The maid came in. Offered me a plate of quince and pippin pie. I'm sure it was delicious, but I hardly tasted it.

I went back to collect young John from the street where I'd left him to play with the local urchins. There was nobody there. I knocked at the door of the house where the gossips had been holding forth.

'You come for your boy.' It wasn't a question. She was scowling.

Constance was right. He hadn't wanted to play. And the other children could see that he thought himself different. The woman had taken him in.

'I give him some bread and an apple,' she said. 'He were hungry. Didn't say nothing. Does he never speak?'

'Sometimes. Not often. His mother died. And her sisters too. So I have to look after him.'

I gave her another penny for her pains, and took John back with me to the Red Lion, where we stayed the night. We'd need money for the journey, and I was tempted to sell some of the jewellery. But thought better of it. The talk throughout the town was all about the fire at Rowley Hall. If someone recognised anything I tried to sell, I could be accused of setting the fire myself. And so I paid for a room for the night with what little money there was left in the purse that Mistress Atkins gave me.

In the morning I found a carter taking bales of wool to Newbury. He agreed to take us with him.

29
A face and no face

The three of us sat together, John on my left, the carter on my right. The road was rising up onto the ridge that overlooked the Clumps when John nudged me. 'Look, Matthew.'

'What?'

'Smoke.'

'Ruins of Rowley Hall,' said the carter.

But the smoke was coming from nearer the river than where the hall had stood. Something wasn't right. I asked the carter to stop and let us off.

'Bench not padded enough for yer lardy arse?'

I told him the boy was feeling sick.

I half recognised the area. The Clumps to our left, the river below. The sun to our right in the southern sky. The smoke could have been coming from a charcoal burner's fire. But I feared something worse.

I took hold of John's hand, and we made our way across meadows. We saw sheep and cattle grazing, we saw a ploughboy leading a shire horse, its flanks steaming in the autumn sunshine. The ploughman – his father? – plodding slowly behind, gnarled hands clenched tight on the handles of the plough. A seething crowd of gulls and crows followed, swooping for unearthed bugs and worms, screeching and quarrelling amongst themselves.

Had they looked up they'd have seen a well-dressed man and boy walking purposefully towards the woodland by the river. But they were both gazing steadfastly ahead, ensuring the plough stayed upright and the furrow stayed straight.

The smoke was rising from the woodland where Rowley's crew had made their wooden shelter. I cannot have spent more than ten days, a fortnight at most, in these woods, and yet I felt a strange nostalgia. Even after the dunking of Agnes and the fire at Rowley Hall, my memory of the wooden shelter was a place of safety, a place where nobody looked askance at my scarred face, where John was a strange little boy who spied on me and hardly spoke, where Constance and I could nestle together and find comfort in each other's warmth and the fleeting sharing of our very different lives.

I could smell the smoke, but see no flames. I stopped. Lifted a finger to my lips.

'What?' whispered John.

'Hush.'

I drew him away from the path, and crouched down behind an enormous old, pollarded beech tree with hollow trunk. And there we waited. John had a thumb in his mouth and was clutching that hand with his other. I put my arm round his shoulder and held him close.

A squirrel leapt silently between branches. Beech nuts fell close to us. I put my finger to my lips, let go his hand and stood up, gesturing for him to stay where he was.

'I want to come with you,' he hissed.

I couldn't leave him. He was too frightened.

'Very well. But say nothing.'

Back onto the track. Every few steps I stopped, and listened. The only sounds came from high in the trees. Crows quarrelling, ravens croaking. And above them buzzards or kites mewling.

We walked the track I'd learnt to recognise until we came to the clearing where the shelter had stood. It had been pulled down and burnt. A few tongues of flame licked over the smouldering fallen beams. All that remained were charred logs and the heavy iron cookpot, which lay on its side beside the tripod it used to hang from.

Despite the destruction, I felt something close to relief. It made sense. Nobody who lived nearby would want their children playing in that shelter, pretending to set up home in the place where Rowley's madness had taken root.

John clung to my arm, as if I could protect him from his own dark memories. Then he gasped, tugged at my arm and pointed. I turned and looked up. A black cat had been strung up in a hangman's noose. And behind it a woman, her feet just inches above the forest floor, hanging by the neck from the bough of a yew tree. We were too late.

I turned John away and led him back the way we'd come, back to the beech tree, where I sat him down, and knelt with him.

'Is she dead?' he sobbed.

'I don't know. But stay here. Even if I cry out, stay here. Only move if I call your name.'

He looked blank, still in shock.

'Trust me, John. Stay here. I will return. Then we shall go to Newbury. And from there to Winchester and Canterbury. We'll go together, John. But only if you swear you won't move from here.'

'I swear.'

'I may call out for help. But don't move. Not unless I call you by your name.'

'I swear.'

I covered him with my cape, and ran back into the clearing to cut her down. I was just yards away when I saw it for what it was: not Agnes, but an effigy. The face carved from a turnip with painted pebbles for eyes, the hair a crude wig. The clothes and shoes were real enough.

The cat was dead, its body still warm.

My thoughts were churning faster than it takes to say these words. The cat I could understand if they thought it was her familiar. But the effigy? Was it there as a warning to Agnes? Stay away, or this will be you.

The place was too silent. The crows and the squirrels had been spooked. And not by the dead cat. I was being watched.

So maybe not a warning? A trap to lure in Agnes? Think your enemy's thoughts. The carter who'd taken us to Abingdon was convinced that Agnes was responsible for Rowley's madness, that she'd bewitched him, and the fire in Rowley Hall was her doing.

My sight was still not as keen as it used to be. But my ears were sharp. Something was moving on the edge of the woodland. A fox, a deer, or maybe a badger? No sooner had I heard it than it stopped.

I breathed in slowly, sniffing the air. Woodsmoke, of course, mixed with the slow decay of woodland in autumn. Fallen leaves, mushrooms, damp moss. And horse. The musky smell of horse. A single horse. There'd be other sounds if there was more than one. But one man alone couldn't have destroyed the shelter. There must have been a crowd of them. Had just one of them stayed behind on watch, with a horse to ride for help?

You trick the cheater by thinking as he does. Let him think you're doing what he wants you to. Destroying the shelter was an act of vengeance. But setting a trap? Suppose it wasn't the witch they hoped to trap? Even a witch can't survive alone. So, they'd reckon there must be sympathisers. Catch a sympathiser and torture him.

Or her.

Then set the sympathiser to catch the witch.

I'd been attracted by the smoke, as a compass needle to a magnet. Exactly as they hoped. In the clearing, smoking logs around me. They saw me as prey. Same as games of cards or dice. Let the cheaters think you're ready to be taken. Never let them get a sniff of your suspicions.

I stood in plain sight in the middle of the clearing, looking at the dead cat and the mock witch in a pantomime of horror.

The rope that held up the effigy ran over the bough and had been tied off around the base of a sapling. I walked slowly towards it. A true sympathiser would want to destroy the power of sympathetic magic. That's what they hoped I'd do. So that's what I would do. Take down the effigy.

Time to say a prayer. I could leave the cat for crows, but a man needs to save his soul. I dropped to my knees and steepled my hands together. And while down low, hidden by scrub and bushes from whoever was watching, I found a long thick stick, and pushed it into the leaves and leaf mould, searching for the tell-tale glint of cheese wire in a snare that had surely been laid. Nothing. I got to my feet. Pushing and prodding with the stick like a blind man on icy cobbles.

I caught a glimpse of blackened metal. I gave it a prod. With a fearsome crack, loud as a pistol shot, the stick flew from my grasp. The black iron teeth of man-trap jaws snapped shut. I screamed in shock and agony. And fell to the ground, gasping as a man whose blood is spurting, pumping over the woodland floor.

Crows and pigeons took screeching to the air.

I threw loose bracken over my leg and the erect clenched jaws of the sprung trap. My screaming growing weaker with every breath.

I saw him coming. A figure running towards me, silhouetted against the light at the edge of the woodland.

My screams fading to snivelling, snot-wet cries.

And there he was. Standing, towering above the poor pathetic witch sympathiser, a dagger in his right hand. I sobbed and I moaned, I whined and I whimpered. He had the look on his face of a man who's not supposed to feel pride, but is delighted to have been proved right.

But there's another kind of man-trap, as he soon found out. My own spring was coiled tight. As he bent down and tried to grab my hair to drag me upright, he tickled this man-trap's trigger plate. I may not be as fast as a metal spring, but I was a deal quicker than him. I wrapped my arms round his legs and pulled his feet from under him. He fell backwards, cracking his head on the woodland floor. His turn to cry out.

I was on my feet. My boot on his right arm. Pinning it to the ground.

'Let go the knife.'

He clenched it tighter. He was dressed as a man of the church. Perhaps he was even the parson that Rowley so despised. Geoffrey Benson, if I remembered right. Keeping my weight on his forearm, I bent down and tried to prise the knife from his grasp. But he was determined. And I wasn't expecting him to be so strong. With his free arm he grabbed at my ankle. If he wanted to play the fighting man, he deserved the respect of being treated like one. I stamped on the hand holding the knife. Stamped hard enough to break bones. Screaming in pain, he loosened his grip. I took the knife from him.

'Stop your damned howling,' I said. 'Or I'll cut out your tongue.' I drew the knife across his cheek. Not deep. Just enough to draw blood. Enough for him to know I could do far worse.

'I meant you no harm,' he whimpered.

'You set a man-trap and you meant no harm!'

'Not to you, sir. We have to be rid of the witch. Thou shalt not suffer a witch to live. It's in the Holy Book. This was for her. Not for you. I would never kill a man.'

'You came for me with a knife, Master Parson. And you set a man trap. You think it can choose who it bites?'

'It wouldn't have killed you.' He looked up at me in terror.

I knelt down beside him. Let him take a closer look at my scarred face. Held his own knife to his throat. 'The jaws of a man-trap crush bones. If I hadn't bled to death I'd have died of gangrene.'

He shut his eyes, and mouthed a silent prayer.

'You not know who I am, Master Parson?'

'No,' he squeaked.

'You not recognise me?'

'No.'

'My face too badly burnt for you to see it?'

He whimpered.

'Because I know you, Geoffrey Benson. And you surely know me. I'm Peter Rowley. You not remember me?'

'Pee … Pee,' he spluttered. 'Peter Rowley's dead. He fell from his brother's horse and never recovered.'

'Oh, but I did. My face is not what it was. But you surely recognise the clothes. Be thankful that you summoned Peter Rowley, and not the witch herself, for she is far more powerful than me.'

'You're not a ghost. You're – '

'The devil incarnate? No, Master Parson. I'm Peter Rowley given new life by my brother Adam's pact with the very devil himself.'

'Adam Rowley, bless his soul, was deceived by the witch.'

I laughed. It started as a gently mocking sneer, and grew louder and more raucous. Laughing as loud as alarums. And that made him truly fearful. Something I learnt from the theatres. There are moments when laughter's more troubling than a great torrent of curses. The colour drained from his face.

'Any true witch could have saved herself from your foolish gin-trap. A true witch has powers you could never dream of.'

'What, what powers?' he stammered.

'How do you think a true witch spends her time? Turning old milk sour? Laming cows or staling yeast? Why would a true witch waste her powers on such fripperies?'

'What powers?'

'My brother, Adam, was strung taut with guilt about my death. You told him to pray. You remember that?'

'I do remember. Of course I do.'

'So Adam prayed. And he prayed again. And then he prayed some more. And he called on God to forgive him. But his prayers were not answered, because he could never confess to what he'd truly done, for it was Adam who caused his own brother's death, Peter's death, *my* death. And so he fell to despair, and in the depths of despair the devil himself called on him. He made a pact, Master Parson, as you will with me. And the devil told him he would send a witch to draw up a deed in blood. If Adam himself set the fire at the Hall, Peter Rowley would rise up and walk from the ashes.'

'No. No. That cannot be.'

'It can. And it is. The fire breathed new life into me. I walked from the ashes, and here I stand before you. That is why you see my face the way it is. A face and no face.'

'That's monstrous. It goes against – '

'Believe it, Master Parson. If you truly feared witches, you would never hound out the poor and the elderly who only offend because they understand those ancient salves and remedies that lie hidden in the hedgerows and the forests. They are helpless, and that is exactly why you persecute them. But a true witch. That is very different. Most unwise to persecute a true witch, for she has real powers; powers that you men of the cloth cannot begin to imagine. Can you read, Master Parson?'

'Of course I can read.'

'Then look at this.'

I removed Forman's charred book from my pocket, opened it to pages filled with mysterious writings and diagrams, and held it in front of his face.

'Read to me, Master Parson.'

'I can't. You know I can't. I don't understand that writing.'

Which was as I'd hoped. I held the charred pages to his nose.

'Breathe deep, Master Parson. You know where this comes from? You recognise that smell?'

His eyes grew wider, his mouth fell open, as he detected the whiff of sulphur and the stench of hellfire.

'As I passed through the flames at Rowley Hall someone, or some *thing,* placed this book in my hand.'

His bottom lip was quivering.

'You want to lure the witch? I can help. Wait here. I'll call her up.'

'No.'

'You not want to see her now?'

'No.'

'Then what will you tell them? Those brave men who burnt down the shelter?'

'Don't know.'

'My advice to you, Geoffrey Benson, Parson of this parish, is take down the effigy, bury the cat, throw your cursed gin-trap in the river, and tell your congregation to stop meddling in what they don't understand. Now. To your feet.' I prodded him again with the tip of his knife. Enough to make him bleed a little more. 'Take down the effigy.'

I watched as he untied the rope and lowered the effigy to the ground.

'Remove the rope from her neck.'

When he'd done that, I had him hold one end of the rope, keep his arms flat against his body and turn round until he was wrapped tight. I led him deeper into the forest, tied him to a tree, pulled a kerchief from his pocket and forced it into his mouth. I searched his other pockets and found a full purse.

Foolish fellow. Who but a fool takes money with them to the woods?

'I hope you're well practiced at saying your prayers, for you will surely need them. But take heed of some advice, Master Parson. If you do not wish to be visited by the forces of darkness, never again meddle in what you do not understand.'

John was where I'd left him, behind the old beech tree. I led him out of the woodland and round to where the parson's horse was tethered.

'What happened to the man?'

'Which man?'

'The man you were talking to.'

'He's waiting for his friends.'

30
The strangest of strange goodbyes

I allowed myself a moment of triumph. Not only had I made the woods safe for Agnes, but I now had a horse, a dagger and a full purse.

I helped John up onto the horse, and led it away from the woodland and down towards a track near the river.

'Where are we going?'

'To Newbury.'

'Don't we have to get back on the road where the carter dropped us?'

'I don't want the ploughman or his boy to see us.'

'Why not?'

'Because we didn't have a horse when we walked past them and now we do. And people make up stories.'

'Why?'

I did my best to hide my impatience. 'Because their lives are dull. Because other people's lives are more interesting than their own.'

'Why's it matter if they make up stories?'

'Because gossip travels faster than the wind.'

'How?'

'I wish I knew. But it does. And that's that. No more questions.'

He was sitting stiffly upright on the parson's mare, clinging to the pommel of the saddle. His legs not long enough to reach the stirrups. For a mile or so he said nothing. Which suited well enough – until I glanced up and he avoided returning my look.

'I don't mind you asking questions. But not now. I need to be sure of where we're going. Now duck your head.'

He hadn't seen the low branch ahead. He bent forward, burying his face in the horse's mane. And that's where he stayed. He wants to sulk, so be it, I thought. He'd been silent for much of his young life. An hour or so more would do him no harm.

The track took us back into the woods. The canopy of leaves grew thicker. Another holloway, with banks on either side and trees arched over. As dark and as narrow as any London backstreet alley. I reached up to take John's hand, to assure him all was well. He didn't stir. He'd fallen asleep.

On I walked, leading the bay mare, its hooves splashing through muddy puddles, picking its way over knotted tree roots. Deeper into the muddy darkness.

Talk to me Constance. Tell me I'm going in the right direction.

She was as silent as John.

Time slowed, seemed to drift and to melt. My feet on the path, one foot forward, the other following. Time passed. I was sitting on a mossy boulder, John still slumped on the mare, the leading rein tied to a tree. We were in a clearing. The sky above was blue, shafts of sunlight lit up a grassy area. I don't recall how we got there.

'You tooken yer time.' Agnes was sitting beside me.

'Was it you led us here?'

'How could I do that?'

'I don't know. I don't understand you.'

'Lot o' things yous don' unnerstand. I sees you got the boy.'

'He's coming with me to Newbury. Then on to Winchester and Canterbury.'

'Pilgrimage, is it?'

'He wanted to come.'

'You tol' me you was a man of yer word.'

'I am.'

'You said to wait, Matthew. Wait for us, you said, and you'd bring us food. 'Swhat you said.'

'It took longer than I'd expected. But that's what I did. I left it here for you. In this clearing. On this rock.'

'Then you be more fool than I took you for. You think Agnes be the only creature lookin' for food in these parts? You think foxes and crows be not hungry too?'

'I brought you food, Agnes. Took longer than I'd hoped. But I brought it. I looked for you. And when I couldn't find you, I left it for you. It was well wrapped. That's more than most would have done.'

'*More than most*? Best you can do?' She gave a small laugh.

'I will never understand you, Agnes. But I've grown to like you. There are others in these parts who don't like you. I took the boy to Abingdon to stake a claim for his inheritance. I heard much talk that Adam Rowley had been bewitched, that the fire at Rowley Hall was witchcraft. They are looking for you. They fear you, Agnes. And when men fear women, it never bodes well.'

'You think I don't know that?'

'I scared them off, Agnes.' I told her about my encounter with Parson Benson, about the effigy and the hanging cat. I wanted to show her the danger she was in. But a smile slipped over her face. A smile which broadened and turned to laughter.

'It's no laughing matter.'

'Oh, but it is, Master Matthew,' she cackled. 'It is. 'Cos you be telling me what I seen wi' my own eyes.'

'You were there?'

'I seen it all.'

'All what?'

'The parson and his gang pullin' down the shelter, burnin' it – jus' like you say – settin' the gin-trap, stringin' up the cat. And that stupid doll. Looked nothing like me. I were there when they left. Back to they's wives and they's chilluns. And the brave parson waitin' to catch the fearsome witch in his trap. I were there, Matthew. I seen it all. I were there when you and the boy come along. I were there when you sprung the gin-trap.'

'Where were you hiding?'

'You and me, Matthew. We both knows stuff. Some of it the same, some of it different.'

'You saw what happened? With me and the parson? You heard what I said to him?'

'I saw what I saw, an' I heard what I heard.'

'Where were you hiding, Agnes?'

'Wouldn't be a secret place if I tells you.'

We sat for a while. I looked up. The sky above, what I could see of it through gaps in the tree canopy, was a deep blue. Heavy frosts coming. A squirrel appeared, looked at us, curious. Neither Agnes nor I spoke. The squirrel went about its business, collecting acorns and beech mast for the winter ahead. The boy slept on, slumped over the mare's neck as if Agnes had given him a draught of poppy juice. Then she turned to me. Her expression had changed. Her eyelids looked heavy. When she spoke it was in that growling she-bear voice I'd heard before when she so mistrusted me. 'You play your games. They makes me smile. They almost makes me laugh. You's not Agnes. You's Matthew, who'll never know what it is to be Agnes. What you said to the parson. It ent true. I see things, yes. But I got no powers, no magic. I ent even got spells.'

'You have great wisdom, Agnes.'

'I know how to hide in the forest. I know how to move about unseen. I knows about leaves and shrooms, herbs and healing. And I sees things others don't. Call that wisdom if you will, and mebbe wisdom get you power in London. But not round here. In these parts power is money callin' on ignorance to do its bidding. All just a game to you. I knows you meant well. What you says about men is truth. When men fear women it don't go well for women. You scared the parson half way out his wits. But even supposin' he believes every word you tol' him, he don't have the brains nor the charms what you have, Matthew. Those other men, those what burned the shelter, strung up the cat and the witch doll, they'll be angry and even more frighted when they see the state of him. He can't stop 'em doin' what they want. He got no more power 'n me. If they believe Adam Rowley was bewitched, then Parson Benson can be too. Give it a week, mebbe two at most. They'll soon be seeking vengeance for the bewitching of Parson Benson. And no Master Matthew to stand in their way this time.'

'I was making the place safe for you, Agnes.'

'I knows what you thought you was doing.'

Young John muttered something in his sleep.

'We must go, Agnes. To Canterbury.'

'You and the boy?'

271

'Yes.' I misread the look on her face. 'I can't stay here to look after you.'

'Just as well. You's a troubled man, Master Matthew. And you bring trouble with you.' I expected her face to be clouded with anger. But she took hold of my hand and smiled. 'I seen a good man in there somewhere. Yous don't mean to bring harm. Trouble is, you bring it just the same. I seen it from the first. 'Tis good you go, 'tis good you take the boy.'

'Then come with us, Agnes.' I never thought I'd say it. But I meant it. 'I cannot leave you here. I have a spare set of clothes for the boy. We could dress you in those. Come with us. At least until we find somewhere safe for you.'

'You think me wearin' boy's clothes will keep me safe? You wants me to pretend to be a child?! You knows your own world, Matthew. You don't know this one.'

'I don't like leaving you behind, Agnes.'

I thought I caught a moment's hesitation, as if she was pondering the idea. I should have tried harder to persuade her. But I didn't. I let her convince me.

'I can't be going with you. I's better on my own. I know places I can go. Let me be. Let me find my own ways.'

Not knowing how to say my goodbyes, I got to my feet. 'Will Constance stay here or come with me?'

'Ask her. I'm not the one she talks to. You alone knows what happened 'twixt you an' her. That will stay with you always.'

'Are you saying she'll haunt me?'

'I knows nothing 'bout haunting. But there's no changing the past. I do know that. I helped your eyes to see again. I helped your skin to heal. But I cannot change the deeds you done, nor unlight fires was lit.'

'And still you talk in riddles, Agnes.'

'Call it riddles, call it wisdom, call it the babbling of a weird ol' crone. But open your ears to hear it, and it be plain as day. Now shut your eyes, hold out your hand.'

She put something on my palm, and closed my fingers around it. 'A hagstone, Matthew. That's what we call it.'

'What do I do with it?'

'Keep it.'

'Does it have powers?'

'It is what it is. A gift from Agnes to Matthew. A thing of beauty. You see things. More 'n you know sometimes. You shown me that at the Clumps. See this. Allow it to be what it is.'

'I thank you, Agnes. I shall treasure it.'

She took my hands in hers, looked deep into my eyes. 'Time will tell.'

'Meaning what?'

'You see more 'n you see. And you knows more 'n you knows. But you and I's from different worlds.'

'Meaning what, Agnes?'

'Meaning no more talk. Be on your ways. And leave us be.'

And thus it was that Agnes and I said our strangest of strange goodbyes.

31
Pilgrims

I'd seen hagstones before. Forman had several. And Hannah had a large one hanging in the old charcoal burner's hovel she called home. But the stone that Agnes had given me was different. It was well rounded and the surface was as smooth as a child's skin. I held it up to the sun between the forefinger and thumb of my right hand, and marvelled at the stone's strange perfection, and at the pleasure it gave me.

I've seen many fine jewels and pearls, but never anything so pure in form, so rare and as flawless as this. The hole in the middle was just big enough to slip my little finger into, although the stone was too big to wear as a ring. I put it in an inside pocket of my doublet. It felt strangely precious.

Agnes insisted she had no magical powers. And who was I to disagree with her? But she had something about her. Something I would never understand. She was mistrusting and other worldly. But there was no malice about her. It was humbling that she should have presented me with such a gift.

By the time we got to the Newbury road, the sun was warm on my face, even though the air was still cold. John had woken from his slumbers and was sitting upright again. I lifted him down from the saddle.

'Are we going to Newbury now?'

'Indeed we are, young man. And from here we'll ride.' I mounted, adjusted the stirrups, for my legs were a deal longer than the parsons, then lifted John back up to sit behind me. 'Wrap your arms round my waist. Hold tight.'

The road was a wide track with hedgerows on either side. In places the ruts from carts were so deep that we could go no faster than a slow walk. But there were decent stretches where it was possible to trot and even to canter. We must have ridden five miles or so when a cart came by, heading towards Oxford. I stopped to talk with the carter. He thought the weather fair, though cold, and likely to get colder. Which is pretty much what I thought too. He thought the road was rough, though not as rough as some. A genial fellow then. And no mention of witches. But if he was dull with his conversation and light on gossip when he met us, he wouldn't be after meeting the well-dressed gentleman and his boy riding a bay mare. Which is why I thought it prudent to feed him the same story that had probably already seeped out from The Bear at Moreton. I asked if this road would take us to Salisbury. It was most important we got there as soon as possible. Could we get there before dark?

He thought it madness to try to get as far as Salisbury in a day. But if the horse didn't go lame we could probably get there by the following evening. I thanked him for his advice, and he trundled on his way.

When Benson's friends found him gibbering mad with terror in the forest, they'd make enough sense of his story to know that a man with a burnt face had ridden off with the mare. The parson might try to stop them from chasing down the Satanically reborn Peter Rowley, but Agnes was right. They'd see it as a challenge to find the mare and bring her back, and give the thief a sound beating, face or no face. But the carter's gossip would send them chasing off to Salisbury.

'Franklin used to let me sit in front of him when he took me with him to Abingdon.'

'You used to go riding with Franklin?'

'He was nice to me,' said John. He picked a handful of grass, then held it out on the flat of his palm for the horse to eat. The mare lowered her head and nuzzled him. It was good to see. The mare and the boy had an affinity for each other. And he clearly had no fear of horses.

'You liked Master Franklin?'

'He was kind to me.'

So different from the picture Rowley had painted. I saw something I'd not seen before. Rowley afraid of his own son and bitterly jealous of Franklin for his ability to connect with the boy. I liked the boy despite his occasional sulks. But I cursed myself for ever telling him that Adam fucking Rowley was his father.

I remounted the mare and lifted John up to sit in front of me.

'Better?'

'Thank you.' His contact with the mare had lifted his spirits. I wrapped an arm round him. We trotted on.

Time passed.

We crested the brow of yet another hill. The sun was low in the sky. The road led down into a valley, and there was Newbury before us. A small town with a river running through it. My original plan had been to stop there for the night, sell Rowley's jewellery, then set off for Winchester the next day. But that was too risky. The horrors of No-face had worked on Parson Benson, but I was already regretting what I'd done. I'd thought myself so cunning, thought I was doing right by Agnes. But if Benson was so frighted that he could hardly speak, they wouldn't wait to heed his warnings. The carter would tell a story about a man with no face on a bay mare bound for Salisbury, but No-Face and the boy with him would surely have to stop for a night in Newbury. A gang of men in pursuit could follow at double our speed. If we stayed the night at an inn in Newbury, they could have us by morning.

We walked on for a few hundred yards and came to a crossroads with a friendly fingerpost. Straight ahead *N'bury 1 mile, W'chstr 28 miles, Soton 42 miles*. That was encouraging. If we could find somewhere to stay nearby, we'd be in Winchester on the morrow. But where to stay tonight? To the right, towards the sunset and the west, *H'ford 10 miles, Bristol 62 miles*. To our left and the east, *Thatcham 4 miles, Reading 20 miles, London 62 miles*.

We headed east, stopping at The White Hart in Thatcham. The ostler took the mare for stabling. There was no need for stories because I had a full purse and a good horse, and we no longer stank of smoke and poverty. But John was still the deaf mute because I hoped that might get us a little sympathy. Maybe it did, but not as much as I'd have liked. The innkeeper and I traded pleasantries, but he was suspicious of my no face. He called a maid and whispered to her. She led us along a narrow passageway, up two sets of stairs to a room on the top floor that was less than half the size of the one we'd had in Moreton. One narrow bed, one chair, a small window that let in very little light. No wash stand, no carpets, nor even rushes on the rough wooden floor and no hangings on the walls, which might once have been limewashed, but were stained green and black with mould. She left her battered lantern with us, and said there'd be food downstairs if we wanted it. As her footsteps were clomping down the stairs, John started: 'Don't like it here.'

'Nor do I, John. But we have to sleep somewhere. We have a roof over our heads, we'll get a meal tonight and another in the morning.'

'Why've we come here? You said we were going to Newbury.'

'Newbury's not safe for us now.'

'Why not?'

'There are people who don't like it that I've protected Agnes. They might catch us in Newbury.'

'Are we safe here?'

'I don't like it here. But yes, we're safe.'

After a few moments silence he asked, 'Did you steal the horse?'

That flummoxed me. What to tell him?

'Your father once said something to me that I will never forget. *How can a man steal what cannot be owned?*'

John asked what that meant – as well he might. And that, too, flummoxed me. I changed the subject. 'Does the mare like us, do you think, John?'

He shrugged.

'She likes you very much.'

He walked over to the window, taking the chair with him to stand on.

'Can we see the stables from here?'

I went to join him. The window glass was so thick and grimy with candle soot that we couldn't see anything much. He went back and sat on the bed.

'Does she have a name?' asked John.

'The maid who showed us to the room? I don't know.'

'Not the maid. The horse.'

'If she does, I don't know it.'

'Can we call her Mary?'

'You think she'll like that name?'

He did. And we went downstairs to eat. The food was better than the innkeeper's manner. We kept ourselves to ourselves. I didn't want anyone putting John's deaf muteness to the test. We were both very tired that night and took to our bed early. John slept through til daybreak, although he kicked me awake every time he had a nightmare.

In the morning we were given a good breakfast. The mare – Mary as she now was – had been well looked after. The ostler told me a way of getting to the Winchester road without passing through Newbury. We made good progress, arriving in the city while it was still light. We found an inn by the river, close by the city mill. I paid for the mare to be stabled, and for a good room on the first floor with a bed that was big enough to sleep through the night without being kicked every time young John had a nightmare.

I'd spent all the money Mistress Atkins had given me, and there were only a few coins left in the parson's purse. We'd need more money to get us to Canterbury. After the business in Oxford I was reluctant to seek out games of cards or dice. I'd need to sell the jewellery from Rowley Hall, and for that we'd need at least a day in Winchester.

'Are you ready for your next lesson?'

John grinned.

'Can I speak this time?'

'If I tell you some lines, do you think you can remember them?'

We practiced in our room before walking out – up High Street to the Butter Cross, where twenty or thirty stalls were set out, giving me a pang of longing for the thrum of life round Cheapside. I bought a small leather bag. We found a quiet corner in an inn, and there I transferred the bracelet, the brooch, the ear-rings and the pearl to my new bag.

'Are you ready?'

'Yes.'

'Yes what?'

'Yes, father.'

'Good. So now we must find ourselves a jeweller.'

In London I knew where to sell anything, I knew who was looking for particular items. I knew who'd ask no questions and still pay a good price. I knew the dealers, and they knew me. If I said I'd bring them a certain something, that's what they'd get. In London I'm known as a man of my word. In Winchester I was nobody. But I did have in my favour the clothes I was wearing, and a young son who was devoted to his mother – whether she was alive or dead. Clear signs of respectability.

In Jewry Street we found a pawnbroker, the three golden balls of his sign gleaming in the morning sun. The shop was so full of items at pawn there was hardly space to stand. So I bade John sit down on a high backed wooden chair.

'What do we do now?' he whispered.

'We wait.'

And while we waited, I looked around the shop. All manner of furniture, some of it well crafted. A rusty old two-handed sword. The wheel of a coach. Children's toys. More clothes than you'd find in most tailors. Doublets, lace bonnets, boots, a dark cape lined in velvet, a red velvet petticoat, wedding silks. And much more besides.

But no jewellery of any kind – at least not on display.

The broker, a small, wizened man, wearing calf skin gloves, as if he didn't want to be contaminated by the goods he'd taken at pawn, emerged silently from the darkness like a spider that had felt a tug on his web.

'You have something to offer me?' he said. 'Or have you come to buy?'

'To buy,' I said. 'Or rather, my son would like to buy.' I nudged John, who got to his feet and duly spoke the lines we'd practiced in our room at the inn. 'I wish to buy a bracelet as a birthday present for my mother. Do you have anything you can show me?'

He rummaged in a drawer and found some glass beads on a string.

'What do you think, father?'

I thought here was a man who didn't trade in jewellery and wouldn't recognise the quality of what I had to offer. So we went on our way.

A little further along the street, swinging from a bracket above the door of a four-storey house was a wooden board painted with a necklace, a tiara and a gold ring. At the bottom of the sign – for those who could read:

Gilthead & Son
Goldsmiths and Jewellers

We opened the door and went in. We could have been in the small hallway of a yeoman farmer's house. A long table stood in the middle of this room on a terracotta tiled floor, with a chair on either side of the door we came through. The walls were all oak-panelled, with a couple of wall lanterns on each, though only one of these was lit. No wall hangings, no rushes nor rugs on the floor. A jeweller's shop with nothing on display – that either meant that Gilthead had fallen on hard times or here was a man so well known in his trade that he had no need to advertise.

I rang the small bell on the table.

A door opened in the wood panelling. A tall man came in, carrying a lantern. He had grey hair, gaunt face and a wispy excuse for a beard. He held up the lantern and peered at me; as curious about my face as I was about the jeweller's shop with no jewels.

'You come to buy, or to sell?' he said.

'You do sell jewellery?'

'I only show to those I trust.'

His eyes were blue, almost that same turquoise blue that was so striking in Frances Howard, and Alice.

'I'm the same, Master Gilthead, which is why I've come to you, for I'm here to sell not to buy.'

John tugged at my arm. 'Father,' he pleaded.

'Not now, boy.'

Gilthead went back through the panelled door, and then emerged with two more lanterns which he placed on the table, then lit them with a taper. I placed the contents of our new bag onto the table. He inspected the bracelet. Then the pearl, the butterfly brooch and the ear-rings. Each time he held an item to the light he gave a studied non-committal grunt, but said nothing. It was a performance, and one I was well used to. I knew the routine. I was hoping he didn't know mine.

'Father,' said John, a little more urgent this time.

'Not now, son.'

'But.'

'Hush you, boy.'

'I'll give you five pounds for the bracelet,' said Master Gilthead. 'Three for the ear-rings, and two for the pearl.' But I could see from the way he feigned a lack of interest in the brooch that that's what he really wanted. I moved it away from the other items, but didn't yet put it back in the bag.

'Father,' John was sniffing. 'We can't.'

'John. Stop it. It's what your aunt wanted me to do.'

At that he burst into tears. The jeweller, who was holding the bracelet to the light, put it down, as if that might silence the boy. It didn't. He started crying.

I took John into a corner and spoke to him sternly. 'Enough of this, John.' Then I crouched down and lowered my voice. John mumbled something in reply.

'I can't hear you, boy.' I cocked my head to one side, so he could whisper in my ear.

'Yes, yes, yes. I understand. But it's already been decided and we've agreed.'

I went back to the table and explained to Master Gilthead that John was still very upset about losing his mother in the same fire that had burnt my face. He tried to be sympathetic, but his eyes flickered across to the butterfly brooch.

'You say ten pounds in total for the bracelet, the pearl and the ear-rings?' I said as I took the brooch from the table and put it back into the bag.

'That's what I offered.'

'What do you say to that, John?'

John sniffed, pursed his lips and nodded.

'I'll sell them to you for fifteen pounds, Master Gilthead.'

Gilthead chuntered. I countered. Up a little, down a little. We came to rest at twelve pounds and ten shillings. As we were about to shake hands, he asked to take a look at the brooch.

'We don't want to sell it.' But I didn't take it from the table.

He held it to the light.

'Father. You just promised we wouldn't sell the brooch,' said John.

I led him to the far side of the room and sat him on a chair. I told him sternly to be quiet and stay there. In the meantime, Gilthead had taken a magnifying glass from a drawer in the desk, and was looking at the tiny jewels that made the eyes. 'How much do you want for this?' he called across.

I went back to him. 'I can't. I promised the boy we'd not sell it.'

'I'll give you twenty pounds,' said Gilthead.

John sobbing almost convinced me.

'Thirty,' I whispered. 'And if you really want it, Master Gilthead, do it quickly before the dam of the poor boy's sorrow breaks.'

'Twenty three.'

'I'll take no less than twenty five.'

It was a shame to sell the brooch because it would have made a fine present for Kate. We struck a deal at thirty seven pounds for everything. I left the shop with a full purse and a wailing boy. Gilthead was glad to see the back of us. We had more than enough to get us to Canterbury without having to sell the horse. If there was a little to spare I could buy something for Kate when we got there.

From Jewry Street we walked to the cathedral church, where I sought out the Deacon, who was deeply moved by our story of the terrible fire which burned my face so badly and took the life of John's dear mother, my beloved wife. In her honour we wanted to make a pilgrimage to Canterbury because that was a place she'd always wanted to visit.

The Deacon suggested a pilgrim's route and places where we might stay. He even gave me names of innkeepers who would offer generous terms to honest pilgrims such as us, who'd suffered such terrible misfortunes.

All in all, a most satisfactory day. Or so I thought.

When we got back to our room at the inn, I congratulated John on his fine performance. 'You remembered your cues, and all your lines. You even played extempore exactly when needed. I am very proud of you, young man.'

He glared at me, his lower lip trembling. Whether he was holding back tears or rage, I couldn't tell, for he threw himself onto the bed and buried his face in the bolster.

'You wanted to be a player,' I said. 'You are very, very good.'

From the bolster came the muffled sounds of crying.

'John,' I put my hand on his shoulder. 'John, what's the matter?'

He tensed, and flicked at my hand as he would at a fly.

'Talk to me. Tell me what's upset you.'

'I'm not really your son,' he said through sobs. 'I'm not. I'm Adam Rowley's son. You told me so yourself.'

'We were pretending, John.' I spoke gently, doing my best to soothe. 'And you were very good. When we get to London, the players will take you as one of their own.'

'Adam said that we shouldn't pretend. It's lying. Adam told us that theatres are bad places. He said that pretending to be what we're not will prevent us from returning to the Fullness.' It reminded me of the way that Constance sometimes parroted Rowley's insane teachings. One moment he seemed to have calmed, the next he started crying again. There was no reasoning with the infection of Adam Rowley's madness wherever it appeared. I held myself in check, and silently cursed Rowley. *Damn your father. Damn his lies. And damn it that you don't despise him, John.*

And that's what you want, is it, Matthew? For John to despise his real father so he can love you all the better?

Rowley's actions killed you, Constance. It would be best for John to forget that Rowley ever existed.

And now he has to put his trust in you, and make his first journeys away from Wittenham across wild country to faraway places that he's never heard of.

It was you persuaded me to bring him.

Don't blame me for doing what you wanted to do. Not me who's forcing him to collude in your games and your deceit.

The boy has to learn how to survive in this world. It's for his own good.

It's for you, Matthew. You get a thrill from cheating.

Gilthead wanted the butterfly brooch. He'd have happily cheated us.

None of it was yours to sell.

If I'd not taken it, that jewellery would all have turned molten and dribbled into the ashes of Rowley Hall.

You've been exploiting the boy. And when you get to Canterbury and you find your beloved Kate, you'll abandon him.

No.

Just as you abandoned me.

No.

Why keep the ring?

Enough.

A gift for Kate?

No.

What then?

I wear it. Don't you see? I'm playing the widower. The ring's my costume.

Is that why you're playing at being the kind father too?

I'm playing the father. I admit to that. But if I'm kind that's because he brings it out of me.

She didn't respond to that.

After good food and a long sleep in a warm bed John was in better spirits the next morning.

The Deacon in Winchester had been most helpful. I followed his directions and recommendations. We stopped at respectable inns and paid for their best rooms and good stabling for Mary. And John assumed the part of my son, the speaking part now, with growing confidence.

It was me who grew increasingly distracted as we came ever closer to Canterbury. How would I find Kate? How would she take to John? Would she even want to talk to this stranger whose face had been burned away in an Oxfordshire tithe barn?

We arrived at Canterbury in late afternoon, stopping just outside Worth Gate. I dismounted, then lifted John down.

'Are we here, Matthew?' The excitement in his eyes that I should have been feeling. 'Are we here?'

'I think so.'

'Is something wrong?'

'No. Of course not. Nothing's wrong. We're here. At last.'

PART THREE

32
Fever and gossip

'Where's Mary?'

'We don't need her now. It's easier to walk.'

The boy had grown fond of her. I wondered if he'd spent more of his young life with horses than with people? Better than spending it with Adam.

'Where is she, Matthew?'

'Where's who?'

'Mary. The horse.'

'We're walking. Canterbury's not a big city.'

We'd arrived just over a week before. And although my head was full of Kate and how to find her, I knew better than to go looking for her that same night. John was tired and barely able to keep his eyes open. The first inn we came to had room for us, but no stabling for the mare. The landlord recommended The White Hart, close by West Gate. They had a stall in the stables for the mare. The ostler took charge of her while John and I found the innkeeper, Master Cooper, a short man with a face as round as a baby's arse and a nose that glowed red as a lantern fuelled on brandywine.

'You have a room for tonight?' I asked.

He looked at John, who could barely keep his eyes open, he looked at my face that was no longer a face. Then he looked at my fine leather boots, well stitched doublet, dark blue cloak and wide-brimmed black hat.

'For you and the boy?'

'And for our horse. I've already spoken to your ostler.'

'Show me your purse.'

I showed him.

'I'll have the maid, Ellen, show you to your room.'

Ellen was just a few years older than John. She barely spoke as she led us up stairs and along a corridor to a room at the back. It was better furnished than any we'd had since we set out on our travels: the four-poster bedstead was curtained, as was the window, the wood-panelled walls boasted hangings and lanterns, the floor had rugs rather than rushes, and in the corner furthest from the door stood a table with a large bowl and a jug of water.

John went straight to the bed and lay down. He was asleep before the maid turned to go.

'Here, Ellen.' I pulled a silver penny from my purse and put it in her palm. Wide-eyed in disbelief, she thanked me profusely and went on her way. I ate well that night, but John was difficult to rouse and said he wasn't hungry. Soon after I went to bed he started coughing and tossing and turning. He threw off the bedclothes, then moaned in his half-sleep that he was too cold. By morning I knew he had a fever.

I'd been dreaming of Kate for months, imagining the day when we'd meet again, yearning for the day when I'd get to Canterbury and knock on the door of the house where she was living. And yet I spent those first days in Canterbury at John's bedside. The silver penny I gave to the maid was well spent. She found a nurse to help me look after the boy.

There were moments when I thought I would lose him; moments when I was shocked at my own distress. Less than a fortnight before I'd wanted to leave him in Abingdon, hadn't wanted him coming with me. At Rowley Hall, he'd thought I might be his father. And that's the story I'd told on our journey. Tell a story often enough, and you almost believe it.

But in the nightmares of John's delirium, it was Adam he called for. Who can ever know the dreams and terrors of others? But I could almost smell the burning flesh as the boy thrashed about in that four-poster bed, sweating for all he'd lost, screaming for Adam and Franklin, Godwyn and Sarah.

There were moments when I wished that I'd persuaded Agnes to come with us, for she would surely have had better remedies than anything the nurse gave to the boy. If anybody could have calmed his terrors, it would have been Agnes. When I was in the room alone with him, I took out the hagstone she gave me, as if that might have powers to heal him. But I didn't know how to use it. I clutched it in my hand, gently placed my hand on his sweating forehead. And felt foolish. Despite that, I did it every day.

I must have looked sickly myself when I talked to the innkeeper. But it was worry I was sick with, not plague nor whatever fever had taken hold of John. I asked if we could stay another night. He was delighted to take my money, and I was too worried about John to waste time haggling over the price.

A second night's stay became a third, and then a fourth. And a fifth. We were there for more than a week. By which time the boy had sweated out his fever and emptied my purse. To this day I still wonder whether the strange powers of Agnes's hagstone had anything to do with his recovery, but he was no longer drenched in sweat, and his appetite seemed to be returning, though he was weak and slept for much of each day. The nurse said he should stay abed for several more days. I could have taken him with me as I searched for Kate. But we had nowhere to stay except The White Hart, so I sold the mare. If I hadn't been so desperate, I'd have got a better price. But needs must. In any other town I'd have found ways to make money. After Oxford I was wary of cards and dice, but I had the picklock wires, and wherever there are locks to be unpicked, there is money behind those locked doors, and valuables too. But we were in Canterbury. And Kate was in Canterbury.

Ellen, the maid, promised to take John food and drink. She was delighted to be asked. I think she'd rather taken to young John – and the small change I gave her.

Although I still carried Forman's casebook and letters between him, Frances Howard and Rochester, I'd not forgiven myself for leaving my precious letter from Kate in The Crown in Oxford. But I'd read it so any times that I still remembered every word. Anne, Doctor Forman's widow, had cared for Kate when she was sick with a fever after being pulled from the River Thames. Her letter said Anne would take Kate with her when she moved back to Canterbury, where Anne was born and her father was a proctor in the cathedral.

The skies were grey and the air was cold when I set off for the cathedral. It was almost as shabby as Paul's in London, though without the hordes of beggars and vagabonds that haunt Paul's. But I wasn't there for shelter or for work – and not for worship either, though I made a show for the benefit of the clergy. I needed someone to tell me where I might find Simon Forman's widow, Anne.

Knowing that my no-face could be an asset, I told a similar story to the one I'd used in Winchester. Canterbury's Deacon was more troubled by my appearance than moved by my misfortunes. But over the years I've learnt many different kinds of patience. And I pieced together the information I needed from his ramblings. Anne Forman had been Anne Baker before she married Simon. Her father had passed away several years before. Knowing that Anne wanted to leave her London life behind, along with her dead husband's infamous reputation as a practitioner of the dark arts, I guessed she might be calling herself Mistress Baker again.

I wanted to track her down as quickly as possible, but the Deacon was proud of his church and insisted on showing me where Thomas-a-Becket was murdered. As we were standing in the transept, a crowd of thirty or forty men, women and a few children, came in through a side door. They entered in silence, and were dressed smartly, as for worship. The Deacon asked me to wait for him while he found a key amongst the many he had on a chain hanging from his belt. He walked over to a small door, which he unlocked. Their leader bowed his head and quietly thanked him. The Deacon unhooked a lantern from the wall and gave it to him. Then the whole gaggle passed through the doorway and into a dark passage. The Deacon shut the door behind them, but didn't lock it.

'Frenchies mostly,' he said. 'A few Dutch. We allow them to worship in the crypt.' Alice and her family were Dutch, I thought, and wondered if she and her brother were amongst them, although I hadn't recognised any faces.

Madam Gossip is a troublesome enemy, but she can sometimes be your friend. In a small place like Canterbury, she knows about the arrival of strangers even before they've removed their boots. She would certainly know about me and John. But she'd also have made it her business to follow the fortunes of a woman who'd left home to marry a man with Forman's reputation. I suspect Madam Gossip knew more about Anne than Anne did herself. And that was how I learnt that she'd come back from London with her only son and a mysterious woman. Some said this woman was a cousin, others thought she was her sister-in-law. All agreed that the two women and the boy had taken up lodgings in a house in Castle Street.

It was just after midday when I knocked on the door of Rose Cottage.

33
A stranger at the door

I knocked, then stepped back and waited.

The clouds were growing heavy, and I wondered whether it might snow later.

I knocked again.

A light flickered in a downstairs window. Footsteps clacking on a flagstone floor. A key turning in the lock. A bolt sliding back. The door opened ajar. A young boy stood looking up at me.

'Good day to you, sirrah.' As if he were the gentleman usher.

'And good day to you, boy.' He smiled. Perhaps he hadn't yet seen my featureless face, which would have been silhouetted against the darkening sky.

'Is your name Clement?'

He nodded, and took a step back, suspicious of this stranger who knew his name.

'I've heard about you, Clement. Good things, I promise.'

I crouched down to his level. He would have to see my face sooner or later. I knew it might frighten him. But keeping it hidden would speak of shame, and that's always frightening to a child.

His eyes widened. But he didn't run away.

'I was in a building that caught fire. I escaped with my life. It took a while to heal. But when it did, I was left with this for a face.' I laughed, a feeble attempt to set him at ease. He sniffed and swallowed, not knowing what to say.

'Is your mother at home?' I asked quietly.

She was. I heard her footsteps descending a wooden staircase. A door opened at the end of the small hallway. She walked through. I stood up to greet her.

'Clement. Come back inside. It's cold.' She had a lantern in one hand. With the other, she gently ushered Clement away. 'Go inside.' He backed off, but only to the staircase, where he climbed a couple of steps and sat down to watch.

'Anne Baker?' I said.

We were standing less than a yard apart, looking at each other eye to eye. I half expected her to slam the door on me. But she was still looking at a stranger, not Matthew Edgworth.

'Anne Baker?'

'Yes?' Clement was standing half way up the staircase, trying to see what was going on.

'I've come to thank you,' I said quietly.

'To thank me?' she said, holding the door tight.

'May I come inside? There's a cold wind, and my face is raw. I'll make no demands on you, Mistress.'

'Yes. Yes, of course. Come in.'

She opened the door and led me through to the kitchen at the back of the house. Thankfully, it was warmed by a bread oven, and not an open fire, for I was still gripped by terrors at the sight of flames.

She gestured for me to sit, but she remained standing.

'Who are you that wants to thank me?'

Should I tell all? Or nothing? Continue with a version of the tale I'd almost learnt to believe? Invent myself as Kate's cousin?

'In August of last year, you gave shelter to Katherine Garnam. You saved her life.'

Her eyes narrowed and her head turned slightly to one side. Still curious, but guarded.

'Katherine couldn't read nor write, and so she dictated a letter which you put to paper. You took it to a carter in Southwark. You asked him to deliver it to Richard Weston at The Mermaid Tavern. The letter was addressed to Matthew Edgworth.'

The colour drained from her face. 'Matthew Edgworth.' She spoke the words in a chilled whisper, as if to do so was to invoke some minor devil. 'You killed my husband.'

'I am Matthew Edgworth, yes, Mistress. But your husband's death was not my doing.'

'I saw you with him. I was watching from an upstairs window.'

How long ago was that? More than a year ago. Imprinted on her memory. The last time either of us saw Forman alive.

'I was talking to him. Not poisoning him. I was horrified when I learnt of his death.'

She shook her head.

'Mistress … Do I call you Anne? Mistress Baker? Or what should I call you?'

'How dare you come here? How dare you talk to my son?'

However vigorously I protested my innocence, what she saw from that upstairs window of the Forman house on the edge of Lambeth Marshes was an argument between the husband who cheated on her and the man she saw as cruel and brutal. She was angry with Simon when he lived – I'd seen it, I'd heard it when I was with them together in Forman's study – and she was even more angry with him for dying. And there always has to be someone to blame.

But she'd written that letter which Kate dictated, and she'd addressed it to me. That gave me a glimmer of hope.

'I came to thank you for giving sanctuary to Kate. You saved her life.'

She nodded a reluctant acknowledgement. 'And now you've said your thanks. Now go.'

'Will you hear me out, Mistress? You've seen my face. That alone will tell you that I am not the man you once thought to be a great deceiver.'

'Say it. Say whatever you have to say, then begone.'

'I was told that Doctor Forman died when his heart failed as he was rowing across the Thames. I knew nothing of his death until several days later. I had my suspicions then that it wasn't a natural death. I feared he'd been poisoned. But not by me. Your husband's death put me in fear of my own life. I don't know who tried to kill Kate. But I know who ordered it.'

Still not meeting my gaze, she said quietly under her breath, 'Katherine spoke of that.'

'The man I worked for was Viscount Rochester. Frances Howard called him Robert. It was he who forced your husband to make poisons. I merely delivered his instructions. Rochester wanted me to kill Simon if he wouldn't do his bidding. I refused. That's why, when I heard of Simon's death, I suspected Rochester ordered it. And that's why I was certain he'd have me disposed of as soon as I was no longer of use to him. Rochester wanted rid of Kate. And he wanted rid of me.'

She looked up. 'Your face? Is that – ?'

It would have been easy to say that Rochester tried to have me burnt alive. But I didn't. I told the truth – or most of it. I told her of feigning my death in Cope Castle, of my broken ribs and smashed hand. I told her how I made my way to Oxford and was walking from there to Newbury when I stopped to rest in a tithe barn which caught fire, and how close I came to death myself. And how I was nursed back to health in a village near Abingdon in Oxfordshire. I said nothing of the cheaters from Oxford chasing after me, and nothing of Adam Rowley's crew and his madness because even I could hardly believe what had happened. I was about to tell how a young boy who'd been orphaned when he lost his parents in a house fire had attached himself to me – but Anne interrupted, and asked if I was hungry.

She produced a bowl of hearty soup and bread to go with it. She relaxed enough to sit down with me.

'You didn't come to Canterbury to thank me for looking after Katherine.'

'I did, indeed, want to thank you. But I also came to find her.'

'Katherine may not want to be found.'

'The letter she dictated – '

'The letter said I'd bring her with me to Canterbury. It didn't ask you to follow.'

'That's not what I remember.'

'I know what I wrote, and I advised her not to ask you to follow. And she was well advised, don't you think? Because even without writing that, she expected you. She believed in you. And you disappointed her. More than sixteen months have passed since I wrote that letter for her.' She was staring at me now. Trying to read what passed for my face. 'Katherine loved you, Matthew, more fool her.'

'It took nine months for that letter to reach me. And that was no fault of mine. I was desperate to believe that Katherine had survived. By the time I finally read it I'd almost given up hope.'

She looked sceptical.

'Katherine asked you to take the letter to the carter who'd worked for me. He would deliver it to the Mermaid Tavern, where I often met with Richard Weston. Yes?'

She nodded. At least we agreed on that.

'But Katherine had never been to any London inns. She'd heard me talk of The Mermaid. But most wharves and docks by the Thames have their own Mermaid. Bill Carter delivered Kate's letter to A Mermaid – but not one that I'd ever been in.' I tried to smile in the hope that would convince her of the truth of what I was saying.

'This is very fine soup. Thank you.' I lifted the bowl to drink the last drops.

Anne was still a fine-looking woman. I'd thought that when I paid my calls on her husband. Her face had filled out a little since last I saw her. Maybe widowhood suited her better than she'd admit to? If I hadn't been so obsessed with finding Katherine, those beautiful emerald eyes would have been most beguiling.

I put the bowl back down. She was staring at my hands.

'You seek out Katherine, but you're married.'

'Katherine is the only woman I have ever loved.'

'And yet you're married.'

I'd been trapped by my own carelessness. Half-truths are always half-lies, however well-intentioned. They're the ones that catch you out.

I removed the ring and placed it on the table. 'I'm not married, Anne. Given the hand that Fate is dealing me, I never will be. I bought the ring from a pawnbroker. I've been wearing it this past fortnight. I've grown so accustomed to wearing it that I'd forgotten I had it on.' If there'd been time and I'd thought for a moment she'd believe me, I'd have told her the truth. But the story made sense, and there was some truth in it.

She looked unconvinced. 'Why? Why buy a wedding ring? Why wear it when you're not married?'

'There's a boy, John, who suffered a terrible loss when his parents were both killed in a house fire. I took care of him for a while.' I couldn't begin to explain what happened at Rowley Hall. 'He seemed to feel safe with me. I brought him with me.'

'You brought a child with you to Canterbury!' She sounded incredulous. 'Where is he now?'

'John is about the same age as Clement. We took lodgings at The White Hart. We arrived about ten days ago. He fell into a fever. I've been with him until this morning. I think it's passed. But he still seems weak.'

'You left him?'

'I hired a nurse when the fever was at its worst. I know what you're thinking. Matthew Edgworth caring for a child.'

'You don't know what I'm thinking.'

'These past few months, I've been as close to Hell as any man can get. You can surely see that in my face. I've not told you the half of it because the truth is too horrific. I've been wearing the ring to convince innkeepers I was a widower. They took pity on me.'

'And now you expect the same from me?'

I expect nothing from you, Mistress Anne. I am grateful to you for – '

'Yes. I know. For the soup and for giving Katherine sanctuary. You're repeating yourself.'

'Would you like me to start again? Tell you the whole truth in all its horrors?'

'I'd like you to leave. Go back to The White Hart and the boy – if he exists. Come back tomorrow. Bring him with you.'

She showed me to the door. Outside, night had fallen, and with it the first flakes of snow.

34
Snowfall

'Where's Mary?'

'We're walking. We don't need to ride.'

'Where are we going?'

'To see a friend of mine.'

'Will he like me?'

'She's looking forward to meeting you. She has a son. Clement. The same age as you.'

That silenced him. It was easy to forget that he'd spent so little of his short life with other children.

More snow had fallen overnight. At least three, maybe four inches underfoot. Icicles were already growing from overhanging eaves.

'Is it far?'

'A few hundred yards.'

'Can we see Mary first?'

'You've been sick with a fever. I had to pay for the room at the inn 'til you recovered, and for a nurse to care for you. There was no more money in my purse. I had to sell her, John. It's not what I wanted.'

'Can I say goodbye to her?'

'I don't know where she is. The ostler knew someone.'

He sniffed, and slowed.

'Come on. It's cold. We need to walk quicker.' I took hold of his hand. He dragged his feet in the snow, and grumped silently until we were standing outside Rose Cottage. I knocked.

'Please, John. Try to smile. I know you're upset. But the woman who lives here might give us food and shelter. Don't sulk.'

'I'm not sulking. Mary liked me. That's what you said.'

'When the snow melts, I'll ask the ostler where she is, and maybe we can visit her.'

He said nothing. No sign of life in the cottage. I knocked harder. Snow slid from the slope of the thatch. No light in any window.

'Aren't they at home?' said John.

'Maybe they're at the back of the house, and can't hear us,' I said. But what I feared was that Anne had thought better of it and was avoiding me. But we walked round the back. And what we saw – no, what John saw, for I was in a cloud of despair and hardly saw the path in front of me – were footprints in the snow. We traced them to a small porch. Inside this, on a bench at the side, was a large round stone used as a paperweight to hold down a letter addressed to Matthew Edgworth. I recognised the hand, for it was Anne's, and it was she who'd written Kate's letter for her all those months ago.

> *Matthew,*
> *Clement and I have gone to speak with Katherine.*
> *We will return to the house before nightfall.*
> *Anne.*

'Can I read it?' said John.

'You can try.'

He recognised Matthew, but none of the other words.
'Show me.'

I read it aloud and traced the words with my fingers.
'Who's Clement?'

'Anne's son. He's about the same age as you.'

'Will he like me?'

'I'm sure he will.'

'Who's Katherine?'

'She's a friend of Anne, who lives here.'

'What do we do now?'

'We find somewhere warm to shelter. Then we come back just before nightfall.'

'Why don't we go in the house?'

'It's not our house, John.'

'But it's cold.' He tried the door. It was locked.

'Can't we pick the lock?'

'Anne is my friend, John. I don't want to frighten her.'

'All shall be shared,' he said, as from a pulpit. 'That's what my father said.' *My job to be my father now that he is dead.* Neither of us had forgotten.

When John and I called into the cathedral in Winchester it was already dark, and his thoughts were elsewhere. He hardly seemed to notice the building itself. When we entered the cathedral close in Canterbury the sun had briefly broken through, and the church seemed to glow. I'd taken little notice when I was there the day before, but John gasped and gazed in awe. His sense of wonder was infectious. Even I was impressed by the sheer size of the place, and the way that it stood alone in all its majesty. Paul's is surrounded by houses and the busy throng of pamphleteers and those crowding to the *Si Quis* door to find work.

'What is it?' said John.

'What's what?'

He pointed to the cathedral.

'It's a church. We're going to seek shelter there until Anne and Clement get home.'

'Why's it so big?'

Why indeed! Adam Rowley would no doubt have had something to say about that, something I might have agreed with for once. Not that Rowley would ever have allowed John near a church.

John had so many questions – most of which I couldn't answer. Why so many statues of people lying down with their hands steepled together on their chests? Why the windows with glowing, coloured pictures? Why the pillars? Why the strange ceilings? I enjoyed his curiosity – until it grew tiresome. Perhaps I should have sought the Deacon and asked him to show the boy around. But I didn't want John to let on that he'd never been to church. We might yet need the Deacon's goodwill.

Eventually, John's mind of many wonders grew weary. His questions and his chattering slowed to a halt, and we settled in a dark corner, where he fell asleep. I covered him with my cape, gave him my knapsack for a pillow and sat beside him, waiting for the day to pass, adrift in wonderings of my own.

I was startled by the clatter of boots on the tiled floor. Without meaning to, I'd brought us to the place I'd been the day before when the Deacon had shown the crowd of Frenchies through the door that led to the crypt.

They waited patiently. The cathedral clock bells rang out three. The Deacon appeared and, just as he had the day before, he handed their leader a lighted lantern, unlocked the door, ushered them through, then closed it behind them. It seemed to be a ritual as regular as Mattins or Evensong. I paid more attention this time, wondering if I might see Alice, her mother or little brother Frans. But nobody was looking in our direction. They filed through the small door, down into the crypt, leaving clumps of caked snow from their boots on the stone floor, snow which slowly melted into puddles.

I nudged John awake. It would soon be getting dark outside. 'We must be on our way.'

'What if your friend's not there?' It was the question I'd been asking myself.

'She will be.'

It must have been snowing for most of the day, softening the features of this town I hardly knew. We walked down what I thought was Castle Street, but snow had turned sharp angles to soft curves. And the sky was heavily clouded. The boy said nothing, but clung to me. For warmth? For comfort? For the promise that I'd take good care of him.

'Is this the house?' He looked sullen. 'John?' He shrugged. The snow had shifted the shapes of all it swathed. And we had no lantern.

'Let's go round the back again. Make sure this is the right house. We'll recognise the little porch.' I tried to sound cheerful. But I was fearful that we might have to seek charity from the clergy, and spend the night huddled in a corner of the nave with the most miserable of Canterbury's beggars.

Snow had drifted up against the left side of the house, but the right side was in the lee of the wind and the path was clear.

I knew before we knocked on the door. It was indeed Anne's house. But there were no lanterns lit inside. What remained of wintry sunlight was fading from the sky, but there was enough to see that ours were the first tracks in the snow. Anne and Clement hadn't returned. I sat down on the bench in the porch.

'What do we do?' said John.

'Hush you. I'm thinking. Come in here for a moment.'

Anne had seemed to soften to me the day before. I'd believed her when she said she'd get word to Kate. Was that her way of ridding herself of a man who brought her nothing but misfortune and trouble?

I got to my feet, knocked on the door. The sound was muffled by snow. I pulled the dagger from my boot, the dagger I'd taken from Parson Benson and banged the hilt on the door.

Nothing. John fiddled in his pockets, then nudged me. 'Matthew.' He showed me a small length of bent wire. One of the picklock keys we'd fashioned back in Rowley Hall.

'Shall I try?' he said.

'I don't think Anne would like that.'

'We can light a fire. We'll be warmer in the house than in that big church place.'

'If she wanted us to go into the house, she'd have said so in her letter. She'd have left a key with a neighbour.'

He already had the wire in the lock, and was fiddling.

'No, John.'

'Why not?'

'I've told you why not.'

'I can do it. Listen.' He moved the lever inside the lock.

'I said no.' I grabbed his arm and pulled it away. He squealed.

I fiddled with the picklock wire to remove it from the keyhole, and realised that he'd already unlocked it. He was indeed a quick learner. I slipped the wires back in, and relocked it. John looked puzzled and resentful.

I don't know what stopped me from finding a stick and giving John the beating he deserved. Maybe I still hoped Anne would soon arrive and I didn't want her to see me thrashing him. Or maybe I feared John might run off into the night and I'd not see him alive again.

'We'll knock the door of the neighbour,' I said. 'I'm sure they'll offer us shelter.'

The neighbour took one look at my face and slammed the door on us.

35
Children's games

John saw the two lanterns before I did. Lights wavering in the darkness and moving towards us as we were walking back up Castle Street. The air was thick with snow, blown horizontal on the wind.

'Anne?' I called.

'Matthew?'

We exchanged no pleasantries in the lane. She led us round to the back, unlocked the door and ushered us in.

There was still a little warmth from the fire beneath the bread oven. She opened the fire door. Embers were glowing. I offered to bring in firewood. She told me where to find the wood store, and gave me a wickerwork basket. I volunteered John for carrying a lantern. He seemed glad to be asked. Clement, who'd not yet spoken, watched John warily and didn't come with us when we went out for the wood.

I cleared the path of drifted snow. We filled the basket with wood, brought it in and placed it by the oven. The fire door was open. Anne had already fed kindling onto the embers.

'Would you get the fire going, Matthew?'

I knelt down to do as she asked. A flame leapt up as the kindling took light. Instinctively, I pulled back and turned my head away. I couldn't put a log on the fire. To my surprise, John took the log from my hand and placed it on the burning kindling. Anne smiled, as if it had been an act we'd planned to show what a good boy he was; to reassure her that she could rely on him to help in the house.

We ate together that night, as the silence of snow fell heavy over Canterbury. The four of us at Anne's kitchen table. Soup and bread, ale and mead.

Anne had been looking for Katherine, as she'd said she would. Traipsing round in the cold with his mother all day had left Clement in a dark mood. I'm sure he also resented us, the unexpected, unwished for visitors.

'Katherine wasn't where I thought she'd be,' said Anne. 'She's moved to Faversham, a small port, about four hours' walk from Canterbury. Maybe an hour on horseback – in good weather. I've sent a message, telling her that you're in Canterbury, and asking if she would like to see you. You and the boy can stay here until I receive her reply – which may be several days because the road to Faversham is blocked with snow.' There was a strange formality about the way she spoke.

It seemed polite to respond in kind. 'Thank you Mistress Anne. That is very generous.'

'You think I'd be so cold-hearted as to throw you out in this weather?'

'No. But I thank you just the same.' And I took a spoonful of soup.

John broke the uneasy silence. 'We used to have a horse. But Matthew sold it.'

'Who's Matthew?' said Clement. The first time I'd heard him speak since we sat down to eat.

'I am.'

'But who are you?'

'Clement! Don't be so rude,' said Anne.

'He's my dad,' said John before I could answer.

Anne raised an eyebrow, but didn't ask the question – not then.

I'd hoped the boys might go to bed before me and Anne, but that's not what she wanted, and I was reluctant to suggest anything that she or Clement might interpret as interference in the way they lived their lives.

There was only one bed in the house, and that was in the upstairs room, where Anne slept with her son. Before going on up, Anne unlocked a heavy oak chest in the downstairs room at the front of the house, and removed three large woollen blankets for me and John. She gave us a lantern, then bade us goodnight, shutting and bolting the door to the stairs behind her.

I laid my cape on the flagstone floor, then folded two blankets over and lay them on it as a makeshift mattress. We wrapped ourselves in the other one, and curled up together for warmth. It was better than huddling with the beggars in the cathedral.

'Say nothing, John. Don't grumble. We have a roof over our heads.'

In the morning, I brought in more firewood. At least a foot of snow had fallen, and in places had been blown into deep drifts. But the sky had cleared and the wind had dropped.

'I have chickens and a pig,' said Anne. 'They'll need feeding. I'll come out with you.'

John and I busied ourselves with shovelling snow, clearing paths to the woodshed and the animal pens. Anne fed the livestock, and was delighted to find two eggs had been laid, despite the cold. We brought enough wood into the house to last for several days. Clement stayed inside. When we went back in, he was sitting at the kitchen table with a book. 'He likes reading,' said Anne. 'Takes after his father.'

There was much about him that reminded me of his father: high forehead, dark eyes and thick black hair which fell in ringlets. It may not be fair to call a child aloof when he was probably just shy and unused to the company of other children. But I saw a boy who'd learnt to expect his mother's undivided attention and resented the intrusion of strangers. I wondered what he'd make of his father's casebook, which I still had secure in the inside pocket of my doublet.

'Your chickens are quiet,' I said.

'They must be flummoxed by the snow,' said Anne. 'But the fox hasn't broken in to the coop. And there are no paw prints nearby. Small mercies.'

I could see that John wanted to talk to Clement, perhaps to play with him. But didn't know how.

'I can read,' said John. My heart sank. I wanted to protect him from his own clumsiness, and was relieved when Anne asked Clement to put his book away while we took breakfast.

'Frumenty porridge.' She ladled out for each of us.

I had so many questions to ask Anne, but felt restrained while John and Clement were with us.

'Do you have any marbles, Clement?' I asked. He nodded, but looked suspicious. 'Shall we play?'

He went upstairs and came back down with a small wooden box full of glass marbles.

'Come on John. The three of us can play while Clement's mother goes about her business.'

We went through to the front room, where John and I had slept the night before. Clement's marbles, with their twisting threads of colour inside glass, were a thing of wonder to John. Even the little wooden box was unusual. It was crafted from a dark wood, with ornately carved patterns on the lid, and lined with dark blue velvet. I wondered if Simon Forman had had it made specially for the boy?

'What rules do you play, Clement?'

'Don't you know them?'

'I know several different games of marbles. Let's play the game you know.'

I knelt down between the two boys. We played by Clement's rules. John picked it up quickly. But Clement won most of the games – which was probably just as well, for I suspected he'd not learnt to lose with good grace. When John's throwing began to improve and the marbles rolled where he wanted them to, I thought that was the time to stop.

'You win, Clement,' I said.

'No, he doesn't,' said John.

'He does today, John. Maybe we can play again tomorrow if we're still here.'

'Are you going to be here tomorrow?' said Clement.

'I don't know.' I said. 'Maybe. Do you have any puppets?'

He shook his head.

'Have you seen a puppet show?'

He had. In the summer they sometimes set up a booth and played in the yard at The Chequer of Hope. John looked puzzled, and on the edge of falling into a sulk. Had Rowley damned puppets as profane enormities?

'Have you seen plays with grown men playing the parts?' I asked.

'The players came last summer,' said Clement. That piqued John's interest. 'Mother took me to see them at the inn near Westgate.'

In the oak chest where Anne kept the blankets, I'd noticed various fabrics – wool, and linen, a small hessian sack, even some small pieces of silk and velvet. The boys watched as I wrapped some undyed linen around my hand. I found a piece of charred wood in the fireplace, and used that to draw two eyes on it. Then, moving my thumb and fingers as a mouth, 'Tell me boy. You have a name?' In a reedy, high-pitched voice.

John looked puzzled.

Clement hesitated before proudly announcing himself.

'And who is your friend?'

'John.'

'What's yours?' said Clement to my gloved hand.

I put the hand behind my back and whispered, 'What do you think his name is? Or is he a she?'

They both shouted out names. All boys' names. 'He's shy,' I said. 'Let me talk to him.'

The hand came out from behind my back. 'They want to know your name.'

I put my hand to my ear, and whispered a muffled gibberish.

'What do you say?' I said to the hand.

More mumbling.

'He says he'll only tell one of you. Clement nudged John forward. I put the hand to John's ear and said, 'Barnaby,' one of the names that Clement had suggested.

'What did he say?' pretending I'd not heard.

'Barnaby,' said John.

314

And so Barnaby gradually overcame his shyness and talked to John and Clement. After a while Barnaby confessed that he was lonely because his best friend was still in the wooden chest. Together we made another hand puppet and gave that one a name. Jenkin. Where Barnaby's voice was squeaky, Jenkin was gruff and impatient.

'Who asked you to wake me up?' Jenkin grumbled.

Barnaby asked for the boys' help in trying to cheer up Jenkin. By now they'd lost the awkwardness they'd had around each other. Together we made up a play – which came to an end when Jenkin lost his temper with Barnaby and started calling him names. And the ruder the names, the more the boys laughed. The kitchen door opened. Anne looked round to see the source of such merriment.

'Stop, stop, stop,' I called to the puppets.

'No, no, no,' chorused Clement and John.

'I tell you, Jenkin, if that be your real name,' said I. 'You are being far too rude. Mistress Anne will be most distressed to see such vulgarity in her good house.'

'Smelly fish-breath,' said Barnaby – to me this time. I pantomimed horror that he'd turned against me. Which made the boys laugh even more.

'I told you to stop. No more insults.' Me, Matthew, to both of the puppets.

A pause. The puppets looked to the boys for approval, which they nodded vigorously. Then turned back to me: 'Warty hog-grubber,' growled Jenkin.

'Knave i' your faces, you rogues,' said I. 'How dare you call me such a thing!'

At which the two puppets froze. They glared at me. Mouths agape. They looked at the boys. Then they started to beat me about the head.

'Help,' I cried. 'Clement. John. Help me. Help! They're attacking me.'

The boys screamed with laughter as they each grabbed an arm.

'Tell them to stop,' I cried.

'You are not to attack Matthew,' said John, though there was mischief in his face as he said it.

I wanted time alone with Anne, and had thought to ask them to make up their own puppet play, but if I left them alone, they'd follow my example and squabbling puppets would soon become fighting boys. I'd enjoyed the uproar, but needed to calm them. So I sat down and asked them to sit with me.

'More puppets,' said Clement.

'Your mother says you like reading.'

'More puppets.'

I unwound the fabric and lay Barnaby and Jenkin down on the floor.

'What do you read?'

He looked quizzical and suspicious.

'Can you show me. Then maybe we can read together.'

He hesitated, then got to his feet and went through to the kitchen and whispered something to Anne. He came back holding a key, then went upstairs. When he came down, he had a book in his hand. To my astonishment, it was a play.

A Midsommer nights dreame
written by William Shakespere

'You read this?' I asked. He nodded.

'You like it?' He nodded some more.

'Did you see it acted when you lived in London?'

'Don't remember. Father used to go to The Globe and The Rose. Mother says he wrote about the plays he saw. But she's never shown me his writings. Father talked about plays a lot.'

'I'm going to be a player when we go to London,' said John.

I squirmed in embarrassment for the poor boy, imagining that Clement would mock him for being fanciful. But he was more interested in showing me how well he could read.

> *"Now fair Hippolita, our nuptiall houre*
> *Drawes on apace."*

'What's a nuptial hour?' said John.

'When they're getting married,' said Clement. He was warming to John. They'd been suspicious of each other, and I was worried that they might fall to fighting, but John's curiosity about the play gave Clement the power of knowing.

'Who is?' asked John. 'Who's getting married?'

'Hippolyta and Theseus. They're a king and a queen.'

I'd seen the play often enough, but never taken much notice of it. It was the spectators I watched. *The Dream* is a perfect play for cutting purses. The laughs come in the same place every time. No better distraction. What I knew was that it had lovers and clowns. Country folk and fairies. And a mischievous spirit called Puck who turned a fool into an ass, and made a queen fall in love with a donkey – which was where the purses could best be tickled.

'Is it a funny play?' I asked Clement. 'Does it make you laugh?'

'Yes.'

'Can you find the funny bits?'

He thumbed through the book.

'Can you read them with John?'

I left them with cloth to make their own puppets and a challenge to see if they could bring *The Dream* to life to entertain me and Anne.

In the kitchen, Anne was kneading dough.

'Enough for just two loaves. The last of the flour.'

'Tell me where the mill is, and I'll get us a sack of flour.'

'Suppose it snows again?'

'Then it will take me a little longer.'

'You're not the man I thought you were.'

'I'm not the man I thought I was.'

She smiled. 'Clement doesn't have many friends. I don't often hear him laughing.'

'I like playing with them.'

She looked down at the dough. Big hands. Strong hands. The hands of a woman who did things for herself. Who didn't rely on a man. She turned the dough and slapped it down on the floured table. 'Who is he?' she said, without looking up at me.

'Who is who?'

'John. The boy.'

'I told you.'

'You told me something. I don't think you told me the truth. Are you his father?'

'No. He's an orphan.'

'Last time I saw you, you were wearing a wedding ring. Today you're not.'

'I no longer need to play that part.'

'So what part are you playing today?'

She lifted the dough. Slapped it back down on the table, raising a light mist of flour. From the front room came the sound of the boys' laughter. Still looking down, she said, 'The part of a kind man who cares for the boys? A good man who ventures out in the snow for a sack of flour? I don't like to mistrust people, Matthew. But I don't know who you are. Your face is a testament to suffering. Your manner with young John tells me more than any stories. And yet.' She stopped herself.

'And yet you still think I had something to do with your husband's death? And you can't forgive me that?'

She continued wrestling with the dough, but said nothing.

'You had every reason to despise me, to keep me away from your husband. I understand that. But I swear to you I've changed. I am indeed the man you see before you.'

'I don't know the man I see before me.'

'And yet you gave us food and shelter.'

'Common decency. Not something you ever knew much about.'

'And yet you took a message to Katherine for me.'

She divided the dough between two baking tins, then looked me in the eye. 'I wanted Katherine to have the choice about whether to see you, whether to accept you back into her life. If I'd turned you away, you'd have found her without my help. It might have taken you a little longer. But you would have found her.'

I walked over to the window. The snow was gleaming in bright sunlight.

'Tell me where the mill is, and I'll get us a sack of flour.'

'You'll need the donkey to carry it back. There's a saddle bag in the stable.'

'I don't have any money, mistress Anne.'

She opened a drawer in the kitchen table and took out a purse. She counted out five shillings. Put it on the table.

'You trust me with your donkey and your money?'

'It's not a matter of trust. I have something you want. You'll come back because you want to find Katherine. That doesn't make you trustworthy.'

I smiled with as good grace as I could muster. She added, 'Jeremiah Millward is the miller. Tell him the sack's for Anne Forman. They know I'm a widow. He always sells to me for a good price.'

I led the donkey through to the High Street. Snow from drifts which had been blocking doorways had been shovelled into piles in the street, which was thronging with the good folk of Canterbury, all going about their business while they still could.

I walked the donkey down to Mill Lane and followed the river upstream. It was in full flow, gurgling and churning as it emerged from the millrace, splashing liquid silver onto low hanging branches bejewelled with ice, gleaming crystal in the morning sun. A hundred yards or so along the lane stood the mill, where a few men and a score of women were queuing to buy flour. The fellow at the front was haggling with the millwife. People glanced at me, stared, then quickly looked away.

I tied the donkey to a post, and walked on round the side to the large double doors which gave access to the ground floor of the mill. They weren't locked. I wanted to strike a deal with the miller, not stand in a queue. The place was uncannily quiet. I called out. My voice echoing through the dark forest of beams and shafts. The only light a beam of bright sunlight from a high window. The place stank of hog's lard, used to grease the water shaft, the cogs and gears. Choking on the heavy, rancid air, I took a step inside. After the brilliance of sun on snow, it took a while for my eyes to grow accustomed to the dingy light. No sign of movement. I called out again. The building creaked beneath the weight of snow above; its ancient beams, made from the masts of old ships, groaning in longing for the sea. The sounds added weight to the silence.

I stood still, trapped in an unexpected yearning for Constance. She'd not spoken since we left Winchester. I'd found my way into the mill to buy direct from Master Millward. But I was thrown back to Constance and the fire that destroyed her family mill. I waited, expecting her to come to me.

Talk to me Constance. Speak to me. What am I doing here?

Something moving. A cat somewhere in the darkness? Or rats? The only sounds came from quietly creaking beams and water in the millrace splashing over the locked down millwheel.

Talk to me Constance.

Nothing.

I stood waiting. For what, I don't know. Didn't know then. Don't known now.

Anne said she didn't know who I was. But nor did I. Seeking Katherine gave me some sense of purpose, and I'd been looking after John as best I could. But there in the darkness of Canterbury's Town Mill I felt utterly bereft because the ghost of Constance, or whatever it was, refused to speak to me.

36
A good husband

I took my place in the queue and waited. And in due course I bought a sack of flour from Jeremiah Millward himself. They'd ground enough corn to fill the loft with flour, to last til New Year, so the miller was working the shop with his wife. That's why the mill had been so quiet. I told him the sack was for Mistress Forman, and he did indeed give me a good price. He even had one of his millhands carry the sack for me and load it on the donkey. In all my dealings with millers I had never encountered one who had an ounce of generosity or kindness about him. Was the world turning upside down?

I feared the boys would be fighting by the time I got back. But Clement was in the kitchen, sitting by the bread oven, reading. John was playing with the puppets on his own. He had all the voices.

Anne thanked me. She seemed almost pleased to see me. Despite everything she'd said earlier, she welcomed me back into the house. I busied myself that afternoon, clearing snow from the paths, and doing various other household tasks.

Of the two boys, Clement was the more solitary child. Perhaps John growing up in the company of Rowley's crew hadn't been as damaging as I'd feared. He had, after all, been well cared for. There was, however, a self-sufficiency about him which troubled me even as I admired him for it.

'Did you like the play?' I asked.

'Don't know. Clement locked it away in the big chest. He said I was too slow.'

'You're not slow, John. You're a beginner. And you're learning fast. Reading takes time. You only started a few weeks ago.'

'He doesn't like me.'

'Did you fight?'

'No.'

'Did you argue?'

'No.'

'I think he likes you. Anne likes you. She told me so. I like you. Clement's not used to anyone else of his age in the house. He's not used to sharing.'

'*All shall be shared.*'

'I know that's what your father said, but – '

'You said it too.'

'I don't remember that.'

'When you got me to climb through the window of the Hall.'

'Maybe. But things are different here.'

He seemed to be about to say something. I sensed he was struggling with a sadness he had no words for.

'And there are other things you've learnt, young John, that you're very good at. Clement knows nothing of them.'

He stared at me quizzically. It wasn't my words he didn't understand, but what he was supposed to do with them.

I woke in the night. I lay still, listening for movement, thoughts racing. Something had woken me. John kicking in his sleep? Snow sliding from the roof? The silence lay heavy. The only sound was John's breathing. For the first time in ages, I started thinking about Rochester. Talking to Anne had taken me back, for it was Rochester who'd had me threaten Forman, Rochester who'd almost certainly had him killed. Did his web of intelligencers reach to Canterbury? Could word have reached him that Forman's widow had an unexpected visitor? If gossip had led me to Anne, gossip could lead Rochester's thugs to me.

Even if I found Katherine in the next day or so, and we married, settled in Canterbury, lived the quietest of lives, we would never be safe while Rochester could have us tracked down. There would come a time when I would have to return to London and fashion my revenge against him.

I took the dagger from under my pillow and crept through to the kitchen. It is what I've always done when I wake in the night. There was warmth from the bread oven. I opened the door, added coals to the embers. I was almost proud of myself for daring to get so close to the fire.

Be wary of pride, Matthew. There were no flames.

Do you mock me?

I merely warn you to be wary. Pride. And your thirst for vengeance. They could destroy you.

I'll not take preaching from you, Constance. I sought you out in the mill. Where were you then?

Are you angry with me for not appearing at your beck and call?

You come to me when I least expect it. Was it you who woke me?

Is that what you think? That I'm here to haunt you?

I don't know what to think.

I leaned forward. Reached across the table to take her hand. The room was warm, but dark. The darkness of ravens' wings at midnight. I put on an oven glove. Opened the fire door ajar to let some light into the room. Pans hanging from a ceiling beam caught the glow of the fire.

Constance?

Sit you down, Matthew.

I reached across to take her hand.

Why are you here? You said you wanted to come to Canterbury for your beloved Kate. But you're already settled with another woman. A woman you never spoke of.

I needed shelter for the boy while we're waiting to hear back from Kate.

How patient. Waiting with a young widow, accepting her food, her hospitality. Enjoying her company. The Matthew I knew was not such a patient man.

Anne knows why I'm here. I've been honest with her.

Honest? Always careful about what you say and don't say.

What I told her about her husband is the truth. And how could I tell her about Adam Rowley? There's nobody alive could understand the true extent of his madness.

She fell silent. But not for long.

Are you growing to like this life?

What life?

The life you have here. It's homely. I see you growing to like it very much.

I'm here to find Kate.

The Kate of your fantasies? The Kate of your dreams?

You think I came all this way in pursuit of a dream?

If Kate was who you really wanted, you'd have found her by now.

I'm doing all I can.

But already you're planning to leave her and return to London.

To ensure our safety.

By putting yourself in harm's way? Rochester's long forgotten about you. That's what you don't like.

People like Rochester don't forget. You can't possibly understand.

You collect a sack of flour. You bring in wood. You play with the boys. You clear the paths of snow. You put coals on the embers to bank up the fire. What I see is a man playing at being a good husband. I see a man enjoying it. I see things, and I hear things, Matthew. And what I see confuses me.

I was up at first cock crow. Before Anne and Clement. I left John to sleep on. I went through to the kitchen. It was warm. The embers in the fire beneath the bread oven still glowing. If I'd conjured Constance in a dream, then I'd banked the fire in my sleep.

There'd been a hard frost in the night. No more snow had fallen, and the sky was clear and already lightening. I fed the chickens and the pig. Collected wood and coal. Walking on frosted snow like crunching shards of splintered glass. But for the moment I was strangely contented. Constance could taunt me all she liked, but I could bide my time.

When I went back inside, Anne was in the kitchen. After breakfast I took the boys outside. Neither of them had made a snowman before. So that's what we did. And wherever there are snowmen there are snowball fights. The squeals of delight and peals of laughter brought Anne to the back door. She looked on in wonder. I left the boys playing and went to stand next to her.

'I didn't know he had it in him to laugh so much,' she said.

Soon after that, John grew tired of snowballs and wet from melting snow. He was shivering. 'You need to get warm, and dry,' said Anne. She gave him a bowl of soup, then took him upstairs to change into some of Clement's clothes. She came back down alone.

'He was shivering, Matthew. I said he could rest in my bed until he's warm.'

'Should I ask Clement to come in?' He'd wanted to make a snowman of his own.

'He's dressed for it. Let him stay out a little longer. I am so pleased to see him happy. He'll come back in soon enough if he gets cold.'

Anne and I alone in her kitchen.

'You're very good with the boys. You'll be a good father, Matthew. Hard to believe you're not already.'

And hard to know how to respond to that. I was minded to turn it into a jest against myself, but she meant it as a compliment, so I thanked her for it.

'You make it easy to be here, Anne. Yet you had good reason to turn me away.'

She gave me a small, knowing smile that gave me permission to say more.

'I didn't kill your husband, but you thought I did. And yet you make us welcome.' She looked away, perhaps considering how much to tell me.

'Simon was a complicated man.' She started slowly. 'You tried to force him to do things he didn't want to do. But he was flattered to include Frances Howard and Viscount Rochester amongst his clients. Lady Frances saw him several times. Private appointments which lasted several hours. You didn't force him to see her. He did that willingly. She was usually accompanied by her friend Anne Turner. Sometimes by her maidservant, Katherine. But the consultations were always private. The friend or the maid had to wait. My job to make conversation. I disliked the Turner woman. But I took to Katherine. She was full of life and had a generous spirit about her. I can see why you fell in love with her. Not so easy to understand why she fell for you!'

'I've often asked myself the same question.'

She allowed herself a quiet chuckle, then her expression changed. 'Simon kept nothing from me. You may not have corrupted him – I know that his dealings with the likes of Rochester were shady at best – but you did threaten him. He was frightened of you. He thought you utterly ruthless. He was frightened of what you might do to me and Clement if he refused to do your bidding.'

'It gives me no pleasure to be reminded of it. But I swear to you I had nothing to do with his death. I would never have harmed you or the boy, and I didn't want him dead.'

I don't know whether she believed me, but she nodded slowly, and spoke in a hushed voice, barely louder than a whisper, 'I also know that Simon had many enemies. And few friends who would speak up for him publicly. He told me things about the Lady Frances he should never have told me. He kept few secrets from me. I often wished he'd kept things more to himself. I didn't need to hear about his every dalliance.'

'Your maid?'

'Susan? Oh yes. One of many. Servants, ladies of the aristocracy, the wives of merchants and lawyers. Young and old. His appetite knew no bounds.'

'But even now you're loyal to his memory?'

'I loved him.'

'Whenever I saw you together, I saw hatred in your eyes.'

'How many times did you see us together?'

'Twice. Maybe three times.'

'What you saw was jealousy. And rage. Not hatred. He loved me, Matthew. He never stopped loving me. He never stopped wanting me. And despite everything, I loved him.'

'You forgave him his infidelities?'

'He never pretended he was anything other than the way he was. That was better than what many women have. I would rather have had Simon than a husband who stayed faithful, but cared nothing for me. In some ways I'm fortunate. I have no brothers nor sisters. My father bequeathed this house to me, and left me a small legacy. Not big enough to make it worth your while stealing. But enough to protect me from penury and the disaster of a second marriage to a man who resented Clement and cared little for me.'

'I don't deny that I threatened Simon. And I apologise for that. But I swear to you I never threatened harm against you or Clement.'

'I can never know the truth of what you said to Simon. But I don't have to forgive you. I'm not going to marry you, not going to share my bed with you.'

We sat for a while, not exactly relaxed in each other's company, but there was a curious absence of resentment in her demeanour.

'I'm surprised you're happy for me to play with your son.'

'He likes you. There is still something in you of that former Matthew, the man who would do whatever he thought was necessary to please his wretched master. But I can see that there is some good in you. Perhaps more than you ever knew yourself. Did it take the burning, the stripping off of half your face, to reveal that goodness to yourself?'

Night came early that afternoon as the sky grew dark with heavy snow clouds. Another foot of snow fell overnight. It took more than an hour the next day for us to dig ourselves out, and most of the morning to clear the paths to Castle Street.

No messenger came to the house that day with word of Katherine. Canterbury had been silenced by snowfall. Cut off from the rest of the world. As the days passed, and the city came back to life, my anxieties grew. Suppose Kate had married another? Suppose she was living with Alice and her family, and Alice had turned her against me. It had been nearly a year and a half since we were last together. Time enough for even the truest love to turn sour. When days stretched to a week, I even began to fear that she might be blaming me for the attempt to kill her at Fleet Bridge.

Anne and Clement were regular churchgoers. It was their custom to attend evensong every day, as well as the morning service on Saturday and Sunday. Once the paths were clear enough of snow to walk safely, they started going to the cathedral again.

'Would you like John and me to accompany you?'

'A widow and her son attending church with a strange man! The gossip would make my life Hell. The neighbours will talk anyway, but they like us. Saint Margaret's church will surely welcome you.

I surprised myself by attending the services at Saint Margaret's with John. As I sat there with him, and the preacher delivered his sermon, I wondered why I'd been so willing to go to church. Maybe to please Anne. More likely to spite Adam Rowley. I said my Amens dutifully, and I prompted John to do the same, but heard nothing of what the preacher was saying.

I asked John what he thought of going to church.

'I liked the singing.'

We stayed with Anne for another fortnight. John and Clement had their arguments, but with a little help and encouragement they sorted things out. On most days, Clement spent time teaching John to read, and even though he quickly grew impatient, he treated John like the younger brother he'd have liked. The city slowly returned to something like normal. But there was still no word from Katherine.

Then came the thaw. I went out one morning and the icicles were dripping, the edges of Castle Street were covered in brown slush. The snowmen had grown thinner overnight. That same evening, a knock came at the front door. A boy, maybe twelve years old, delivered a letter to Anne.

She read it, then handed it to me.

Katherine Garnam likes that Matthew Edgworth is alive.
She likes to see him. He must go to The Weavers House. *It is close by King's Bridge. We lead him.*

'How far to the weavers' house?'

'Less than half a mile. Ask for Katherine, and someone will take you to her. The last I heard she was in Faversham. It's ten miles or so from here.'

'Faversham?'

'Ask her. The letter says she will be pleased to see you. For now, be satisfied with that.'

37
To Faversham

We'd got no further than High Street when John asked, 'Where are we going?'

'We're going to meet our guide.'

'Where are they going to take us?'

'Faversham.'

'Where's that?'

There were times when I yearned for those days back at Wittenham when John lurked in the shadows and hardly spoke a word.

'I don't know. We'll find out soon enough.' I spoke slowly and quietly – doing my damnedest to suppress my impatience.

'Is it far?'

'I don't know. Anne thought about ten miles.'

'Can we get Mary back?'

Five shimmering feet of icicle broke from the eaves above, crashing down onto the cobbles just inches from where John was standing and bursting into a thousand shards. It spooked a drayman's horse, which reared. Half a dozen baying dogs appeared, snapping at the horse's legs. The drayman cracked his whip to shoo them off. A butcher arrived, shouting at the drayman to lay off his dog. I pulled John into a narrow alley to get him away from the affray.

'Can we?'

'Can we what?'

'Get her back?'

'I'd have to buy her back. And even if they were willing to sell, I don't have any money.'

'She likes me. And you sold that brooch in Winchester. You got lots of money for that. You said I was very good at playing that part in the goldsmiths.'

'John. Enough. I don't have a brooch to sell. We're going to the weavers' house, and from there to Faversham. I'll hear no more about it.'

He scowled.

'Don't sulk.'

'I'm not.'

'Then don't.'

'Why don't we go to a goldsmith here in Canterbury?'

'Because I don't have anything to sell.'

'I do.'

'What?'

He reached into a pocket and pulled out a small, jewelled brooch. 'See.' He grinned. 'We can find a goldsmith here and sell this.'

The commotion in the street had already melted into weary squabbling, but I led John further down the alley. I didn't want us to be overheard.

'Where did you get that?' hoping he'd brought it with him from Rowley Hall.

'I remembered what you taught me.' Which is what I feared. 'Upstairs, in their bedroom, there was another of those big chests, like the one where they kept the blankets and the cloth to make the puppets. I used the picklock wires to open the wooden chest. I've been practicing, Matthew. Just like you said.

It was easy. Inside it was a little wooden box. And that had a lock too. That was more difficult. But I did it.' He was talking fast. 'Can we? Can we find a goldsmith?'

I crouched down to talk to him eye to eye. 'What else did you take? From the jewel box.'

'Only the brooch.'

'Good.'

'I thought you'd be pleased. I thought you'd be proud of me. I didn't break anything. I even locked it all up again afterwards. Just like you said.'

'I am proud of you, John. Let me look at it.' It was a nice piece. He had a good eye. The brooch was valuable. It might be months before Anne noticed it was missing. And I could get a good price for it. Maybe not enough to buy back the mare, but I'd need money to set up with Katherine. The ring was still in my pocket, along with Forman's casebook and the letters. But they were the only things of value I still had.

'Matthew?'

'I'm thinking.' And what I was thinking was that Anne had been good to us. I couldn't repay her generosity with theft.

'Can we find a goldsmith man?'

'Maybe later.'

After Kate and I were reunited, we'd go back, the three of us. And while Anne was busy outside with the livestock, I'd put the brooch back in the box where John had found it. For now, we had to get to Faversham and Kate.

The weavers' house backed onto the river. I knocked the door and waited awhile before it opened. A woman stood before us. Short in height and gaunt of face. She wore a long brown leather apron and a worried expression. She might have been expecting us – but she backed away and looked at me wide-eyed when she saw my no-face.

'My name is Matthew Edgworth. The boy is John. Anne Forman said to come here.'

Her nod said she was expecting us, if not the way I looked.

'Anne told me that if we came here, someone would take us to Katherine Garnam.'

'Enter, please.' The accent was French. We walked into a simple, unfurnished hallway, little bigger than the pantry at Rowley Hall. She pulled the heavy front door shut behind us, locked it, and slid the bolts back. Even before we left the hallway, we could hear the muffled clatter and clanging of machinery. She opened a door to a room which was as long as the house, and throbbing with industry At least a dozen men and women were working looms and spinning wheels. The wooden floor shuddered as they stamped down on treadles, regular as soldiers on the march, but in time with no-one except themselves. The squealing of wheels that needed greasing, thwack of shuttles thrown back and forth, treadles banging up and down. I was put in mind of the female factory at The Bridewell, where I'd taken Alice for her own safety. More than two years ago now. I'd brought Alice and her family here to Canterbury. I half expected to see one of them now. Was she here, in this room? Was Alice to be our guide?

John stood and stared, bewildered and open-mouthed.

'Come,' said the woman who opened the door to us. She walked us through the weaving room to a kitchen, where a man was sitting on a bench. She said something to him – most of it in French. I understood our names and the word Faversham. The fellow stood up and turned for the back door.

'*Alors*, we go,' he said. 'Now. *Vite. Vite.*'

'Go,' said the woman. 'Go with Guillaume. He take you.' She flapped her hands at us to follow him out into the yard, where a two-wheeled cart had been loaded with bales wrapped in hessian. A donkey had already been harnessed to the cart. Guillaume, the carter, climbed up, and beckoned for us to follow. I pulled John up to sit beside me, where he slumped and he grumped. I could deal with his foul humour later. If he chose to stay silent, so be it. I could pass the time by talking to the carter. But if he did have any English, he chose not to use it on the road to Faversham.

I'd thought the weather was turning, but the morning thaw had been but brief respite from the bitter cold. The wind had blown snow into drifts which reached over the tops of gates and turned hedgerows into hillocks. On the road itself, the snow had been compacted and rutted. The donkey picked its way as nimbly as a goat, but every time the poor beast veered off to one side, the carter vented a tirade of incomprehensible abuse. I waved my hands in what I hoped was an appropriately French response. He grunted.

We entered a forest, where the road was less rutted, but time passed ever slower. The cart groaned and squeaked as it lurched from side to side. The donkey plodded on. John sat sullenly silent. The carter grumbled to himself in French. I shut my eyes and thought of Kate. I'd left London four months before, imagining that Kate and I would be together within days. And now, finally, we were just an hour or so apart. I allowed myself to conjure memories. Her soft skin, her sweet kisses. Our meeting in Saint Olave's churchyard. Kate on horseback, riding alongside Lady Frances. Chaste thoughts, indeed. Yearnings would become reality soon enough.

We emerged from the forest. And I began to notice the world around us. I had sorely missed London those past few months; but even on the coldest, brightest midwinter day, London's streets are too busy for snow to lie pristine for more than a few minutes once the sun has risen. Here, the whole rural landscape was transformed from the dark, bleak, angular greys and browns of winter into a wilderness of purest white. Everything softened, rounded, feminine, though I confess it might have been the prospect of seeing Kate which made it seem so.

And on we went – until we arrived in Faversham, where we stopped at a warehouse by the quay, and helped Guillaume unload the bales of woven silk.

'Et maintenant nous allons dans la Rue de l'Abbaye. Oui? Yes?'

'To Katherine Garnam?'

'Oui. Elle est là.'

We trundled on for another half mile or so, stopping at a large house in a wide street. Guillaume knocked the door. We waited. I allowed myself to hope.

But it was an older woman, not Kate, who opened the door. She and Guillaume greeted each other, then he walked through into the house. Her greying hair had been tied up beneath an extravagant coif. Her skin was pale and wrinkled, but free from pocks and scars. Her eyes were still bright.

'My name is Isabelle.' I was relieved she spoke English, albeit with a strong accent.

'I am here to see Katherine Garnam.'

'Katherine. Yes. I know. She speaks of you. It is cold on the cart of Guillaume. *Oui?*'

'Yes.'

'First you must be warm. And the boy, I think he is cold also. You come with me to the warm place.'

We followed her through to the kitchen, a much larger kitchen than Anne's. I call it a kitchen because there was a bread oven and a range, pots and pans hanging from the beams, plates on shelves, a butter churn by the back door, a large cooking pot bubbling on the range. But there were also two long tables in the middle of the room with benches down each side. Guillaume, the carter, already had a bowl of soup in front of him with a chunk of bread. A young woman was sitting at the other table, giving suck to a babe in arms. For a moment I thought she was Kate. I was startled, delighted and caught in a web of nerves. Then she looked up, caught sight of my face and immediately looked back down at the baby. Not Kate.

'*Asseyez vous*. Sit down please,' said Isabelle.

John didn't wait for my say so. He sat straight down, next to Guillaume.

'*Avez vous faim*?' said the woman by the range, as she ladled stew into Guillaume's bowl. Isabelle translated.

'Yes,' said John. 'I am very hungry.'

And then to me: 'Come. Sit you. Eat with us. *Oui*?'

John beamed up at Guillaume, as if the man were his friend, as if the two of them had spent the journey from Canterbury in constant gossip. The fellow liked the attention, and patted John on the head, but had no more to say for himself than he had on our journey. John started talking as if he'd known the man for years. Guillaume, smiled and nodded. It shouldn't have surprised me as much as it did – the boy had grown up in the company of adults although he'd spent very little time with children. The miracle was that he'd managed to make a friend of Clement.

'*Voulez vous manger?*' The woman with the stew – to me this time.

'I'd like to see Katherine,' I said to Isabelle.

'But you are cold and hungry.'

'I am. But I would like to see Katherine. Maybe she and I can eat together.'

An exchange of looks between Isabelle and the other woman.

'Then come.'

I walked over to John, and told him I was going to meet my friend.

'You are safe here. I'll be back soon. I promise.'

38
Hope House

Isabelle led me out of the kitchen, up a narrow wooden staircase to a long landing, where she knocked on a door, as if she were an usher to nobility and wanted to be sure Lady Katherine was ready to receive her guest.

The door opened ajar. A woman's voice. A quick whispered conversation.

Isabelle turned back to me. 'Katherine is asleep.'

'I'd like to see her. Is she sick?'

More whispers.

'You can enter. But you must not wake her.' Isabelle stayed outside as I went through. A wooden chair had been placed beside the bed, where a woman lay asleep.

Her hair was lank, her cheeks were sunken. Her hands were bony, the hands of a woman much older than Kate. Her face, her hands as colourless as chalk. If this woman was truly Kate, she'd aged ten years in the eighteen months since I'd last seen her.

'Kate?' I whispered. She didn't stir. Had I arrived too late?

A hand on my shoulder, easing me away from the bedside. I didn't take my eyes off my beloved Kate.

'She has had a fever. We thought she might not live.' The voice was familiar. 'She is still very weak. But she is recovering.'

I backed away, still watching Kate's breathing, slow and regular, but oh so quiet.

'She needs to rest.'

I knew the voice. I looked round. I knew the eyes, the mouth. 'Alice?'

She was staring at me.

'I was burnt in a fire – '

'There's no need for you to explain,' she said. 'Anne Forman wrote of it.' The Alice I'd known had all the voices but not these formal tones.

So much all at once. Kate, and now Alice. My past catching up with me, or me catching up with it.

'How long has she been sick?'

'Several months. But she was weak before that. Her fever was so bad we thought we would lose her. She is stronger now, but she needs rest. When we told her you had come to Canterbury, she asked to see you. But you will have to be patient.'

'I want to be here when she wakes.'

She gave this some thought before removing a blanket from a wooden chest.

'Warm yourself. I will ask Isabelle to bring you some food.'

When Isabelle returned, she brought me a bowl of stew, a chunk of bread and a tankard of ale on a wooden tray. The two women spoke again in French.

'The boy, John, is downstairs,' said Alice. 'Isabelle says he is asking where you are.'

'Will they look after him?'

'People here are good with children. There are many children. We have our own school.'

I'd seen John's look of terror at the sight of the other children when I left him that afternoon in Abingdon, but I shut that from my thoughts. He'd managed with Clement. The time to worry about John would be after Kate had woken, and she knew I was there for her.

I sat beside the bed, waiting. Alice stayed with me, as chaperone to Kate. And then she took some knitting from the blanket chest, and sat clattering her needles like a dull, honest housewife. A simple action, so normal for some, but it seemed almost as strange as Rowley's madness, for this was the woman who had played the fine lady Frances with such aplomb just two years before.

Alice knitted, while I waited dutifully at Kate's bedside. Alice knitting, me waiting. Neither of us speaking to the other. Like an old married couple.

The afternoon slipped away. Alice lit candles and a wall lantern. Kate was breathing steadily. Alice's needles clattered as regularly as the workings of a wall clock.

I was dozing when Kate started whimpering, which startled me awake. She surfaced from sleep slowly. It was the moment I'd been yearning for. I'd imagined it in so many ways, but always with the Kate I'd known, the Kate whose every smile sang with life, the Kate who glowed with health. She opened her eyes, saw my face that wasn't a face.

'Alice,' she screamed. 'Help me.' As if Alice could make the nightmare disappear.

The click-clacking needles stopped. Alice came over, gesturing for me to move back. 'It's Matthew.' She took Kate's hand in hers. 'Matthew Edgworth.'

Kate stared at me. Her eyes had a hint of cloudiness about them, like fish too long on the slab.

'Matthew?' Kate whispered. 'That's not Matthew.'

'You are safe, Katherine,' said Alice. 'It is him. Matthew Edgworth.'

'How can he be Matthew?'

'I was in a fire. My face was burned.'

Silence. She shut her eyes. I thought she was shaking her head. I thought I heard her groan. 'No.' And then, still with her eyes shut, 'Is that truly Matthew?'

'Yes. It is him,' said Alice.

Kate opened her eyes.

'It is me, Kate. Truly. I am Matthew. I swear to you, Kate.'

'He will not harm you, Katherine. I will stay here with you.'

Kate looked at me then, gazing into my browless eyes, trying to see past the featureless skin that surrounded them.

'I've lost my face, sweet Kate. Burned off in a fire. But my love for you is as strong and as fresh as ever.'

She smiled faintly. I squeezed her hand very gently. She seemed so delicate that I feared I might break bones.

'Can you leave us together now, please, Alice?' I said.

'Say whatever you want to say. Say it quietly if you will. But I must stay here.'

Kate didn't question this. So nor did I. Alice resumed her knitting. Alice, the woman I'd rescued from a Petticoat Lane whorehouse, turned guardian of Kate's morality.

I had dreamt that being with Kate again would be a reunion to treasure for the rest of our lives, a time when we wrapped arms around each other and revelled in holding and being held. This was not that reunion. But we did talk, even with Alice in the room with us.

'I have yearned for you, Kate. From the moment you left my lodgings, I yearned for you.' I so wanted to seal that yearning with a kiss. Kate looked quizzical. 'I know, and I am truly sorry. It must have seemed like I abandoned you. Lady Frances accused me of kidnapping you. I looked everywhere for you, Kate. I hoped you might be in hiding. Then I heard that a cart had knocked you into the river Fleet. I knew it wasn't an accident. I refused to believe you were dead, but I came so close to despair.'

'I sent you a letter. Anne wrote it for me.'

'I know that now. But it didn't reach me for months.'

I squeezed her hand, then stopped myself. Her bones felt so fragile.

'I'm sorry I ever doubted you, Matthew. I wanted to believe in you. But ...' Whatever she wanted to say was interrupted by a bout of coughing that left her out of breath.

Alice came over and said quietly. 'Katherine, you mustn't try to talk too much.' She gave me a look that I took as a warning.

She said nothing for a while, then whispered, 'I confess it, Matthew. I lost faith in you.'

'Hush, sweet Kate. Alice is right. Don't try to talk. Not now.'

I sat beside the bed for a while, her hand resting on mine. I told her of walking to Oxford and getting caught by the cheaters in the barn at Wittenham. I told her that I'd been nursed back to health by good people in a nearby village. But I thought it best to wait until she'd recovered her health and her strength before telling of the ragged crew, and the vile atrocity that Rowley wreaked upon them in the name of his Promised Land.

I don't know how long I talked, but it was time enough for the candles to burn down and for Alice to replace them from a cupboard in the corner. Despite the foetid stink of tallow, I was relieved they weren't beeswax.

I had so many questions for Kate – above all, why she'd chosen to come to Faversham, rather than to stay with Anne – but she whispered, 'You're here.' And she smiled. And everything else could wait.

There were times when she shut her eyes, and I wondered whether she was slipping into sleep. Until finally, soon after Alice had changed the candles a second time, she did. Alice came over and quietly suggested it was time for me to leave.

'I'd like to stay here. I can sleep in this chair.'

'Leave her be, Matthew. You can spend time with her again tomorrow.'

I got to my feet, and she went out into the corridor with me. She shut the door quietly behind her, then said. 'She is pleased to see you, Matthew. But I needed to be certain she wanted to see you before sending word back to Anne.' There was a warning in that. Kate might have accepted that I didn't abandon her, but Alice had known a rather different Matthew, and was unlikely to forget that.

It wasn't until I walked back into the kitchen, and was met by the smell of mutton simmering with herbs and ale, that I realised how hungry I was.

John was sitting on his own. He saw me. I smiled at him. He stared down at a book on the table. The carter, Guillaume, was nowhere to be seen. Isabelle was stirring the stew. A woman I'd not seen before was kneading bread dough. I thanked Isabelle for looking after John. She'd taken him to the schoolroom while I was upstairs with Kate. But school had finished for the day.

'He has never been to school, have you John,' I said. He ignored me.

'He is a little *timide*,' said Isabelle.

'Shy?'

'Yes. But he is good boy.'

'I thank you for looking after him.'

'*Ce n'est rien.* We eat soon. After, I show where you sleep.'

'How did you like school, John?'

He shrugged.

'Did they give you a book?'

He shook his head.

'You were reading when I came back down. Just now.' He'd hidden the book.

'Can't read.'

'You can. You learn quickly. You can read some words. And some will soon become many. In no time at all you'll be reading as well as me.'

He shook his head.

'What were you reading? Just now.'

He shrugged. 'You don't like me learning fast.'

'I told you before. I'm proud of you. Very proud.'

'No you're not.'

'John. Just show me what you were reading.'

'Why?'

'Because I'm interested.'

'You said I learnt quickly to pick locks. Then you didn't like it.'

Isabelle glanced across. I lowered my voice: 'Show me the book.'

'You'll be angry. I don't like it when you're angry.'

'I'll be angry if you don't show me.'

I'd considered asking Anne whether John could stay with her and Clement, but now that we were here, with other children and a school of a kind, I thought this place would be perfect for him. He might not like it at first, and he might have to learn a little French or Dutch, but no harm in that.

'John, show me the book.'

He was sitting on it. He lifted a leg and put it on the table. *A Midsummer Night's Dream*. The copy of the play that Clement inherited from his father. No point asking how he'd got it, for I knew very well, and I didn't want to humiliate him. But I vowed to myself that we would take it back. Together. And he would apologise to Clement and to Anne.

'How much of it can you read now?'

'A little. They don't talk to me.' I smiled, thinking he meant the people of the play – until I caught the look of sadness on his face.

'Have you tried talking to them?'

'They speak a funny language.'

'French.'

'Why can't they speak English?'

'They're from France. And some of them from Holland.'

'Why?'

'Ask them, John. Some of them speak English.'

I opened the playbook and found a scene to read with him. He said, 'You're not my father are you?'

'No. I'm not.'

'She said you are.'

'Who did?

'The teacher woman. She speaks some English. She asked me to join in. I said I didn't want to. She said, *Your father will be back soon.* And I said, no he won't. He's dead. And she said, *He's only upstairs.*'

'That's right. I was upstairs.'

'Are you?'

'Am I what?'

'My father.'

'No, John. I am not your father. But I will look after you. I promise you.' Better than your own father ever did, I thought.

'I don't want to be here. You said we'd go to London, and I could be a player.'

'We will go to London.'

'And will I be a player?'

'Yes, of course you will. But first you have to learn to read.'

The outside door opened. Four men walked in. The first men I'd seen, apart from Guillaume, since we arrived. Their faces were as dirty as the nightmen or the coalmen in London. They'd attempted to wash their hands, but the grime from whatever work they'd been doing was ingrained. John looked at them wide-eyed, and fearful. They barely cast a look in our direction, but sat down at the long table.

Isabelle asked me and John to sit at that same table, then she went into the entrance hall and rang a bell. The women and children soon appeared, including the young mother and her baby. All except for Kate and Alice, who had evidently appointed herself as Kate's nursemaid. They all queued for food, then sat on the benches. One table for men. The other for women and children – except for John, who was allowed to sit with me.

Isabelle ladled out a bowl of stew for each of us. The other woman gave us each some chunks of bread and a tankard of ale. The men hardly spoke a word. I recognise exhaustion when I see it. The rest of the room soon filled with chatter.

'Is that what my father meant by speaking in tongues?'

'There were things your father spoke about that I didn't understand. If we're here a long time, perhaps we can both learn to speak French.'

'I don't want to be here a long time.'

Later, while talking to Alice, I discovered that the men all worked in the nearby gunpowder mills. In winter, they left for work before dawn and returned long after sunset. The older boys had to work there too, though only for half a day at a time. It took a while for me to understand how this strange community worked. At that moment, I confess my only real interest was that Kate and I had been reunited. We were being well looked after. John might get some schooling. And Kate was making a good recovery. I wasn't thinking further ahead than that.

The single women, the married couples and their children slept in rooms on the first floor. Isabelle wanted John to sleep in a room with the other boys, but he pleaded with me, and I persuaded her that he should stay with me for at least that first night. We were each given a truckle bed in the room on the second floor of the house where the unmarried men slept. It should have been more comfortable than blankets on the floor in Anne's house, but there were eight of us in that room at the top of the house – five French, a Dutch, me and John. The men all snored loudly and the place was sour with the fermented, sickly stench of years of night farts. Sleep came quickly for John. It eluded me.

I lay awake, thinking about what lay ahead, trying to pick my way through a tangled web of doubts and fears, hopes and memories. Kate had been pleased to see me, but she wasn't strong enough to make decisions for herself. I wanted nothing more than to be with her, but I was no nursemaid. I felt duty bound to protect young John, but if we were to stay here, he would have to find the courage to join in with the other children. When I did finally drift into sleep and fell into fitful dreaming, I was shocked to find that it was Alice who was waiting for me, taunting me with fractured, splintered memories of the journeys we'd taken together. London to Chartley. Audley End to The Bridewell. Southwark to Canterbury. The teasing, the flirting, the sparks of sparkling wit, the flaring temper and the desolate melancholy. Maybe she remembered me differently. But there had been something between us I never really understood, something I could never quite forget.

In the morning I talked to John.

'Do you really want to be a player at a London theatre?'

'Do they allow boys?'

'There are companies of players who are all of them boys, so it will be good practice while we're here for you to play at being a good scholar.'

'What do you mean?'

'I will ask if you can join the class.'

'Don't want to. They won't like me.'

The men got up and left for work before dawn. School started after breakfast in a room on the ground floor. I asked Alice, who had appeared for breakfast, to explain to the teacher, a woman called Françoise, that John spoke no French, but would like to join the class again. Françoise smiled and welcomed him. She spoke enough English to introduce him to the other children. He looked miserable but took his slate and chalk and sat down at the front. The other children all stared at me with that look I've grown accustomed to. And children, who are rarely embarrassed about staring in the way that adults often are, don't try to hide their curiosity.

Kate was awake when I arrived. She was sitting up in bed. She said she was pleased to see me. Her smile reminded me of the warmth and vitality of the woman I'd known before, like a footprint left in sand. Recognisable, but fading. She had very little strength in her hand, but her attempt to squeeze mine was as loving as anything we did together when we shared a bed.

'I was so frightened, Matthew,' she said. So quiet I had to strain to hear. Her eyelids looked so heavy. 'I was so worried about what they might have done to you.' She had been worried about me!

'I'm here now, Kate. We're both safe. Talk to me later. When you're stronger.'

'I am stronger already. How long can you stay?'

'I will never leave you, Kate. I swear it.'

I sat with her, holding her hand. Alice helped me ease her back down into the bed. I wished I could somehow speak with Agnes, ask her advice about how to speed Kate's recovery, though what Agnes would have made of Hope House I'll never know.

'Will she sleep for long now?'

'Sometime an hour, sometimes all morning. Go back down. Be with your boy if you want to. I'll be here for Katherine.'

'I'd rather stay.'

352

We sat in silence for a while. I was watching over Kate, but conscious that Alice was looking at me, as if making an appraisal. Then she said, 'The boy. Who is he?'

39
The test

Alice was stick thin and frail the last time I saw her, some twenty months or so before. Her face had now filled out, her eyes had regained their lustre, and she'd recovered all that spirited self-possession that had been beaten out of her in The Bridewell.

I moved over to sit with her. She'd been polite the day before, but I knew how uncomfortable she was with my presence in the room. She laid her knitting on the lid of the chest, and set aside the charade of good manners.

'Who is he? The boy you call John. Why bring him with you?'

'He lost both his parents in a house fire.' It was hardly a lie. Godwyn and Sarah might as well have been his parents.

'He was an orphan, and you took it upon yourself to care for him? Such a kind man. Such a caring man. I don't believe it. That is not the Matthew Edgworth I knew in London.'

'I've changed.'

She harrumphed. 'Your face is scarred. I can see how badly burned you were. That doesn't make you a different man. I should tell you now, I didn't want you here. I still don't.'

'You have good reason not to like me, Alice.'

'I have good reason not to trust you. I have good reason not to believe a word you say.' She spoke very quietly. I turned and looked over to Kate, who slept on.

'I wouldn't expect you to trust me. But I was never as wicked as some liked to paint me.'

'Why is the boy with you?'

'It's complicated.'

'I heard what you told Katherine.'

'I told her no lies.'

'That doesn't make it the truth. When I knew you, Matthew Edgworth, you were the consummate deceiver.'

'I know what you think of me, Alice.'

'Katherine wanted to see you. I didn't think it wise. I thought you'd abandoned her.' She waited for me to respond. I chose not to. 'I'll ask you again. Who is the boy? I'm no fool. I don't want half-truths. They're often worse than lies.'

I took my time before answering, and took care not to raise my voice. 'I, too, was orphaned at about John's age. The only way to survive was to live by my wits.'

'At everyone else's expense. You put me in The Bridewell, and left me there to rot.'

'I put you into The Bridewell for your own safety.'

She gave me a withering look.

'I worked for Lord Rochester. Taking you to Chartley Manor was to enable his affair with Frances Howard.'

'Do you think I'd forgotten? You think because I'm not English I'm stupid?'

'No, I – '

'And you called Chartley a palace. I remember that too.'

'That is not what I said.'

'*Would you not rather work in a palace than a common house?* Your words, Matthew. And then that other palace. The one they call The Bridewell. A House of Correction and you

355

called that a place of safety! *You'll be there just a few days.* Those were your words too. I don't forget. I will never forget.'

There was rage in her eyes, though both our voices soft as silk. And there was Katherine, just a few feet away. Sleeping peacefully. Alice intended her barbs to hurt. But she didn't want me to walk away.

'Apart from Frances and Rochester, there were only five of us ever knew about the exchange. You, me, Katherine, Colquhoun (Rochester's steward) and Bradshaw (his coachman). Rochester commanded that all of us be silenced. And Doctor Forman, too, I'm sure of it. So you and Katherine were to be drowned in the Thames – and that's where Rochester thinks your corpses lie. Forman was poisoned. Bradshaw fell down stone stairs and cracked his head open. The only reason I'm still alive is because I fled from London.'

'And Colquhoun, the steward?'

'Who knows? I'd be surprised if he's alive. Rochester thought you were dead, Alice. I put you in The Bridewell until I could get you safely out of London.'

She shook her head and scoffed. '*Just a few days* is what you said. Just a few days and I might have believed you. I was there for more than six months.'

'It wasn't safe to get you out.'

'You forgot about me, damn you. You had better things to think about.'

'You survived, Alice.'

'I will never forgive you for leaving me there so long.'

'I don't expect you to. But I did get you out. And I brought you and your family to Canterbury. You're safe.'

'Do you take me for your wretched bitch to lick your hands and thank you because you stopped kicking me?' Her look of momentary triumph fell quickly to disappointment when I chose not to respond. She seemed about to say something else when Kate stirred. I went over to the bed and knelt beside it. Kate slept on. I laid a hand on her forehead, which was warm, but not hot. My worry, nay, my dread, was that the fever would return, that my dreams of a life with Kate would be snuffed out as soon as they'd been rekindled. I bowed my head and rested it on the bolster. If I could have prayed, I surely would have done. But my silent prayers have never been met with anything but silence. If Alice hadn't been present, I'd have laid Agnes's hagstone on her forehead.

'I didn't want you here,' said Alice.

'I know,' I whispered without looking up.

'But Katherine wanted you. And even I know that you are not wholly bad.' I moved back to the edge of the room. She was staring at me.

'Your face.'

'You don't have to look at me.'

'Were you burned in the same fire that killed the boy's parents?'

I hesitated. What to tell? How much to tell? She was right about half-truths. I've said it many times myself. It's the mongrel half-truth, half-lie that snaps at your heels and brings you down. She had every reason not to trust me. But why should I trust her?

'Matthew. It's a simple question. Were you? In the same fire?'

'No. No, the fire that nearly killed me was about two months before.'

She waited.

I shut my eyes, unable to look at her while I admitted, 'I was reckless, greedy and impatient. I brought it on myself. There. A confession of my foolishness. Is that enough for you?'

'Tell me no lies, and no half-truths.'

'I was fleeing from London. Fleeing from Rochester's thugs, from whoever knocked Katherine from Fleet Bridge intending to drown her, from whoever pushed Bradshaw down the stairs, cracked open his head. I made my way to Oxford. I planned to make enough money from the scholars to give me and Katherine a good life.'

'Another of your stories, Matthew?'

'This one's all true. And I've no reason to invent it, for I don't come out of it well. I took money from a gang of cheaters. I thought I had the better of them.'

'You cheated the cheaters?'

'I wanted money to get me to Canterbury, money to look after Kate when I got here.'

'You thought Katherine would like that? Being looked after with stolen money?'

'You asked for the truth. I took from cheaters – and saw to it that they were shamed.'

She was about to say something, but held herself back. She was searching my eyes for truth and lies. But what could she read in a face with no eyebrows?

'I thought myself more cunning and sharp-witted than any I might encounter outside of London. I was proud and arrogant, which made me careless and stupid. I paid for it dearly. I took a rest in a barn a few hours south of Oxford. I fell asleep. The cheaters caught up with me. They set the barn alight. They would have burnt me alive.'

'But Matthew, being Edgworth, turned the tables and escaped, leaving his attackers to die in the inferno!'

'If you want me to tell truth, don't mock me. None of them died. And I was pulled from the flames by ... I don't know who rescued me. I remember nothing of that. Just the flames. And the heat. And wanting to live. I'm told what happened. But I don't remember it. Except that there were people working in a nearby field.'

'People?'

'It was harvest time. Men and women cutting corn. My memory of those weeks after the fire is like looking at shards of a broken looking glass. I glimpse fractured moments. Many of them make little sense. I was nursed back to life by two women in a darkened room. At first I couldn't see them. Didn't know who they were. Didn't know where I was.'

She lifted her hand. I thought she was about to touch my face. To assure herself the story was true? Or maybe a gesture of an apology for mocking me earlier? Then she put her hand to cover her own mouth. Now it was me who couldn't read her.

'Living in darkness in the company of strangers, not knowing whether I'd ever see again, struggling to breathe, my throat so sore that I could hardly speak. Believe me, Alice, any man would be changed by that.'

Her head moved, the merest hint of sympathy. 'And the boy?'

'The boy, John. John Robins I call him. His story's even stranger than mine.'

'We have time.'

And so I told her about Adam Rowley, the landowner, the man who had lost his parents and his brother. Adam who had fathered a bastard child with a maid on a nearby estate, and paid two of his own servants to bring up the child as their own son. Adam, who never admitted his own paternity. John the child in search of his father. Alice smiled wryly, for she had surely heard such tales before, though never anything quite like Rowley's descent into the madness of his crazed belief that he could lead his followers to his apocalyptic Promised Land.

'So the boy John didn't lose his parents in a fire?'

'He lost Sarah and Godwyn. Good people both of them. They raised him as their own from when he was just a few weeks old. They both died in a fire, far more terrible than the one that so nearly killed me.'

I told her how I cursed myself for not understanding earlier what Rowley planned to do. I told her how I rescued John and Agnes from the fire, but had to leave others to perish. The telling of it left me drained and raw.

'And you blame yourself for all those deaths?' Her tone had changed. She sounded softer, gentler.

'Rowley confounded me. I knew he was dangerous. Knew he was mad. But I never worked out what he had planned. I thought the worst would be destitution for his sorry band of followers. I thought he'd abandon them when things started to go wrong. I thought he'd forget about his crazed vision of the mystical Promised Land, and walk back to the life of wealth and privilege he'd always known. I curse myself because I always knew that something was wrong. But I could never have conceived that he was planning for us all to be born again through fire.'

'Could anybody have imagined that?'

'I didn't confront him. And I should have done.'

'You went back into the burning hall to rescue John?'

'And Agnes.'

'Agnes? Who is Agnes?'

'One of the women who nursed me back to something like health.'

Alice seemed to retreat into her own dark memories. After what seemed like an age she spoke slowly: 'I have never met a man like your Adam Rowley. But I know about burnings. And I know about people who are driven to madness by their beliefs. That's why we are here. It's why I was in London. It's why you found me in the House of the Vixen. And it's why I hated you for calling me a whore.'

I nodded my understanding of what she said.

'The people who burnt our houses were driving us off our land. No promised land for us. They despised us, thought of us as lower than livestock because our beliefs were different than theirs. The same Christian God. Just different ways of worshipping Him. So I understand what it means to flee in fear of your life, and to take orphaned children with you and look after them as your own.'

'John knew that Sarah and Godwyn weren't his true parents. When he first saw me, he thought I might be his father. That's what he wanted me to be. He never knew that Adam Rowley was his father.'

'Does he know it now?'

'I've told him many times. But who knows what he believes? The child is a stranger to himself, and to all he meets. He knows about the fire, but he also knows that the adults he grew up with thought of Adam Rowley as some kind of Messiah. He remembers all that. And he's deeply troubled by it.'

'Was there nobody could look after him in Oxfordshire?'

'Rowley kept his band of disciples – and yes, I think that's what they were, disciples – he kept them separate from the nearby village. John grew up without the company of other children. He wanted to come with me.'

She took her time before asking gently, 'Do you think of yourself as his father?'

'I do my best to look after him. But I am not his father. And I tell him so.'

A long silence, broken only by the sound of Kate's regular breathing which sounded like purring. Breathing in through her nose, out through pursed lips.

'Would you like to be?'

'Would I like to be what?'

'His father.'

I shook my head. 'He's confused. He doesn't really know what he wants. And I know nothing about bringing up a child.'

'He adores you, Matthew. I've seen the way he looks at you.'

'I can act like his father. But he needs a mother more than he needs me.'

'Maybe.'

I waited.

'Maybe you have indeed changed, Matthew. You are not the man I knew before. But that doesn't mean I will ever learn to trust you. And forgiveness isn't mine to give.'

It sounded like I'd passed some kind of test. Perhaps now would be the time to ask why Kate was in Faversham, and not still with Anne in Canterbury.

Alice looked at me, weighing up how much to say. 'Katherine and I shared a room at Chartley for ten weeks. She was good to me. We became close friends. When Anne brought her to Canterbury, Katherine asked her to find me. I told her about this place, and she chose to join us here. I was pleased to return something of the care she'd given to me.'

Alice spoke quietly and slowly, choosing her words carefully, lapsing into that strange formality she'd adopted when I first came into that room. Perhaps I was not the only one to lapse into half-truths at times.

40
A glimpse of paradise

I was beginning to understand something of how this strange community worked. They called themselves Huguenots. I had to ask what that meant. 'Reformed Protestants,' I was told. That meant nothing to me. But they were welcoming, they weren't Puritans, they weren't Adam Rowley. And nobody spoke of a Promised Land. Most of them had escaped from persecution in France. A few, including Alice and her family, had fled from France to Holland, only to be driven out of Holland too. Some had come to Canterbury where they'd set up their weaving business; others to Faversham, where most of the men worked in the gunpowder mills. After the Hell they'd suffered, Faversham was a glimpse of paradise.

Where most large houses have dining and withdrawing rooms on the ground floor – and perhaps a library and a study for the master of the house – this had its kitchen and dining room, a schoolroom and a chapel. Somebody said they thought the house had once been the refectory for Faversham Abbey. Isabelle said they called it their house of hope. The outside walls were stone built, where most of the others in Abbey Street were timber framed. The chapel was different to any I'd seen before. Instead of pews set out in rows, as I've seen in the chapels of the grand houses – with the front row reserved for the master of the house, his lady wife and their children – here there were plain wooden benches arranged in a semi-circle around a pulpit. The men wore hats, the women coifs and bonnets. Even the children covered their heads. John and I had to borrow hats, but they were keen for us to attend.

The bedrooms were on the first and second floor. A staircase at each end of the house.

From mad Rowley to this. And all to be with my beloved Kate.

She was the only one who didn't attend chapel. But once a day one of the men, whom I took to be a preacher, said prayers at her bedside. When Alice came down for a service, one of the other women took a turn at Kate's bedside. There was always someone there. I was never allowed to be alone with her. I could have taken offence. But being near Kate, even with someone else in the room, was better than arguing my way out of the goodwill they all felt for us.

I heard Kate's name spoken in chapel, but I understood little else of what was going on. I dutifully mumbled my Amens and nudged John to do the same. I was curious about the services. There were prayers, bible readings and the singing of psalms, but not much speechifying. I hummed along with the psalms, but John had learnt the words in the little schoolroom, and seemed to enjoy singing. Despite this, when he and I were alone, he insisted he was miserable.

'Why do I have to sit with French children all morning?'

'Because they're looking after us, and that's what they do.'

'When are we going to London?'

'I don't know. But we will. I promise. I will take you to London. But for the moment I have to stay here.'

His questions kept coming. 'Is London near here? How long will it take us to get there? Can't you take me to London and then come back to look after your friend?' For John, London had already become a kind of Promised Land.

Time passed. Hours became days, and days drifted by, one to another. And all the time I watched for Kate's recovery, noting how long she sat up in bed, how much time she spent sleeping, the light in her eyes, the strength in her hand as she squeezed mine. Others in the community came to see her. By the time that first week had passed, each of the women had visited several times. Kate seemed cheered by her visitors, and particularly the young woman, Elise, who was nursing the babe in arms. When I asked her about Elise, Kate smiled. 'I have few words of French, dear Matthew, so she is a mystery to me. But I like her very much.'

'And the child? The baby boy?'

'Thomas.'

'He has an English name?'

'It's a French name too.' She pronounced it with a French accent, and laughed. 'He is such a lovely boy.'

That stirred me to such deep joy. Kate's laughter was something I'd treasured in the days we had together in London. The pleasure she took in the child's presence held such promise. She would recover. She would be strong again. We would be wed. All that talk of *Do you want to be John's father?* I couldn't stop myself. I dared to imagine the time when Kate and I would have our own children together, my own paradise on earth.

By the end of that first week in Faversham, John started asking if we could go back to Canterbury. 'I liked Anne and Clement. They didn't talk funny. I didn't have to sit down for most of the day.'

'We will see them again, John. When Kate has recovered, we'll go back to Canterbury, all of us.' *And I will return Clement's playbook and Anne's brooch*, though I didn't say that to him.

A boy of about the same age as John had been staring at me from time to time since the day we arrived. One morning after breakfast he came up to me. 'Good day to you, sir. Are you Mister Matthew?'

'I am indeed.'

'My sister tells me who you are. Do you remember me? My name is Frans.' His words chosen with care and spoken slowly. I should have recognised him before. Alice's younger brother. I'd brought him to Canterbury on the cart with Alice and her mother. I lifted him up and whirled him round. He laughed and squealed with excitement. I had to put him down because I was making myself feel turn-sick.

'Again.'

'Maybe later. Let me get my breath back.'

'Yes. Yes.' He was holding his arms out.

'John first,' I said. 'Then you can have another go, Frans.'

I put my hands under John's armpits and lifted him up.

'Ow. That hurts.' He was scowling, seething with jealousy. 'Don't want to. Put me down.'

'Can I? Can I?' said Frans.

'Later. Best go to school now.'

'Is John coming?'

'Yes. But I need to talk to him first.'

Frans ran off to the schoolroom. I found a quiet corner where I could talk to John without being overheard. 'He can be your friend, John.'

'No, he can't. I don't want him to be my friend. I don't like him. Clement's my friend.'

'Frans can be your friend too. He likes you.'

'Doesn't.'

'You could teach him English.'

'He talks funny.'

'He already speaks some English. You could teach him more.'

He shook his head. 'Don't want to.'

'Maybe read the play with him.'

'You don't understand.'

I took him by the hand and dragged him to the schoolroom. I opened the door and ushered him through. About a dozen children, boys and girls, the youngest perhaps about seven years old, the oldest a girl of nine or ten, were sitting on chairs in a semi-circle facing a woman who was standing with her back to the wall, an echo of the arrangement in the chapel. The children had slates and chalk. The woman was talking to them in French.

Frans was sitting at the end of the semi-circle. An empty chair next to him with slate and chalk lain on the flagstone floor in front of it. Frans grinned and waved. John gave me a venomous look before trudging over to take the seat.

When I went into the dining room for supper that evening, John and Frans were sitting together. I sat close enough to hear they were talking, but not close enough to hear what they were saying. I don't know what happened between them that day, but from then on, they became inseparable. John even asked if he could sleep in the large room with Frans and the other boys, instead of with me. Strange as it might seem, I missed him. But it meant I could stop worrying about him, and that gave me more time with Kate.

After passing what I thought of as Alice's test I thought she might allow me to be alone with Kate, but no. Alice always stayed with us. And I became so accustomed to her presence that I took no more notice of her than I would of a ticking clock.

I helped Kate sit up in bed, she seemed less tired. 'When I first got to Canterbury, I spent every day expecting your knock on the door. I was certain that you'd follow me, so when several weeks passed and you still hadn't arrived, I feared you must be dead; that they'd taken you down in the way they tried to kill me.'

'They would have done if I'd not convinced Rochester I was already dead.'

'Does he still believe that?'

'Colquhoun, his steward, killed me. Rochester watched as my life blood drained onto the floor of a room in the stable block at Cope Castle.'

'So the man I see here is a ghost I've conjured from my dreams?' She said it with that mischievous grin I remembered so vividly, the surest sign yet she was regaining her health.

'I'd schooled Colquhoun to use a stage dagger.'

'So you're not a ghost?'

'You tell me.' I leant over and kissed her.

'No, dearest Matthew. I don't think you're a ghost.'

We looked at each other. Her eyes were still tired, but there was life in them, and joy in the twitching dimples on her cheeks. We spoke no words, but we knew what we were thinking. She wanted me in her bed. And I wanted her more than I have ever wanted any woman. Alice's presence kept us chaste. But the kiss convinced me that Kate would recover her health and we would have the rest of our lives together. We had waited for each other, yearned for each other, feared for each other's welfare. We could wait another few days.

'You remember when you told me, in your lodgings in Water Lane, that both of our lives were at great risk?'

'I remember it well.'

'I didn't really believe you. Not then. It felt like a game. A way of persuading me to leave Lady Frances and come to you.'

'Did you think I would lie to you, Kate?'

'No. No, I don't mean that. But I believed that you would never allow yourself to be outwitted by Rochester. Then we got to Canterbury and there was no sign of you, no word from you. The knowledge that you were so cunning and resourceful gnawed away at the last morsel of hope. And I confess it, Matthew, I feared you'd forgotten me and found another.'

'I never forgot you, Kate. And I never will.' I kissed her on the forehead. She reached up and drew my lips down to hers again.

'Anne told me that I should let go my memories, my hopes and my yearnings. She said loving you was a fantasy.'

'I am here, Kate. This is me. Not a fancy. Not a ghost.'

'Anne feared for my life in those days after I was dragged from the river. She said it was a miracle I survived. I say it's because there was always some part of me knew you would find me.'

That gave me such cheer. But that night I lay awake, and I couldn't stop thinking of what she'd told me. It brought back a dark rage against Rochester which I thought I'd left behind. It wasn't yearning for Kate that kept me awake that night, but planning my revenge. Kate wouldn't like it, and nor would Alice. But I had to destroy him.

Frans took to John in a way that Clement never did. Clement had been willing to spend time with John, but had no need of anyone's company except his mother's. But Frans quickly grew to adore John – something John had never known before. They sat together in school and at mealtimes, they played together when school had finished, for they weren't yet old enough to work in the mill. There were no glass marbles in Hope House, but John made his own with pebbles and stones, and he taught Frans what Clement had taught him. I often saw them on the street outside when it wasn't raining. Frans had taught John to play a game he called Apple Ball. They took turns to poke a stick into a rotten apple and fling it over the creek. On one rainy day I found them in the kitchen with Clement's copy of *Midsummer Night's Dream*, and John giving Frans instructions on how to act. Not a day passed without John asking me for help with his reading, and what some of the words meant. He was learning to unpick words as enthusiastically as he'd learnt to pick locks.

It was such a relief to me that the boys enjoyed each other's company so much – not least because Alice delighted in their friendship as much as I did. 'I have not seen Frans so happy in all the time we've been in England.' Frans being happy made Alice happy. And that worked well for me and Kate.

John and Frans were odd little people, both of them. They seemed to thrive on their differences from the other children in the community. But despite this, John took readily to the services held every evening in the chapel. It was he who chivvied me to be there on time. I asked what he liked about it so much.

'The singing,' was all he said at first. But after the service I sometimes heard Frans giving his English version of some of the bible stories.

'Do you say the prayers?' I asked.

John shook his head. 'I say Amen. Everyone says Amen. Even you say Amen, Matthew. What's it mean?'

'That you agree. That you want the prayer to be in your name too.' I was parroting what I'd been told when I was his age, when I, too, was curious about prayers and God and churchgoing.

'Even if you don't understand?'

'Yes.'

'Is God happy about that?'

'I don't know. Ask the people who lead the prayers.'

One evening, after leaving the chapel and bidding the boys goodnight, I went up to Kate's room. I opened the door very quietly, not knocking in case she was asleep. Alice was sitting by the bed. Neither of them noticed I was there. They were talking in whispers, but I heard what I heard. Kate said, 'I want to tell him. He should know.'

'No Katherine. Don't tell him. We agreed.'

I tippytoed back into the corridor. Then I knocked and opened the door. Kate was sitting up. She smiled at me. I said nothing about what I'd heard. I would ask what she wanted to tell me when we were finally allowed to be alone.

The next morning she said, 'I would like to try to walk.'

Alice and I lifted her to the edge of her bed, where she sat with her feet touching the floor. She needed both of us to help her stand, with one arm round my shoulders, the other round Alice. She couldn't balance without our help. The bones of her arms dug into my shoulders. She weighed less than John or Frans.

We helped keep her upright as she slid her feet on the floor, shuffling slowly forward. She asked to go to the window and look out. What she saw on that drear afternoon was the dirty grey water of Faversham Creek and grimy melting slush on the path by the river. She sighed. I thought she might want to retreat to her bed and not try walking again til a sunny day in May. But her sigh was an 'Oh' of pleasure. 'There were times I thought I would never see the outside world again. I want to walk in the rain. I want to run. I want to gallop across meadows.'

The thrill of hearing her enthusiasm encouraged me to talk about the lives we might have together. How many children would we have? Kate thought five. Three boys and two girls. Where would we live? In Canterbury because Kate wanted to be close to Anne, and it had some of the bustle of a small city.

And all the time Alice click-clacked in the corner. The silent witness to all my promises. No comments, no questions, no tuts of doubt or disapproval. Clickety clack, and occasional barely heard whispers as she counted her stitches. I'd been so obsessed by Kate's health that I hadn't thought til then to ask Alice what she was knitting, though it was clearly precious to her.

'A christening gown for baby Thomas.'

'Elise is fortunate that her babe is so loved,' I said.

'We are all fortunate to live together as we do. But Elise has had her share of loss and sorrow.'

There was a moment when Alice left to visit the privy, without asking anyone else to take her place. I asked Kate what she was keeping from me.

'Nothing.' But her cheeks had coloured.

'What was it you wanted to tell me?'

'All sorts of things I've told you, Matthew.'

'I have a confession, Kate. I overheard you say to Alice, just a couple of days ago, *I want to tell him*. And Alice told you no. What was it, Kate?'

She swallowed and looked away.

'Promise me you will never tell Alice what I tell you.'

'I swear it.'

'She didn't want you here, Matthew. That's why it took so long to get a message back to Anne.'

I took Kate's hand and gently squeezed it. 'That doesn't surprise me.' And I wanted to believe her, even though I knew it was only half true because Alice herself had already told me that she hadn't wanted me there. But whatever it was they were hiding could wait. The time we had together was too precious, and Kate's recovery too fragile to spoil it by confronting her. And it was indeed the most precious time. Days passed, and then another week. The chill grey of January turned to the delicate promise of a warm sunny day in February. Kate was eating more, her face was filling out, she was able to walk to the window without our help. We sat together on her bed, talking – mostly about the life that lay ahead of us, the life we would share together. Such simple joy. The future seemed so rich in possibilities.

And then one day, she asked Alice if we could take a walk outside. I carried her piggy-back down the stairs. In the kitchen they greeted her like a lost child returning home. Isabelle found her a thick woollen cloak, hat and gloves.

'Is it far to the churchyard?' Kate asked. She'd seen it from her bedroom window.

Alice and I took most of her weight as we walked a hundred yards or so up the lane. When we reached the churchyard, Alice offered to wait by the gate so Kate and I could be alone. We made our way slowly up a gravel path beneath an ancient yew tree to a bench against the wall of the church porch.

'Remember Saint Olave's?' said Kate. Saint Olave's churchyard, close by Mountjoy's shop, where we first kissed.

'Is that why you wanted to come here?'

She smiled and gave me a knowing look that left me to decide what to do with it. I knelt before her and took her hands in mine. 'Will you marry me, Kate?'

She laughed. Laughter like singing. The most beautiful sound.

'Is it funny?'

'I'm laughing with joy. Of course I will. There is nothing I would like more.'

Then we both laughed. Alice turned in surprise. Seeing our joy, she ran to us and clasped us by the hands. The three of us together. Children dancing in a ring.

41
Flesh and Blood

Atishoo, atishoo. All fall down.

Even as we were standing there in the churchyard, Kate's laughter turned to coughing.

'It's nothing,' she insisted. 'Really. I'm not ill. I'm just not used to laughing.'

But it wasn't nothing. And as we walked her back to Hope House, she had to stop every dozen steps or so as another bout of coughing took hold.

Alice said she didn't blame me for Kate's relapse, but she thought it best I leave her alone for the rest of that day. 'Let her relax and sleep. She will be better in the morning.'

I sought out John and Frans. They were making the most of the late afternoon sun, down by the creek with a trug of apples, taking it in turns to throw them as far as they could. I found some flat stones and showed the boys how to throw them low over the water till they bounced and skimmed. Frans got one to make three jumps before it sank. John threw his too high or too low, and he quickly grew impatient.

'When are you going to take us to London?'

'I can't leave while Katherine is ill.'

'Frans wants to come with us. He wants to be a player too.'

Frans nodded vigorously. 'Can I? Can I?'

'We can't go yet.'

'When?'

'When Katherine's better.'

'When's that?'

'Soon.' Earlier that same day I'd have said that in good faith. I no longer believed it.

'How far away is London?' said Frans.

'Fifty, sixty, a hundred miles. I don't know. A long way.'

'Is it as far as Canterbury?'

'Further.'

'How will we get there?'

'We'll probably find a carter who's going to London, and beg a ride.'

'Can't we get horse?' said John.

'That would be quicker. But we'd need two horses. And I don't even have the money to buy one.'

I ate supper that night with John and Frans. Afterwards, Isabelle gave me a tray to take food up to Alice and Kate. Alice ate her supper. Kate was asleep. I put a hand on her forehead, which was hot and moist.

'Has the fever returned?'

'I don't know,' said Alice. But her face told me that she feared the worst. 'You should spend the rest of the evening with John.'

'I don't want to leave her.'

'There is nothing you can do.'

'I want to stay here with her.'

'Matthew, she is very weak. She has never properly recovered from the near drowning.'

'I know.'

'You should rest. Be the father to young John that he wants you to be. He needs you more than you know.'

'I want to stay with her tonight.'

'There is nothing you can do.'

'I can be with her. I wasn't with her when she needed me before. I can be with her now.'

Alice took hold of my hand. 'You do know?' she whispered.

'Yes. I know.'

She asked Isabelle to bring lamp oil and candles. They spoke together quietly in the corridor. Whatever it was they said, I couldn't hear the words. But I knew.

I sat on one side of the bed, Alice on the other. Kate was burning up, her breathing heavy and rasping, her palms and forehead clammy with sweat. Alice and I took turns to wipe her down, to cool her with wet cloths, then dry her with towels. Occasionally Kate coughed. We sat her up in bed. But she was hardly conscious.

Where was Agnes now?

Time passed. Minutes? Hours? Unaware that I'd slipped into sleep, I was woken by Kate calling out. Hoarse. But oh so urgent. 'Matthew, save him from the fire. He's burning. Matthew, get the child.' She was sitting up. Arms flailing. 'Save us. We're drowning.'

Alice trying to calm her. Wet flannel on her face.

'Don't drown me. Where is Thomas? Bring Thomas. Let me hold him.'

Alice upped and ran from the room. 'There is no fire, my sweetest Kate. No fire. No water. Not now. You're safe. I'm here.'

'I'm burning, burning. Save him. Why's he drowning?' Burning one moment, drowning the next. Our lives churning together in her fevered turmoil.

Alice returned with Elise and baby Thomas. I gave up my seat to Elise.

'He's safe, dear Kate,' I said. 'He's here now.'

'Don't take him from me. Don't let him drown.'

Elise looked at Alice. A questioning look. Alice nodded. Elise passed the babe to Kate, who held him to her, his tiny head resting in the crook of her arm.

'Will she live?' said Kate.

'He is Thomas,' I said. 'A boy, not a girl.'

The child started to cry. Elise moved forward, ready to take the babe back. But Alice put a hand on her arm. Everything so slow and gentle. Kate tried to hum a lullaby.

The child's cries softened to whimpers, and Kate's humming faded. Her delirium seemed to pass, and she fell back into sleep.

'Let Thomas stay there,' whispered Alice. 'He soothes her.'

I stood by the door, watching. Baby Thomas lying on Kate's breast, his head turned to one side. Elise and Alice sitting beside her, one on each side. A vision of peace. No need for fathers. Alice was right. Nothing I could do. The babe started crying again. Elise picked him up, cradled him in her arms, and left the room so as not to wake Kate. I took her place at the bedside.

I had no sense of time passing. All I saw and heard was the slow rise and fall of Kate's breathing, which had weakened to a frail wheezing.

It was dark. I was holding Kate's hand. Alice was sitting on the other side of the bed. Everything was the same, except that our world had frozen. And in that frozen world Kate took a gasping breath. And then a wheezing, groaning exhalation, which sounded almost like some ghastly crackling. On and on it went, til every last breath of air in her lungs was gone.

Then she was still.

Nothing moved.

Silence swelled to fill the room with nothingness.

Silence.

Alice didn't speak.

One of the tallow candles spluttered and spat.

Silence.

We knew. We looked at each other. Alice held the back of her hand to Kate's nose. I felt for her pulse.

I didn't cry. Not then.

'Would you like me to leave you with her, Matthew?'

I nodded.

I took her hand and lifted it. The hand that had held mine just hours before. I kissed the hand that was Kate's hand. There was still some warmth in it. 'Kate.' I wanted to talk to her. There was so much to say. But the only words I could find were, 'Kate. I love you so much. I love you now. And always will.'

I couldn't cry. Not then. The well of tears was too deep.

There were no last rites. She'd been ill for months. And yet when it came, when death came, it came so suddenly.

I remember very little of the next few days. I saw John and Frans, but had little to say to them. They seemed content in the worlds they were creating for themselves.

Alice wanted me to attend the prayer meetings they held in the Chapel. I sat there, not hearing what was being said, standing up when they stood up, sitting down when they stood down, saying Amen when they said Amen. They prayed for Kate's soul, I'm sure of that, for I was alert to her name, as if hearing her name spoken aloud might bring her back. They might even have prayed for me. But that drifted past me.

The people of the house were kind. They let me eat with them, they let me continue sleeping in the room with the other unmarried men, they let John sleep with Frans and the other young boys. But there was no reason for me to be there. I had come to the house for Kate. I was there for Kate. My future had been with Kate. And now that Kate was dead, my future was missing.

I went back to the churchyard where I'd proposed to Kate. Sat on a bench beneath the yew tree, gazing at nothing for hours in that chill, drear February. If only I'd brought Agnes with me. If only I'd left London sooner. If only I'd not been so foolish as to fall asleep in that damned barn in Wittenham.

If only …

If … I took John to London, I could honour my promise to him, introduce him to one of the companies of boy players. It would be a way of showing Kate that I am true to my word, proving to her that I could have been a truly good father. And then?

Then I'd be free to put on heavy boots and throw myself from Fleet Bridge.

There was nothing else to live for.

I'd made my decision, and I was calm. I went back to the house. Isabelle was at the range, taking bread from the oven. Elise was chopping vegetables for a stew. Maybe they saw a calm, contented Matthew come back in. Maybe they thought I'd had some kind of epiphany in the churchyard.

Baby Thomas was asleep in his cradle. I took a chair and sat beside it. Elise looked over. I rocked the cradle gently back and forth. Elise smiled at me. I smiled at her. I looked down at little Thomas.

And saw Katherine. His eyes were hers. His nose was hers. Suddenly so clear. Kate was his mother, not Elise. And if Kate was his mother, I was his father. Why had I not seen it before? Elise was his wet nurse, not his true mother. That's what Alice had meant by *Don't tell him.* Don't tell him, Kate, that little Thomas is your own child, and Elise is nursing him till you're strong enough to care for him yourself. Don't tell him, Kate, that Matthew is Thomas's father. Of course, don't tell him because Matthew can't be trusted.

'May I hold him?' I asked. He was our son. He was all I had of Kate. Moments before I was thinking I had no future. But Thomas was the future. Our future. My love for Kate would live on in him. As he learnt to walk and then to talk and play at marbles, as he laughed and giggled and danced, Kate would be there in everything he did.

'Little Thomas. May I hold him?' I repeated.

Elise didn't understand. She turned to Isabelle and said something in French. I said 'Thomas' in what passed for a French accent, and gestured that I would like to hold him.

Isabelle and Elise both smiled, humouring me. Such a sweet natured man who had suffered such loss.

'Peut-être you wait, Matthew?' said Isabelle. 'He sleeps. He is quiet. It is a moment of peace.'

A moment of peace. All I wanted was to hold my own child. I lifted him from the cradle as I'd seen Elise do many times. I supported his bum with one hand and held his head with the other.

Elise cried out, waving her hands for me to put him back down. Did she fear I might steal him away or dash his head on the flagstone floor?

'No, no, Matthew. Put him down,' said Isabelle, trying not to scream.

Elise ran over, flapping her arms. What a stupid thing to do. Why frighten the babe?

I shut my eyes. I shut out their foolish panic. I breathed in the smell of little Thomas's hair and the milky softness of his skin. He could fart and shit in his swaddling clothes. He could throw up all over me. He'd still be my own sweet Thomas, he'd still be all I had of Kate.

'Matthew, Matthew. Please. Please.'

I heard the door open, glanced up to see Isabelle rushing out. Elise beside me, pleading in words I didn't understand. Her hands outstretched. I smiled at her. Then shut my eyes again. I knew enough French to say, 'Non.' And held tiny Thomas to me all the more firmly. He cried out. He bawled. But that's what babies do when people frighten them. I did what any good father would do. I held him firmly in the safest place he could be. I rocked to and fro.

'Hush, hush, hush,' I whispered. Elise could plead all she liked. She'd been a good wet nurse. And she could give suck to him again – when the time was right. But a boy child needs time with his father. His cries were getting louder. Poor mite. But Elise would soon see sense.

I didn't hear the door squeal open. A hand on my shoulder. Alice.

'Give him to Elise, Matthew. Please.'

I ignored her.

'Matthew. Please. He is hungry.'

'I'm not going to drop him.'

She looked at me as if that had been a threat.

'He is safe with me. Look. He's safe. He's not used to me. That's all. That's why he's crying. He needs time. That's all.'

'Matthew, he's distressed. Give him to Elise. Let her feed him. Then you can hold him again.'

'He needs time to get used to me.'

'He needs his mother, Matthew.'

'I know. He does. But she is dead.'

A look of confusion crossed her face.

'No need to pretend any more. He's my son, isn't he. That's what you didn't want Kate to tell me. I am his father. I will always be his father.'

She looked perplexed.

'Stop pretending, Alice.' I was whispering, but dear sweet baby Thomas, he knew how upset I was. Of course he knew. We were flesh and blood. My flesh and blood. Kate's flesh and blood. He was screaming. Screaming for his real mother. Screaming for me. His cries were my cries.

Alice laid a hand gently on my shoulder. 'Let me take him, Matthew. I know you are a good father.'

An angry father, furious at the deception that Kate had been forced into. But there was nothing to be said – not at that moment, not with my baby son doing my raging for me.

'Let Elise feed him,' said Alice. 'He's hungry. He needs milk.'

The child's cries were deafening.

'You can hold him again after he has fed,'

I spoke into his ear, 'I love you little man. We know don't we.'

Then I allowed Alice to take him from me. She passed him to Elise, who ran from the room.

'Where is she taking him?' Until that moment I'd been holding back. Now I was shouting. *'Don't tell him.* Why not, Alice?'

'What are you talking about?'

'Kate wanted to tell me. But you forced her to lie to me. I overheard you. All this time. My own son. And you wouldn't let her tell me. Even after she accepted my proposal, you kept it from me.'

She met my gaze, and waited. Until I ran out of rage, and broke down, sobbing. We were alone in the kitchen. I sat down. Alice beside me.

'Katherine had a miscarriage,' she said quietly. 'While she was with Anne Forman. Her child, your child would have been a daughter. But she was stillborn. That's what I didn't want her to tell you. Not while she was still so weak. Because I feared your rage.'

'Why would I be angry with Kate?' I sniffed.

'Your rage against whoever knocked her from Fleet Bridge. I didn't want Katherine to see that rage. I knew it would distress her.'

I slumped in the chair, put my elbows on the table, rested my forehead on my hands. 'Who is Elise?' I said from behind the shelter of my own hands.

'A widow, Matthew. Her husband was killed in an explosion at the gunpowder mill. Thomas was born just a week after her husband died. He never saw his own son.'

'And my daughter never saw the light of day.' I spoke quietly, more to myself than to Alice, 'Rochester wanted Kate dead. Rochester murdered our child. But it was me who killed her, me who walked her to her death.'

Alice pulled her chair closer. 'You are indeed a good man, Matthew,' she said quietly.

'No. No, I'm not.'

We sat for a while in silence in that communal kitchen, just the two of us, me and Alice. She gave me a kerchief to blow my nose. When Isabelle cautiously opened the door to come back in, Alice asked her to give us a little longer.

'John and I will take our leave in the morning.'

'You don't need to go.'

'You've been very good to us. All of you. But I have to leave this place, Alice. You're good people, and you've treated me better than I ever deserved.'

'Kate wanted you here. You mustn't blame yourself for her death.'

'I took her to the churchyard.'

'*We* took her to the churchyard,' said Alice. 'You and me. She wanted to go. That wasn't your doing.'

'It is all my doing, Alice. I destroy everything I touch. Everything I go near.'

'You can stay with us. And the boy, John, too, he will be safe here. He is a refugee from fire, Matthew, like me and my family. We do not ask you to become one of us. But here you will be with people who understand your grief.'

'I'm not French. I'm not Dutch. I'm not a Huguenot. This is not for me.'

'Then at least stay with us until after Kate's funeral.'

And I would have done. I would have allowed myself to be persuaded if Frans hadn't sought me out later that same afternoon.

'Matthew. I show you something. Yes?'

'Yes, if you like.'

'Not here. It is secret. Come you with.' He was bubbling with excitement, his hands flapping. 'Come. A secret place. Where nobody see.'

He took me to a small shed at the back of Hope House. Coiled ropes were hanging from wall hooks, hessian sacks lay neatly folded and stacked on a wooden shelf as if they'd been pressed and folded by a fastidious washerwoman. A heavy tarpaulin had been rolled against the wall. The air was thick with the smell of hemp and tar.

He slid his hand into the pile of sacks, and pulled out a small leather bag, which he gave to me. 'Look. Look.'

I could hardly see his face in that dim light, but the excitement in his voice told me what I didn't want to know.

'Open it. Open it.'

A brooch. A bracelet. A pearl necklace. Silver coins. A signet ring.

'There. Now we buy horses and we ride to London? Yes?'

'Where did these come from?'

'The Manor House. John show me.'

'What did John show you?'

'He show me pick locks.'

'Where is John. Where is he?'

'He teach me. All shall be shared, he say. He teach me, Mister Matthew. He say I very good.'

I did my best to stay calm. 'Frans, may I keep these for a while so I can look at them in a stronger light?'

'Yes please.' He handed me the leather bag.

'These things are very valuable.'

'Yes,' he said, with such pride, such innocence.

'Can you find John?' I said. 'We should talk about this together.'

He ran off, leaving me holding the bag, my thoughts in utter turmoil. I felt shamed, guilty, distraught. I, Matthew Edgworth, who had taken gold and silver from the finest houses in London, I was ashamed. This was somehow even worse than John thieving from Anne and Clement. Not because it was from a Manor House. I couldn't give a damn about that, so long as they got away with it. But because John had been Frans's teacher. Frans declaiming Rowley's *All shall be shared*. John had inducted Frans into his very own sect. In my head I'd railed against Rowley, but it was I who'd used the phrase when I taught John to pick locks – never for one moment imagining that it would turn into doctrine.

I was minded to give them both a good thrashing. And I surely would have done had Frans brought John to the shed. But I waited for them, and neither of them came near.

I waited until I heard the bell that Isabelle rang for supper. I pocketed the little leather bag with the jewels and the brooch and I walked back to the house. I sat with the other men at supper. John and Frans glanced nervously across at me as we ate our meal. I was glad that nobody spoke English and my no-face was so hard to read. It was the custom that nobody left the table before everyone had finished eating. We stood up and a closing grace was intoned, giving thanks for what we'd just eaten. We all said our Amens, then I moved quickly, grabbing John firmly by the arm.

'Come with me. I need to talk to you outside.'

'I want to go with Frans.'

'Don't argue.' I was trying to be quiet. But several people noticed.

Outside, it was cold but not raining. The sky was clear and there was half a moon to see by.

'We're leaving tomorrow. You wanted to go to London. I will take you to London.'

His lips quivered. I thought he might cry. He shifted from one foot to another. 'I want to stay here with Frans.'

'We're not staying here. We can't. Not now.'

'I like Frans. He's my friend. Can he come with us?'

I took the bag from my pocket. Held it in front of him. He looked away. 'You taught Frans to pick locks. The two of you stole this from the Manor House.'

'I only taught him what you showed me.'

I grabbed him by the shoulders and shook him. 'Do you have any idea what they would have done with you if they'd caught you?' I was shouting by then. And John was crying. Above his sobbing I heard a shout. 'Matthew? John?' Alice's voice.

I reined in my temper, but held him firmly. I didn't want him running off.

'Do you still want to be a player, John?' I said quietly.

I just made out a 'Yes' between his sobs.

I knelt down beside him, holding back my anger. 'If we stay in Canterbury, you will never see a playhouse or a tiring house where they keep their costumes. I made you a promise. I always keep my promises.'

Alice kept her distance.

'Would you like that?'

'Don't know,' he whimpered, on the edge of tears.

Later that evening, I was sitting with Alice in the kitchen. Everyone else was in bed. It had been her suggestion that we talk. And after everything that she'd done for Kate, I agreed. I owed her at the very least an honest good bye.

'What's between you and the boy John is your business, Matthew. But Frans is as distressed as John, and he won't tell me why.'

I dearly wanted a glass of brandywine. But there was none in the house, nor sack, nor canary. Only small ale which was always served in moderation and I was growing tired of moderation.

'John and I are leaving in the morning.'

'I know you were angry with him, Matthew. But is that fair punishment?'

'It's not punishment. It's what he wanted. He wanted to go to London.'

'If you say so. But Frans? Why is Frans so distressed?'

Where to start? 'Not long ago you told me plain that when you knew me in London you saw me as the consummate deceiver.'

'As indeed you were.'

'And I was cruel to you, Alice. And I regret that now. I am truly sorry.'

She made to say something.

'Hear me out,' I said. 'I don't ask for forgiveness. I don't expect it. But now I want to do right by you. So I will be honest with you. I taught John to pick locks. I needed his help. And if

I'd not taught him, we'd not have survived. It's how we escaped the fire at Rowley Hall. But I regret it. For John learns quickly. And now he's shared that skill with Frans. John's taught him to pick locks. Don't be angry with Frans. I have to take John away, Alice. If I don't, Frans will not grow up well. This is all my doing Alice.'

'What is your doing?'

'Together they thieved from the Manor House.'

She caught a breath.

'I have to take him away. It's not right that he stays here. Not right that I stay here. This is a godly community. The kindest, most generous group of people I've ever met.'

'You hardly know us, Matthew.'

'Well enough to know that I don't want to destroy you.'

'We try to live good lives. But we are none of us saints.'

'John's done it before. He thieved from Anne Forman. I could give him a thrashing he'd never forget, and he'd still do it again. People round here see you as a threat. You're hard-working and cause no trouble, but people always blame strangers for things that go wrong. This is your safe haven. But it can't be mine. If a theft is traced back to this house, you'll all be hounded out. We have to leave you, Alice.'

'Given time and patience, John can learn different ways.'

'That's as maybe. But we're leaving. In the morning. I made a promise to him several weeks ago that I would take him to London. I have to honour that promise.'

And that, I knew very well, was less than a half-truth. Because I had to be in London to take my revenge on Rochester. I had fondly thought that if Kate and I could settle in Canterbury, maybe even bring up John in our own family, then I could have let things go. But I had to feed the fire of my revenge. I would destroy him utterly. Nothing would stop me.

I smiled at Alice. I stood up and wished her good night.

As I walked past her, she reached out and took my arm.

'When you have honoured your promise to John, we would welcome you back, if you want to come back.'

EPILOGUE

On 26th December 1613, Robert Carr, otherwise known as Viscount Rochester, was married to Frances Howard. The wedding was a lavish affair, largely paid for by King James, who bestowed on them the titles Earl and Countess of Somerset. Rochester (formerly plain Robert Carr, now Lord Somerset) was James's personal favourite, and the King was so well disposed to them that he had personally intervened to speed the annulment of Frances's previous marriage to the Earl of Essex.

But Rochester or, as we now should call him, the Earl of Somerset, had amassed a store of enemies whilst courting the King's favours. Just three months before their wedding, one of those enemies, Sir Thomas Overbury, died in the Tower of London. The coroner said he died of natural causes, but rumours circulated that he'd been poisoned and that the Somersets were somehow involved. But that was just rumour – as were the stories that they had both visited the notorious Doctor Simon Forman. With the King as their friend and supporter, gossip was easily silenced.

On 28th February 1614, Matthew Edgworth set out from Faversham in Kent for London. He was accompanied by the boy known as John Robins, and he carried with him one of Doctor Simon Forman's casebooks and letters in which Forman chronicled his dealings with Frances Howard and Viscount Rochester.

HISTORICAL NOTES

Paradise Burning is a work of fiction, woven around and emerging from the historical records.

PEOPLE

ROBERT CARR was a page to the Earl of Dunbar when he met Thomas Overbury in Edinburgh in 1601. The two became close friends and travelled to London together. Carr soon became King James's personal favourite and was appointed as Gentleman of the Royal Bedchamber. Whilst there is some dispute about whether the relationship between the King and his favourite was sexual, it was certainly passionate, as is clear in many of James's letters. In March 1611, James ennobled Carr, making him **VISCOUNT ROCHESTER**.

FRANCES HOWARD was the daughter of Lord Thomas Howard (Earl of Suffolk). In 1604, she was married at the age of fourteen to Robert Devereux, 3rd Earl of Essex. The arranged marriage was intended as a political reconciliation between two immensely powerful families. In 1610, Frances Howard met Robert Carr. They began a passionate love affair. Although Frances's marriage to Essex was never consummated, he was intensely jealous of her and refused Frances's requests to have the marriage annulled.

Henry Howard (Frances's great uncle) persuaded King James to set up a Nullity Commission. Proceedings started in May 1613. The Commission finally agreed in September 1613 that Frances's marriage to the Earl of Essex should be annulled on the grounds that the husband was impotent.

On 26th December 1613, Frances Howard and Robert Carr were married. What happened after they were married is explored in the third volume of this trilogy.

Rochester's close friend **THOMAS OVERBURY** was an intelligent and skilful political operator. Rochester relied on Overbury for advice which he passed on to the king as his own. Overbury was initially amused by Carr's fascination with Frances Howard. He even helped compose letters for him to write to her. When the relationship became more serious, however, he strongly disapproved. In April 1613, he was imprisoned in the Tower of London on a trumped-up charge of treason, which had probably been initiated by Rochester. Overbury died in the Tower on 15th September of that year. The strange circumstances of his death and the subsequent murder trials became known as 'The Overbury Affair' and was one of the great scandals of the Jacobean age.

SIMON FORMAN was an excellent, if maverick, doctor. His enemies accused him of being a sorcerer and necromancer. He was heavily implicated in the Overbury Affair – even though he had himself died two years before Overbury's death in September 1611. It seems likely he had a heart attack, but the circumstances of his death are very curious; and there was much speculation at the time that he had been poisoned.

Many of Forman's casebooks survive (most are stored in the Bodleian Library in Oxford). They give us a wonderful first-hand account of late sixteenth / early seventeenth century medical practice. They also contain vivid first-hand accounts of theatre-going (including visits to The Globe to see *Pericles* and *Macbeth*) and detailed references to Forman's own numerous adulterous relationships.

Although he remained active as an astrologer and a doctor until the week of his death, the whereabouts of those casebooks he kept for the period from 1610 until his death in 1611 is not known. It was during this period that Frances Howard consulted with him.

ANNE FORMAN (née Baker)

Anne Baker was born in Canterbury. Her father was a proctor at the ecclesiastical court in Canterbury. She and Simon Forman were married in 1599, when she was seventeen years old (and he was 30 years older than her). Their son, Clement, was born in 1606.

It's not known for certain what Anne did after Simon Forman's death, although she did sell the house they had in Lambeth. It seems likely she returned to Canterbury with Clement.

The **AGNES** who appears in *Paradise Burning* is a fictional character, but the fear of witchcraft in Abingdon is well documented. Mary Pepwell and Elizabeth Gregory were tried for witchcraft at Abingdon in March 1605. Both were acquitted, but the case came to the attention of King James.

The 'real' **JOHN ROBINS** is first heard of in the historical records in 1649, when he is written about as one of London's most prominent and infamous Ranters. Ranters were the most extreme of the radical sects that emerged during the English Revolution of the 1640s. More moderate sects which emerged at this time included the Shakers and the Quakers. The John Robins who appears in *Paradise Burning* is a speculative character. I was intrigued by how events in his childhood could have laid the grounds for what he subsequently became in adulthood.

Nothing is known about his early life. By his own accounts, he was a man of 'little education'. He claimed to have inherited some land in Oxfordshire, which he sold. He was known to fellow Ranters as someone 'claiming to be something greater than a prophet'. He was commonly spoken of as 'The Ranters' God' and 'The Shakers' God', and was effectively deified by his followers.

His wife said that she expected to become the mother of a Messiah. It seems that Robins viewed himself as an incarnation of the divine being. He asserted that he'd appeared on earth before as Adam. He claimed a power of raising the dead. He acted as a cult leader and put forward a scheme for leading a host of 144,000 persons to the Holy Land. Robins publicly declared that 'Lord Jesus was a weak and Imperfect Saviour, and afraid of death'.

On 24 May 1651, Robins, his wife, and eight of his followers were apprehended at a meeting in Moorfields, and jailed for blasphemy. Robins remained in prison for more than ten months. In February 1652, he wrote a letter of recantation to Oliver Cromwell, the Lord Protector of England. He was then freed, and he returned to Oxfordshire, repurchased his land, and lived quietly. Although he said before leaving London that he expected to 'come forth with a greater power', he was not heard of again.

ADAM ROWLEY and all of his crew (except for John Robins) are fictional characters. His 'preaching', however, draws heavily on the tirades against inequality and hypocrisy of the radical sects that came to prominence during the English Revolution. Although this is in some ways anachronistic, the ideas that emerged in the 1640s, and were promoted by the radical sects, grew from ideas and strands of belief which had been around for many years. It took the apocalyptic chaos and uncertainties of civil war to bring them to prominence.

PLACES

All the taverns and inns mentioned in the novel – in Oxford, Abingdon, Moreton, Thatcham, Winchester and Canterbury are still standing and at the time of writing still functioning as hostelries.

ROWLEY HALL is a fictional house in a real landscape. The layout and appearance of the house and its estate is very loosely modelled on Yelford Manor, a late C15th manor house in the hamlet of Yelford, about twenty miles north west of Wittenham.

THE CLUMPS. The neolithic earthworks near Long Wittenham, where Agnes takes Matthew, are now known as Wittenham Clumps. The earliest earthworks on the site date back to the Bronze Age. More banks and ditches were added during the Iron Age. The artist Paul Nash described the view from The Clumps as 'a beautiful legendary country haunted by old gods long forgotten.'

CANTERBURY. The Huguenots first arrived in Canterbury in the years following the Saint Bartholomew's Day massacre in Paris in 1572, coining the term *réfugiés* (people seeking refuge) to describe themselves. By the end of the 16th century the French Huguenot settlement was well established in Canterbury, and Protestants fleeing persecution in the Spanish Netherlands started to join them. Matthew refers to this group as Dutch, though strictly they were Walloons, and it is they who brought with them silk weaving skills.

Canterbury's Huguenot congregation was first allowed to worship at St. Alphege Church. As their numbers grew, they were invited to use the Western Crypt of Canterbury. The silk weavers' house by the river, to which Anne Forman directs Matthew, was part of the Huguenot settlement. It is now The Old Weavers restaurant.

FAVERSHAM is about ten miles north west of Canterbury. In the early C17[th], it was a significant seaport. In this period, the majority of Huguenot refugees came to Canterbury, but some also settled in Faversham, Maidstone and Dover. Chart Gunpowder Mill was established in the 1550s. It was one of the earliest gunpowder mills in the UK. It has been restored and is open to the public in the summer months.

THE FORTUNATE ISLES are often referred to in plays of the period. They were semi-legendary islands in the Atlantic Ocean, variously treated as a conveniently remote geographical location and as a winterless earthly paradise inhabited by the heroes of Greek mythology.

ACKNOWLEDGEMENTS

The typeface for the title and chapter headings is IM Fell DW Pica Pro. The Fell Types are digitally reproduced by Igino Marini. www.iginomarini.com

The episode with the puppets at Anne's house in Canterbury draws on the scene in final act of Ben Jonson's *Bartholomew Fair*.

Many thanks to Christine Aziz, Tracy Baines, Ann Bauer, Rib Davis, Tim Grana, Mike O'Byrne, Judith Ramm, Stevie Simkin, and Debbie Weinstein – all of whom have read extracts and early drafts of the novel and offered insightful observations and generous encouragement.

ADDITIONAL MATERIAL

Additional information about the background to the novel can be found at:

http://www.brianwoolland.co.uk/paradise.html

Readers who sign up for the mailing list will receive advance information about the final novel in the trilogy.

Edgworth mailing list info: edgworth1612@gmail.com

Praise for *The Invisible Exchange*

Matthew is a great character. He has a distinctive voice, he's engaging and fascinating. He's playing power games all over the place. His point of view is intriguing. *The Invisible Exchange* is a real page-turner.

Lesley McDowell
author of *Unfashioned Creatures*

Equal to any Andrew Taylor or CJ Samson, if not better.

David Howgego

A wonderful book. I was compelled by the force of the story and the complex and fascinating narrator. There is so much that causes you to pause and drink in the historical detail, the wonderful turns of phrase, and brilliantly drawn sense of place.

Caroline Doherty
author of *The Belfast Girl*

The Invisible Exchange bashes the historical genre up against the thriller, with a central character and a main plot line unknown to recorded history. By placing an underground fixer, Matthew Edgworth, at the centre of the story, Brian Woolland turns the novel into a real page-turner, while also subtly exploring how the dominant aristocratic and royal narrative of text book history is not the only one. Matthew's surname says it all – he may live on the edge, but that doesn't make him worthless. The picture my imagination formed of him was Ian McKellen as Bosola, in Philip Prowse's National Theatre production of *The Duchess of Malfi* back in the 80s. Like Bosola, Matthew is dependent on the aristocrats whose dirty work he performs, but sees through their self-seeking machinations. Like Bosola, he encounters Bridewells and Bedlams, wise women and whores. In one particularly vivid sequence, he enters an almost psychedelic world of the subconscious, when he looks into the scrying mirror of Dr John Dee. That mirror has Aztec provenance, and is now in the British Museum.

The novel begins with a variant of the "bed trick". It's a narrative device as old as the Bible, but most common in plays from the Jacobean era, the period in which the novel is set. The bed trick crops up in Shakespeare's *Measure for Measure*, and in Middleton's *The Changeling*: but its most sophisticated outing is in John Marston's *The Insatiate Countess*. Frances Howard was, of course, a Countess at the centre of a sexual scandal – *The Changeling* draws heavily on her story. Marston himself puts in a cameo appearance in the novel. Like Bosola, Matthew Edgworth is a malcontent – a common figure in Jacobean drama, and the title of yet another Marston play.

So *The Invisible Exchange* is also an entertaining piece of playful post-modernism, but without the ostentatious whizz-kidding. You don't have to get all the allusions to be engaged and compelled by Matthew's story – but if you unravel some of the literary puzzle, it makes you realise how culture and narrative do not simply respond to an historical moment, but serve to shape it. It's this that makes *The Invisible Exchange* as contemporary as it is historical.

Michael Walling
Director of *Border Crossings*

ABOUT THE AUTHOR

Brian Woolland worked as a wine merchant and a photographer; as a teacher in mainstream education and in a therapeutic community for maladjusted adolescents before becoming an Advisory Teacher for Drama, and then taking a post at the University of Reading in the Department of Film, Theatre & Television.

He now works freelance as a writer, educator and theatre director. He is widely published as an author of educational and academic books. He has also enjoyed success as a playwright – with ten plays commissioned and produced by professional companies, and four published in book form. He has led theatre and creative writing workshops throughout the UK and in Greece, Hungary, Austria, Jordan, Palestine, The Lebanon and Australia.

When Nobody Returns and *This Flesh is Mine* were co-produced by London based Border Crossings and Ashtar Theatre of Ramallah, Palestine.

Paradise Burning is the second volume of a trilogy set in early seventeenth England, which begins with *The Invisible Exchange*.

He is currently working on the final volume in the trilogy.

Printed in Great Britain
by Amazon